Serendib

White Plague

Serendib: White Plague

Cover design by Carmen Dougherty
Layout by Rhiza Press

Print ISBN: 978-1-76111-105-1

Published by Rhiza Edge, 2022
An imprint of Rhiza Press
PO Box 302,
Chinchilla QLD, 4413
AUSTRALIA
wombatrhiza.com.au

NATIONAL LIBRARY OF AUSTRALIA

A catalogue record for this book is available from the National Library of Australia

Serendib
White Plague

PATRICIA WEERAKOON

To my publisher Rochelle
without whose friendship,
support and encouragement,
I would have not found my
voice as a fiction writer.

CHAPTER 1

Kalgoorlie, Western Australia, 2030

'Dear God, Edward. What have you done?'

The tension of the last few weeks crashed in on Jonathan Ashley-Cooper. Every muscle on his face contracted in a mask of frustration. His eyebrows furrowed in fury. It wasn't a video call, so Edward couldn't see him, which was a good thing. If they were actually talking face-to-face, things could have been much worse.

'What have I done? What have *I* done …?' A short burst of laughter came through the phone. Edward's voice rose in pitch. 'Jonathan, I did it for the company. And for you.'

'For me? For *me*?'

Jonathan realised he had subconsciously mimicked his employer's manner of speech. That's what happened when you weren't just workmates, but also long-term friends. Correction—*had once been* workmates and long-term friends. Both of those relationships were over now. Probably forever.

Disgust rose in a bitter tide and clogged his larynx. Jonathan wrinkled his nose. 'How dare you imply that I was involved in your … your malicious … *scheme.*' He spat out the last word. '*You* handed it over to the Geneva lab. *My* research, Edward. *My* work. You did it without consulting me. Why call me now? Why?' He stopped. Waited for a response. None came. Seconds passed.

'Jonathan, have you seen the newspapers? News channels are all reporting rampant HSV encephalitis virus infections in Europe! Now spreading to the UK and the USA! Even South Africa. People are dropping like flies! We have to do something. Fast.' Edward took a ragged breath. 'You read the text messages I sent you?'

'Yes.' The word stuck in Jonathan's throat. He'd read all fifteen of the messages. They detailed a spiralling global catastrophe. 'It's not my problem, Edward. You seem to have forgotten that I handed you my resignation letter.' He hesitated for a moment. 'Anyway, what makes you think the current infections came from the HSV virus I modified in the lab? How do we know it's not some other strain of virus affecting brain tissue?'

Edward took a slow stuttering breath. 'The infections have been traced back to a cluster of encephalitis virus infections in Geneva. There were major international conferences on there at the time it started. The delegates carried the virus back to their countries. The WHO is tracing the genetic code of the virus right now. My contacts tell me that they're close to linking it to the Geneva lab.'

'Great. Just great! The lab to whom you sold my research data and our virus cultures!' Jonathan snarled.

'Listen to me Jonathan. The situation is very grave. What do you think happened?'

'How would I know, Edward? I know what was in those virus cultures when you sent them to the Geneva lab. The encephalitis virus I modified in the lab. What I had was harmless to humans. I have no idea what they did with it after that. And I have no idea why they did it.'

The tone of Edward's breath changed. Became rapid. Harsh. Moments passed in silence. Silence apart from the faint static on the phone. When Edward spoke again, his voice was laced with anxiety. 'Jonathan, we have to do something to stop this. Be reasonable. You're part of the team. You're the most valuable member of the team. Heck—you *are* the team, Jonathan. You discovered that virus. You developed the cultures. We're lost without you.'

This time it was Jonathan's turn to snort a laugh. His wife, Anne, and son, Stephen, turned to stare at him. He waved to them and turned away to continue his conversation.

'I wanted you to stay on with Ellis Enterprises and work with the

Geneva team, Jonathan. You know that.'

'And I refused, Edward. You know that. I tried to explain it to you when you first suggested the collaboration. It was too early to share our work with anyone, much less the Geneva mob. Think back, Edward. Remember what I said?' He took a deep ragged breath. Then spoke slowly, emphasising every word. 'I. Don't. Trust. Them.'

Jonathan moved the phone away from his ear to muffle the curses spewed out by Edward.

'Edward, I am four weeks into my long service leave.' Jonathan deliberately injected a sense of indifference into his voice. 'I'm on the other side of the continent. Travelling with my family in a caravan. Most of the time we've had no mobile cover. We haven't bothered to keep up with the news. And we've kept our phones switched off for the precise reason that both Anne and I are on holiday from work!'

'Okay, Jonathan,' Edward snapped back. 'You want me to take responsibility? I'll do it. But right now, it doesn't matter how it happened. Or even who's to blame. We need to find a solution. I need you back in the lab, Jonathan. No one in the world knows this virus like you do. You're probably the only researcher who can do something to stop this … this … demon.'

'A demon your friendly scientists in Geneva created.' He didn't try to keep the sarcasm out of his voice.

'Jonathan—don't make me grovel. You are the only one who can work on a vaccine and treatment.'

'No.'

'You mean, you …' Edward's words were rushed. Panicked.

'I mean,' Jonathan responded, 'I will not come back at your command. I handed you my resignation letter, Edward. I meant every word in it. You can get your friends at Maius Bonum and their henchmen in the laboratories in Geneva to work on it.'

'Maius Bonum? What the hell are you implying, Jonathan?'

Jonathan bit back a curse. 'Don't treat me like an idiot, Edward. The connections are obvious when you know where to look. I am done with you and your machinations of powerplay. I've washed my hands of the consequences of your actions. I'm not coming back to Ellis Enterprises.' He paused and took another deep breath. 'Find yourself another scapegoat.'

'What can I say to make you change your mind, Jonathan? Is it money? Personnel? I can arrange for you to have the funds you need. The best people to work with you.'

'No.' Jonathan cut him short. 'There is nothing you can say to make me change my mind, Edward.'

Edward's voice was dull. Weary. 'Is that ... is that your final word?' he mumbled.

Jonathan stabbed his phone's power button, terminating the call.

He didn't need to wait for the genetic tracing. It was his virus. The basic info Edward had texted him was enough to tell him that.

He had designed it to be a lifesaver. The Geneva lab had converted it into a deadly virulent monster. Edward's one act of greed had released a demon into the world.

He looked across the car park to where his wife and son stood at the edge of the Kalgoorlie Boulder Super Pit with his good friend, Vijay Jeganathan.

Shoving the phone into his pocket, he jogged over to them.

God help them all.

CHAPTER 2

Kalgoorlie, Western Australia, 2030

Heart racing, young Stephen Ashley-Cooper leaned forward to gaze into what looked like a gigantic meteorite crater. A frisson of excitement rippled up his spine. This was where he wanted to be. It was what he was studying for and dreaming of. He pulled out his phone and clicked. The pictures would go on Instagram and Facebook, Snapchat and Twitter. They should bring him a tsunami of likes. He chuckled and tagged it *#superpit*.

The Kalgoorlie Boulder Super Pit wasn't a meteorite crater. It was evidence of humanity's skill at wrenching riches out of the bowels of the earth itself. And that's what Stephen was determined to do. He wanted to be part of the team that ripped the precious metal out of the ground. It was a primal urge. It was gold fever.

Dr Vijay Jeganathan had driven them deep into the mine crater, right to the rim of the pit. The general public didn't get to come this close. But Dr Jeganathan was the executive mining engineer at the company that owned the Super Pit. And he was a long-term friend of Stephen's dad. So, he could pull Stephen and his parents some favours.

Dr Jeganathan placed his arm around Stephen's shoulder. 'At over three-point-five kilometres long and one-point-five kilometres wide, the Golden Mile Super Pit is one of the largest open-cut gold mines in the southern hemisphere,' he lectured in his sing-song accent. He swept his other hand in an all-encompassing gesture. 'Look like Lego toys, don't they!' He gestured to the yellow and orange vehicles scurrying around in the area of the afternoon blast. 'Go on, get as many pictures as you want.' He chortled. 'Down there—' he pointed to the bottom of the pit, 'it's almost a kilometre deep. That—' he pointed to a shovel digging into the blasted ore and rock, 'that can scoop sixty-six tonnes at a time into its bucket. And, over there—' he pointed to a row of trucks 'those dump trucks can each carry over two hundred and forty tonnes at a time. Pretty impressive, eh?'

'Yes, sir.' Stephen watched the miners and other staff in protective vests as they darted antlike around the vehicles. He pulled out his phone, recorded a short video, and put it on Snapchat.

'So …' Dr Jeganathan kept his arm on Stephen's shoulder. His fingers tightened. 'Your father tells me you want to be a mining engineer?'

'Yes, sir.' Stephen turned to Dr Jeganathan. 'It'd be totally awesome to work in a place like this.'

'Well, it's hard work. Often twenty-four-seven! But very rewarding. You must come spend the summer vacation with us in Kal.' He chuckled. 'It'll be refreshing to have someone I can talk technical with. Our sons are both planning to do medicine like their mother. You got on well with them at the birthday party, didn't you?'

'Yes, I did. And thank you, sir. Thank you for the invitation.' Stephen kept a polite smile on his face. But he knew it would never happen. A long-distance friendship was okay. But an Ashley-Cooper could never spend a summer break with an Indian family.

His mind spun back to the conversation in the caravan on their way to Perth from Adelaide. They had spent the night at a crummy caravan park in Norseman. The dodgy facilities didn't bother them because their own caravan was as good as a two-bedroom luxury apartment.

It had been late. 10 pm. They had been on the road all day. His parents had assumed he was asleep in his bunk bed. Instead, he had been scrolling through TikTok and Instagram. Revelling in all the adulation he was getting for his social media posts about his travels across Australia.

Concern and weariness had threaded through his dad's voice. 'Anne, can we just stay at Vijay's place for a couple of nights? He's been so accommodating. He even arranged his schedule to take Stephen to the Super Pit and the Fimiston processing plant. And they've organised Padmini's birthday party a week early so we could attend. Her relatives have flown in from Switzerland and France and who knows where else!' He stopped and laughed. 'Vijay said that Padmini had pulled out all her old British recipe books. She wants to cook for us!'

'That's the problem, Jon.' Stephen knew that clipped tone of voice. When Mum spoke that way, she brooked no disagreement. 'We accept their hospitality in Perth. Then when they visit Sydney, they'll expect us to entertain them.'

His dad had sighed. 'Is that such a bad thing, Anne? They *are* civilized, you know. He's an executive mining engineer at Kalgoorlie Consolidated Gold Mining. She's a consultant physician, for goodness' sake.'

'Don't patronise me,' she had snapped back. 'Of course, they're civilized. They both spent as much time as we did in London. But … but … they're so … so Indian.'

'Meaning?'

Dad, Stephen had pleaded silently, let it go. You know you can't change her views about it.

'They're vegetarians. And they don't drink any alcohol,' Mum had continued. 'They speak loud and fast. And that accent. And the head wobbles. *And* they smell of the curry they immerse themselves in.' Even facing away from them, Stephen had sensed his mother's delicate shudder. 'If we stay with them, then we have to reciprocate by letting them stay with us. We would have to host a dinner party. Introduce them to our friends in Vaucluse. Invite them to church on Sunday. Imagine how uncomfortable *that* would be. A long-distance friendship is fine. But, Jon, we have to set some boundaries.'

Stephen had pulled the pillow over his head. He didn't want to hear any more. It's not that his parents were racist. No. Not really. They didn't hate people of colour. Or Indigenous people. They attended the Sorry March. Supported international missions. Mum helped out occasionally at the English language classes at their church. His parents had paid for their Indian home-help Devi's surgery. No. That wasn't it. They were just uncomfortable with people who were different. That's it.

He had drifted off to sleep thinking of how awkward it would be if he were to invite his Year 11 Advanced Information Technology class over for lunch. Mum would have a fainting fit when she realized that he was the only white-skinned boy in the group. His parents wanted him to be best mates with the kids of their friends. Their *white* friends. But he couldn't. The other white boys at school were all misogynistic snobs. His parents wouldn't want him to be with them if they knew about their drug-fuelled, porn-watching parties and their social media profiles.

Dr Jeganathan's voice dragged him back to the present. 'Call me Uncle Vijay, son. No more of this 'sir' or 'Dr Jeganathan'. Do you understand?' He let go of Stephen's shoulder and jabbed his index finger at Stephen's chest.

'Thanks, sir—sorry, Uncle Vijay. Yes, I'd love to summer with you after the exams.' He was going to be eighteen next year. Surely, his parents wouldn't stop him from doing something that would further his career.

Dr Jeganathan turned to Stephen's mum. 'Anne, your son sure is an intense academic. Just like Jonathan was.' His laugh was a full-throated, uninhibited rumble. 'I remember the late nights he spent in the virology lab in Oxford.' He waggled a finger at Mum. 'Although, it was probably the southern belle, fellow doctoral student rather than the viruses that kept him up at night!'

Dr Jeganathan didn't seem to notice the flash of irritation in his mum's blue eyes.

'Hey, Dr … eh, Uncle Vijay. Do you mind if I make another video?' Without waiting for his response, Stephen hit the record button on his phone. He flexed the biceps of his left arm and leaned towards the pit. 'Superman at the Super Pit!'

With another burst of laughter, Dr Jeganathan moved to stand behind him. He flexed both arms. 'Do it again, Stephen!'

His dad jogged over to join them. 'Vijay,' he puffed, 'do you know anything about a breakout of encephalitis?' His voice was tight with worry.

Dr Jeganathan moved away from Stephen and tilted his head. 'If you're asking about that so-called new HSV strain encephalitis, there's been news about cases in Europe. Our relatives who came down from there for the birthday party mentioned it. This morning's news reported a few cases in Melbourne.

A spike in cases was reported across Europe. The WHO is contemplating declaring it a pandemic. I guess they learnt the importance of quick action after the COVID experience of 10 years ago!' He stopped and shrugged. 'I figured you would know about it. You're the expert.'

'Stephen, Anne—' His dad's face was set in an expressionless mask. But Stephen could pick up on his anxiety by the tightening of muscles around his eyes and the sheen of sweat on his upper lip. 'We need to get back to the hotel.' His fingers were clasped talon-like on the mobile phone.

'Jon!' Mum narrowed her eyes and tossed her hair back. 'It's only two o'clock. Vijay promised to take us to the mining museum.'

'Sorry.' Dad shushed her with a touch to her arm. He turned to Dr Jeganathan. 'Vijay, I'm sorry.'

Dr Jeganathan patted Stephen's dad on the back. 'No worries, Jonathan. I'm just happy you visited with us. Padmini would have been heartbroken if you missed her forty-fifth birthday celebration yesterday!' He chuckled and nudged Stephen's dad. 'Although, I think she likes people to think it was her fortieth!'

Dr Jeganathan led them over to his Toyota Landcruiser. 'Son,' he addressed Stephen. 'You driving yet?'

Stephen grimaced and glanced at his dad. 'Only in our old Beamer!'

Dr Jeganathan patted the bonnet of the vehicle. 'I'll give you driving lessons on this when you visit next summer. This is what we call a mine spec vehicle.' He pointed to the front. 'Bull bar, spotlights.' He gestured to the antennae from two small boxes. 'Eighty channel UHF radio and VHF radio. Lots more interesting additions. A real beast. Although a quiet one with its electric motor!' He opened the front seat next to the driver. 'Jump in the front. I'll give you your first lesson.'

Stuck between a slow-moving grader and a water tanker, the drive back to the staff car park was slow. Dr Jeganathan pointed to the parts of the grader and explained its role in clearing the mud roads after the blast and picking up the debris from the dump trucks.

Only half-listening, Stephen studied his dad's face reflected in the driving mirror. Dad's eyes were fixed on his phone. His reaction to what he was reading was obvious from his tensed shoulders, pursed lips and the frown lines on his forehead. He met Stephen's eyes in the mirror and mouthed, 'it's okay.'

At the staff car park, his dad clicked the remote to their Jeep Grand Cherokee before Dr Jeganathan parked his vehicle. 'Come on, Stephen. Anne,' he called out. He leapt out of the car, turned to Dr Jeganathan and held out his right hand. 'Vijay, thank you for everything. Sorry we have to rush off.'

Ignoring his outstretched hand, Dr Jeganathan stepped out of the driver's seat and wrapped Dad in a hug. 'Jonathan,' he muttered, 'You're upset. I don't know what exactly it is. I'm guessing it has to do with the virus. Keep strong, okay?'

Stephen watched, open-mouthed, as his conservative, no-touch dad returned the embrace and whispered something in his friend's ear.

Dr Jeganathan stepped back and held his dad by his shoulders. He wobbled his head in assent. 'I don't understand, but I will follow your advice.'

'Anne.' Dr Jeganathan called out to Stephen's mum, who had sauntered to their car. 'I hope you'll let Stephen come and spend time with us next year after his HSC exams. We'll take good care of him.'

'I have no doubt you will, Vijay. However, he has a year to go.' She glanced at the car. Dad was in the driver's seat and had the ignition turned on. 'We better get going. Jon seems to be in an outlandish hurry.'

Dr Jeganathan held the front passenger door open for Stephen's mum, then looked at Stephen. The intensity of his gaze surprised Stephen. 'You take care of your father, son,' he said in an undertone. 'He needs you right now.'

CHAPTER 3

Rawlinna,
Western Australia, 2030

A palpable fog of angst hung between his parents on the drive from the mine to the hotel. Stephen tried to ignore it. He snapped photos of the picturesque old outback buildings lining the Kalgoorlie streets. Uploaded them on Instagram. Added a few tweets about the mine.

Dad's tensed shoulders and white-knuckled death-grip on the steering wheel, coupled with the worry lines around his mouth and on his forehead, should have conveyed his mood to Mum. Apparently, it didn't.

'Really, Jon,' she complained. 'What's so important that we can't spend one more day touring Kalgoorlie? It's such a pretty little city!' She stared out of the window.

A faint shake of Dad's head was the only response. She turned to face him.

'Don't look away! Talk to me, Jon!' She clasped his forearm. 'What the—? You're tense as a board.' She stopped. Her voice was softer when she continued. 'Who was that on the phone, Jon? Was it Edward Ellis? What did he say?' She frowned. 'Has it to do with the virus you asked Vijay about?'

'Anne, can you please let me think?'

Mum jerked her hand away, slid over in the seat and looked out of the window again. 'Fine,' she snapped.

They drove in silence to the hotel and parked by the caravan bay. Dad tossed the caravan keys to Stephen. 'Help your mum pack. I need to make a call.' He dashed off into the hotel.

When Stephen and his mum reached their hotel suite, his dad was pacing up and down the balcony, the phone pressed to his ear. His other hand made frantic stabbing gestures in the air.

Stephen flung the wardrobe open and shoved his clothes into his backpack. He pulled out the roller bag his mum used and gave it to her. She unzipped it and started folding her clothes. 'I knew something was brewing!' she grumbled. 'He comes home and announces that he's taking long service leave. Then drags us across the continent. Makes you miss school. And me … me …'

'Mum,' Stephen stopped packing and straightened up. 'You finished marking and grading student exams. You're on uni break. You're always whining that Dad's a workaholic.' He grinned at his mother to soften the words. 'And Dad knew I was dying to visit the mine sites in West Australia. He said his long service leave was overdue. Maybe it was just chance?'

His mum's lips lifted in amusement. She turned and ruffled Stephen's hair. 'My wise son.'

They finished packing in silence.

The balcony door slid open. 'Sorry, Anne, Stephen. We have to hit the road. Now!' Dad flung open the wardrobe door and crammed his clothes into his carry case. Then, ignoring Mum's cry of protest, he shovelled all the toiletries in the bathroom into a plastic bag and tossed it to Stephen. 'I'll check us out and get the caravan connected. Meet you at the front of the hotel in ten.'

Mum sneezed into her elbow. She grabbed a handful of tissues. 'Just what I need,' she sniffled into the tissues. Stephen swung his backpack on his shoulder and grabbed her roller bag. 'Come on, Mum. You can rest in the caravan. I'll sit up front and navigate.'

'No,' she mumbled. 'I need to talk to your dad. I know there's more to this whole trip than just a family getaway.' She sniffed and shoved another handful of tissues into the pocket of her trousers.

They rolled their luggage out of the hotel to where Stephen's dad was waiting for them. The Jeep's engine was humming, the caravan was attached, and his dad had a grim, impatient look on his face. He jogged over to them, grabbed their cases, and tossed them into the caravan. Stephen got in the back seat of the jeep while his mum slid into the front passenger seat. Dad hurled himself into the driver's seat, slammed his door shut, switched on the engine, and took off while he was still buckling his seatbelt one-handed.

They travelled in silence, heading south on the Goldfields Highway away from the city of Kalgoorlie. A little past the city limit, his dad swung the car left onto a smaller road. The signpost read 'Mount Monger Road.' Mum grabbed Dad's arm, causing the car to swerve. Dad swore and swung the steering wheel back. Mum glanced at the positioning device on her phone. 'Jon, what do you think you're doing?' she shrieked. 'We need to continue on Goldfields Highway to the coast road!'

'No.' His dad's voice was brusque. 'We're going through Rawlinna.'

Mum stared at her phone. 'Rawlinna? For God's sake, Jon. Why?' she snapped back. 'There's nothing there.' She glanced down at her phone. 'I can't find a caravan park. Nothing. And it'll add hours to our trip to Adelaide.'

The car and caravan juddered into a pothole in the road.

Mum sniffled, then sneezed into her elbow.

From the back seat, Stephen handed her the box of tissues.

Dad drove in silence. His fingers were rigid on the steering wheel.

His mum sighed. 'Jon, darling,' she whispered, her voice now threaded with worry. 'What is it?' She placed her fingers over his on the steering wheel. 'I've never seen you like this. It's got to be that phone call you had. It *was* from Edward, wasn't it? What's going on in Sydney, Jon? Has something happened at the lab? Do they want you back there?' She tightened her fingers on his. 'Why not go back to Perth and fly to Sydney? I'm sure Vijay won't mind holding the car and caravan for us.'

Dad slowed and swung the car around another pothole. He took his left hand off the wheel and wrapped Mum's fingers in his. 'Yes, Anne. I need to explain.' He glanced in the mirror at Stephen. 'You too, son.' He sighed and shrugged his shoulders. 'Things are happening that I could never have foreseen. In my wildest dreams. Or—' His voice dropped a notch, 'in my worst nightmares.'

'Jon,' Mum's voice rose in pitch. 'You're scaring me.'

Dad dropped Mum's hand to grab the steering wheel and swing the car around another rut on the road. He took a deep breath and let it out in a shuddering sigh. 'Anne, you know about my research on blood-brain barrier transmission in the central nervous system.' He glanced in the mirror at Stephen. 'That, for the mechanical-minded, is the filter that keeps the bad stuff from getting into the spinal cord and brain.'

'Yes, Jon,' Mum mumbled through her sniffles. 'That's why Edward Ellis headhunted you for his lab. He knew that your research on how some viruses get into the spinal cord and brain and others don't is internationally recognised.'

Dad nodded. 'You know I was testing on mice.' He glanced back at Stephen. 'Because we're not allowed to test on human subjects.'

Stephen grinned. 'Awesome! They do it in the movies! That's always how they create the supervillain. Some crazy scientist goes and tests his super-drug on himself.' He laughed. 'Or he goes and tests it on someone else. And that guy becomes a monster.'

At the word monster, his dad flinched. Then he took a deep breath and let it out slowly while shaking his head. 'Anyway … I was studying how different species of mice respond differently to various strains of encephalitis. That's a brain disease,' he said, glancing at Stephen in the rear-view mirror. 'Kind of like a brain fever.'

'I know that,' Stephen muttered.

'Anyway,' his dad continued, ignoring him, 'I wanted—I wanted to—progress to eventually looking at how people from some ethnic groups get affected by the particular virus strains and others don't.'

Stephen pulled a puzzled frown. 'Why research that? It sounds kind of racist.'

'IT'S NOT RACIST!' Dad yelled and slapped his hand on the steering wheel. Mum jumped in her seat and stared at him. 'Sorry,' Dad muttered and released another deep breath. 'I was trying to develop testing methods, okay?' he continued in a more subdued tone. 'And medications. And vaccines. Ways to help people. By diagnosing them early. And develop vaccines and medications precisely tailored to the ethnic group.' He continued to speak as the Jeep lurched along the rutted dirt road. 'We had this modified virus. It came from the Herpes Simplex Virus.' He glanced in the mirror at Stephen. 'The one that causes shingles.'

Stephen nodded.

'Our research assistant Rachel called the modified virus HSV Cousin or HSV cos. The name stuck. Anne, you remember Rachel, don't you?'

'Yes,' Mum mumbled. Her voice sounded thick and hoarse. Her sinuses must be really congested. 'Rachel Thomas. The one with the really cute two-year-old son, Paul.' Mum sneezed and rubbed her eyes. 'But what has this got to do with us taking the Rawlinna route home, Jon?'

Dad was quiet for a few seconds. Stephen glanced out the window. Outside their air-conditioned, mobile metal oasis, the dry Australian bush stretched out as far as he could see, flat as an ironing board. It was covered with low mallee shrubs with their leaves, dark green and tough. A few short, hardy red-bark gumtrees stood their ground against the dry landscape. The sky above them was cloudless and bright blue.

Dad sighed again. The car slowed even further. 'Something else happened. I didn't want to tell you. I knew it would upset you.' He rubbed his face with the palm of his hand. His voice dropped. Every word was weighted with torment.

'The virus, HSV cos. It could cross the blood-brain barrier in a specific species of mice. We were ready to start human trials. It was all laid out. But we didn't have enough money in the project budget. That next phase needed a big injection of finance.' He stopped for a moment to navigate the Jeep and caravan across a wide ditch. Then he continued. 'Edward called me into the office on the first of February.'

'That was two days before we left on our road trip!' Mum hissed. 'For God's sake, Jon! I asked you what the rush was! You said it was because you had leave. And that management had ordered you to take it. And that you were dying to get the new caravan on the road.'

Dad shrugged. 'At that meeting, Edward told me he had sold the patent for the research process.'

'What!' Mum's head snapped to the side to stare at Dad.

'And the samples of our modified virus cultures.'

'He can't do that!' Mum twisted in her seat to face Dad. 'It's your original work! Your ideas! We can sue him!'

Dad shook his head. He coughed and reached for a tissue from the box Mum held. 'Yes, he could do it. He showed me the small print on my contract. I couldn't ... didn't have any authority to prevent it.' Dad shrugged again. 'He'd sold it to an international research company based in Europe. In Geneva, Switzerland. My material was already on its way to their lab. I couldn't stop any of it from happening. Legally, all I had was—' His knuckles tightened further on the steering wheel. 'An option to work with the team in Geneva.'

'Who'd he give it to? Who's this Geneva company?'

'I think they're linked to a group called Maius Bonum'.

'Maius Bonum?' Mum wheezed. 'Meaning the greater good? Who're they?'

Dad made an angry growling sound in the back of his throat. 'They market themselves as medical philanthropists. Seeking world health and prosperity and all that.' He coughed and cleared his throat. 'But I think they're a bunch of white supremacists who are afraid of the rising power of developing countries like India and China.'

'And now they've got your research on ethnic-specific infections. And can do what they want with it!' Mum slumped back in her seat. 'Why would Edward do that?'

Dad's voice was little more than a hoarse whisper. 'Money? Power? Or maybe he's linked with Maius Bonum.' His voice rose in volume. 'I don't know. I don't know!' he shouted.

'Jon, please,' Mum clasped Dad's hand.

Dad got control of himself again. His voice dropped to a whisper. 'I gave Edward my resignation. He refused to accept it. He told me to take time off to think about it. So ... here we are.'

'Dad.' Stephen had to know. 'What did Edward say to you over the phone? At the Super Pit?'

'Apparently, things are happening that no one expected. He wanted me back in Sydney. Back in the lab. He sounded frightened. Even terrified. I think he knows more than he was willing to tell me on the phone. He booked us tickets on this afternoon's flight from Perth to Sydney.'

'So,' Mum coughed into a tissue. 'Why are we in the car on a side road to Rawlinna and not on a flight to Sydney?'

'Because ...' Dad slid a look at Stephen in the rear-view mirror. 'After talking with Edward, I made another call. To Rachel. And I need time to think about what she told me.' He stopped speaking and remained silent as the car and caravan continued bouncing along the rough Rawlinna Road.

Mum rested her arm on the window and dropped her head into her elbow.

'What did she say, Dad?' Stephen prompted.

'Rachel said that there were reports of an HSV related strain of encephalitis in Europe and the United States. She said it sounded like it was from our encephalitis HSV cos virus. It was very infectious. And that it seems to infect mainly white-skinned people. Apparently, they're calling it the 'White Plague'. She wouldn't, or maybe couldn't, say more.' He stopped and rubbed his forehead. 'What's even weirder is that she warned me that Edward has used his influence to contact the police in this area. They're on the lookout for us. On all the main routes between Perth and Adelaide. They've been instructed to intercept us and get us back to Sydney. By force, if needed!'

'That's absurd! What are we, a bunch of criminals?' Mum coughed yet again.

'No. We're not the ones who committed a criminal act. Edward took care of that!' Dad sighed. 'If the infection is in the community, and spreading as fast as Rachel said it is, it won't be long before it's a global catastrophe. The Prime Minister is likely to declare a national emergency. Maybe he already has. He won't want another crisis like COVID 2020.' Dad stopped for a few seconds. His voice was laced with weariness. 'Come to think of it, the order to get us to Sydney may have come from a source higher than Edward.'

'Maybe we should go back to Perth?' Mum took a shuddering breath.

Dad sighed and glanced at the map on his phone. 'Maybe you're right.' He sighed. 'There's a smaller road from Rawlinna to Adelaide. I'll take that. It should get us to Adelaide by nightfall. We can reconsider our options there.' He frowned and concentrated on the road.

Mum broke into a fit of coughing.

Dad slowed down and pulled to the side of the road. 'Anne,' he reached over and touched her forehead. 'You're running a temperature. Go lie down in the caravan for a while.'

Mum swallowed and sighed. 'My throat hurts. A little nap would help.'

Dad walked with Mum to the caravan. He came back with two carry mugs of coffee. 'Jump up in the front with me.' He grabbed a tissue and sneezed. 'Bummer, I think I'm coming down with the same thing Mum has.'

A sudden thought entered Stephen's mind. 'Dad, is it possible that you could have caught that 'White Plague' brain bug you described?'

He was silent for a couple of seconds. 'No.' he replied. 'We weren't exposed to anyone with the disease. Vijay said they've only reported cases in Melbourne.'

They drove on. Away from the flat bush into a pine tree forest. In time, the trees they were driving through thinned and gave way to bronze-copper gimlet gum, silver saltbush and blue bush scrub.

Dad sneezed and yawned. 'We're entering the Nullarbor now.'

Stephen grabbed his phone and clicked. He put the pictures on Facebook, Snapchat and Instagram. *#Nullarbor.*

Stephen dozed. Then jerked awake at the sound of his dad coughing.

Dad had his hands clasped tight on the steering wheel. Every line of his face and body radiated anxiety. 'Dad!' Stephen reached out to touch his dad's arm. He stifled a gasp. Dad's skin was hot and wet with sweat. He glanced at his dad's face. The red flush and sheen of perspiration confirmed it. His dad was sick.

Dad slowed and reached into the side pocket of the door to pull out what Stephen recognised as the satellite tracking communicator. He handed it to Stephen. 'Press the red button,' he wheezed. His voice was brittle, fragile with worry. 'It's an emergency transmitter. It'll alert authorities that we're in trouble. Then dial triple-0. Tell them we're just short of Rawlinna. Both your parents are unwell.' He coughed. 'Give them my name.' He sighed. 'For all you know, they may be looking for us!'

Stephen switched on the communicator. He stared at the screen. The words were in stark red upper case. 'NO SIGNAL'. He switched it off, waited a couple of seconds, and turned it on again. 'NO SIGNAL'.

'Dad,' Stephen stammered. 'There's no connection.' He pressed the red emergency button anyway. 'NO SIGNAL'.

His dad picked up his mobile phone from the holder on the dashboard. 'What the heck!' he muttered. 'No connection?' He pulled the car and caravan off the road.

He should go for help. Stephen clicked his seat belt off and looked around. The sun was a harsh golden ball, low on the distant flat horizon. The sky bled crimson and orange over the never-ending saltbush and occasional mallee shrub. There was nothing else. Nothing but the white limestone gravel that carpeted the Nullarbor Plain.

Except ... shimmering in the distance ... what looked like a small cross on the roadside. He squinted and stared through the heat haze. No, it was a road sign. At the beginning of a narrow dirt side-road.

Stephen opened the door of the car and jumped out. The dry, hot air burned his nose and throat. He gasped, then took a deep breath and ran towards the road sign. A hewn wooden post pointed down the side-road. It read, 'Rawlinna Sheep and Cattle Station'. Stephen shaded his eyes against the harsh rays of the setting sun and looked down the road. In the distance, he could see the outline of a cluster of buildings. A light blinked on. Silver blue. The intensity of the light waxed and waned.

Stephen dashed back to the car. 'Dad.' He opened the driver's side door. His dad was slumped on the wheel. 'Dad! Dad!' He shook his shoulder. 'Come on, Dad, let's go to the caravan. I can see Rawlinna Station. I'll run over there and alert the flying doctors.'

Stephen slid his arm around his dad's waist and coaxed him to walk to the caravan. He settled him in the bed next to his mum. Stephen grabbed his leather jacket and a torch, dragged on his leather walking boots and slipped his phone into the side pocket of his jeans. He shut the door of the caravan and set off at a jog down the road to Rawlinna Station.

The dry, brown-grey dust sprayed up and around him. It coated his clothes and invaded his face and hair. The red-orange globe of the sun slung lower on the horizon. The white noise of the twilight cicada chorus only accentuated the desert stillness. The crunch of his feet on the sand was the only sound.

He kept his eyes fixed on the silver-blue light. It blinked brighter. It seemed to beckon him.

He was hallucinating. He must be sick too.

Gasping for air, Stephen ran faster toward the light. It was his only hope.

CHAPTER 4

Serendib, 2131

'This cannot be happening!'

A spike of adrenaline flashed across fifteen-year-old Aletheia Joseph's neural pathways. She bit down on her lower lip and swallowed the scream that threatened to burst out of her. She couldn't control the harsh rush of her sharp indrawn breath. It quivered and sank in the pure silence that surrounded her.

She blinked and looked again at the Cognitive Visual Unit display in front of her. On it was an image representing the use of Laplace transform to solve complex differential equations. It was shot through with a purple and silver streak. The streak had nothing to do with mathematics. And everything to do with the existence and stability of the universe she currently inhabited. Sweat broke out on her forehead. She slid back and grasped the arms of the shell she was seated in to keep her hands from trembling. The shell softened and shaped around her fingers. Sensing her tension, it rubbed and soothed. It didn't help. She felt her heart race. Her breath caught in her chest.

Holding her head still, she slid her eyes around the learning pod. The walls of the dome-shaped pod radiated the fluorescent blue light that encouraged attentiveness and focus. Their learning Guide, Miss Chitra, dressed in the blue-green silk saree of an advisor, stood in her customary place at the front. Ally looked over the group again, checking if anyone else looked disturbed.

Everyone else in the pod, all fifteen of the scholars, sat back in their custom-designed shells, arms folded, white silk tunics and trousers shimmering and drifting in the light breeze that flowed through the gills that served as air vents in the dome. The shells were seats designed with an inbuilt motion detector and response unit. Each shell had its own inbuilt artificial intelligence, which enabled it to detect the emotional status of the person seated in it and respond appropriately. None of the shells appeared to be dealing with excessive stress right now. Except hers. The other scholars were relaxed, their collective attention focused on solving the equations flashing across their personal CVU's.

Nobody had noticed Ally's reaction. Yet.

She fixed her gaze on the purple and silver interference. 'Go away.' She marshalled her neural control centres and focused on the streak. 'Go. Away … Please.' She silently signalled her CVU. 'Not now. Please. Go.' Nothing changed.

Ally took a half breath and held it. She concentrated her thoughts on her body's response. She had to slow her heart rate. Calm her breathing. The Guide would know if she panicked.

The streak blurred and changed into a mauve aura that pulsed across her CVU.

She looked around the learning pod again. Everyone else was concentrating on their maths. So, it was only her.

This was good. It was also bad. Very bad.

She needed to get out of the learning pod and talk to Appa.

Nathan, her best friend and study buddy sat in the shell next to her. He reached over to grasp her arm. Ally gasped and looked at him. His grasp tightened. 'Ally,' he whispered. 'Where are you?' He pointed to the Guide at the front of the pod. 'The Guide is channelling you! She's almost yelling! I can feel it.'

Ally dragged her eyes away from the CVU to look toward the front of the pod. The Guide's stare pinned Ally to her shell. 'Aletheia,' the Guide vocalised. Her voice was low, but conveyed a mix of concern and apprehension in the one word. 'What is happening to you? Your CVU is completely distorted. Your brain's cognitive thought patterns are unreadable.

You aren't responding to my communications. Are you feeling unwell?'

At her spoken words, every other scholar rotated in their shell towards Ally. The Guide very rarely vocalised to an individual scholar. One-to-one communications were conducted by direct mind contact and channelling. To speak to an individual during a learning session was an extraordinary event. It signalled a disruption in interpersonal mind contact communication. A very rare occurrence among the citizens of Serendib. Even worse, was the suggestion that she was unwell. A hint that Ally's brain-body coordination wasn't functioning as it should. That hurt. Ally knew that in her position, that was impossible. The Guide probably knew that too.

Ally dragged herself away from the grasp of the shell and got to her feet. It released her with an obvious reluctance. She concentrated on relaxing her vocal cords. Her voice when she spoke was low and calm. 'Aunty Chitra,' she silently channelled the Guide with the familiarity permitted to the female scholars. 'May I please be excused for a few minutes? I need to recalibrate my CVU.'

'Well,' Guide Chitra channelled back silently. 'We are at a critical point in our complex differentials.' She stared at Ally. The Guide's concern for her vibrated through her signals. 'But if anyone can catch up—you can.' Ally inclined her head in assent and then looked into the Guide's eyes. The unspoken message burrowed into her consciousness. 'I don't believe there is anything the matter with your CVU. And I know that you are not unwell. We will discuss this later.' Ally flashed back acceptance of the Guide's comment and turned away. She controlled her urge to rush out of the learning pod.

Ally heard the Guide's silent instruction to the others as she walked to the exit portal of the pod. 'Scholars, let's get back to our learning.'

The wall of the learning pod slid open with a whoosh and ejected her into the harsh white light of the tropical sunshine. She stepped away from the exit and stood under the shade of the araliya tree. The sweet fragrance engulfed her. That, together with the sight of the velvet-white flowers with their deep yellow sun-shot heart, eased her tension. Just a fraction.

Ally closed her eyes and concentrated. She switched on to the neural communication lobe in her brain and channelled the frequency of Saint Paul Thomas, the spiritual leader of Serendib. Saint Thomas was her great-great-grandfather. He was 'Appa' to her. Saint to the rest of Serendib. He responded to her call within two seconds. Ally placed her palms together at breast level in the traditional Serendib greeting to an elder. 'Appa, Vannakam.'

The image in front of her shimmered and consolidated. Standing at a hundred and seventy centimetres and weighing around seventy kilograms, one hundred-and-three-year-old Saint Thomas was not a big man. But what he lacked in stature, he made up for in authority and charisma. One glance from the platinum grey eyes could reduce the toughest citizen of Serendib to a blubbering mess. But right now, his eyes were a deep charcoal grey of contemplation. His silver and grey tunic and trousers shifted in the breeze as he raised his palms to return Ally's greeting. 'Vannakam, Aletheia.' His lips twitched. 'Your CVU not working?' His trimmed grey beard glimmered in the sunshine.

'Appa. You knew this would take place, didn't you?'

Saint Thomas slanted his head in acquiescence. 'I expected it. You know that, Aletheia. Just not so soon.'

'Appa, what will happen? Will it change everything?'

'Aletheia, Aletheia, you are impatient. Everything is too inclusive of a word.' He stopped and shook his head, setting the silver threads in his shoulder-length hair quivering. 'You are young. Maybe too young to take on the responsibilities this will entail.'

Tears sprang to Ally's eyes. 'Yes, Appa. I am young.' She reached her fingers towards the image shimmering in front of her. 'But it will be a long time before I have to take over leadership of Serendib. You will be here with us …'

'But not forever, Aletheia. Not forever.' He stopped her with a flick of his fingers. 'And when the time comes, you *will* be ready.' The grey eyes sharpened. Turned from charcoal to flint.

Ally straightened her spine and stood erect. She brought her palms together again and bowed her head. 'Yes, I will be ready.' She paused, lowered her head further and looked at him through the veil of her eyelashes. 'Appa,' she whispered. 'Can we not ignore it?'

'Ignore it?' Saint Thomas snapped.

Ally didn't look at him. She didn't need to. The energy of his displeasure radiated in waves toward her.

'Aletheia,' Saint Thomas' voice was low and laden with care. 'What are the creeds we live by?'

'Faith, hope and love. But the greatest of these is love,' Ally whispered.

'What would you say is the most loving thing to do?'

'We cannot ignore the cry for help,' she whispered. 'We have to open the way. What will it look like, Appa?'

'I will turn on the cross-temporal illumination. We can open the time portal only for a short length of time. At twilight their time. To do more would be too destabilising.'

Ally frowned. 'Destabilising? For us? How?'

Saint Thomas chuckled. 'No, Aletheia. Serendib is safe. It will be disrupting for them. In the Before.'

'But, Appa, are you sure this is the only way? How can we be certain that it will be for good? How can we be certain the time is right? How … how can we be sure that it will be the right person? The Chosen One?'

'We will know, Aletheia. *You* will know.' Saint Thomas chuckled again. 'Come, come, Aletheia. I am supposed to be the doubting one.' He pointed a finger towards the learning pod. 'Get back to your lesson.' He glanced up at the sun dropping into the horizon, a shining orb in the red-and-orange-streaked sky of the Nullarbor plains. 'I will open the portal and call for the light.'

'Will I be involved in … in whatever happens, Appa?'

Ally felt a feather-like touch on her hair. She raised her hand and came away with a fresh araliya flower in her fingers. The golden centre in the blossom reflected the glow of the setting sun.

'The blessing of the araliya blossom. Aletheia, I think you have your answer.' Saint Thomas's gaze softened. 'Go back to the learning pod child. You have my blessing, too.'

The learning pod opened to allow Ally access. None of the scholars looked up when she entered. She slipped into her shell. It enfolded and accepted her. She bit her lip and controlled her breathing as she initiated her CVU. It flashed in front of her, clear and full of the complex differential equations she had missed. Nathan's soft message to her slipped into the edge of her consciousness. 'Ally, are you alright?' She slipped back a response. 'I'm fine. Tell you about it later.'

Within a few minutes, Ally had whizzed through the equations the scholars had worked on in her absence and was working in sync with the group. The Guide glanced at her. 'Well done, Aletheia.' Her words of approval slipped into Ally's brain's self-esteem zone.

The scholars worked in silence. They moved from complex mathematical equations to gene mapping and the history of microbial forensics. The blue lights emanated by the walls of the pod changed to a warm mauve. Then a soft glowing lilac. It indicated the end of learning for the day. The Guide sent her evening message to the scholars. 'Well, enjoy the evening muscle-building sessions, scholars. Take some time to relax and enjoy the sunset. I will see you all tomorrow.'

Sixteen shells whooshed as they released their hold on the scholars.

THUD. THUD. THUD.

Someone or something was banging on the wall of the learning pod. The access slid open. The scholars and the Guide stared as one at the opening. Ally felt the collective low rhythm of the group's neural wave pattern shudder, then spike.

Scholars and Guide stepped back and away from the opening.

All except Ally.

Heartbeat racing, palms damp with sweat, Ally stepped forward toward the opening of the pod.

The time had come.

It was beginning.

CHAPTER 5

Rawlinna, Western Australia, 2030

'Oh God … dear God … please help me …'

Stephen didn't pray much. Actually, not at all. That was until now, as he dashed down the dusty track towards the broken-down buildings of Rawlinna.

'Please, God,' he panted as he ran. 'Don't let my parents die. Please. I'll do anything. Anything. Just. Help. Me.'

He skidded to a stop in front of the tall red-bark gumtree which stood sentinel to a weatherboard building. The bleached, worn-out sign on the side of the building read 'RAWLINNA SCHOOL'. The paint on the building was sunburned and peeling, and many of the boards were splintered. The wooden door hung half-open from rusted broken hinges. A rush of desert wind made the door squeak and swing shut with a bang. He looked around. There was no life. Nothing. Except for the dim glow of the naked light bulb which hung over the school door. The light which had guided him here. A light in the middle of the Nullarbor. He must be hallucinating.

As he stared at it, the light bulb seemed to increase in brightness until it glowed with a silver-blue effervescence. Stephen bolted forward the last couple of steps to the wooden door. He raised his fist and banged on it. Once. Twice. Three times. Harder. Louder. 'Help. HELP. HELP,' he screamed.

The door swung open.

Stephen stood frozen at the entrance. He must still be hallucinating.

He took a slow shuddering breath. The air was sweet and pure. The oxygen hit to his brain was intoxicating. He swivelled his head and looked around. His heart pounded in his chest. Every muscle in his body tensed, then trembled. He took a shuffling step forward.

The slanting surfaces of the dome-like structure he had entered shimmered and pulsated. The reddish-mauve light bathed the space in the dome and the people in it with a purple aura. Multiple pairs of black eyes were fixed on him. The breeze from behind him drifted in and ruffled their black hair and gently wafted over the silky, silver-white loose tunics and trousers they were dressed in. They stood tall and still. Then, in a synchronized move, they drifted away from him towards the back of the dome. Their dusky-brown faces were fine-boned and beautiful. But, at that moment, they were showing varying expressions of apprehension and anxiety.

One girl stepped forward. Her skin was much fairer. More olive than brown. Wavy black hair cascaded down over her shoulders to below her waist. Almond-shaped, deep brown-black eyes shaded by long eyelashes met his. Stephen opened his mouth to speak, but found himself speechless at the intensity of her gaze. She wasn't looking at him. She was looking into him. She slid closer. The smell of frangipani surrounded him. The corners of her perfect, bow-shaped lips turned up in the mere hint of a smile.

Her voice when she spoke was little more than a whisper. But he felt it in his soul. 'Welcome to Serendib, Stephen.'

Stephen opened then shut his mouth. He swallowed the lump that had formed in his throat. He coughed. Cleared his throat. 'I … I … need … need help. Wait! How do you …?' he rasped. 'How do you know my name?' Stephen stared wide-eyed at her. 'Where am I? And—who … who …'

Her smile widened, showing the tips of perfect white teeth. 'No, Stephen.' She kept her eyes locked on his. 'Don't say anything. Relax. Breathe.' His heart rate settled. His breathing calmed. Her eyes burrowed deeper into him. 'Stephen, who do you see in front of you?'

'Boys and girls. Teens. And … and … one adult. A lady,' he stammered.

She reached forward and took his hands in hers. From any other girl, this would have seemed overly familiar. But with this girl it felt right. 'What do they look like, Stephen? What are they wearing?' she continued. His fingers curled around hers in an involuntary move.

'They look … look …' He glanced around, then lowered his voice to a whisper. 'Indians … maybe. Young. All very beautiful. They're not angry. Not frightened. Confused, maybe. And … and … dressed in …' he stopped. Scrunched his eyes shut and opened them. 'They're in blue jeans. The girls with pink blouses and boys in white shirts.' Stephen stopped and blinked. 'It's not what I saw when I first came in!' he stammered.

She let go of him and tilted her head. 'Good.' She turned to face the silent group behind her. 'Aunty Chitra,' she spoke in a soft, sing-song voice. Every eye was now on her. 'Scholars. Stephen is visiting with us. I am vocalising so he can hear and understand what I am saying. As you can see, he has travelled a long way. He needs to consult with the Saint. I will take him there.'

One of the boys stepped towards them. He stared at the girl. 'Ally, what are you doing?'

She looked in silence into the boy's eyes for a few seconds. The boy wobbled his head in a move that reminded Stephen of Dr Jeganathan. 'Okay, I'll see you later at vitu.'

She swung back to Stephen. 'Come on.' She took hold of his right hand. 'We need to get out of here.' Stephen looked down at her hand. Slim, long, olive-skinned fingers. Pink crescent nails naked of any colouring.

'Where … where am I?' He stammered.

'Hush.' She tightened her fingers around his. Stephen gasped. A jolt of primal energy ripped up his arm to his brain. He tried to pull his hand away. 'Don't worry.' She held on. 'What you're feeling is normal. It's a time thing. A cross-temporal clash of sensory surfaces upsets the nerve conduction patterns in your skin. You'll get used to it.' She part-coaxed and part-dragged him towards the opening he had just come through. 'My name is Aletheia Joseph, Stephen. But all the scholars—sorry, you would say classmates, call me Ally.' She swung round to stand between him and the opening of the dome. 'Stephen, the place we are going out to is very different to what you came in from. Accept what you see. Please. And,' she rolled her eyes, 'try to keep calm. Handling your anxiety is exhausting me.'

He pulled her back and stopped her from leaving. 'Ally, or whoever you are. I need medical help for my parents. They're sick. Very sick. Our caravan's on the main road. I need to call the flying doctors. My phone has no connection! Can I use your phone? Or—' He looked back at the others inside the dome. They stood silent, staring back at him. '—maybe from one of your friends?'

She groaned and continued to drag him out of the dome. 'Your parents are not the only ones who need help,' she muttered. 'Helping them is what this is all about. Come.'

Stephen stumbled out of the building behind her.

For the second time within a few minutes, he stood frozen. His heart rate accelerated again. Waves of panic raced through him. He felt himself hyperventilate. This could not be. A tall frangipani tree laden with white-gold flowers stood where the red-bark gumtree had been. Behind it, the fronds of tall palm trees laden with what looked like green coconuts wafted in the breeze. The air around him which a few minutes ago had been dry, hot and laden with dust had the warm, soft feel of a tropical sunset. The girl, Ally, tightened her grip. She kept moving away from the building they had left. Stephen staggered along with her. Somewhere in the recesses of his brain, he realised that the dry, dusty mud road he had travelled here on was now a paved pathway. It had a grassy border lined with frangipani trees and bushes redolent with jasmine blossoms.

A few metres away, a fair-skinned, golden-haired woman in a grey suit knelt at a flower bed full of rose bushes. She looked up and waved. 'Ally,' she squealed. 'I want to show you my drawing!'

Ally waved back. 'Later, Cindy.' She held on tight to Stephen. The woman got to her feet and hopped from one foot to the other. 'You promise? You promise, Ally?'

Ally shushed her with a regal wave. 'I promise. You finish with the rose bushes. Then go home. Be a good girl.' The woman turned back to the flower bed with a giggle.

'Ally. Where am I? Who are you?' Stephen tried to drag his fingers away from her clasp. Unsuccessfully. She had a strong grip for a girl. 'What happened to the buildings in Rawlinna? The gum tree? and who was—'

She stopped and raised her left hand to her forehead. 'Please, Stephen, stop thinking and clear your mind for a few minutes. Your thoughts are giving me a headache.' She wrinkled her nose at him. 'Apart from your opinions about the strength of my grip being mildly sexist!' She sighed and looked into his eyes. 'Stephen, when you came through the door at Rawlinna, you crossed a time portal. You are in Serendib. The year is 2131.' She silenced his protest with a raised hand. 'Yes, 2131. Over a hundred years from your time in the Before. You came here looking for help. And we will help you. I'll explain everything. I promise.' She pointed to a wrought-iron seat under a frangipani tree. 'But now, please sit there and try to relax, Stephen. I need to make contact.' Her lips curved in a cheeky grin. Her eyes twinkled. 'How would you put it? I need to take you to my leader. But I need to talk to him first.' Her eyes continued to hold his gaze. Stephen felt the tension in his muscles ease. He sank into the seat. It softened under him and shaped to his body.

'What the—' He tried to get up. The seat hollowed deeper. It moulded around his bottom and massaged his thighs. He raised his hands in the air, trying to pull himself free.

Ally gasped and grasped his right hand. She traced the birthmark he had on his palm with the tip of her index finger. 'The star,' she whispered. 'Stephen, were you born with this?'

Flushing, he pulled his hand away, and rubbed the hand on his jeans. 'Mum says my nanny used to try to wash it off,' he muttered.

Ally smiled. 'Yes, Appa was right. As always.'

He gave up trying to get off the seat. 'Ally, what's happening?'

She quietened him with the same regal gesture she had used on the woman earlier. 'Shush for a while. I need to concentrate.'

She turned partly away from him and shut her eyes. Long, curled black lashes shimmered on her cheeks. Black hair cascaded and twisted in the breeze. Her body seemed to thrum to a rhythm he couldn't hear. Stephen couldn't tear his gaze away from her. She was the most beautiful thing he had ever seen in his life. He should record this. He pulled his phone from his pocket.

Ally pivoted back to face him. 'Don't even think about it!' she hissed. 'It will not record anything.' She slapped her right palm on her forehead. 'What is it with you young people in the Before? A life revolving around yourself.

Self-aggrandization. Instant self-gratification. iPhones. iPads. The iGen, I believe you were called!' She pointed to his phone. 'Put that—that thing away and keep still for a few minutes.' She turned to face away from him.

A shimmer of gold light appeared in front of her. Ally bowed her head and brought her palms together at her breast. It was the greeting he had seen Dr Jeganathan's wife use when welcoming her elder relatives at her birthday party. Ally raised her eyes and focused on the shimmer.

Stephen watched in wonder as emotions flashed across her face. The furrows of indignation on her brow smoothed. Her eyes narrowed in query and then widened in awe. Her lips went from pouty discontent to a moue of acceptance. Her eyes pooled with tears and she shook her head, biting her lower lip. Her body tensed and straightened. Finally, she raised her chin, stared into the shimmer and nodded. A quiet gesture of acquiescence.

Bowing her head, Ally brought her palms together again. The golden shimmer softened. Then vanished.

Ally stood for a few seconds with her head bowed. She took a deep, shuddering breath, blinked a couple of times, and turned to him. Tears still sheened her eyes and clung diamond-like to her eyelashes. She looked at Stephen. She blinked a couple of times, her body relaxed, and she laughed. It was a dulcet tinkle of distant bells. The sound reached into his soul, comforting and calming. She dropped down onto the seat next to him. 'Thank you, Stephen.'

'Thank you?'

Ally laughed again and leaned toward him. 'Yes, thank you. Thank you for telling me that I am the most beautiful girl you have ever seen.' She picked up his left hand in her right. 'I hope you don't mind my holding your hand, it helps communication. In the beginning, anyway.' She continued with what could be construed as a soft giggle. 'Thanks also for saying that you could sit here forever holding my hand!' She laughed. 'I will have to teach you to block your thinking.' She stood up and pulled him to his feet. 'Or maybe I won't. I don't get too many compliments around here!' Then she frowned and shut her eyes. She sighed. 'The … the leader made connection. He wants me to stop … how do you say it in the Before … fooling around and to speak with you about ….'

'Ally,' Stephen interrupted. 'My parents. I need help.'

Ally massaged her forehead and dropped back on the seat under the tree. 'Your parents will be okay, Stephen. I promise you.'

'They need urgent medical help.' He sat down beside her. 'I can't just sit here with you. They may be dying!'

'Stephen, there's only one way to save your parents and … and …' she paused and tightened her grip. He heard her unspoken words in his head. 'And the world as you know it.'

'Ally …'

'Hush, Stephen. You have to stay with me. Things will seem strange. Everything. The environment. People.'

'It can't get any weirder,' he muttered.

'Oh, please be quiet and listen,' she asserted.

Her exasperation whipped through his brain and forced him into silence.

'For your information, Stephen, it will, to you anyway, get even weirder, as you describe it.' She stopped and fixed her eyes on his. 'Good. I have your attention. Now, stay quiet, clear your mind and pay attention. I will take you to our spiritual leader. You will hear me address him as 'Appa'. It means father in Tamil. He lets me call him that though he is actually my great-great-grandfather. To everyone else, including you, he is Saint Paul Thomas. Saint Thomas. Or, simply, the Saint.'

'Ally,' Stephen interrupted her, 'you said we are in 2131. But how? And what is this place? Where am I … we? Who are you? And who is your leader?'

'You are where you have to be, Stephen. And I repeat—your parents will be fine.'

He tore his eyes away from hers. He felt the rip in his soul. 'That tells me nothing!'

She let go of his hands. A cold wind tore around and through him. He felt alone. Afraid.

Ally spoke in a whisper. 'There is nothing to be afraid of, Stephen. And you're not alone. I will be with you. I have told you what you need to know—for now.' She reached out and placed a finger on his chest. 'Please.

You have to trust me. Are you ready to proceed?'

His heart and mind flooded with a deep sense of peace at her touch. 'Yes,' Stephen responded. Yes. Somehow, he knew that he could trust this girl.

'When you first walked into the learning pod—the school to you,' Ally continued, 'I manipulated your perception. You saw us dressed as was comfortable and normal to you. I did it because I sensed that you were teetering on the edge of a panic attack. Appa chastised me for doing that. So, from now on, you'll see and experience things as they are here in Serendib.'

Stephen blinked. He saw her as he had the moment he had first stood at the opening to what he now knew was called the learning pod. 'How … how did you do that?' he stammered.

Her silver-white, silk-like tunic and trousers shimmered in the last rays of the setting sun. 'Hmm, how can I explain it to you? Think of it like the creation of a temporary hallucination.'

'I feel like I'm going crazy!' Stephen rubbed his forehead with his palm.

She placed her hand over his on his forehead. 'No Stephen,' she breathed. 'You are more alive and rational than you have ever been in the Before of 2030.'

She dropped her hand and faced him. 'One very important thing. Soften your heart, Stephen. Be receptive to new feelings. New emotions. New challenges. Where you come from, your culture is narrow-minded. Individualistic. You people in the Before look inward. You think you can find your authentic self by feeding your desires. It has made you hard-hearted. Even bigoted.' She placed her right index finger on his shoulder. 'No. Don't say anything. I know that you aren't happy. You can't accept the status quo of your family … school … your classmates … even your church. The values they espouse. Their attitudes. You want to make a difference. And you are sad. Sad because you don't know what to do.'

Stephen blinked. This strange and beautiful girl had just read his mind. He should have been angry or annoyed that she had done it. But here, in this strange world with her, it seemed right that she should do it. He considered what she had said of him. Was he sad? He knew he was confused. Conflicted. He was torn between his parents' and friends' behaviour and his loyalty to his Asian and coloured friends. He remembered the many times that he had tolerated the snide, racist comments of his white classmates. The ethnic jokes. He had even joined in the laughter. He felt a tingle of self-loathing.

Ally sat watching him.

After a few moments, she reached out and ran her finger down his dust-encrusted jacket. She rested her palm over his heart. 'It's okay, Stephen. I understand how you feel. For now, clear your mind. Let the past go. Stay in this moment. Look around you. Listen. And learn from what may feel impossible. Accept that which may seem unacceptable. Now, we need to go to our vitu, our home. We'll get you cleaned up. We can then visit Appa—Saint Thomas.'

A whoosh of wind rustled through the branches of the frangipani tree. Flowers shaken free by the gust blew down on them. Ally caught one in her hand. 'The araliya flower.' She cupped her palm to cradle the blossom. 'You call it frangipani, or plumeria. Here in Serendib, we consider what just happened a blessing. Come.'

Ally walked back to the dome—or learning pod, as she called it. She placed her palm on the surface. A panel slid open. She picked up two white objects that looked like medium-size skateboard decks with no wheels attached to them. She placed both on the ground between them. And tapped the front end of each.

'Jump on. We need to get moving.'

'But … but how?' Stephen stared at the boards resting on the path.

'Oh, ye of little faith!' Ally stepped on one and held her hand out to him. 'Step on to it, Stephen.'

Stephen placed his feet on the other board as he would on his skateboard at home. He took her extended hand. 'Whoa!' The boards lifted off the ground and started moving.

'I believe you call them hovercrafts?' She threw her head back and laughed.

Her joy floated into Stephen's brain. His heart felt a little lighter. He gave up trying to rationalise what was happening. Her smile told him that she approved.

Together they whizzed down the paved pathway. On either side domes shimmered orange and red in the gentle rays of the setting sun. Plants and flowers provided swathes of colour around the domes. Dark-skinned women dressed in shimmering multicoloured silk in the style of the Indian saree, and men in two-piece suits in a similar silk material, stared with amazement at Stephen and waved to Ally.

She stood relaxed on the device. Her hair blew a black shimmering cloud around and behind her. Gray-suited, white-skinned men and women walked and skipped along on the edge of the road. They called out to Ally. Ally beamed and waved back.

'How does this thing know where to take us?' Stephen yelled out to her. He tensed the muscles of his back and stuck his free arm out to keep his balance.

'I tapped the route into the skimmer.' Ally replied. She glanced back at Stephen. 'Oops, sorry. Too fast for you?'

'No,' Stephen grimaced, wobbled, and then regained his balance. 'I'm fine,' he spoke through gritted teeth. 'Just fine!' He was an experienced skier and surfer. He would master the use of this tiny, hovering skateboard.

Ally laughed.

The skimmers turned and stopped in front of a silver-white dome, and then sank to the ground.

Ally let go of his hand. She touched the surface of the dome. A section slid open. She turned to Stephen with a faux curtsy. 'Welcome to our vitu—our house, Stephen.'

Stephen stepped in. Ally followed.

The dome slid shut behind them.

CHAPTER 6

Serendib, 2131

They stood inside the front door. Ally watched as Stephen ran his fingers through his hair. His curly, golden-brown hair was tangled and encrusted with Nullarbor desert sand. His leather jacket and jeans were crinkled and dusty. He looked down at his clothes. The pupils of his cobalt blue eyes dilated, and a red flush invaded his pale cheeks. He looked tired, stressed. A mess. She knew that he felt it, too.

A wave of empathy flew across Ally's emotions. Stephen's adrenaline levels were high enough to explode from his ears. She reached out and placed her palm on his cheek. 'Stephen. Relax.' She made eye contact with him. 'Hey, your friends call you 'Coops', don't they? Maybe I should call you that!' She let her fingers trail down his cheek.

His eyes dilated further. 'How do you … Never mind.'

'Relax.' Ally took a step closer to him. 'You may even enjoy what you are about to experience.'

Her parents bustled towards them. Ally dropped her hand and stepped in front of Stephen.

She sent a mind message to her parents. Talk. Don't connect. He cannot get our messages. As yet. Her parents wobbled their heads in acceptance of her instructions.

'Aiyo, pillai … child, all the people on the way are contacting me. Complaining that you are holding hands with a noncy on a double skimmer.' Her mother prattled to Ally. 'My brain was bursting with worry. Then Saint Thomas contacted and told us not to be concerned.'

Ally held back a chuckle. Whatever Appa had said must have impressed her mother. She had dressed in her festive orange silk saree, and taken time to get the ceremonial pottu decoration on her forehead, even slicked on some lip gloss.

Her father was dressed in his standard evening wear of silk veshti and shirt. He moved around Ally. 'Aah, you are the boy from the Before. Welcome to our home, son. Welcome. Come, come. Dinner is ready.' He wobbled his head and waved his hand toward the living area.

'Stephen, meet my parents. This,' she gestured to her mother, 'is Amma.' She then pointed to her father. 'And I call my father Thatha.'

Stephen wiped his palm on his jeans and shook her thatha's hand. 'Thank you, sir. I'm sorry. I've been on the road. I—I'm not dressed for a visit. For dinner.'

'My goodness, Stephen. How very polite.' Thatha shot a look of wry amusement at Ally. 'You can teach our hoyden daughter some manners. Come.' He drew Stephen through the arch that separated the entrance foyer of their vitu from the living and dining area. 'Saint Thomas said you would probably like a shower and a change of clothes.'

'Sir,' Stephen interrupted. 'Sir, I need medical help.' His voice rose a notch. He spoke in a rush. The words tangled with each other getting out of his mouth. 'My parents need a doctor. They're in our caravan. It's on the main road. Please, can I use your phone? Call triple-0, the emergency hotline? I need the flying doctor. Ambulance. The rangers. Someone. Now! They may be dying!'

Thatha looked at Ally, his eyes clouded in confusion. 'Phone? Emergency hotline? Ambulance? Flying doctors? Caravan?' He frowned at Ally. 'What is he talking about?'

Ally shushed them with a gesture. 'I will explain later, Thatha. Right now, as you rightly said, Stephen needs a shower.' She dragged Stephen towards the guest cell of their home pod.

Nathan, seated in a home shell, watching the hologram of the evening newscaster called out, 'I brought over the sets of clothes you wanted, Ally.'

'Thanks, Nathan.' She hustled Stephen into the guest cell.

Ally stopped just inside the opening to the cell and waved the opening shut. 'Great,' she muttered. 'I hope none of our neighbour's notice I'm in a sleep-cell with a noncy!'

She reached up and placed her hands on Stephen's shoulders. 'Sit. Please.' She dragged him down on the double shell in the corner and dropped down beside him. The shell started the usual massage routine. 'Oh, stop it!' she snapped and slammed her hand, palm-down on the armrest. The movement stopped. 'Stephen. Listen to me. Listen carefully. First, and most importantly, your parents *will* be alright. You feel like you've been away a long time, but it's only been minutes since you left them. Probably less. Please trust me on this. It's very important that you do this.'

'Ally, what the heck do you mean? It's been over an hour. How can they be alright? It's more likely that they're dying!' He dragged out his mobile phone from the pocket of his jacket. 'What the … it's got to be broken.' He shook it. Then tapped the screen. 'It's stopped at five pm. That's just after I left the caravan. It can't be.' He dropped his head in his hands.

Ally placed her fingertips on his shoulder. She pressed down, conveying her strength to him as best as she could.

Stephen raised his head. The movement was slow. Wary.

What she saw in his eyes clutched at her heart. Ally reached into him with calming vibes. She attempted to push down the spikes of fear and pain racing through Stephen's nerves and neurons.

'Ally,' he stammered. 'Who are you? Where am I? How can it be 2131?' He scanned the room. 'What's this place?' Panic flashed through his conscience making him shudder. 'What's happening?'

Ally crisis-connected with Saint Thomas. He sent back an immediate response. Sharp and short. 'Stephen.' She held his gaze, forcing him to stay connected. 'You're in Serendib. As I told you earlier, we are a hundred plus years from your time in the Before. Serendib is the Asia and Oceania headquarters for IPI. The International Peace Initiative. The Asia-Oceania collaborative is called Samaataanam.'

'What …?'

Ally stayed linked to Saint Thomas. 'Be gentle with Stephen,' he channelled.

'Stephen,' she lowered her voice to a whisper, using mind connection over words. 'Samaataanam means tranquillity, peace and reconciliation. It forms the basic tenets of our society. The Africas call themselves Amani and the Americas and Europe are Shalom. You don't know it now, but you are destined to be a part of this collaboration in your future.'

'No.' He shook his head as if to rid himself of an unwelcome bug sitting on him. 'I've got to be dreaming! I'm in the Nullarbor!'

'We are in the Nullarbor, Stephen.' She received a message from Saint Thomas. 'And, maybe it's better that you see this as a dream. For now. But—,' she stood up and pulled him up with her. 'Dream or not, you need to clean up, have dinner and visit with Saint Thomas.' She walked towards an opening in the wall and motioned to him to follow her into the adjoining space. 'You stand here,' she pointed to a corner, 'and you'll be showered.'

'Showered? How?' Stephen stammered, and looked up at the roof of the cleaning pod.

Ally laughed and rolled her eyes. 'No, not by me! Or anyone else!' She pointed to the roof. 'Sorry, no old-fashioned showerhead either! Relax. You'll enjoy the experience. And,' she chuckled, 'no towels either. You'll dry off. That,' she pointed to a small, silver ball attached to the wall, 'will shave you if you pick it up and touch it to your face.' She passed her hand over a small, recessed button. A chute opened. 'Drop your clothes into this. There are several fresh sets of everything in the room for you to choose from after you dry off.' She turned away. 'I'll be in the gathering area.'

Stephen reached his hand out to stop her. 'Ally, what's a noncy?'

His anxiety flowed in waves towards her. 'A noncy is someone who isn't coloured.' She hurried to the opening. 'Connect with me if you want anything. No. Correction. Call me if you need any help.'

Ally returned to the gathering area and slumped onto the vitu shell next to Nathan. 'I'm exhausted!' She glanced at the hologram, currently reporting on the weather. 'Did I miss anything?'

'Of course!' Nathan's elbow dug her in the ribs. 'A report on the future leader of Serendib riding helter-skelter with a handsome, if somewhat bedraggled, noncy.'

'That's not amusing, Nathan.' She sank into the shell, permitting it to massage and comfort her. The knots in her spine and shoulder loosened.

Nathan picked up her right hand and glanced at the purple birthmark on her palm at the base of her thumb. 'I don't like this, Ally. I know you're keen to live out your destiny. But should Saint Thomas put you through this now? You're fifteen. This contact with the Before is tiring you out. I had a couple of our fellow scholars connect with me. They said you're completely off all communication channels.'

'Nathan.' She entwined her fingers into his. 'Thank you for worrying about me. But I'm strong. You above anyone else should understand that I have to do this.'

Nathan sighed. He slid an arm over her shoulders and hugged her.

'The boy from the Before has a name, Nathan. He's Stephen. Stephen Ashley-Cooper.' Ally exhaled slowly and leaned into Nathan. She accepted the comforting energy he directed to her. 'I had to read Stephen's thoughts, Nathan. It wasn't difficult, his brain patterns are so basic. Totally unsophisticated. Primitive.' She shuddered. 'What drained me was keeping his emotional circuits from going into a neuronal meltdown. He has to be in a relaxed brain pattern when we meet Appa.' She pulled her feet up. 'So much depends on it.' She breathed out slowly. 'It's going to be a long evening.'

'Do you want me to come with you?'

'Hmm, no.' She shook her head. 'It's between Stephen and Appa. I'll only be there as an observer.'

Hands entwined, Nathan and Ally sat in silence, watching the hologram discuss cloud patterns over central Australia. 'Wow.' Ally sat up straight. 'Stephen made contact! He's a fast learner.'

'He has the best teacher,' growled Nathan.

Ally sat up straight. 'He says he's dressed. Wants me to check if he's done things right.'

'How hard can it be to wear a veshti?' Nathan grinned.

Ally dropped Nathan's hand. She rounded on him. 'You didn't!' she cried.

'No!' Nathan burst into laughter. 'I left two good sets of tunics and trousers, together with the required undergarments.'

Ally punched Nathan on the shoulder and pushed off the shell. 'I'll go get him.'

The sapphire blue silk of the tunic and trousers were a perfect complement to Stephen's fair complexion and the cobalt blue tint of his eyes. The clothes were a near-perfect fit, the silk tunic hugged pectorals and biceps that had been unnoticeable under his leather jacket. He had left the top buttons on the tunic open. While not the standard way to dress, it looked good on him. His damp hair reflected burnished gold in the dome's luminous lighting and curled at the collar of the tunic.

For the first time, Ally noticed his strong arched brows and thick eyelashes. The distinct cheekbones and angular jaw made her think of pictures of soldiers from the Before. He stood tall. He looked like a warrior ready to take on whatever lay ahead.

His nerves were calmer than earlier, but still shooting spikes of anxiety. No. Correction. There was a challenge in his expression. Stephen's full lips turned up at the corners. The movement spread through his face to crinkle his eyes.

She focused on his pupils, giving him a chance to connect. It was rudimentary, but he was getting through. Ally gave him time to unravel the messages. She felt his words. 'Do you approve, Ally?' The challenge was unmistakable.

She suppressed the unfamiliar jolt of energy that whipped through her emotional brain.

His smile widened, dimpling his cheeks. 'Thank you, you do like it!'

'I believe 'wow' would be a suitable response?' She gestured to him to precede her out of the guest room.

Stephen placed his hand on her arm to stop her. 'Ally, I think you know that I'm confused and anxious. I don't pretend to understand what is happening. But I feel that I can trust you. So, I will follow your instructions. But please, please help my parents.'

'Thank you for your trust.' She placed her other hand over his. 'Your parents will recover. I promise you that. Now, let's have dinner and go meet Appa.'

Nathan walked up to them and cuffed Stephen on the shoulder. 'I believe an appropriate greeting would be, 'G'day mate! Howzit going?"

Ally giggled at Stephen's attempt to disguise his abhorrence at the greeting. 'Nathan, I don't believe that is an appropriate manner in which folk in Stephen's class greet each other in the Before.' She glanced at Stephen. 'Correct?'

'Sorry,' Stephen stammered. 'I didn't mean to be rude. You're right, it's not the customary greeting.'

Thatha bustled up to them. 'Come, come, children. The thosai and sambar are getting cold.'

Ally caught Stephen's eye. 'We don't sit at a table with cutlery and crockery.' She pointed to the silk cushions on the floor. 'We sit cross-legged on the floor.'

'And,' Amma interjected, 'we eat with our fingers. But I have the utensils for you.' She handed Stephen a plate with a fork and knife.

Ally kept silent during the meal.

Stephen picked at his food.

Nathan and Amma chatted about the latest information from the African and Asian chapters of IPI.

Thatha scooped thosai into his mouth. He kept glancing at Stephen.

'The flowers are beautiful this year.' Amma mused. 'The noncy's have done a great job.'

Stephen frowned. 'Noncys. The non-coloured.' he looked at Ally and shifted his eyes to Thatha. 'Mister Joseph, forgive me if I'm being indiscreet.' Stephen placed his plate on the dining mat. His voice was low but determined. 'Are the white-skinned people here in … in Serendib … in some way different to you folk?'

Thatha shifted on the cushion. His throat wobbled as he swallowed. He cleared his throat. 'Stephen, no. Ask. I will tell you what I can. It is all because of what happened a long time ago to the white people. The white-skinned became really nice … nice-natured.'

'You mean friendly? But there's more, isn't there? I didn't see any whites in the classroom with Ally.'

Thatha shut his eyes, then spoke slowly, weighing up every word. 'They … the whites … noncys … are not able to keep up. So … they …

they have special learning hubs. Due to what happened a long time ago, their brains don't develop past happy childhood days.'

Ally listened as Thatha parroted the words Appa had instructed him to say. 'You'll meet our leader soon, Stephen. Saint Paul Thomas will explain it all to you,' he finished in a rush.

Stephen frowned. Ally could feel his mind slotting pieces together. He put his fork down on his plate, uncrossed his feet, and rose in a dancer-like fluid movement.

Ally couldn't help but stare.

Stephen looked at Ally. The corners of his lips twitched. 'I play rugby, tennis and cricket. I'm a state-level swimmer. I've got to be flexible.'

He turned to her parents. 'Mrs Joseph, Mr Joseph, I really appreciate your hospitality, but I think it's time I met your leader or guru or whoever. I need answers.' His voice firmed. 'Now.'

Thatha's black eyes softened. He sighed and scrambled up off the floor. 'Young man, you have a good heart and a strong spirit.' He tapped the side of his head. 'I can sense it.' He chuckled. 'If you were one of ours, I would have proposed a marriage between you and our Ally.'

'Thatha!' Ally choked on the tea she was sipping.

She felt Nathan bristle with outrage.

'But,' Thatha continued, 'as it is, I am afraid you may end up with more questions than answers. Go, go. And God go with you.'

CHAPTER 7

Serendib, 2131

It was the time of day when all of Serendib rested from work and learning. But today, Ally would not rest. She had a mission to accomplish.

The vitu home pods on either side of the paved path glowed in shades of bronze, orange and amber. They radiated the energy they had absorbed during the day and reflected the activities and moods of their occupants. A few radiated the gentle mauve of a family already asleep.

She tapped the route to Appa's nexus pod into the skimmers, then stepped on hers and held her hand out to Stephen. 'We have a fair way to travel.'

Stephen stepped onto his skimmer and waited for the air cushion to lift. He kept his hands by his side. 'No, Ally. I'll follow you. You go on ahead.' His lips tensed in concentration. 'I'll manage,' he muttered.

'Of course, you can manage, Stephen.' She smiled. 'You're a … what do you call it in the Before … a surfer dude, aren't you?'

Ally's eyes met and held his. His brain waves were no longer spiking and erratic. Instead, they now blazed on high alert. Stephen was ready. Appa had been right. As always.

They travelled in silence. Stephen rode by her side. She kept her eyes on the paved path and avoided eye contact with Stephen. It would give him time to prepare.

The skimmers veered left and away from the domed, tropical city of Serendib. Ahead lay the stark expanse on the Nullarbor Plain. Kangaroos stood silhouetted in the distance and a wombat ambled by in the saltbush on the side of the path. Somewhere in the distance stood the dark shape of a camel.

The glitter of a myriad of stars in the vast black sky was interrupted only by the sultry glow of the low hanging moon. Night in the desert never ceased to fascinate Ally. Stephen's eyes were raised to the sky. He felt it too. Ally felt a flicker of connection from her heart to his. She tamped it down. No. Not wise. Not now. Not ever. Affection was dangerous. She had a job to do. Success depended on her remaining objective.

They travelled farther. She sensed Stephen's mounting tension and sent out calming vibes the best way she knew. She hummed the evening chant of her people. 'The heavens declare the glory of God; the skies proclaim the work of his hands. Day after day, they pour forth speech; night after night, they reveal knowledge.'

The skimmers sped on. And on.

The dome ahead of them blazed bronze and gold. It flashed a ray of light that lit the paved path ahead of them and banished the darkness of the Nullarbor night.

'Where did that come from?' Stephen exclaimed.

'Appa turned on the luminescence of his nexus pod. He knows we're near.'

The skimmers eased to a stop at the dome.

Ally stepped off. She went up to the shiny surface of the dome and stood with her palms together and head bowed in her customary posture of respect. A glimmer of pride went through her brain when Stephen, with a sideways glance at her, imitated her posture perfectly.

'Don't be surprised at anything that happens,' she connected to him. 'Stay brave.'

A flicker in his eyes indicated that he had received her message and understood it.

The entrance slid open.

'Stop chatting and come in, children,' Saint Thomas called out. He connected with Ally at the same time. 'You will be an observer. If this is to work, you cannot influence him. It has to be his thoughts. His choices. Finally, his decision.'

Ally sent back a message of assent.

The spacious, dome-shaped chamber was arranged in meeting mode, with four double shells in a circle and a small table in the centre. The rest of the chamber was bare. The walls radiated the blue glow of concentration.

Saint Thomas sat in the shell facing the entrance.

'Come in, Stephen.' His only acknowledgement to her was an almost imperceptible nod of his head. He remained seated. Stephen approached with his head held high. He looked straight at Saint Thomas. 'Good evening, sir.'

Saint Thomas' eyes flickered to Ally. 'He is strong. Patient. Wise,' he channelled. 'He doesn't know what he can achieve—as yet. He is a worthy candidate from the Before. And you know that he is the Chosen One.'

Ally nodded. She read in Saint Thomas' eyes approval of how she had calmed Stephen and prepared him for the meeting. She clamped down on her fears that Stephen was not yet strong enough to deal with what lay ahead, but not before Saint Thomas picked up on her feelings.

Saint Thomas' dedicated noncy, Jake, dressed in the standard grey two-piece suit, sauntered in with three glasses of fresh coconut juice. 'Good evening, Saint,' he sang out in the high, childish voice of the adult noncy. 'You said you had a meeting. I thought you might like something cool to drink.' He placed the glasses on the table and glanced at Ally. ''ello, Ally.' He wiggled his fingers in her direction. 'Where did you find this gorgeous young man?' He tittered. 'And all dressed up, too!'

'Thank you, Jake.' Saint Thomas reached out and patted Jake's arm. 'Why not call it a night and go home to your lovely wife?'

Jake hooted in laughter. 'Yes, she'll be all set to party when I get home early. Thanks, boss.' He squealed and scampered out of the room through an opening at the back of the pod.

Stephen's eyes followed Jake's every movement. He was looking, listening, and learning.

'Have a drink, Stephen.' Saint Thomas gestured to the glasses on the table. 'And relax.' He gestured to a shell.

'Sir,' Stephen remained standing and held Saint Thomas' gaze. He didn't flinch at the penetration of the steel grey eyes. 'I don't know who you are, but you're obviously someone of authority here. I don't know why you're keeping me here or what you want with or from me. But, right now, all I care about is getting help for my parents. They're both very sick and in a hot caravan on the main road.' He dropped his voice, his words now slower. 'Get. Them. Help. Please, sir.' He stopped, took a deep breath, and exhaled. Slowly. 'After that … after that, I will do whatever you want me to do. Sir, you have my word.'

Saint Thomas' eyes tunnelled into Stephen's. Ally shivered. A brain wave from him clipped the corner of her consciousness. 'You are too involved. Disentangle yourself. Stay objective.' She accepted his orders and cleared her mind.

The silver threads in his beard shimmered. 'Sit.' He pointed to a shell. Stephen stared back. Then sank into the one closest to Saint Thomas. Saint Thomas' voice carried the authority of the ages. 'Stephen Ashley-Cooper, you are very bright for a Before and yet woefully ignorant. You have much to learn.'

'Sir, my parents?'

'Aah, you are worried about your parents. That is good. Very good. But unnecessary. They will live and be cured. I can't say the same for everyone else in your world.'

'Sir, I don't …' A glance from Saint Thomas' grey eyes stilled Stephen.

'You don't understand now. But you will. You will. You have a few days, maybe a week here with us.' Appa snapped his fingers. 'But it will be a few minutes in the Before. In your time in 2030.'

'How …' Stephen managed only the one word before he lapsed back into silence.

'Stephen,' Appa leaned forward. His dark, age-lined hand reached out and rested on Stephen's shoulder. 'As Aletheia has told you, we are in 2131.' He increased the pressure of his fingers. 'You will return—if you return to the Before within a few minutes of your leaving.' He stopped and took a deep breath. 'Your parents will recover. I give you my word. My word as the spiritual head of Samaataanam. And on my lineage as descendent of Thomas the Apostle of Kerala.'

Ally's brain waves crested. That was information he rarely shared.

'He's smart,' Saint Thomas' thoughts reached her. 'We can only hope he has the strength.'

Stephen sat still. Silent. Pale.

‘I’ll help him,’ she flashed back.

Saint Thomas bored into Ally’s brain. He nodded. ‘That you will, Aletheia. That you will.’

‘Stephen,’ Saint Thomas’ voice was low, his tone radiated comfort and assurance. ‘You want to help your parents recover from this malady that has overcome them. And you need our help to do this.’

Stephen’s nod of assent was barely perceptible.

‘We will help you. But to accomplish this, you need to play your part. It will require you to be lion-brained and lamb-hearted.’

‘Courageous and humble.’ Stephen’s words were slowly articulated. Barely audible.

Ally fired a ray of encouragement and strength towards Stephen.

The ray of energy was intercepted by Saint Thomas. ‘No, Ally.’ He connected in silence. ‘This has to be his mission. You can only support him. You cannot direct or lead him.’

He spoke to Stephen. ‘Stephen, what you experience here may make you feel broken-hearted and crushed in spirit. But you will emerge a better man. Stronger and ready for the job you will do.’

‘Sir—, Saint Thomas, I don’t understand! Why me? Why now? And what do you mean by a job? All I want is medical help for my parents.’

Saint Thomas held Stephen’s eyes for a few seconds. ‘You want more, Stephen. You don’t know it yet.’ He nodded slowly. ‘You will learn. You will understand. It is as it is.’

Stephen tore his gaze away from Saint Thomas. ‘What do you want me to do?’

‘Look at me, Stephen.’ It was spoken in a tone that brooked no disagreement.

Stephen raised his eyes to meet Saint Thomas’ gaze.

‘Yes. You are almost ready.’ Saint Thomas’ eyes drilled into Stephen’s. ‘First, clear your mind of your concern about your parents’ health. They will recover. Do it. Now.’ Seconds passed. ‘Good. You are ready. Now, answer me. Stephen, what do you know of your parents’ family history?’

Stephen blinked and shivered, as if drawn out of a trance. ‘My parents’ family history?' He hesitated, shrugged, and continued. 'I know a little. My father's British. He and his mother, Nana Janet moved to Australia when he was three.'

'When your grandparents divorced.'

Stephen frowned and then continued. 'My mother's American. Well, she was American, she's an Aussie citizen now.'

'They are both from wealthy families.'

Stephen's eyes took on a look of reminiscence. The emotion flicked up the corners of his lips. 'They tease each other about that. They were both scholarship students at Oxford working on their PhD in virology and immunology. They both thought the other one was poor and didn't talk about their own family wealth till they were engaged.'

'Your mansion in Sydney. The ski lodge in the Snowy Mountains and the luxury holiday home on the coast in Gerringong. The vineyard in the Barossa Valley. Have you ever wondered where the money came from?'

Stephen grimaced. He shook his head. His voice when he spoke was a little more than a whisper. 'No, sir.' Ally caught his eye. His brain waves were spiking again. She sent calming thoughts. 'It's okay. He's a kind man. Trust him. It is important that you do.'

This time, Appa let the thought waves through.

'They joke about their money coming from plantations in very different countries from very different sources. I don't know any more. I … I kind of take it for granted, I guess.'

Saint Thomas' grey eyes flashed. He withdrew his hand. Stephen flinched and leaned back in the shell. 'And you never thought to investigate how these plantations generated the family millions?' he probed. 'Whose toil and sweat lined the velvet and silk pockets of your ancestors?'

Stephen's looked from Saint Thomas' face to Ally. She sensed the deep memory zones of his brain stir. 'Sir,' he struggled to keep his voice steady. 'I never … never thought about it. Never …' He stopped and swallowed. 'Never asked.'

Ally's empathy lobe threatened to kick into overdrive. She clamped it down. This was not a time for emotion. She had to be ready for action.

Saint Thomas stood up. Stephen rose with him. 'No, you didn't think.' Saint Thomas' voice was steel. 'You accepted the upper-class white privilege as your right.' He reached out and placed his right palm on Stephen's chest over his heart.

'Sir—'

Saint Thomas' voice gentled. 'But you will think, Stephen. You will. And you will act. It is your destiny.'

Flint-grey eyes under bushy silver eyebrows burrowed into Stephen's conscience. Ally watched as memories hidden in the recesses of his brain swam to the surface. He remembered his visit to the Byrne family plantation bungalow in Virginia. He spoke in a semi-trance. 'I spent two months as an exchange student last year with my family in Virginia. There were things I wasn't happy with. But … but …' He stopped and looked away.

Ally read his thoughts and articulated them for him. 'You wanted to ask questions about how they lived. The photographs of their ancestors on the wall.'

Stephen nodded.

The old man reached out and placed his palm on Stephen's chest again. It was a touch of comfort and calm. Ally watched as the tide of distress in Stephen's brain ebbed and receded.

'Sir—' Stephen croaked out the word.

Ally stepped to the table and passed him the glass of cloudy white fluid. 'Drink,' she commanded.

Stephen sipped. He then gulped down the coconut water she had handed him.

He turned back to Saint Thomas. 'Sir, what is it you want from me?'

'Beati of Serendib call me Saint Thomas.' He laughed quietly. 'Although I must say my history is anything but saintly!'

'The blessed ones of the land of unexpected benevolence,' Stephen murmured.

'Good, very good.' Saint Thomas tilted his head. A smile tilted his lips. 'And you will now have a taste of this benevolence. Come.' He gestured for Stephen to follow him and walked toward the wall of the nexus pod. The curved surface glowed blue and purple. A streak of light twisted and shimmered across it.

Ally scooted around Stephen to stand next to Saint Thomas. 'Are you sending him to kutumpam?'

He stopped and turned to her. 'Enlightenment, Ally. He needs to experience his roots.' They stood toe to toe; eyes locked. Seconds passed in silence. 'Maybe you are right.' Appa sighed. 'You can go with him. It will be part of your training to take my place when the time is right.'

Ally reached for Stephen. He slipped his fingers into hers. She felt the tremor of fear mixed with anticipation coursing through him.

Stephen followed her and Appa through the opening in the surface of the nexus pod.

CHAPTER 8

Virginia, USA, 1860

The sun was a brazen gold sphere high in the sky. A hot, moist wind blew across the manicured lawn, whipping up sand and dust. The dust whirled around them and invaded his throat. Ahead of them stretched a dirt path with two parallel ruts of hardened mud with a grassy strip in the middle.

Stephen coughed and looked around for Saint Thomas.

'What happened to … to the Saint?'

'Appa has gone back to Serendib, Stephen.'

'Gone *back*? Where the heck are we?'

Stephen stared at the building at the end of the dirt path.

The three-story red-brick house stood sombre and sedate. The two-story portico was supported by white columns. The entrance at the centre of the lower floor verandah was framed by long, rectangular windows. Similar windows on the second story stood open. Lace curtains fluttered in the breeze. The sloping slate roof was broken up by dormer windows and two large brick chimneys. Tall oak trees stood on either side of the house.

A sense of foreboding slithered up his spine and spiked into his brain. His head spun. Stephen gasped for breath. He staggered. 'What … I don't understand …'

Ally wrapped her fingers around his. He clung to her. 'Look at me, Stephen,' she commanded.

She pierced his mind with her gaze. He calmed.

'I feel like I should know this place,' he faltered.

'Good. I'll be with you the whole time. Hang on to my hand.' She chuckled. 'I don't want to leave you behind in 1860!'

A strange familiarity crept into his brain and joined the feeling of foreboding. '1860? Dear God.' He stuttered. 'This is my mum's family home in Virginia! Just a long time ago.'

'Yes, Stephen. This is the Byrne family plantation in 1860.'

'I visited last year,' Stephen whispered. 'It's the family house. They still call it the mansion. It hasn't changed much.'

'Yes. Your mum sent you here to get to know her family. You went to school with your cousins, Nat and Anthony.'

'Ally,' Stephen cleared his throat of the dust. 'Why're we here? How?'

Ally glanced around, then dragged him towards a stone bench on the manicured lawn. 'Time to sit and talk, Stephen. I can't tell you why we're here. That's something you have to figure out. But I can tell you how. I'll make it short. You have many things to experience in the window of time Appa has granted us.'

Stephen dropped onto the cold stone bench.

'Stephen, have you heard of parts of your brain that are called silent areas?'

'I read somewhere that we use only about ten percent of our brain.'

'The other brain areas aren't as silent as you think. Some of the areas in the frontal lobes,' she tapped her forehead, 'store the memories of past ancestral experiences. These memories are passed down through generations. Spoken history and intuitive experiences.' She stopped and smiled. 'I guess the closest you know of it is the science of neural epigenetics.'

'How's all that related to this?' He pointed to the house.

'Don't interrupt, Stephen.' Ally batted her fingers at him. 'Appa mined into these areas in your brain. You'll use those areas to experience your roots. We call it revisiting family. In Serendib, it's called the kutumpam experience. Kutumpam is the word for family in Tamil. The language of Serendib. Pay careful attention, Stephen. And,' She stopped and shut her eyes for a second. Then opened them. 'I should have anticipated it. Appa isn't connecting. We're on our own.' She took his right hand in both of hers. 'Stephen, immerse yourself in what happens. Allow yourself to be *here*. In the moment. Look. Listen. Feel. And learn. It's important you do. Please. A lot depends on it. On you.'

Stephen groaned. 'Okay. I'll do it. At least, I'll try. Only because I trust you, Ally.' He turned her right hand over. 'I thought I saw it earlier. You have a birthmark like mine!'

Ally placed her open palm next to his. 'Not like yours, Stephen. Identical.'

'What does that mean, Ally?'

'Every second or third generation a child is born with this mark on their palm. The person has a special destiny.'

'I think I know what it means for you. You obviously have an important role in your world of 2131. But what does it mean for me?'

'That, you'll have to find out, Stephen.'

The sound of horse hooves and the rumble of wheels on the gravel interrupted them. A four-seater carriage drawn by two tall black Palomino horses came into view and clattered toward the front of the house. A black man in worn, white linen shirt and brown khaki trousers sat in the driver's perch. On his head was a tattered brown hat. By his side sat a girl with a café au lait complexion. She held a basket full of fruit on her lap. Dressed in a cotton print dress, she sat erect, her face turned up to the sun. Her head was bare and covered with tight black braids. Her perfect features could have been sculpted by an artist.

The two white men in the back, judging from their raised voices and extravagant gestures, were engaged in a heated debate.

'What if they see us?' Stephen muttered.

Ally giggled. 'You don't have to whisper, Stephen. They can't see or hear us.'

'Ally, are these my ancestors?'

She smiled at him. Her caring and concern reached out to him, calming his confusion—a little. 'Meet your many-times-removed grandfather Stephen, and his father, Alexander Byrne. Maybe you were named after the younger one?'

The carriage drew close to the house and stopped.

Ally jumped up and dragged Stephen with her. 'Come on, you need to hear what they're arguing about.' Hand in hand, they ran up the path and stood by the carriage.

The girl slipped down and placed the basket on her head. The black man jumped off the seat and opened the door to the carriage. The younger of the two white men climbed out of the carriage onto the mud path. Slim and clean-shaven, with sharp lean features and flyaway gold hair, he was dressed in a knee-length cutaway jacket with a waist seam and a striped pair of fitting trousers. His leather boots were mud-encrusted.

Supporting himself on his cane, the older man heaved his bulk out of the carriage. Dressed in a loose long double-breasted jacket and trousers, his leather boots were also caked with mud. Feet planted apart; he looked up at the taller younger man. The older man's flat nose and handlebar moustache quivered as he turned a fierce green-eyed stare on the younger.

'Stephen, I will have you know that your behaviour today at the auction was totally unacceptable. I will not have you insulting me and your fellow plantation owners that way.' Spittle sprayed on the young man's coat.

'Father.' The younger man didn't move. His icy blue eyes met and held the older man's gaze. 'You told me we were to purchase a couple of new slaves. You gave me no warning of the putrid conditions. The dirt. The inhuman treatment. A slave auction!' His voice rose. 'Father, they are human beings. Humans with chains around their necks. Even the women. We wouldn't even keep a dog restrained that way! The auctioneer described these people—people, Father—like they were animals for sale.' He turned his head and spat on the ground. Ally and Stephen jumped out of the way of the spray of spittle. 'That old man Sherwin was salivating while prodding that young woman. Poking her body like she was a piece of meat. I had to say something. How could you stand there bidding as if you were buying a horse? How could you? How could you?' His voice broke on a deep sob.

Stephen clenched his fist. 'Slaves. They kept black slaves.' He realised he was squeezing Ally's fingers. 'Sorry,' he clenched his teeth. 'I've seen enough. We need to leave.'

'No! We have to stay for the time allocated and you have to watch.' She shoved him closer to the two men. 'Listen.'

'I should have realised you were too lily-livered to take it! It's your mother's fault! She is the one who insisted we send you to that fancy school up north. Come back speaking like a bloody Northerner! That way of talk has no place here. You behaved like some abolitionist at the sale yards today!' the older spluttered, spraying more spittle on the younger. 'Why do you think I dragged you away early? You were shivering and sweating up a storm. After the way you insulted the plantation owners, you would have been pummelled to jelly if we had stayed any longer.' He guffawed. 'I got you out before you vomited, didn't I?' His voice got louder and gruffer. 'Grow up, boy! You are my heir. Sadly, the only one I have! You will be doing the buying at the auctions soon.'

'No!'

The older man shrugged and continued. 'You will,' he growled. He swept his arm in a wide arc to encompass the house and the rolling fields that stretched into the distance. 'Who do you think plants and harvests the tobacco and cotton other than *your* slaves? Look around.' He prodded a finger in the younger man's chest. 'This is your destiny. You will do as I say.' He turned and walked a few steps towards the front door of the house, then looked back. 'There was a useful breeder coming up in the next lot. I wanted her. Now that fool Newham will get her.'

The girl with the café au lait complexion walking a few steps ahead of them shivered. The baskets on her head trembled.

The younger man reached out and grasped the arm of the older. His eyes fixed on the straight back of the girl. 'Father!' he spluttered. 'Don't.'

The older man guffawed and slammed his palm on the back of the younger. 'You like her, don't you, Stephen? She sure is a pretty wench. For a mulatto.' He clapped the younger one on his shoulder. 'Well, Alice is all yours, son! Take it as my gift to you for your 21st birthday. Use her as you wish. Enjoy yourself as much as you want. Make sure you breed some good quality products for us.'

Still laughing, the old man hauled himself up the steps onto the verandah.

The girl slipped around the side of the house and vanished to the back.

CHAPTER 9

Virginia, USA, 1860

These were his ancestors. This was where his mother's money was acquired and her values were spawned. Anger and disgust coiled snake-like in the pit of his stomach. The venom of his inheritance spun through him. White American. White British. White Anglo-Saxon Australian. He looked at Ally. Her dark complexion glowed in the afternoon heat and humidity. Black hair cascaded and twisted in the breeze. Brown-black eyes met his, conveying understanding, pouring her strength into him. Her words came back to him. Look. Listen. Learn.

'God, Ally. Haven't we seen enough?'

She shook her head. 'No.' She dragged him closer to the young man. 'There's more. Listen.'

The black man who had driven the carriage stood at the head of the horses. The reins held loose in his fingers. 'Massa. Me take carriage to barn? Get horse ready for Massa ride in afternoon?' His words carried a guttural accent threaded through with anger.

The young white man stepped towards the black and grasped his arm. 'Don't try that on me, Tom. You and I both know you can speak better English than that.'

The muscles on the arm of the black man tensed and his fingers tightened on the horse's reins. He was strong. The thought came unbidden to Stephen. The Black could flatten the young white in a flash. Ally's response crept into his brain. What do you think would happen if he did?

'Massa Stephen heard boss Massa. He own me. He own Alice. You own me. And now you own Alice. Why you think I talk like you?'

'Dammit, Tom.' The young white man stepped closer to the Black. The black man didn't flinch. He was taller and the young white man had to look up at him. 'You and I studied together. We played together. Grew up together. And God knows, you are far brighter than I am or could ever be!'

The black man pulled his arm free and stepped back. 'We no study together, Massa Stephen. You study. You treat me as toy. Play teach me. English. Teach me count. Only game. Game for young Massa Stephen. Now you grow up. You soon boss. We slave.'

The white man stepped back. 'Tom! How can you say that? We were … we are friends. You Blacks are humans in your own right. You are not and never will be my property.'

The black man stood tall. The black pupils in the ivory white eyes glinted. The ancient pride of his people radiated from him. 'You people and my people no be friends, Massa Stephen. Not now.' He looked around him. His thick lips curled in a sneer. 'Maybe never.' His voice dropped to a gruff whisper. 'Maybe never.'

'No, Tom! You are wrong. I am not like my father. I will make a difference. Wait and see.'

The black man's eyes lost the gleam of anger, softened to sadness. His body loosened and slouched into a posture of servitude. He raised his right hand to the brim of his hat and bowed his head. 'I take carriage to barn, Massa Stephen.'

'Tom!'

The black man turned and led the horses away from the house on the continuation of the dirt road towards the stables.

'Tom, stop!' the young man trotted after him. 'Stop.'

Ally and Stephen followed.

The black man walked in silence till they reached the stables. He stopped and ran his hand over one of the horses.

'Tom,' the white man pleaded. 'Please, I need you to help me settle back here. Your advice. I need …' he sighed. 'I need a friend, Tom.'

A shudder rocked the body of the black man. He spoke without turning to face the white. 'Massa Stephen, you try be my friend make things worse for me. Make bad. Very bad.'

The white man walked around to stand between the black man and the horses. 'What are you talking about, Tom? What would be very bad?'

Stephen turned to Ally. 'What's he talking about?'

'Shush,' she hushed him with a wave of her hand. 'Listen.'

'You gone two years, Massa Stephen. Boss Massa make new overseer. You know. Johnno.'

The young white man gasped. 'Black John? My father appointed Black John as the overseer?'

The black man nodded.

'Why would Father do that? He has always had white overseers. Dear God, Tom. Black John is a cruel pig.'

The black man shrugged. Then winced. 'Boss Massa give Johnno whisky. Tell him do anything to make black people obey.'

Ebony black eyes sheened with tears met and held the young man's blue ones. The white man's voice was barely a whisper. Stephen and Ally shuffled closer to listen.

'What did he do to you, Tom?'

The black man ripped his shirt off and turned around so the white one could see his back. Raised red and purple welts crisscrossed the man's body from shoulder to waist. 'He want my wife. I say no.'

Stephen grabbed Ally's hand. 'The overseer whipped Tom for refusing to hand over his wife to be raped?' he rasped.

Ally nodded. 'Plantation rules, Stephen. Productivity at any cost. Slaves are dispensable. Profits are not.'

The young white man staggered back. He swung round and ran back down the path towards the house.

Stephen and Ally followed.

He slowed as he approached the house. Then, with a muttered curse, he leapt up the steps leading to the verandah.

The front door swung open and the light-skinned black woman they had seen earlier stepped out. Her night-kissed skin, high, sculpted cheekbones, and green eyes were a heady mix. Her lips set in a sultry pout. Then slipped open to show even, white teeth. 'Massa Stephen,' she purred. She rested her right hand on her hip and stuck her chest out in what was a deliberately provocative gesture. 'Boss Massa and ma'am are waiting lunch.' With a flick of her cotton skirt, she stepped aside to allow just enough room for the young white man to sidle past her and enter the house. She followed him in and shut the door.

'The poor guy,' Stephen murmured. 'He doesn't stand the chance of a snowflake in hell.' He frowned. 'She didn't look like she liked it when his father gifted her to him.'

'She didn't like it. She doesn't now.' Ally's response was tense with innuendo.

'Then why is she playing the seductive temptress?'

'Because the Boss Massa instructed her to do so.'

'But why?' Stephen stammered.

'But nothing, Stephen. She's a slave,' Ally hissed. 'If she refused, Boss Massa would use other means to make sure she propagated.'

'How?' He winced. 'Ally, what are you implying?'

Ally shrugged. 'Come on, let's go join your family for dinner.'

Stephen eyed the shut door. 'What do you suggest? We knock and say, "Good afternoon, we are visiting from a hundred and seventy years in the future"?'

Ally smiled. 'Over two hundred and seventy-one, to be precise. But who's counting? I have a better idea.'

She stepped up to the large, oblong window and fiddled with the sash. It slipped up. Grinning, she gestured to him. 'Come on.' Together, they clambered in.

'Ally,' Stephen looked down at her. 'Did we have to scramble in through the window?'

She shook her head and chuckled. 'No, but it was way more adventurous than walking through walls and turning up in the dining room!'

They followed the sound of voices and cutlery to the dining room.

The family sat around the round mahogany table. The same one

Stephen had sat at for meals a year ago. What was different was that a trio of slaves, two men and a woman, moved around them. They carried steaming tureens of meat, chicken and vegetables. The slaves stopped at each of the family and served the contents of their individual dishes onto the plates with the grace of a choreographed dance.

Father and son had been joined by two women. Both dressed in elaborate satin dresses with tight bodices and full skirts. The older one had her hair drawn back in a tight chignon, while the younger had her golden hair parted in the middle and dangling like curling vines on either side of her pale face. No one at the table acknowledged the service of the black slaves.

'My ancestors sure didn't bother with thank you!' Stephen grumbled.

'Why would they, Stephen? Blacks are slaves. An inferior breed, hardly human. Servants. Serving their white master.' Stephen cringed. Their Indian home help in Sydney, Devi. Their Turkish chauffeur. The Islander gardener whose name he never could remember. The Chinese guy who ran the corner store where he and his mates picked up an occasional Coke. He never talked to them. Never said thank you. He took their service as a given. A right.

As his ancestors were doing.

The older man stuffed a slice of meat in his mouth. He gulped his wine from the goblet by the side of his plate. Slammed the glass down. One of the slaves stepped up immediately to refill the goblet. 'Your son—,' he pierced another piece of meat and shoved his fork towards the older woman. Gravy dripped from the meat onto the white linen tablecloth.

'Your son doesn't approve of the slave auctions. He thinks we need to treat Blacks better. Give them more freedom!' He guzzled down more wine. 'Stephen can't understand that they would be lost without our help. It would be like releasing a pet dog into the wild. We give our slaves houses, clothes, and food. What more would a black man want? Our slaves are better off here than in some jungle eating bugs and slugs like savages.' He turned to the tall, middle-aged black man in a white shirt and brown trousers refilling his wine goblet. 'Isn't that so, boy?' He barked at him.

The black man bowed from his waist. 'Yes, Massa.'

'See?' The older man glared at his son. 'Our slaves are happy.' No one else joined in his boisterous laughter.

'Father,' the young girl turned innocent blue eyes towards her father. 'Our slaves are not from the auctions, are they?'

'No, Maryanne.' The older man looked with fondness at his daughter. 'A few are. But most were born here. Don't bother your sweet head with it. You are sweet sixteen only once!' He chuckled. He looked at his wife. 'Good breeders, these blacks. Good life they have here too! A good life of food, sex and play on our tobacco and cotton plantations.'

'Good life?' The young man, Stephen, slammed his clenched fist on the table. 'Brought in shackles to this country—America, the so-called land of the free, on squalid ships! Stripped naked and sold in auctions in conditions not fit for animals! Forced to sleep on a wooden pallet on a dirt floor in a hut with a leaky thatched roof! Compelled to work in the fields from dawn to dusk with no pay! Whipped if they don't obey! Depend on you,' he pointed a trembling finger at his father, 'their … their … Massa,' he spat out the word, 'for their clothes and daily ration. You call that a life? A *good* life?'

'Enough! Shut up, Stephen!' the older man roared. He dragged himself out of his chair and reached for his walking stick. His chair rocked and fell back with a resounding crash. One of the slaves rushed up and set it upright. He waved his stick at his son. 'Get out of my sight. You speak like a bloody abolitionist. How dare you. Get. Out.'

'Or else what, Father? Will you whip me too?' The younger man folded his linen napkin. He placed it on the table and stood up. 'All right.' He stared straight at his father. 'I will leave. I will go to my room and pack.'

'You have nowhere to go,' the older man blustered.

'My friend Isaac has offered me a job in New York.'

'In New York? Go into business with a Jew? No! Never. Not a son of mine.'

The older lady stood up. She wound her way around the table and placed her fingers on her husband's arm. 'Alexander, calm down. Stephen is young. He is emotional. A dreamer. Do you not remember how it was for us at that age?'

He looked down at her. His expression softened. 'Yes, yes, my darling. He is young.' He dropped back in the chair.

'Father,' the young man stood tall and steady. His eyes narrowed and glinted in anger. 'May I be excused?'

His father pushed himself out of his chair. The male slave, the one he had addressed as 'boy' hastened to help him. 'Yes, yes. Don't do anything rash,' he yelled after his departing son. 'We can talk. We can talk. I will be in my study.'

The younger man left without looking back.

Stephen and Ally followed him.

The young man cursed and bounded two steps at a time up the stairs to the second floor.

Stephen and Ally ran up the stairs behind him.

The young man swung open the door to his bedroom. 'Alice,' he gasped. 'What are you doing here?'

'Your father gave me to you.' She reached up and started unbuttoning her blouse. 'He said you can use me as you want.' The faux civility in her voice didn't cover the anger and disgust.

Stephen backed away from the door. 'Ally, we should leave. This is so nasty!'

'Hey, preppy boy, are you chicken?' She tightened her hold on him, dragging him back into the bedroom.

The young white man reached out and slapped the black woman's hand away from her blouse. 'Stop it, Alice. I am not going to do anything to you. It was a stupid statement my father made. He was angry.'

Tears coursed down her cheeks. She didn't wipe them away. 'Why, Massa Stephen? Don't you find me pretty?'

'Alice. You are pretty. Very pretty. But I can't. We grew up together. You, Tom and I. We played together.' He walked across the room and dropped into an armchair by the window. 'You are like a sister to me,' he whispered.

'That was then, Massa Stephen. You were a child. You are adult now. You must accept what your father says.'

'Alice,' he mumbled. 'Are you asking me to make love to you?'

Tears continued to track down her cheeks. Her lips twitched in a grimace. 'Make love. What a beautiful word. No. Not make love, Massa

Stephen. Have sex. Please. Do it.'

'But why? Why, Alice? Why would you want me to … to do that?'

'To take me, Massa Stephen? To … to rape me?' A sob rose deep from her soul. 'Because if you say no, you send me away, Massa boss say he will do it.'

The young man dropped his head in his splayed fingers. 'Damn him. Damn him.' He sat in silence. The girl Alice stood mute and still in front of him. A minute passed. Maybe two. Slowly he raised his head. His eyes glowed with purpose. Deep determination. 'Stay with me for a while, Alice. We need to talk. We will beat him at his own game.'

'Son, we are leaving for church.' His mother called out from the bottom of the stairs.

'No,' the young man called back. 'I am not coming to church today.'

'But everyone is looking forward to seeing you.'

His father's loud guffaw interrupted her. 'Leave him be woman. He's otherwise occupied.'

Alice flinched.

The young man muttered a curse.

CHAPTER 10

Virginia, USA, 1860

Ally grabbed Stephen's hand. 'Come on, time to go to church.'

He tried to pull free. 'Ally, I've seen enough. Can we go back?'

She held on. 'One more Stephen. Appa is very keen you see this.' She tightened her hold. 'Hang on.'

They stood at the arched doorway of a red-brick building. Stephen looked up and around. The steep pitched roof was held up by stout oak beams. The afternoon sunshine filtered through multicoloured stained glass windows. The all-white congregation, the women in coloured and frilled silk dresses, and the men in formal suits sang lustily with piano accompaniment:

"God moves in a mysterious way,
His wonders to perform;
He plants his footsteps in the sea,
And rides upon the storm.
Deep in unfathomable mines
Of never-failing skill;
He treasures up his bright designs,
And works His sovereign will."

Stephen looked back to where the carriages were lined up. Each with a black slave standing by it. He turned back just as a grey-haired, portly man dressed in white robes and a purple shawl climbed up to the elevated podium. He raised his hands to the roof and said in a booming bass voice, 'In the name of the Father, Son and Holy Ghost'.

The people in the pews droned, 'Amen.'

Stephen turned to Ally. 'How much longer, Ally? I don't do church much.'

She shook her head and rolled her eyes. 'I know. You play rugby on Sunday mornings.' She pointed to the man on the podium. 'We can leave after the message.'

The man slammed his fist gavel-like on the podium. 'You are all aware that there are rumblings of discontent at what is seen by some as slavery. My dear brothers, we must stand firm in what we know is the truth.'

There were murmurings of 'Yes. Yes. Amen.' in the pews.

'You heard in the Bible reading from the book of Genesis chapter 9. The youngest son of Noah was cursed. It was said of his descendants "The lowest of slaves will he be". It is right and true. It is, as you sang, one of God's mysterious ways in the world.' He stopped and nodded at the people. 'It was decreed that we, the descendants of Shem, be the landowners and leaders, and the African descendants of Canaan be the simple-minded followers. Some call this slavery. We call it, doing our duty.'

Stephen spoke through gritted teeth. 'He's using the Bible to justify slavery and cruelty. How could he do that!'

Ally turned to face him. 'People have always used the Bible to justify their desires and actions, Stephen.'

'But here? To justify slavery? This is pure evil!'

A flash of lightning ripped through the sky. Thunder rattled the window and growled across the room.

Ally tensed. Then tugged at Stephen. 'Come on, Stephen. Time to leave.'

Hand in hand they ran out of the church and into the thunderstorm.

CHAPTER 11

Serendib, 2131

Saint Thomas sat in his shell. A book lay open on his lap. 'Welcome back, children.' He shut the book and waved it at them. '*Roots, The Saga of an American Family*, by Alex Haley. Great read.'

'I've read it, sir.' Stephen glanced at the shell next to Saint Thomas. 'May I sit?'

'Sit, son, sit.' Saint Thomas motioned to the shell.

Stephen dropped into the shell. The shell massaged his back. Stephen rubbed his forehead. Then looked at his palms as if he expected to see the bloodstains of his ancestor's deeds on his hands.

'Drink.' Saint Thomas pointed to the two tall glasses of cloudy coconut water on the table. 'You children have worked hard.'

Stephen reached for the glass and gulped down the refreshing liquid. It washed away the grime and dust in his throat. It did nothing to ease the fog of shame that engulfed his heart and soul. He placed his elbow on the arm of the shell and dropped his head in his palm.

Ally dropped to her knees by his side. 'Stephen, are you okay?'

'I didn't know. I didn't think that ...' his voice drifted off.

'Stephen, relax.' Ally whispered in his ear.

Saint Thomas hushed Ally with a wave of his hand. 'He needs to speak, Ally. Acceptance first. Then enlightenment.'

'I'm named after a slave trader.' Stephen felt the disgust and repulsion rise tide-like from the very depth of his soul. 'He was ready to take that woman, Alice, a mixed-race woman.' He sat in silence for a few seconds.

Then spat out, 'My blood is tainted.'

Ally stroked his fingers. It helped.

The shell Stephen was slumped in moved under him. It massaged and soothed. But this time, it failed to help him relax.

'Stephen, look at me,' Saint Thomas commanded. Stephen sat up in response to the command in the black eyes. 'Stephen, your namesake was an amazing man. What you saw that day was only the beginning.'

'What? How? He was ready to rape that black woman!'

'That day, after you left, Alice told Stephen the truth.'

'Truth?'

Saint Thomas shushed him with a gesture. 'She was his half-sister.'

Stephen gasped. 'Green eyes on a black woman. Like the old man. Alice was the young man Stephen's father's daughter by a slave woman. Dear God, it would've been incest if the son had sex with her.'

'It didn't matter in the plantations,' the Saint continued. 'He, your namesake, pretended that he had slept with her. Even thanked his father. Then, with the help of his friend, the Jewish merchant from New York, he arranged for her to escape.'

For the first time since he had returned from the plantation experience, Stephen's tension and anxiety lessened. 'Wow! My ancestor Stephen was an abolitionist!'

'He didn't think of himself that way. He visited the slave cabins in the evenings. His father joked that being with Alice had piqued his sexual appetite! But what the old man didn't know, was that his son was arranging for some of the slaves to escape on the underground railway.'

'A railway? In 1860's Virginia? But how?'

'No. Not a steam train! It was a secret network of passageways and safe houses organised by the abolitionists and used by runaway slaves to reach the Free North. Sometimes, even Canada.'

'Didn't his father suspect?'

'No. The young man was suitably angry when a slave escaped. Even pretended to whip Alice when she was accused of helping one of them. He joined the slave catchers in chasing down runaway slaves. Usually leading them in the opposite direction.'

'Thank you for telling me, sir.' Stephen sat forward and tented his fingers. 'But it hasn't changed,' he murmured.

'What hasn't changed, Stephen?'

'Sir, I visited the Virginia plantation last year on a two-month exchange program. I went to school with my cousins, Nat and Anthony. Even spent time partying with them and riding around the plantation. I didn't see. I just didn't.'

'See what, Stephen?' Saint Thomas prompted.

The words rushed out of him. The guilt of his ignorance. The racism and ugliness of the 21st century in Virginia, USA. A different, more sophisticated version of the slave trade of the antebellum south.

'There was not one person of colour in the school I attended with my cousins while at the plantation. Not one on the district rugby team they play in. I didn't ask why. I accepted it. Assumed that it was what it was. One day, my cousins and I were at the local store. We were kidding around. A couple of Black kids were there. Pretty much doing what we were. Nothing illegal. The police came in. A couple of white guys with all their firepower. I remember wondering why they picked on those kids and not us. They dragged the boys out. Dumped them in the paddy wagon. I asked my cousins.' He stopped and shuddered. 'They laughed.'

'Son.' Saint Thomas reached forward and placed his palm on Stephen's chest over his heart. It calmed him. His heart rate slowed.

'In the plantation, my aunt and uncle had lots of parties,' Stephen continued. 'Soirees, they called them. Their friends were all white, upper-class landowners. The chauffeurs of the cars were black men. So were some of the waiters they hired. I went to church with the family. All whites. Not one Black in the congregation.'

They sat in silence for a few seconds.

'Tell us, Stephen.' Saint Thomas spoke softly. 'What are you thinking now?'

'Standing in that plantation bungalow in 1860, it twisted my heart. I've got to help. I can't change history. But, the future ... surely, that's different.

I think … I think it was what Tom said to my ancestor, to Stephen. His words will stay with me forever. "You people and my people no be friends, Massa Stephen. Not now. Maybe never." Yes. That's what he said.' Stephen looked up at Saint Thomas. 'That's when I made a decision. It's wrong. Wrong! And I can make a difference. I know I can!'

Stephen pushed himself off the shell. An enthusiasm he hadn't thought he possessed coursed through him. His fists clenched. 'I can make sure that the "maybe never" changes. Black and white can and should live and work together.' He stopped. Took a deep breath. Unclenched his fists. 'What am I thinking? How can I make a difference?' His shoulders slumped. 'A high school student in Australia with aspirations to be a mining engineer.' He looked from Ally to Saint Thomas. 'But I have to. I have to do something.'

Ally and Saint Thomas ignored him. They were looking at each other. It was as if Stephen was not there with them.

'Yes, Ally,' Saint Thomas said aloud. 'You are right. He could be the one. But there is more.' He locked eyes with Ally again. 'No, he has to do this next one alone.'

Stephen looked from one to the other. 'Wait a minute! I thought we were done? What about my parents? I've got to go to them. Get help.'

Saint Thomas batted away his concerns. 'Your parents are fine, Stephen. I gave you my word. And I never go back on it.' He pointed a finger at Stephen. 'Concentrate on the now. You are with us for a purpose. And you will have to experience it. In full.' He reached forward and placed his fingertips on Stephen's forehead. 'Do you not feel it?'

'It's not just Blacks in America, is it?' Stephen mused. 'There's more you want me to see. Experience.'

The old man drew his fingers away from Stephen's forehead. Stephen felt weaker for it.

'Yes, Stephen, your father's people. A visit to your paternal family.'

'But my father's people owned tea plantations in Sri Lanka. There was no slavery there.' He stopped. He was no longer sure about anything. 'Was there?'

'Not as you saw in the Virginia plantation, Stephen. But you will see. You will see.'

'Sir, my parents?'

'Stephen,' his voice rose a semitone. Stephen felt the old man's irritation radiate from the Saint's brain into his. 'They are sleeping. A few more minutes will make no difference.' His eyes met and sank into Stephen's brain. 'We'll let your parents rest for a while, shall we? We have only a small window for the next experience.'

He turned to Ally. She shivered. Her eyes filled with tears. They shadowed with pain and remained fixed on Stephen. 'Stephen, I am not …' She flashed a glance at Saint Thomas, 'I am not permitted to come with you.'

Stephen clung to her fingers. 'I need you, Ally.'

'No.' She disentangled her fingers from his. 'You are stronger now. Last time we were observers. This experience is different. More interactive.' She touched her lips to his forehead. 'I will be praying for you. I will be here when you return.' She turned, and with a swish of her silken tunic, walked to the door and out of the room.

The old man chuckled. 'Don't look so bereft! She will be back in a blink. When you return from your island paradise. Come on. Your great-grandfather, James Ashley-Cooper, is looking forward to a visit from his Australian nephew. You don't want to miss your train.'

CHAPTER 12

Sri Lanka, 1937

They stepped out of the nexus pod and onto a railway platform crowded with brown-skinned men and women.

The announcement rang out, loud and strident, probably to make up for the hiss and wheeze of the big-wheeled steam locomotive at the head of the train and the racket made by the crowd struggling to board the carriages. The terms strung together meant nothing to Stephen. But he listened. And learned.

'The train on platform four is the day train to Badulla. It will stop at Polgahawela, Māwanella, Nawalapitiya, Diyatalawe, Hatton, Nanu Oya, and all stations to Badulla.' It was repeated in a language he didn't recognise.

Saint Thomas patted Stephen on his shoulder. 'Here's your baggage.' He placed a brown leather case by his feet. 'And your first-class ticket.' He pressed the printed paper into his palm. 'James Ashley-Cooper, the superintendent of Udatännà tea plantation will pick you up at the Diyatalawe station. You are on a grand tour from Australia visiting the family tea plantations in Sri Lanka. You are here to experience the work done by a creeper.' He turned away. Then looked back. 'Oh, and by the way, it is 1937. And the British call this little colonial outpost Ceylon.'

Stephen glanced down at his baggy brown trousers, brown leather shoes, and open-neck white shirt. The coat he had over it resembled his school rugby blazer. The crest on it was unfamiliar.

When he looked up, Saint Thomas was gone.

Stephen stood rooted to the spot Saint Thomas had deposited him in. He understood now what Ally had meant when she had said that this time it was interactive. He was here. In Sri Lanka. Standing on a railway platform. And the year was 1937. He was on his way to a tea plantation.

What the heck was a creeper on a tea plantation anyway?

He heard Ally's voice in his head. '*Look, listen, learn.*' He tried to connect. There was no response. This time he was on his own. It would be a moment in Serendib's time, but here, in Sri Lanka, his return would depend on the speed with which he learned about his heritage. So, he didn't have much choice. He would follow Ally's advice and immerse himself in the moment. The sooner he got back, the better his parents' chances of recovery.

He took a deep breath. Then gasped. The heat and humidity pressed down on him like a damp blanket. Sweat gathered and trickled down his neck. Not the immersion experience he had hoped for. But he would have to put up with it.

Stephen slipped off his blazer and slung it on his shoulder.

The scene on the railway platform was what he might have described to friends in Sydney as the Easter show on steroids. Dark-skinned men, some dressed in multicoloured shirts and trousers and others in skirt-like garments, dragged bags and suitcases bulging with clothes, fruits, and packets of what looked like food. They pushed, shoved, and mingled with women in equally bright dresses and the wrap-around garments he recognised as sarees. Children darted between them like dressed-up, hyperactive, little brown squirrels.

A cacophony of conversation swirled around him. So loud he could feel his eardrums reverberate. He picked out a few words in English. Others were spoken in languages he didn't recognise. Drawing on his knowledge of geography, he assumed it would be Sinhalese and Tamil. He laughed when he heard a little child scream 'Appa' and scuttle toward a man. It would seem that the word for father hadn't changed from 1937 Sri Lanka to 2131 Serendib. Men walked up and down the railway platform hawking food, carrying their produce of sweetmeats and fruit in cane baskets on their shoulders. Their rhythmic calls of 'vadai, vadai, vadai,' 'kadalai, kadalai' and 'thambili, thambili' added a musical cadence to the otherwise raucous din.

'Sir, are you Mister Stephen Cooper, sir?'

Engrossed in the sights and sounds, Stephen jumped when the heavily subcontinental accented voice spoke close to his ear.

'Sir, sorry, sir. You didn't hear when I speak quietly, sir.' The slim dark-skinned man dressed in somewhat crushed brown khaki trousers and a brown shirt was about Stephen's height. He brought his palms together in a similar, if somewhat less elegant, version of Ally's greeting. He bowed at the waist. 'Sir, Vannakam, sir. My name is Kandiah, sir. I am the assistant tea maker at Udatännà Estate, sir. *Peria dorai*, that is the superintendent Mister Ashley-Cooper, asked me to accompany you on the train to Diyatalawe. Sir.'

Stephen held his right hand out. 'That's very kind of you, Mister Kandiah. It's convenient that you're returning to the estate today.'

The man ignored Stephen's outstretched hand and continued to hold his palms together. His voice dropped. 'Sir, you are new here, no? And young, also.'

'Yes,' Stephen replied.

'Sir, that is why you don't know. You British never shake hands with us natives. You don't even touch us.' There was a hint of bitterness in the mumbled words.

Stephen dropped his hand. 'I see.' He didn't.

'And, sir,' Mister Kandiah continued. 'I am on leave. sir. My wife and son live in Colombo.' His whole demeanour brightened. He stood up straight. 'My son is on a scholarship at St Matthias College, sir.'

'Why're you returning to work if you're on leave?' Stephen picked up his suitcase. 'I can get on the train and get off at … I believe it was …' he glanced down at his train ticket. 'Diyatalawe.'

'No, sir. No, sir. The superintendent sent me a telegram. He didn't want you to travel alone, sir. You are from overseas no, sir?' He wobbled his head in the gesture Stephen was now familiar with. 'Sir, it is all right, sir. I will never have a chance to travel in first-class again, no?' Mister Kandiah chuckled and took the bag from Stephen. 'Sir, come, sir.'

'Mister Kandiah,' Stephen looked around the building they were in.

'Sir, Fort Station, sir. Main place for all the trains going in all directions from Colombo, sir.' He made an expansive gesture to encompass the sandstone walls and arches. 'Sir, you British built the station in about 1910, to carry tea and coffee from the hill country to Colombo. This is what is done now also, sir.'

Stephen looked and absorbed his surroundings. The metal arches were imposing and the intricacy of the whorls and curls were evident even under layers of grime and soot. The wooden doors were adorned with ornate brass handles and stained-glass panels. It was a little bit of old British architecture in this colonial outpost.

'Sir, come, sir. The train will leave soon, sir.'

Stephen followed Mister Kandiah. He stopped at a carriage with 'FIRST CLASS' emblazoned in intricate gold lettering on the side. The carriage was empty, and no one seemed eager to enter it. This was in stark contrast to the crowds clambering into the other carriages. Mister Kandiah opened the door and gestured for Stephen to precede him into the carriage. He followed Stephen's gaze. 'Sir, the natives all travel second-class and the coolies in third, sir. No one will bother you here, sir.'

Stephen climbed the steps into the carriage. He turned to take his suitcase. 'Sir, no, sir,' Mister Kandiah scrambled into the carriage after Stephen. He placed the suitcase in the overhead rack.

The multiplicity of 'sirs' in Mister Kandiah's conversation was beginning to irk Stephen. In his head, he heard Ally giggle. '*Patience, Stephen. Patience.*' She had taken residence in his brain, but wouldn't let him connect. She had some explaining to do when he got back.

Stephen sat down by the window on the leather seat covered with white linen. The seats were arranged in pairs with a central corridor. The two of them were alone in the section. Stephen gestured to the seat across from him. 'Sit down and tell me about this trip and the tea plantation.' He turned his face towards the irregular pulses of air from the fan that rotated sluggishly from the roof of the carriage.

'Sir, no, sir. I will tell you everything you want to know. But I can't sit with you, sir.'

'Why the heck not? Do you plan to stand all the way? And can you please tell me your first name? I'd prefer to just call you that."

'Sir, you can call me Kandiah, sir. That is what *peria dorai*, the English boss calls me.' He wobbled his head again. 'Sir, I can't sit with you because it is not proper for a native to sit with a white man.' Mister Kandiah pointed to the seats across the corridor in line with the one Stephen was sitting on.

'I will sit there when sir does not want anything.'

'And stand when I do ask you something?'

He wobbled his head. 'Sir, yes, sir.' The twist of his lips was more sneer than smile.

'Mister Kandiah.' Stephen placed the emphasis on the mister. 'Are you telling me that you, a Sri Lankan citizen, a native of this country has to address the Britisher as *sir*? That you have to *stand* when spoken to by a white man?'

The head wobbled, but Stephen caught the flash of resentment in the beady black eyes. 'And—' Stephen continued. 'You don't like it, do you?'

Mister Kandiah straightened and looked directly at Stephen. 'Sir, I am a Tamil. My people and the Sinhalese are the original inhabitants of this country. We are proud to be the natives.' His gaze was unwavering. 'But you, sir, you are the white raj.' His voice rose in pitch and volume. 'You are the conquerors. The rulers. What we like doesn't matter—for now anyway.' He stopped and dropped his eyes. 'Sir, sorry, sir,' he mumbled.

The carriage juddered. With a loud drawn-out whistle and a bone-rattling jerk, the train laboured out of the station. A cloud of steam and smoke drifted from the locomotive, partially obscuring the platform.

Stephen pointed to the seat opposite him. 'Mister Kandiah, please sit down.' The man perched on the edge of the seat. 'Please relax.' Stephen waited till the man slid back into the seat. 'Mister Kandiah, you and your people will have freedom.'

The man wobbled his head. 'Sir, someday, sir. Someday.'

'And as long as we are fellow travellers, please stop addressing me as sir.'

'But sir. That is not right, no, sir?'

'Shush.' Stephen waved his fingers in front of Mister Kandiah's face. 'Stephen would be good. But I guess that would be asking too much. How about you address me as Mister Cooper.'

The head wobbled again. 'Sir, if you say so.'

Hot dust and soot-laden steam invaded the carriage. Mister Kandiah jumped up. 'Sir—Mister Cooper, sorry,' He hooked his fingers in the brass knobs and dragged the glass window shutter down on Stephen's side and then his. With a rueful expression and a wry twist of his lips, he settled back in the seat opposite Stephen.

'*Well done, Stephen.*' Ally's voice sounded in his head. 'Glad you approve,' he said under his breath, not knowing if he was getting through to her.

The carriage swayed and gathered speed. The whistle of the steam locomotive was muffled and distant. Stephen leaned forward, clasped his hands, and rested his elbows on his knees. 'Mister Kandiah, we're probably going to be on this train together for a while.'

'Eight hours, sir—sorry Mister Cooper.'

'Well, how about you tell me a little about the countryside we're passing through?'

Mister Kandiah wobbled his head. His eyes brightened. He slid forward in his seat. 'To start, this train is called Uderata Maniké. It is Sinhalese and means the lady of the hill country. We are now leaving the capital city of Sri Lanka, Colombo. The train goes to a place called Badulla. We will get off at Diyatalawe.'

The train chugged out of the capital. The grey smoke and soot-stained buildings were replaced by lush green fields. Bright flowers swayed in the backdraft of the train. Some Stephen recognised. Bougainvillea, frangipani. It brought memories of the frangipani blossoms in the trees in Serendib. Others he couldn't name fluttered past in their colourful glory.

Mister Kandiah pointed to a terraced green field. 'Paddy, sir ... Mister Cooper,' he stammered. 'The ground is broken up by buffaloes. Look! Look!' He pointed to where a man walked behind two immense grey animals with graceful, curved horns yoked side by side to what looked like a ploughshare. The man's brown upper body was bare, and a piece of cloth was wrapped around his groin.

'Amazing,' Stephen mumbled.

Lulled by the soporific effect of the rocking carriage and the sultry circulation of the air by the fan, Stephen dozed.

Ally stood by him. 'You are doing well, Stephen.' She touched her fingers to his cheek. 'Keep strong.' He felt the butterfly touch of her lips on his forehead.

CHAPTER 13

On the Udarata Menike, Sri Lanka, 1937

The train ground to a halt. The shriek of locomotive wheels on metal rail tracks ripped through Stephen's brain. Jerked awake, he grabbed the armrest of the seat to stop himself from sliding off the seat.

'You are awake, sir … sorry, Mister Cooper.'

The sign outside the soot blurred window read, 'Māwanella.'

People from the crowded platform pushed and clambered in and out of the other carriages, but no one approached the one they were in.

'I have ordered chicken sandwiches for lunch, Mister Cooper. But I think I know a drink that you will enjoy.' He slid open a window and hailed a man carrying a bunch of large green fruits. He gestured and gave the man a few coins. The man lopped off the top of one and popped in a straw. Mister Kandiah handed it to Stephen and purchased one for himself. 'It is called Thambili. A word for young coconut. Very refreshing.'

Stephen was transported back to Saint Thomas' presence. The juice was the same cloudy white drink he had drunk with Ally. He raised the coconut to Mister Kandiah in a gesture of appreciation. 'Thanks. It's delicious.' They sat opposite each other, enjoying their drinks in silence. The white man using a straw and the native slurping the juice from a hole in the coconut.

With a cloud of steam and salute on the whistle, the train hauled itself out of the station. Mister Kandiah stuck his head out of the window and pointed to a sentinel-like pile of large rocks atop a mountain range. 'That is Mountain Utuwan, Mister Cooper. In the 1800s a man called

Utuwankande Sura Saradiel or, hero of Mount Utuwan, used the caves there as a hideout.' His eager smile signalled a story.

Stephen opened his window and leaned out. The brisk air, significantly colder than when they were in Colombo, whipped around his head. 'What made this man a hero, Mister Kandiah?'

'He and his group, they robbed the carriages and coaches that the British or their Sri Lankan minions travelled in. They gave whatever they took to the poor villagers.' He wobbled his head and smiled. 'They never stole from the poor.'

Stephen chuckled. 'A Sri Lankan Robin Hood!'

'Yes, Mister Cooper.' His voice took on a wistful inflection. 'If he was alive today, he may have led a rebellion.'

The thought flashed across Stephen's mind. *Which you, Mister Kandiah, would have liked to join.*

'Can you blame him?' Ally's voice slipped into his conscience. 'No,' he tried to channel back. 'Well done,' she responded.

The railway restaurant attendant placed a tray of chicken sandwiches and a steaming pot of tea on a fold-up table between them. He also produced a bowl of hot water, soap, and a towel.

'Thank you,' Stephen glanced at the plastic name tag, 'Sunil. That's lovely.' He washed and dried his fingers.

The young man bowed from his waist. He picked up the bowl of dirty water and left the carriage.

Stephen picked up a sandwich and bit into it. The subtle combination of flavours, chilli, coriander, and others he couldn't identify, teased and then engulfed his taste buds. 'This is amazing!' He reached for another. 'Mister Kandiah, you've got to try the sandwiches.'

He wobbled his head. 'I thought you would like the mix of curry powder, turmeric, chilli and mayonnaise. Kind of South Asia meets England.' He picked one and relaxed in his seat.

'Mister Kandiah,' Stephen injected a tone of casual interest into his voice, 'tell me about yourself. Where were you born? Where'd you go to school? How'd you get to the tea plantation?'

Mister Kandiah swallowed and laughed quietly. 'What you really want to know, Mister Cooper, is how a native Sri Lankan, or Ceylonese as you Britishers like to call us, can speak the Queen's English!'

'No ... I am ...'

Mister Kandiah silenced him with a raised hand. 'It's all right. I'm happy to tell you.'

'Touché,' whispered the familiar voice in his head. 'And if you are wondering about French, I speak over twelve languages.'

'Great!' he muttered.

'Did you say something, Mister Cooper?'

'No. No. Just surprised at how delicately the sandwiches are made. Please go on, tell me.'

'I was born on a tea plantation,' Mister Kandiah continued. 'In an estate called Watakälé. It belongs to the same company as Udatänná. Oriental Produce. My father was the teamaker there. The teamaker looks after the manufacture of tea in the factory. He wanted something better for me. So, he sent me off to live with his brother, a businessman in the hill country capital of Kandy, and his wife. They had no children. I went to a missionary school, Trinity College. Studied in English. Played Rugby. Even became a Christian to please my favourite missionary English teacher!'

'Why'd you come back to the tea plantation?'

'Camelia Sinensis, that is the tea bush, it's in our blood. And,' he gave a mocking laugh, 'my father had a plan for my life. He went to the Superintendent of Watakälé and asked that I should become a creeper. He dreamed of his son going into planting. Wanted me to become a *sinna dorai*. Doing better than him in the tea trade. A *sinna dorai* is Tamil for junior boss.' He explained. 'What you would call an assistant superintendent.'

'What happened?'

'The old man superintendent, Mister Irvine, laughed in my father's face.' Anger dragged down the corners of his mouth and sparked in his eyes. 'He sat at his office table with his pipe in hand and told my father that no native brat will go above clerk or teamaker. Not on his watch, anyway.'

Stephen struggled to find the words for an appropriate response. 'Why do you stay in the plantation and work there?'

The bitterness fled and his face softened. 'I wanted to get married. I met my wife in our church in Diyatalawe. Her parents live in town. She didn't want to leave the hill country. The assistant teamaker's job comes with a lovely little house. I took the job. Once we had our baby, it was too much trouble to change jobs. The teamaker is retiring. Hopefully, I will be promoted.'

'So, you continue to live with colonial oppression.'

Mister Kandiah wobbled his head. 'We don't see it as oppression, Mister Cooper. We see it as something to be tolerated ... for now.' His voice deepened and took on a tone of earnest expectation. 'But, like you said already, things will change. They will. Meanwhile, my son will get a good education in Colombo and move up in the world.'

Stephen inclined his head in agreement. It seemed unkind to respond that Mister Kandiah's father had hoped the same for him.

Picking up the teapot, Mister Kandiah poured out the tea into a cup. 'Milk? Sugar?'

'Black please, no sugar.' Stephen accepted the cup.

'Ahh, good choice.' Mister Kandiah poured a cup for himself. He sniffed the liquid, stared at it, and then sipped. He rolled the liquid around in his mouth. Then swallowed. 'Good. Good. I told the railway restaurant keeper that we wanted a good BOP leaf brew.'

Stephen frowned. 'What's BOP?'

Mister Kandiah stared open-mouthed at Stephen. 'You don't know? BOP is Broken Orange Peko. Say it like peck-oh. It is a high-country tea with flavour,' he pointed to the tea in his cup, 'a golden colour, and,' he raised three fingers to his lips and mimicked a gesture like blowing a kiss, 'just the right amount of flavour and strength.'

Stephen sipped and stared into his cup. 'It's different to anything I've had.'

'Yes, yes. When you are a creeper, you will learn to do what I did. It is called tea-tasting.' He stopped and wiggled his forefinger at Stephen. 'Ahh, you think tea is tea, no?' He drained his cup and set it down. 'You have much to learn!' He pointed out of the window. 'We are coming to tea country. No dust now.'

The air swept into the carriage, cool and crisp. It carried a floral, slightly aromatic smell.

Stephen could feel the locomotive labour as the rail track became progressively steeper. It wound around mountains and through deep cuttings in the hillside. The sides of the hills and the valleys were crowded with bushes; large, dark vermillion green leaves at the base of the bushes gave way to lime green shoots covering the top and shimmering in the wind.

Stephen stuck his head out of the window and sniffed.

'The smell of freshly plucked tea leaves, Mister Cooper.' He pointed to a green field close to the rail track where rows of women were moving through the bushes. They had multi-coloured cloth wrapped around their bodies and oversized wicker baskets slung by a rope over something like a rough blanket on their head. 'Tea pluckers, Mister Cooper. That man,' he pointed to a dark-skinned man in shirt and trousers with a towel wrapped turban-like over his head, 'he is what is called the *kangani*. The supervisor.' The man's hoarse shouts carried over the sound of the wheels.

Stephen leaned out and watched the fingers of the tea pluckers flutter like brown butterflies over the bushes, throwing leaves over their shoulder into the baskets on their back.

The scream of the whistle echoed on the hills as the locomotive toiled around a mountain.

'They pluck the new shoots.' Mister Kandiah held up three fingers. 'Two leaves and the bud only.'

'Are these women also natives? Oh, sorry—Sri Lankan?'

Mister Kandiah guffawed. 'You will have a lot to learn!'

'What do you mean?'

'They are Indian Tamils, Mister Cooper. Poverty-stricken South Indians. Brought here by your ancestors in the 1820s for indentured labour in the tea plantations. No citizenship. No status. No place other than in the tea plantations. We call them *malai makal.* Tamil words for people of the mountains.' He guffawed. 'Sri Lankan Tamilians will be insulted if you think the coolies are Sri Lankan!'

'Sorry,' Stephen murmured. He craned his neck to watch the women till they slid out of sight.

Poverty-stricken. Desperate. Displaced. Transported from their country.

Memories of the slaves in the southern plantation in Virginia tantalised the edges of his memory and merged with the Indian women on the hillside.

'Ally, help me to understand,' he tried to connect with her. There was no response. Just her sigh.

The locomotive climbed higher into the tea country.

Around him, fluffy white strings of waterfalls tumbled down steep cliffs. Range after range of mountains, like a petrified blue-green ocean, faded into a purple haze in the distance.

He would learn more when he got to his destination. Stephen pulled the ticket from his pocket – Diyatalawe.

CHAPTER 14

Udatänná Estate, Sri Lanka, 1937

The steam locomotive drew to a shuddering halt at the station. Large black lettering on a white signpost read 'DIYATALAWE'.

Stephen looked out of the window. The platform teemed with black and brown bodies carrying and dragging bags and hessian sacks of clothes, fruit, vegetables and other sundry items. People pushed and jostled to get into the third-class carriages.

Mister Kandiah picked up Stephen's suitcase and opened the door. He drew himself straight and spoke with a stiff and formal voice. 'Sir, superintendent *peria dorai* will meet you here, sir.' He signalled for Stephen to precede him down the steps to the platform and followed with the luggage.

After the relative quiet of the first-class carriage, the noise of people screaming to and at each other swamped his senses. The pungent smell of unwashed bodies clogged his nose. He grabbed the white linen hanky tucked in his pocket and covered his nose. Then jumped aside when a man dressed in worn trousers and threadbare knitted jumper with a towel wrapped around his head hawked and spat thick red sputum on the edge of the platform.

Mister Kandiah followed Stephen's gaze. 'Sir. Not blood, sir. The Indian labourers, coolies as you will call them, chew a leaf called betel. They add Areca nut and lime. You will see that everywhere in the tea fields, sir.'

Stephen stopped and turned. 'Mister Kandiah, why've you gone back to calling me sir?'

'Because we are now in Diyatalawe, sir. On the train we could pretend that you and I could talk as equal human beings. Now, sir, you are the British master and I am the native.' He pointed to the entry arch. 'And Superintendent *peria dorai* Ashley-Cooper will not approve of any sign of familiarity between us—sir.' He touched his forehead in a faux salute.

Shamed into silence at the implication of Mister Kandiah's words and gesture, Stephen looked to where he had pointed.

The six-foot-something height of the white man dwarfed the uniformed station master who cowered by his side. Dressed in brown khaki trousers, a cream open-necked shirt, a striped blazer and a pith hat resting on his golden hair, James Ashley-Cooper exuded authority and British arrogance. Grey eyes honed in and locked with Stephen's blue.

'Stephen!' He strode across the train platform with his right hand extended. The shifting sea of humanity parted in front of him like the Red Sea in front of Moses. The chatter diminished in intensity. He waved his left hand in a dismissive gesture at Mister Kandiah. 'Put sir's bag in the car, Kandiah,' he commanded.

Mister Kandiah bowed his head. 'Sir, yes, sir.' He picked up Stephen's bag and scuttled off towards the portal. The word 'exit' was painted over it in English and in another alphabet he didn't recognise – probably Tamil.

'Well, a relative from the Antipodes come to check out our little colonial outpost. Welcome, welcome.' The handshake was firm and hearty. 'My wife, Elise, and I should come visit your Kangaroo land sometime. God knows she could do with some cheering up.'

'Mister Ashley-Cooper,' Stephen looked around for Mister Kandiah.

'No, no. James to you, Stephen.' He patted Stephen on the shoulder. 'We are family. I don't know how old you are,' he pointed a finger at Stephen, 'but, given you are on the grand tour to determine your future, I would put you at—seventeen?'

'Yes, I'm seventeen,' Stephen replied.

'Well, I am thirty-two, we could almost be brothers!'

Not really, Stephen mused, *given you are my great-grandfather. In his head, he heard Ally chuckle.*

Stephen followed James out of the station into a courtyard. A gleaming black four-door sedan stood right by the exit. Stephen recognised the crest on the bonnet of the car. It was of a woman leaning forwards with her arms outstretched and wing-like clothing streaming behind her. He smothered a chuckle. His great-grandfather was wealthy and pretentious enough to drive a Rolls Royce Phantom on tea plantation roads. A dark Indian in a white peaked cap, coat, and a skirt-like garment, which he now recognised as the local sarong, stood by the car.

Stephen touched the crest. 'Great car.'

James laughed. 'We have to maintain company standards. Oriental Produce has plantations in Sri Lanka, India and South Africa. It is a matter of prestige. What we drive, how we dress. Even who we marry.'

The white-suited chauffeur rushed around the car and swung the back door open. He held the door handle in one hand and raised the other hand to his forehead in a salute. James slid in.

Stephen reached for the handle of the front passenger seat of the car. 'Sir, no. No, sir.' The chauffeur ran around the car to open the other back door. Stephen placed one foot in the car and turned to the man. 'What is your name?'

'Sir, Sundar, sir,' he stammered.

'Sundar,' Stephen looked into the hooded black eyes. 'Thank you.' He slipped in and allowed the man to shut the door. The chauffeur scuttled round the car and jumped into the driver's seat. The motor switched on with a grunt and the car purred forward. A couple of Indian men dragging a cart leapt out of the way.

Stephen looked around. 'James, what about Mister Kandiah?'

James sniggered. 'Honorifics are redundant when addressing the natives, Stephen. We must maintain a decorum in dealing with them. Keep the Ceylonese in their place.' He gestured at a green-painted closed truck with a large white emblem of three leaves painted on the side. 'Kandiah will travel in the estate lorry. The lorry delivered the packed tea chests to the train.' He pointed to the emblem. 'The Oriental Produce logo. I would have preferred it in silver, but the fools painted it white!'

They drove through the town of Diyatalawe. The road was narrow and lined on either side with open-fronted wooden huts selling every kind of merchandise from sweetmeats and sarees to bananas and broomsticks. Dark-skinned men, women, and children together with dogs, cats, goats, and an occasional cow, meandered onto the road and crossed at will in front of the car.

They left the town behind. The car drove up the mountain road between undulating hills covered with the emerald green carpet of tea bushes, interrupted by tall spreading eucalyptus trees. Mud tracks curled through the hills like dusky brown ribbons.

'Slow down, Sundar,' James commanded. The chauffeur slowed the vehicle to a crawl.

A bend in the road brought into view a multi-storey silver building perched on the side of a hill. 'Feast your eyes, Stephen. That is Udatännà tea factory.' His voice took on a tone of conscious pride. 'The most progressive in the high-country tea estates in terms of tea manufacture techniques.'

'And that,' he pointed further up the hill, to the green roof and white walls of a house partly hidden by a grove of tall trees, 'that is our bungalow.'

'Go,' he barked at the chauffeur. The car picked up speed.

The road curled down into the valley and followed a stream. On the opposite bank of the stream were clusters of structures. They resembled sets of filthy stables. Scrawny chickens and goats wandered between the buildings. The odour of unwashed bodies, food waste and rotting garbage invaded the car.

'Look, listen and learn.' He heard Ally's voice in his head.

Children in tattered and mud-stained clothes played in front of the buildings. They stopped and gawked as the Rolls Royce slid past. Some ran along the stream, keeping up with the car, shouting and waving. Older girls squatted by the stream that separated the road from the buildings. They seemed to be washing clothes in the polluted water.

James reached over Stephen and wound the window up. 'These are the line rooms. The Indian labour live here. We call them coolies. We have provided the line rooms with common toilets and communal taps. But the coolies won't use them. They use the stream for washing, ablutions and God knows what else!' He waved his fingers in a dismissive gesture. 'They have no sense of hygiene and their rooms are filthy.'

Stephen knew the answer, but he had to hear it from James. 'Indians?

But why Indians?'

'The native Ceylonese won't work like these,' he pointed to the line rooms. 'Too bloody proud! The Indian coolies were brought in the 1820s from South India. They were the dregs of society there. As you can see, we care for them here on the plantation. They know nothing else. And they work for a wage which keeps tea manufacture viable and … the profits up.' He smiled at Stephen. 'Don't look so shocked. They are happy. Better off here than in their native India. It's like they were born for this type of labour.'

Stephen reined in the sharp retort that shot through his brain. No, he was here to look. To listen and learn.

The car continued up the hill away from the line rooms, leaving the squalor and smells behind. The sun was sinking over the mountains when they drove up to the superintendent's bungalow.

Stephen looked around. He felt like he was in a dream. The velvet lawns and manicured hedges. The rows of rose bushes redolent with luscious blooms of red, pink and white. The bungalow with the stone steps leading to a wide wrap-around veranda. The green wooden door frames and stained-glass windows. It was all vaguely familiar. The memories came sliding into his brain. They were the scenes in the pictures on the walls of his Nana Janet's retirement villa in Sydney. This was where his grandmother had lived with her husband William. The grandfather he had never met.

The chauffeur stopped the car at the stone steps. He leapt out and opened the door for James. Stephen opened the door without waiting for the chauffeur. He got out and walked round to join James. An Indian boy in a white sarong and long-sleeved shirt came running from the side of the house. James pointed to the boot of the car. 'Take the master's bag to the visitor's room, Raman,' he commanded.

The young man bowed at his waist and touched his forehead in a self-effacing manner. 'Sir, yes, sir.'

James and Stephen walked together up the steps and into the house. Stephen stifled a gasp. The blue velvet-covered sofa with matching wingback easy chairs. The brick and brass fireplace and the round mirrors with carved wood frames. They were all as he had seen in Nana Janet's photos.

James led Stephen down a short corridor. He flung open the door to a room. 'This is the guest bedroom. Raman will run a hot bath for you. We dine at seven.' He walked to the door and looked back. 'And, Stephen, we dress for dinner. It's important to maintain the proprieties of life.'

The young Indian, Raman, stood at the door of what Stephen assumed was the bathroom. 'Sir.' He touched his forehead. 'Sir bathe now, sir?'

'Yes, please, Raman.' Stephen smiled at the Indian boy. 'Raman, do you enjoy working here?'

'Sir,' Raman mumbled. 'Better than factory, sir. I wanting to marry. *Peria dorai aiya*, giving clothes and all, sir. We living in bungalow backside, sir.'

'You have rooms here. It must be better than the line rooms?'

Raman touched his forehead again. He scooted into the bathroom. Then came back and laid a fluffy white towel on the bed. 'Water all hot, sir.'

A steaming hot soak in the claw-footed bathtub refreshed Stephen. He came back to the bedroom to find that Raman had unpacked his suitcase. Laid out on the bed were high-waisted grey woollen trousers, a silk shirt, leather braces and a matching double-breasted jacket. Polished leather shoes stood at the foot of the bed.

With thirty minutes to go to dinner time, Stephen stood at the window.

'Very dapper,' Ally teased in his head.

'Your choice?' he concentrated his brain waves to respond.

'You're getting good at this! Of course, it's my sartorial selection. Imagine what you would've been wearing if I left it to Appa!'

The last rays of sunlight slanted through the shade trees on the tea fields, turning them into a tapestry of green, gold and grey. Stephen watched as the mist clambered up the mountains, snuffed out the colours, and replaced them with a soft blanket of black. One by one, the trees came back to life with the blink and glitter of thousands of fireflies. A distant chirping became a chorus of cicadas.

At that moment, Stephen knew he would be back. He would do what his ancestors would not do. No Indian or native Sri Lankan would stand up for or salute the white man. Honorifics would not be needed. Not for the white man. All men and women would be equal.

Ally whispered in his brain. 'Well done. I am forbidden from connecting till you return. Go well and go with God, my friend.'

'No!' Stephen spoke the word out loud. 'I need to know you're with me.'

There was silence in the room. Silence in his brain. He was on his own.

He glanced at the grandfather clock by the wooden dresser. Five minutes to seven.

Well, the quicker he understood his history here, the sooner he could get back to Serendib. The sooner he got back to Serendib, the faster he would get help for his parents.

***

The woman was seated in the low wing-backed chair; a wine glass held in her delicate long fingers. The dark-green silk clung to her body and flared out to rest in shimmering folds at her ankles. The skin-hugging wrist-length sleeves and raised shoulders gave the impression of a modest covering, except for the neckline which exposed a hint of seductive cleavage, an emerald pendant drawing attention to it. Her golden hair curled at her neck and framed an interesting, if not beautiful, face. With her delicate looks, she could have been a Lladró figurine in Nana Janet's collection. She turned her stunning deep blue eyes towards a young white man who leaned solicitously toward her.

James stood at the window with a glass filled with golden liquid. 'Come in, Stephen.' He raised his glass. 'Whisky? A Glenfiddich direct from the highlands.'

'No thanks, James,' Stephen glanced at the arrays of drinks on the side table. 'Maybe a fruit juice. I enjoyed a … *than* … *thanbeeli* on the train.'

The woman's laugh glided across the room. 'James, give the boy the coconut water!'

James handed Stephen a glass with the white cloudy liquid and gestured to the woman in the chair. 'Meet my wife, Elise. She's been here ten months and is already bored with life in what she calls the tea jungles.' He turned to the other young man, seemingly not noticing the flash of irritation on his wife's face. 'Did you know, Roger, that the natives call the plantations a *thotta kaadu*? Tamil for jungle! Survival of the fittest!' He sniggered and drained his glass.

'This,' James pointed to the young man, 'is my creeper, Roger Hands. He has been here a few months longer than Elise and is getting used to our ways. A creeper, by the way, is a trainee superintendent. With time, Roger will claw his way up through *sinna dorai*, meaning assistant superintendent, to *peria dorai*, big boss superintendent.'

The young man was slim and tall with an expression of intense concentration on his pale, somewhat nondescript face. Curly golden hair hung to the collar of his shirt. He was dressed in a dark blue woollen suit. 'Welcome to Udatännā, Stephen.' His handshake was tentative. His smile forced. 'I understand you will join me tomorrow to learn the ways of the plantation?'

'If I may?' Stephen responded.

'Of course. You are an Ashley-Cooper. James tells me you are on tour to check out your birthright!'

'Thank you,' Stephen glanced at James and Elise. The air vibrated with unspoken tension. There were undercurrents in the relationship between these three. He wouldn't be here long enough to find out.

'Sir, dinner is ready, sir.' The young Indian man who stood at the door was dressed in a white long-sleeved shirt buttoned to the top and tucked into his white sarong. A leather belt with a polished buckle circled his waist. His feet were in open-toed sandals. His black hair was slicked back and his face expressionless.

'Thank you, Appu.' James turned to Stephen. 'That stately and stern young man is our chef extraordinaire, housekeeper and general factotum. We call him Appu.'

Elise seemed to need help getting out of the deep chair she was ensconced in. It was the creeper Roger's hand she reached for.

The dining table was set with delicate blue and white crockery and silver cutlery. A bowl of red roses lay at the centre. Elise walked ahead of the men to the dining room. She seated Stephen opposite her, with James and Roger on either side. Appu stood at the door to what Stephen assumed was the kitchen. She gestured to him with a flick of her fingers to indicate they were ready.

The Indian girl who brought in the dish of sliced roast meat looked younger than Ally. She was dressed in an ankle-length red skirt and a red figure-hugging top that showed off her budding body and displayed a generous amount of flesh between it and the skirt. 'And this,' James' grey eyes softened as they rested on the girl's face, then slid down her body, 'is Malar. She came to work here as a servant last year. Appu has trained her well.' He looked across at Elise. His expression changed from fondness to challenge. 'We can't live without her, can we, my dear?'

Elise's fingers trembled as she served herself from the dish Malar held. She waited till Malar had moved away from her. 'She is a servant, James. We can always replace her.' Arrogant disdain dripped from every word.

Malar's back stiffened. Her fingers clenched on the dish she held. She kept her eyes down as she held the dish to the others. Then, with a purposeful swish of her skirt, she slid a glance at James and sashayed back to the kitchen.

'That girl is getting intolerable.' Elise's lips tightened. Her pupils turned to blue ice.

'Relax, darling,' James guffawed. 'As you so wisely said, she is only a servant!'

Roger cleared his throat. 'James, did you want Stephen to come to muster with me?'

James laughed louder. 'Ever the peacemaker, Roger. Yes, I believe it would be good for Stephen to experience as much as he can in the time he has with us.'

Yes, the more he learned, the sooner he could go home. And to his parents.

'What time do you start muster?'

'Smart man,' James chuckled. 'He didn't ask what it was!'

Roger turned to Stephen. 'I will be here a little before six in the morning. Wear something warm and hardy. We will be walking. The mud roads are slippery and there are blood-sucking leeches in the tea bushes.'

James and Roger discussed tea manufacture for the rest of the meal. Withering times, pruning schedules, planting of eucalyptus shade trees, and the difficulty of keeping the temperature in the fermenting room constant. The discussion turned to maintaining profit and keeping down expenses.

'James,' Roger's voice was tentative, almost pleading. 'Have you looked at the plan I submitted for repairs to the line rooms?'

James guffawed. 'Have you been listening, Roger? Or even heard what I just said? We do not spend on trivialities.' He snapped his fingers. 'The coolies have lived this way for decades. They are happy as they are. We give them food, shelter and money for their alcohol and tobacco. Stop mollycoddling them!' He stared at Elise across the table.

Elise pushed her chair back and stood up. 'I'm tired. I think I will retire early.'

Stephen sat there, taking it all in. He looked and listened. And learned.

CHAPTER 15

Udatänná Estate, Sri Lanka, 1937

A soft tap on the door woke Stephen. Raman slipped into the room and placed a steaming hot mug of coffee on the table by the bed. 'Sir, *koppi*, sir.'

Stephen picked up the cup and let the thick, fragrant brew slide down his throat. Raman opened the suitcase and started rummaging through it.

'Raman, what're you doing?'

Raman looked up with an expression of bemused amusement. 'Sir going muster, no sir?' He shook out what looked like a below-knee-length pair of shorts and tucked it under his arm. He rifled through the suitcase and drew out a khaki shirt, brown jumper and a long coat not unlike an Australian Driza-Bone. He unfolded them and laid them on the wing-backed chair. He dug deeper into the bag and came up with a pair of thick woollen socks and leather boots. He pointed to the bathroom. 'Hot water ready, sir.' He scurried away before Stephen could say thank you.

Stephen took the hint. He picked up the clothes and went to the bathroom.

He came back to the bedroom, bathed and dressed. A fresh cup of coffee was on the table together with two freshly cut egg sandwiches.

Cradling the hot coffee and munching on a sandwich, Stephen stood at the window and looked out into the garden and beyond. The first rays of sunlight crept over the mountain tops and teased away the mist that swathed the dusky grey peaks. He slid open the window and allowed the crisp air with the hint of tea and eucalyptus to sting him awake.

Roger was waiting for him when he emerged from the bedroom. He had two cane walking sticks with him. He offered one to Stephen. 'You will need this to get through the tea bushes. And put this on your curls.' He picked a pith, helmet-like hat from the hatstand and gave it to Stephen.

Stephen kept pace with Roger as he tramped along the mud path. A couple of Indian men walking ahead of them looked back and stopped in their tracks. They muttered something to each other and stepped into the shallow drain on the side of the path. The men took the turban-like wrapping off their heads and stood with heads bowed. Roger strode past without acknowledging them.

Stephen murmured a good morning and looked back at the men.

'Factory workers on their way for the early shift,' Roger explained.

'But … why …'

'A sign of respect, Stephen. Head covering is not appropriate when addressing the white boss. And a coolie cannot share the path with a superior. It's the way we keep the status quo.' He looked at Stephen and laughed. 'Relax. You'll get used to it.'

They walked side by side for a couple of seconds.

'So,' Roger glanced at Stephen, 'what do you think of your relatives?'

'I can see that James runs a tight ship.'

Roger stopped. He spun around to face Stephen. 'Stephen, you are young. Naïve.' He sighed. 'I was like you when I first started.' The undercurrent of bitterness in his words surprised Stephen. 'I don't know why you are here, but I assume you are looking into taking over this plantation or another one like it one day.' His voice cracked with emotion. 'I hope to God you do a better job than James!'

'The estate seems successful,' Stephen ventured.

Roger laughed. 'Of course, it's successful! James makes sure of that!' He pointed back at the Indian men who, having climbed out of the rain-filled drain, were wiping their bare feet on the grass. 'James would have their hide if they showed disrespect!'

'He wouldn't do anything physical, would he?'

'Whip them?' Roger grimaced. 'No. But he would refuse them

employment for a day, a week. A month if they dare to question him. The coolies live day to day. A hand-to-mouth existence. They have no other source of income. They would probably prefer the whip.'

He pointed down into the valley. Strings of women in sarees with bare flesh exposed on their chest and cane baskets tied over rough cloth headdresses wound their way up along the mud path from their line room homes. The bellowed commands of the Indian man walking with them swirled up from the valley. The women responded by breaking into a jog. 'The *kangani* has probably told them that I would report them late and they will have their pay cut.' He pointed to the Indian man. 'By making one of their own the supervisor we remove ourselves from having to deal with the women directly. He bears the brunt of their displeasure.' He gestured toward the women climbing up the mud track. 'The women will start plucking after muster and go on working till dusk. Every day. All year. In all weather conditions. Get a few rupees for the tea leaves they pluck. That too, only if they meet the required weight. Seen their accommodation?' He pointed to the line rooms hugging the stream. 'They live—and die—in squalor. No medical care. No education for the children.'

Stephen remained silent.

They walked together to where the women were now lined up and waiting. Roger pointed to them with his walking stick. 'I, the white master, will now tell them where in the plantation they will work today. They will obey.' He swung around and looked at Stephen. 'Wonder why I'm telling you this? Because something has to be done, Goddammit! Something!' The angry glitter in his eyes softened. 'Elise tried when she first came. She wanted to open a primary school. A creche to care for the babies. To educate the women on health care. Parenting. Budgeting. She was so full of hope. So many dreams. I tried to dissuade her. Tried to explain what James was like.' He shook his head. Sadness laced his words. 'She was so in love with James. So very gullible. So … innocent.'

'What happened to her plans?'

'James laughed at her. Called her a romantic. An impractical dreamer. He told her that he didn't marry her to, as he called it, babysit the coolies. You heard him at dinner yesterday. Then,' His voice rose in pitch and intensity, 'he has the hide to insult her with his keep!'

'His keep?'

'The girl, Malar.' Roger spat out the words. 'He had her established when I came. He chose her from the tea fields when she was just fourteen. She had just started as a tea plucker. He had the audacity to have her in the house when he brought his bride back from England! Elise is only twenty-two. James swept Elise off her feet when on his furlough in England. She trusted him. She didn't want to believe anything bad of him. But he doesn't care about her feelings. Doesn't care that Elise knows about his relationship with Malar. And I wouldn't be surprised if he does the same with Raman's wife!' His laughter was mirthless. 'The plantation version of the *droit du seigneur*.'

Stephen swallowed the bile that rose in his throat. 'Malar is his mistress?'

Roger's lips twisted in a grimace. 'Nice euphemism.'

Stephen's mouth twisted in disgust. 'But, but she's a child!'

Roger turned and stared at Stephen. 'Learn and learn fast if you intend to come here as the *peria dorai* boss, Stephen.' He stopped and sighed. He threw his hand in the air. 'Why am I telling you all this? You will do as James does. Treat the Indian coolies as ignorant brute beasts. More savage than human. Use. Abuse. All to fill the Oriental Produce coffers.' He pointed to the factory. 'And keep native Ceylonese in their place. Dependent on the white man for their salary, their accommodation. No savings. No references if they dare question or leave their job. All that matters is the quality of the tea and the prices in the London auctions.'

Stephen winced. This was how his paternal ancestors made their money. The dollars his parents and he now enjoyed.

'Aiya, aiya!' Raman came running up the hill towards them. He was waving a piece of paper. 'Telegram coming, sir.' Gasping he thrust the paper at Stephen.

Stephen looked down at the words. Typed in the abbreviated language and stilted text of the 1930s it read, 'Father sick. Come home. Now.'

'Sorry, Roger.' He held the paper out to him. 'I need to go.' He looked around at the coolie women lined up and waiting for muster. There was a look of patient forbearing on their dark faces. He studied the *kangani* striding in front of them. His eyes shifted to the filthy line rooms in the valley. Finally resting on the imposing silver edifice of the tea factory.

'Thank you for explaining things to me.'

'Sir, come. Sir, come. Missing train, sir! Rain also coming, sir!' Raman shouted.

A peal of thunder and a flash of lightning heralded a thunderstorm.

Roger shook Stephen's hand. 'Will you be back?'

'Yes,' Stephen declared. 'Yes, I will be back.'

CHAPTER 16

Serendib, 2131

Ally sat in the shell opposite Saint Thomas with her feet drawn up. The long red skirt and white blouse were both embroidered and beaded in silver and gold. Her hair curled round her face and flowed in waves to her waist. She had a white and gold frangipani blossom tucked behind her right ear. She chuckled and pointed to Stephen's trousers and long woollen socks.

'My goodness, Stephen, you look like a real British country gentleman!'

Stephen whipped off his pith helmet and put down his walking stick. There was nothing he could do about his clothes.

'You left me!'

Ally glanced at Saint Thomas. 'I wasn't supposed to be with you. But I managed a small concession.'

'Sit down, Stephen.' Saint Thomas signalled to the shell next to him. 'Help yourself to some thambili. It would seem you have developed a taste for it.' He gestured to the pitcher and glasses on the table.

Stephen dropped into the shell. He stretched his legs and allowed the shell to massage and stroke. The tension in his muscles eased and the anxiety that raced through his brain lessened.

'What did you learn, Stephen?' The musical lilt of Saint Thomas' words swept over him, a calm port after the emotional storm he had experienced at Udatännȧ.

Stephen looked at Ally. 'How long have I been away?'

She uncurled herself and poured him a glass of thambili. 'In 2030 time, you spent a minute in Virginia and a little over two minutes in Sri Lanka.

In Serendib time,' she scrunched her eyes, 'about two hours, twenty-eight seconds. Give or take a few nanoseconds.'

'Stephen,' Saint Thomas prompted. 'We need to talk. And you need to be honest with me.'

Stephen kept silent.

'Yes, I can sense the waves of emotions swirling through your neurons, Stephen. You are wondering what you should say. You are confused about the reason you are doing what you are doing. But all this will be of no use to you, your world, and ultimately to us, unless you are able to gather your thoughts and feelings together and express them.'

'Appa, he needs time.' Ally scrambled off the shell and sank to her haunches by Stephen. She placed her hands on his.

'We don't have the luxury of time,' Saint Thomas snapped.

Ally's touch gave him strength. Their eyes met. 'It's okay.' Waves of assurance washed into his brain from Ally. 'Trust Appa.'

Saint Thomas shook his head. 'No. He has to do this himself, Aletheia.'

With a twist of her lips that wavered between a scowl and a smile, Ally turned back to the shell. She sank into it with a sigh.

'Every human being,' Stephen spoke slowly, the words dragged from neurons deep in his conscience, 'has an intrinsic value. We are the privileged few in the world. We have to understand this. We've stopped slavery as I saw it at the plantation. But it's not enough. A true world community will stand above colour, ethnicity and country.' He stopped and glanced at Saint Thomas.

The old man beamed at Stephen. 'Good, good. Go on.'

Stephen shut his eyes and concentrated. 'Equality. Fairness. Economic parity.' He felt thoughts and emotions drift together from different parts of his brain. 'Common good. Common purpose.' Concepts coalesced into coherent ideas. Then sentences.

'No. I wasn't accurate in saying there is no slavery. We have global human trafficking. Sex trade. Sweatshops, porn production. I wrote a paper on that last semester.'

'And a very good one too. You were given an A-plus on it.' Saint Thomas wobbled his head.

'I haven't got it back. How did you …'

Ally giggled.

Stephen turned to her. He shook his head and smiled. 'Of course, you know!' He swung back to Saint Thomas. The look in the old man's eyes sobered him. 'But Australia is multicultural,' Stephen rationalised. 'We don't have racism. Not really.' Thoughts of his mother's words floated into his memory. 'Well, very little. We accept and treat all people equally. Mostly. There are a number of scholarship students in my school from India, China, Vietnam, Sri Lanka. The Year 12 prize last year went to an Indian boy. Migrants even play on our sports teams. Not rugby but cricket.'

'Methinks,' Ally interrupted, 'he protests too much.'

'Stephen.' Saint Thomas's words crept into his conscience. 'Are you and your people in Australia accepting of all people? Think about it. What about persecuted people seeking refuge?'

'Illegal immigrants?' He met Saint Thomas's gaze. 'Boat people? They're looked after in refugee camps while their applications are processed. Aren't they?'

'Not everyone who comes for refuge comes by boat, Stephen. And they are in immigration detention centres. Looked after is not the phrase I would use for how they are treated there.'

'But …'

'I know, Stephen, I know,' Saint Thomas cut him off. Your parents have discussed this with you. How these people are economic refugees, here in Australia for a better life. They take Australian jobs, academic positions at universities. Even medical school places that are not rightly theirs. Your mother will not go to the medical centre closest to home because the doctor is Sri Lankan.' Saint Thomas' eyes tunnelled into Stephen's. A tear appeared at the corner of the old man's eye. 'Stephen, Stephen. You don't have to say anything. I know you are not comfortable with your parents, especially your mother's attitude. You don't approve of the way your Australian friends treat the Asians and Indians. The racism in their snide and derogatory comments directed at people of colour upset you.' The sympathy in his gaze reached into Stephen's heart. 'You wanted to do something. But didn't know what or how.

And then, when you told your friends that you thought their behaviour was un-Australian,' Saint Thomas shook his head. 'They laughed at you.'

Saint Thomas stopped. He rested his head back in the shell. Stephen watched as the sides of the headrest massaged the old man's neck.

Ally's eyes, filled with love and concern, rested on Saint Thomas. 'Ferreting into emotions is draining for anyone,' she murmured to Stephen.

'Even more so for your one-hundred-and-three-year-old great-great-grandfather!' Saint Thomas muttered.

'And Appa is doing more than just ferreting, Stephen. He is helping you to connect and analyse your neuronal processes—your thoughts and ideas.'

'So little time, so little time. God help us,' Saint Thomas murmured.

'Amen,' Ally whispered in response.

They sat in silence. Seconds. Minutes.

Stephen looked at Saint Thomas. 'Sir. What now? I need to get back to my parents.'

Saint Thomas pushed himself out of his shell. 'Well children, one more trip. And then,' he sighed. 'Then decision time.' He gestured to Stephen. 'Come.'

The side entrance slid open. Saint Thomas and Ally stepped out, Stephen following them.

He was back on the rough, white limestone gravel path. The single red-bark gum tree stood sentinel by him. The sun was a shimmering golden globe low on the eastern horizon. The sky was a cerulean blue expanse without a single cloud.

The arid landscape of the Nullarbor with the seemingly never-ending mallee shrub surrounded him and stretched relentlessly into the distance. The whistle call of the wedge-tailed eagle circling over him split the silence of the desert.

He looked back and then around.

There was no evidence of Serendib.

CHAPTER 17

Rawlinna Detention Centre, Western Australia, 2030

Stephen looked down. He was no longer in the silk suit he'd had on in Serendib. Neither was he in the clothes he'd had on when he returned from the tea plantations. He was dressed in a black blazer with a sharp white trim, a white shirt, and a black-and-white striped tie. His creased grey trousers rested on polished black shoes. He glanced at the crest on his blazer. The oak tree with a branch weighted down and the motto embroidered under it – 'Inclinata Resurgo—Though fallen, I will rise again'—confirmed it. He was dressed in his school uniform.

He felt her presence. Smelled the frangipani fragrance that accompanied her.

'Come on, Stephen,' she nudged him in his ribs. 'We have places to go and things to do. No time to stand gawking at the Nullarbor plain.'

The black below-knee pencil skirt and white blouse, matched with black stockings and leather boots, screamed taste and elegance. Her blazer was a matching pair to his. Her curls were barely restrained by what looked like an oversized ivory hair clip. A couple of stray strands had escaped and framed her dark face. The almond-shaped black eyes were lightly accentuated with kohl and her lips were sheened with gloss. Ally twirled and curtsied.

'Nice school uniform!' Stephen blurted out.

She stopped and frowned. 'Oops. Appa wants us to move on.' She touched his arm and gestured to the gravel path. 'Your chariot awaits, sir.' Tinkling laughter bubbled out of her and enveloped him.

'Chariot? What—wow!'

The vintage grey Subaru Forester was covered with dust and streaked with desert sand. He pointed to the car. 'Where'd you get that?'

'Oh, the folk at Rawlinna cattle station let me borrow it when I fly in to visit with my recluse great-great-grandfather who lives just off their property.' She rolled her eyes. 'It's such a relic. A museum piece.'

'Your great-great-grandfather would be Saint Thomas?'

'Hmm …' She walked around the car and opened the driver's side door. 'Lives on his little property. A hermit lifestyle in his old age. It gives us a useful link when we want to visit the Before.' Ally climbed into the driver's seat and reached across to open the passenger side door. 'Hop in, Stephen.'

'You've got a driver's license?'

Ally laughed. 'For the year 2030? Of course!' She gestured to the cubbyhole in the front panel. 'Check it if you want.'

'But you don't live in 2030!'

'So,' Ally chuckled. 'You thought you were hallucinating when you first saw me. Hallucinate me back into your world of 2030!' Her laughter flowed around him.

Stephen groaned. Yes, he might as well continue hallucinating. At least in this dream he was in wonderful company.

Ally reached for the gear shift. 'This manual driving's a bummer. Oh, and by the way, I'm glad to contribute to your sweet dreams.' She drove down the mud track towards the main road.

Stephen shook his head. 'Okay, Ally, we're back in 2030. Where're we heading? And, why?'

'We flew into Rawlinna station this morning. You and I are school prefects at Saint Christopher's College in Sydney ...'

He glanced at the crest on her blazer. 'That's my school!'

'We know that, Stephen.' She smiled. 'And you'll be head prefect next year.'

'How do you … oh, never mind.' He looked around at the endless desert scene. 'Ally, where're we heading today?'

'I thought you'd never ask! You and I are leading a group in school for inter-racial collaboration and harmony. It's called the "Cornerstone Project". We're here to meet a caseworker from the Australian Department of Immigration and Multicultural and Indigenous Affairs, or DIMIA for short.'

'I know what DIMIA is,' Stephen mumbled. 'But, why?'

'Because she's taking us into the Rawlinna detention centre for Unlawful Non-Citizens.'

'A camp for boat people? Illegal immigrants? There's no refugee camp in Rawlinna. They're held in offshore camps. Manus. Christmas Island.'

Her laugh was not the rich tinkle he had come to love. Rather, it emerged from a deep place of sadness. 'You believed the media reports, didn't you, Stephen? The media reports that people who come illegally are kept in holiday-style, custom-built camps in an island paradise while their applications are considered by sympathetic case officers.'

'Maybe not quite paradise. But I had no reason not to believe the reports.'

'No, you didn't. Why would you? An only child of privileged bourgeois professional white parents. Born with the proverbial silver spoon stuck in your mouth. Nannies. Chauffeur. Private schooling. Why would you?!' Her fingers tightened on the steering wheel.

Stephen squirmed in his seat. 'Okay, Ally. I get your point. That's a pretty good description of who I am. But I'm here with you, aren't I?' He turned sideways in his seat to stare at her. 'Ally, what do *you* want me to do?'

'Wait.' She slowed down. They continued in silence for a few seconds. Ally sighed. 'Appa just gave me permission to answer your questions as I …'

'Ally, start by telling me why …'

She silenced him with a side glance. 'I will answer as I'm able. Only Appa has the truth.'

'I'll take anything you can give me,' Stephen muttered. 'Ally, why am I here? How did I get here? What do you want from me?'

Ally's forehead creased. She half closed her eyelids. 'Stephen, do you know anything of ancient Christian history?'

Mystified, Stephen nodded. 'Some.'

'Thomas, one of the apostles of Jesus, reached India in around AD 52. He landed in Kerala. Ever since the original Saint Thomas landed in India, every third or fourth generation, one of his descendants is born with the mark.' She took her right hand off the wheel and turned her palm towards Stephen. 'The one with the mark is considered the Chosen One.'

'You're the one in your generation. And your Appa, Saint Thomas?'

'He has the mark.'

Stephen rubbed the birthmark on his right palm. 'I'm not a descendant. How come I have it?'

'We always knew that there would be one from the Before who would come to us. We weren't sure how we'd know the person. But you have the mark. It confirms that you are the one chosen for the connection.'

What is this … this … connection?'

'The connection is with the link between our time in Serendib and the Before time … where you're from. Your time in 2030. From childhood, I was educated by Appa. Trained to deal with the event if it happened in my lifetime.'

'Am I the event?'

'Not exactly. We knew that there would be a time shift. The person who would come to us would be the one who would be able to initiate the change in the Before that we all pray for.' She shook her head and sighed. A few curls escaped the hold of the clip and caressed her neck. 'No one knew the time or how it would happen, and every generation hoped and prayed for it. But they also hoped it would not be in their lifetime.'

'My coming in search of help is that event?'

'You said it. These are the two key concepts. Help and search.'

'I came looking for help for my parents. Which I still haven't got.'

She batted away his words. 'Be patient, Stephen. You'll be back with them in a few more minutes, 2030 time. Appa promised you that they'll be fine. You need to trust him.'

'I do trust the Saint, Ally. But why are we here? Please. Help me understand.'

'The world as you know it …' She let go of her steering wheel and opened her arms to encompass the wide barren land they were driving through. 'This world needs help.'

'My world,' Stephen muttered. 'The world of 2030.'

'Yes.'

'I agree, our world needs all sorts of help! Climate change, poverty, starvation. Even racism,' Stephen continued. 'But where does the search come in? What are we searching for?'

She was silent. He connected with her. She blocked him from her thoughts.

'Ally,' he placed his fingers on hers, 'please, don't lock me out. I need your support now.'

Her fingers tightened on the steering wheel.

'Dear God, Ally!' Her distress reached out octopus-like and coiled through his emotions. She blocked him again.

'Ally, what is it? I haven't seen you this upset in the time I have been here.'

She kept her eyes on the road. Her voice was low. A whisper. Stephen strained to hear her. 'We've spent less than five minutes of *your* time together, Stephen. You don't know me. Don't know my world.' She sighed. 'My brain patterns were spiking because Appa is stopping me from telling you more than you can take in right now.'

'I don't understand.'

Ally twisted the steering wheel and the car turned onto a mud track. 'You will. Soon. For now, promise me that you'll search into your soul for those deep feelings and emotions you have hidden. And remember. Listen, look and learn. And, Stephen ....'

'Yes, Ally,' he prompted.

'You'll need to be both wise and compassionate. As shrewd as a snake and as innocent as a dove.'

They drove in silence for a few minutes.

In front of them, stretched out in the dust of the Nullarbor, was a two-metre-high, chain-link metal fence with coiled barbed wire at the top. Stephen squinted and stared. It was a double fence with a moat-like space between the two.

'Ally, what the hell is this place? A prison? You said we were to visit a refugee camp.'

She slowed and stopped the car near a dusty metal sign. It read 'Rawlinna

Refugee Detention Centre' and below it in small print, 'Department of Immigration and Multicultural and Indigenous Affairs'.

Stephen opened the door and stepped out. The dry desert wind whipped around him. Sweat beaded on his exposed forehead. 'Wow, it's hot!' He gasped.

Ally jumped out of the car and walked over to stand by him. She raised her face to the sky. 'Nudging thirty-eight degrees.' She looked at Stephen. 'Welcome to the five-star accommodation for foreigners and refugees, in the middle of the Nullarbor desert.'

CHAPTER 18

Rawlinna Detention Centre, Western Australia, 2030

People ambled around in what looked like a mud courtyard inside the double fence. Two children dressed in ragged trousers and shirts ran up to the inner fence. They curled their fingers claw-like on the metal links. 'Hello, hello,' one called out. 'You take me to beach?'

Stephen frowned. 'Why …'

'Hope, Stephen. Hope,' Ally responded. 'All that's left for the children. If they don't have hope, they have nothing. Only the empty darkness of despair. Daily, from dawn to dusk.'

Stephen walked up to the fence. 'Aiya. Aiya,' one child yelled. 'Sweets? Biscuits?'

A black Hyundai drove up in a cloud of dust and parked next to their Subaru. The door swung open and the six-foot-something driver stepped out. The white cotton short-sleeved shirt fit snug on the chest, exposing muscular biceps and pectorals. Emblazoned on the pocket of the shirt was the Australian Commonwealth crest of the six-state shield with emu and kangaroo on either side. Bold black letters spelled out 'DIMIA' below the crest. The driver reached into the back seat and dragged out a black briefcase and an Akubra hat.

'Time for another adventure, Stephen,' Ally said out loud. 'And that's Georgiana, the caseworker we'll be with for a couple of hours.' Her giggle reached across into his brain. 'Yes,' Ally connected. 'It's a woman. They send the tough ones here.'

The woman's features would have passed for a pugilist in a man. Ally giggled again into his brain. 'You were right on your first guess, she's a female boxer.'

'Well, we better be nice, then!' he channelled back.

The woman crammed the Akubra on her short-cropped brown hair and strode towards them. She stretched out her right hand to Ally. 'You must be Priscilla Thomas. The Indian embassy pulled some strings to get you here. My boss impressed on me that the only reason he consented is because your father, the ambassador, is in negotiations with the immigration minister to repatriate some of the people.' She poked a finger at the people crowded at the wire fence, staring wide-eyed at them. 'God knows we need to get rid of some.'

Stephen smothered a smile as Ally's response flickered from her brain to his. 'Pretentious, arrogant prig!' Ally shook the woman's hand. 'And you must be Georgiana,' she responded. Her voice dripped sweetness. 'Thank you so much for allowing us to sit in with you at the interviews.'

The woman hooted with laughter. 'Georgiana! Haven't been called that for a while. Just call me Georgie.' She looked Ally up and down. 'Gluttons for punishment, you two!' She turned to stare at Stephen. 'And you, young man, would be the head prefect of your college. We were shown the article you two wrote.' She laughed again. 'Dreamers. Dreamers,' she mumbled. 'Never mind.' She raised her voice. 'Let's get in there and give you a reality shot of the sludge that passes for those seeking political asylum. Come on.' She strode ahead of them to the double-padlocked entry gate.

They drew closer to the fence. Stephen could see the faces and bodies of the people inside the compound more clearly. Partially emaciated figures in old clothes. Dishevelled, uncombed hair. Unshaven and gaunt faces. But it was the eyes that reached into his heart. Eyes devoid of all expression. Vacant. Spent. Desolate. Every muscle and sinew in Stephen's body tensed. A tremor rent his body. His government treated people this way. And he didn't know. A thought flitted across his brain. He hadn't bothered to find out. He hadn't cared.

Ally sent calming vibes to him. 'Relax. Breathe. Remember, emotional involvement is not what you're here for. Observe and learn.'

Stephen took a deep breath, then gagged in the dust, heat and the musty sweat-seeped smell that reached out to them.

Two men in khaki uniforms shoved their way through the gathered crowd of people inside the compound. On the front pockets of their uniform were the words 'Australia Security Services'. If Georgie was a pugilist, these specimens looked like overfed bouncers verging on sumo wrestlers.

The men unlocked the inner gate. They shoved people aside and locked it from the outside. Stephen glanced at the wide leather belts the officers wore. On them hung a radio, handcuffs and a leather truncheon. 'Ally,' he channelled, 'what is this place?'

She sighed. 'Look. Listen and learn.' Waves of encouragement and comfort flowed from Ally to him.

One of the men opened the two padlocks on the outer gate and ushered the three of them into the area between the fences.

'Zach,' Georgie addressed one of the men, 'what the hell is happening?'

'Those bloody Tamil fellows are back on the roof protesting. Maybe you could talk to them.'

'No,' she snapped back. 'I'm the case officer, not a negotiator. You folk are the officers paid to do that. Now get us to the interview room.'

The other man pulled up his phone and shouted something into it. Stephen picked up some of the words. Crowd. Unruly. Reinforcements.

Two others, both females, in a similar uniform to the officers, approached the crowd gathered at the gate. They swung their truncheons. People in the compound yelled and scurried out of their way.

The male officer, the one that Georgie had called Zach, opened the padlocks on the inner gate and ushered the three of them in. The other officer locked it behind them.

They were immediately surrounded by people.

'Please, madam.' One grey-haired Asian man shoved a paper at Georgie. 'I've been here for six years. Please help.'

A middle-aged dark-skinned woman held out a toddler. 'Take my child. He know prison only. Take. Take.'

A shout made Stephen look up. Two slim, dark-skinned men were seated on the roof of a shed-like building. 'We appeal to the UNHCR,' one yelled. 'We want our human rights.'

Stephen felt a touch on his palm. Small fingers crept into his. He looked down into the face of the little boy whom he had seen earlier at the fence. 'Aiya,' the child whispered. 'You like me? I come with you.' Tears streaked the smudges of dust and dirt on the child's face. Stephen's heart squeezed in his chest. Tears burned behind his eyeballs.

He felt Ally's fingers on his arm. He felt her strength override and subdue his emotion. 'Keep calm, Stephen.' Stephen smiled at the child and pulled his fingers free.

The four security officers surrounded them and ushered them into a building marked 'OFFICES'.

'Georgie,' one of the female staff in the office called out. She gestured to two young women and two men of indeterminate age sitting in the corridor. 'There are four scheduled for you today to make decisions on. More if you have the time!' She opened the door to a room with a sign on it that read 'INTERVIEW ROOM'. 'I put in two extra chairs like you instructed me to.' She walked to the door and looked back, 'So, which of them do you want to talk to first?'

Georgie dumped her briefcase on the floor and sat down at the table. She gestured to two chairs placed at an angle to hers. 'Sit down, folks. Make yourselves comfortable.' She pulled off her hat and tossed it on the briefcase. 'This could take a while.' She pulled out a file from the briefcase. She glanced at the woman at the door. 'Hayley, send me RD4268.'

Stephen stared at the file. 'The refugees are identified by numbers?'

Georgie chortled. 'Hey, you can't expect me to read their names! Much less remember them.' She flicked the file open to the first page. 'For example, this one is called Selvaa … Lak … lakshii … mee Pri … priya…'

Ally leaned forward and read 'Selvalakshmi Priyadarshini Balasupramanium.'

'Don't worry,' she connected with Stephen. 'They don't tattoo the numbers on their arm.'

'But it's so wrong,' he sent back to her. 'Insulting. Dehumanising.'

Her response floated into his conscience. 'Maybe that's why they do it?'

CHAPTER 19

Rawlinna Detention Centre, Western Australia, 2030

The officer, Hayley, opened the door and stood aside. 'In you go, girlie.'

Georgie flicked through the pages of the bulging file in front of her and then looked at the girl. Her eyes raked over the girl from head to toe. Damn the woman, it was a look calculated to denigrate and dismiss. 'Sit,' she ordered, jabbing a finger at the chair placed across the table from the three of them.

The young woman was dressed in a faded blue and white cotton saree and blouse. Her dark oval face was framed by straight black hair, pulled back in a braid that stretched down to her waist. Unlike the many other detainees they had seen and smelled on entering the camp, the woman's face, hands and clothes were clean and had a faint soap smell. She took a few hesitant steps towards them.

'Sit,' Georgie barked. She shoved a finger at the woman. 'Speak English?'

The woman slid down on the chair and raised her eyes to meet Georgie. 'Little,' she whispered. Her gaze was direct. Head held high. Uncowed. With a hint of pride. Ally's thoughts floated through his. 'She and I come from the same ethnic stock. We are proud of our bloodline, Stephen!'

'I asked for an interpreter,' Georgie groused. She turned to Stephen. 'Could you pop out and ask one of the staff to find me a Tamil interpreter?' Stephen pushed back his chair and stood up.

'Don't bother to get an interpreter, Georgie.' Ally gestured to Stephen to sit down. 'I speak Tamil. I'm happy to help.'

Stephen flashed a teasing thought to Ally 'Sure. Tamil and over a dozen other languages.' Ally's smile told him that she had received it.

She looked across the table and spoke to the woman. 'Selvalakshmi, my name is Ally,' she addressed the woman in Tamil. 'You can tell me anything in Tamil. I will listen and tell you what the lady Georgie says. I will then tell her your reply in English.'

'Call me Selvi, *thangachchi*, sister.'

Stephen blinked. Ally was speaking in Tamil, as was the woman, but her words were registering in his conscience in English. Ally's lips twitched. She sent Stephen a message 'Surprised again?'

Ally moved her chair closer to the woman and looked at Georgie. 'What would you like me to ask her?'

'Ask her to tell me why she is here, and how she came here.'

Ally turned to the woman and repeated the question in Tamil.

'I told the other people everything. I had two interviews.'

'I think,' Ally responded, 'this lady wants to check what you said. Think back and keep your story exactly to what you said earlier.'

The woman took a deep breath and exhaled. 'I was born in a small village called Nilāvarai in the Jaffna district. I had one brother. My father was a farmer. He had chillies and onions in his field. Then the war happened. You know about the war, *thangachchi*?'

'I know about the ethnic war in Sri Lanka between the majority Sinhalese and minority Tamils.' Ally continued to speak to the woman in Tamil and slipped the woman's words to Stephen in English.

'My father was taken away by the Tamil Tigers to fight. My mother and I tried to keep farming. My brother was only three. But it was hard. And we have just enough to eke out a living. And then,' she stopped with a sob, 'in 2016, when I was twenty-two, the Tigers came for me.'

Ally stopped the woman at intervals and translated for Georgie.

'I learned to use guns. To fight. To put in land mines. I carried a cyanide capsule on a rope around my neck. We lived rough. Villagers fed us. Or else we took what we wanted.' She stopped. Tears trekked down her cheeks and dropped unhindered on her breast. 'Many of my friends died. I wish … I wish I too had died.' She dropped her head in her hands. 'Sorry, *thangachchi*.' Her breathing quickened. A sob tore out from a deep place of anguish.

'It's all right.' Stephen felt the waves of courage and comfort Ally directed to the woman. Maybe the woman felt it too. Her facial muscles relaxed. 'And then it all went to hell. We were betrayed. We had no ammunition. No food. We were locked into a small part of land. Us and ordinary, poor Tamil people. No food. No water. No medicine. Only shooting. And bombs and fear … and pain. I … I lost my cyanide capsule.'

Ally translated for Georgie. Her tone and words mirroring the distress of the woman. Georgie's face remained bored as she flicked through the papers in the file. The horror and sadness of the woman's story didn't seem to make any impression on her. 'Tell her to continue,' she instructed.

'I was captured.' The woman's voice broke on a sob. 'They … they … the soldiers … they shot my friends. I … was raped. We were crowded in a camp. Small rooms. We had to go to the river to bathe. The soldiers went with us. They stood and watched while we changed and bathed. They watched and laughed.'

She paused and Ally translated.

'I had a baby. In prison. They gave me some milk for him. I couldn't feed him.' The ghost of a smile flitted across her face. 'One guard was kind. He brought me milk powder. Later baby food. He said that he had a baby like my boy. My beautiful Rajan. A child of sadness.'

'Ask her how long she was in the Sri Lanka prison camp,' Georgie rasped.

'My child, Rajan, was three years old. It would have been the year 2023.'

'Why did she not go back home to her family?' Georgie responded to Ally's translation.

'I went back to the village. My father had died in the war. I had been promised in marriage to a man in the village. He lost a leg in the war. Now had a small shop. He didn't want me. My mother called me a vesi—a prostitute. I had nowhere to go. That night, I stole the jewellery. It was to be my dowry. Then I ran away from Jaffna with my son.' Her face paled and her breath quickened. Stephen filled a glass of water from a bottle on the desk and gave it to her.

'Thank … you,' she responded in English.

'What did you do after that?' Ally prompted.

'I went down to Sinhalese territory. To Anuradhapura. That is where the Sinhalese army man, the one who helped me, lived. He came and took us to his house. His wife looked after us. But they couldn't keep me and my son. I was a Tamil terrorist. His wife worked in the government. She would have got into trouble. They are good people. The wife got me a passport. They told me that if I got to Australia as a refugee, Australia would accept me and give me asylum. They pawned the jewellery for me and bought airplane tickets and clothes. Then I took a plane to … to Adelaide.'

'And?' Ally prompted.

'I said I had been assaulted. I said I could not go back and asked for asylum. My visa was not right. They took me to a room and questioned me. Took me to a hotel and then …' she shrugged. 'Here.'

There was a knock on the door. They heard the voice of a child shout 'Amma. Amma.'

'Aiyoo, my *pillai*. My child!' Selvi jumped off her chair. 'Sorry. Sorry. He gets frightened if he doesn't see me.'

Hayley opened the door to the room. '*Amma*!' A boy dressed in blue shorts and a T-shirt ran in and flung himself into Selvi's arms.

'Sorry, Georgie,' the woman Hayley said. 'I know you don't like interruptions, but …'

Georgie dismissed her with a brusque wave. 'Shut the door.' She turned to Ally. 'According to our informants in this woman's home of …' she glanced at the file, 'Jaff… Jafa… Jaffana, her mother and the one-legged man she says she was to marry both say that she ran away with a Sinhalese soldier and came back with the child.'

Ally's fingers clenched. Her eyes narrowed and flashed onyx black sparks of temper. Stephen concentrated all his energy to send her calming vibes. She flashed him a glance and relaxed. 'Thank you,' she connected.

Georgie flicked through a couple of pages in the file. 'We need proof of what happened. The government hasn't got her name on the list of war detainees. And we have it here that she won't give us the name of the man who helped her.'

'Can you tell them the name of the Sinhalese soldier?' Ally asked in Tamil.

'Aiyoo, no, *thangachchi!* I can't do that! He helped me. I cannot … I will not betray him.' The words ripped out of her. 'The government will kill him for helping a Tamil Tiger.'

Ally translated.

'Sri Lanka is a democracy. They have set up a war crimes tribunal. There is no reason for her to keep the name from us. We have no other way of confirming the story that she was tortured.'

Ally addressed the woman in a gentle calm voice. 'Selvi, *acca*,' she said, addressing the woman by the Tamil word for older sister. 'The army men attacked you. Do you have any injuries? Scars?'

'Yes, *thangachchi*.' Tears tracked down her face. She touched her breast and then looked down at her lap. Ally's eyes glazed with tears.

'Georgie, she was assaulted by the Sinhalese army personnel.' Her voice trembled with emotion. 'They gang-raped her. It was a brutal attack. She says that she has the scars on her breasts and her genitals to prove that it happened.'

'Good, good.' Georgie scribbled in the file. 'I'll have the medical officer examine her later today. If the scars are in keeping with her story of assault, she may stand a chance for a bridging visa. You can tell her.'

The woman stood up. She brought her palms together in the now familiar salute. 'Thank you, thank you, madam,' she said in English. She held on to the boys' hand and scurried out, shutting the door behind her.

'There have been more people killed and tortured in ethnic infighting in the last decade than there were in the two world wars.' The comment flitted from Ally to him.

Georgie slid her chair back and looked at Ally and Stephen. 'Well, what do you think?'

'I have read up on the Sri Lankan ethnic war.' Ally spoke with controlled precision. Stephen sensed her tight control of the emotional roller coaster flying around her brain. 'Her story rings true.'

Georgie looked at Stephen. 'And you, Mister Cooper. What do you think?'

'I think she should be allocated a lawyer to help her make a good case for a visa.'

'Mister Cooper!' Georgie chortled. 'Why don't you go back to Sydney and send a lawyer out here to these god-forsaken cattle-yards that pass for a refugee camp?'

CHAPTER 20

Rawlinna Detention Centre, Western Australia, 2030

Georgie sat scribbling notes in her file.

Ally observed Stephen's thought patterns. Stephen's brain waves were spiking all over his cognitive and emotional brain as he tried to consolidate the information dumped on him. The fact that the government had a detention centre in the middle of the desert where summer temperatures top 40 plus degrees Celsius. The conditions. The sadness. Hopelessness. The assault on Selvi and the fact that she may not get a visa was devastating him.

Ally didn't interfere. She observed as his brain waves calmed, settled, and consolidated into concrete thinking.

'You don't want to be a mining engineer anymore?' she connected.

'No. I need something with more focus.'

'Focus?' Ally pushed.

'Hmm, prepare myself for things I feel I need to do. International law, economics, international affairs.'

'Well, that's that.' Georgie slapped the file shut and shoved it in her briefcase. She proceeded to drag out another slightly slimmer folder marked RD4364. She flicked it open. 'Name Aminia Buk … Buk … hari; sixteen years old, from Far-is … allah … bad in Pakistan. Been here for eighteen months. She speaks Punjabi. Damn, I asked for an Urdu translator.'

'Faisalabad,' Ally muttered under her breath.

Stephen's amusement reached out to Ally. Out loud, he said, 'No problem, Georgie. I'm sure Priscilla would be delighted to act as a translator. Again.'

Georgie swung round in her chair. 'You know Punjabi?'

Ally tilted her head in assent. 'I have travelled with my father all over the world. My mother insisted we learn the local languages of places we lived in.'

'Good. Good.' Georgie reached into her briefcase and pulled out another file. 'You wouldn't be able to handle Dari and Pashto, would you? The next case for today is an Afghan.'

'I have a working knowledge of them both.'

'You're a gem, Priscilla. You could come work with us when you graduate.'

Georgie pushed her chair back. She strode to the door and flung it open. 'Hayley,' she hollered. 'Send in RD4364.'

The woman was dressed in traditional Punjabi women's wear of shalwar kameez. The loose trouser-like garment and shift-dress-like top were clean and clung to her slim figure. The cotton scarf-like dupatta lay over her shoulders and covered her hair. Stray curls framed a dark face. She looked more like twelve than sixteen. On her feet were a pair of sandals, now old and worn, but still showing evidence of the intricate leatherwork and embroidery that had gone into their manufacture.

'Sit.' Georgie pointed to the chair.

The girl walked to the table. She raised her head and looked at Georgie. Ally met and held the girl's eyes. She had been prepared for fear, anxiety, stress. But all she found in this girl's long-lashed black eyes was peace. Ally dug deeper. The girl was calm. Eighteen months in a detention camp from hell and she was at peace. The girl's brainwaves spoke to Ally. 'I am where I am for a purpose.'

At that moment, Ally understood.

The girl sat down and looked at Georgie. Ready for fear and angst, Georgie, clearly discomfited by the girl's expression, was quiet for a few seconds. She cleared her throat and looked down at the notes in the file. 'Aminia Buk ... Buk ... hari.' She turned to Ally. 'Tell her that you will interpret what I say.'

Ally sent out mental vibes to Aminia. To her surprise, Aminia responded with a scrambled acceptance. 'The lady will ask questions in English, Aminia,' she said in Punjabi. 'I think you understand English, but it may be better if you speak through me. Do you understand why?'

The words translated simultaneously to Stephen.

Aminia sat silent.

'Ask her to tell us how she came to be here.' Georgie flipped the papers in the file. 'I want everything. Names. Places.'

Ally spoke to the girl. 'You heard what she said. Think carefully about what you said in your earlier interviews and say the same thing. She is looking for discrepancies in your story.'

'My name is Aminia Bukhari. I am sixteen years old. I lived with my parents and my two younger brothers, Wasim and Imran, in an upper-class suburb of Faisalabad. My family were—are high caste Rajput Muslims. My father owns a textile mill and garment factory. He employs mainly Chura caste people. These are low-caste people who come from the villages to the city for work. I attended an all-female private school called Faisalabad Grammar School.' She stopped and waited for Ally to translate for Georgie.

'The Abbas family worked for my father in the factory. They had one daughter, Layla. Layla's father, Faisal, borrowed money from my father when she was very ill as a baby. It was a lot of money. They, Layla and her parents, have to work for my father till the money is paid back.'

'Bonded labour,' Ally commented silently to Stephen. 'In its most typical manifestation, a worker, usually an adult man, takes a loan or salary advance known as "peshgi" from an employer, labour contractor or landlord. Then the debtor, and often family members as well, are obliged to work for the lender for reduced wages until the debt is repaid. They are paid a pittance for the work and stay in debt till they can no longer work. Or die.'

'Layla and her mother walked me to school every morning and picked me up after I finished in the afternoon.' The girl continued. 'There was a small building which we passed every day. One day, there was a white man at the door. He greeted Layla and her mother. They told me that I must not tell my parents. After that, they tried to make me take another route to school. I refused. We kept passing the building and often saw the white man. After a few months, I insisted that they tell me about the building and the man. I threatened to tell my parents about it. Although I would never have done that!'

Ally translated for Georgie, then swung back to Aminia. 'Was it a church Aminia? And the man, was he an English missionary?'

'Layla told me. She and the family were Christians. They begged me not to tell my parents. I didn't.' Her eyes shone with an inner fire. It lit a matching flame in Ally's heart. 'What I did was go to visit the church on my own. I told my parents I had late classes after school and met with the missionary. He explained it all. Even gave me an Urdu Bible. I became a Christian. Nobody knew until … until my little brother found my Bible and gave it to my mother.' She stopped and took a deep shuddering breath.

Ally translated.

For the first time since she entered the room, tears glittered on Aminia's lashes. A couple escaped and tracked down her cheek. She made no attempt to wipe them away. 'My mother came to my bedroom. I told her that I had found the church and talked to the people there. I told her I was a Christian. I told her how it had changed my life. That the man Jesus was God's son. My mother told me to shut up. She slapped me. She cried. A lot. She said that she had to tell my father. To have a child become a Christian was a shame on the family. A shame on the Rajput caste. She said my father had two choices.' She stopped and sighed.

Ally slid forward in her chair. She reached forward and touched Aminia's arm. 'An honour killing or an arranged marriage.'

'He would have to kill me to save the family name. Or else, I would be married. My mother named a man. He was fifty years old. There was one way she could save me. She said she would burn the Bible. No one needed to know what happened … that I was a Christian.'

'Did they follow through on the marriage?' Ally prompted.

'I said no,' Aminia whispered. 'She didn't let me go to school that day. I decided to run away. I asked Layla to help me. She was afraid. So …' She looked down at her clothes, 'I waited till my mother left the house. Then I packed a few of my favourite clothes and my jewellery and went to the church.'

Ally translated for Georgie. Then turned to Aminia. 'Was it safe for you in the church?'

Aminia grimaced. 'The Pakistani pastor was terrified. My father is an influential man. He would report them for kidnapping me. For stealing my jewellery. The church would be burned. The pastor and the white missionary would be beaten, maybe even killed for helping me. The pastor's wife put me in what is called a three-wheeler—a sort of small hire car and sent me to her cousin's house in a small village near Lahore. They were kind. Poor, low-caste, street-sweeper people. They prayed with me and blessed me. I stayed there one night.'

She stopped while Ally translated.

'They gave me a skirt and blouse to wear. It was safer than looking like a Pakistani while travelling in India. I travelled by overnight train to Chennai in South India. A lady met me. She said she was part of the mission there and put me on a bus to a place called Dhanushkodi. There I got on a boat and went to Sri Lanka. I was so frightened on the fishing boat.' She stopped and laughed. A sad and empty sound.

'I didn't know what was ahead! The fishermen left me with a Tamil girl in a place called Mannar. Another overnight bus ride and I ended up in a refugee camp run by Catholic nuns in a town called Negombo.' She looked at Ally. 'Do you know any of these places?'

'Yes, Acca, sister, I have been to India, Sri Lanka and Pakistan.'

'You will understand how tired I was. And frightened. I stayed there at the convent refuge.' She paused and counted on her fingers. 'I was there for thirty days. The nuns heard from the people who had helped me in India that my father was checking on where I was. They told me that the only way I would be safe is to come to a Christian country like Australia. I gave them my jewellery to sell to buy a ticket on a boat. If it could be called that.' Ally stopped her and translated for Georgie.

'I spent fifteen days with about sixty other people in a small wooden boat.'

'How large was the boat?' Georgie growled.

'I'm not sure; it must have been about forty feet long.'

'What did you eat?' Georgie continued.

'They had tinned fish and meat. And bread. But the bread went stale. They cooked rice. Or I should say half-cooked rice. The nuns gave me packets of biscuits. I shared these with some small children who were hungry. We ran out of water. Had no food.' Aminia fell silent. Ally could see into Aminia's memories. Pain. Hunger. Thirst. Desperation. And then through it all an overlay of peace. 'I knew—I thought—I was coming to a Christian country,' she whispered.

Aminia took a deep breath and let it out in a shuddering sigh. 'We were picked up by an army boat. The men were kind. We were given food and water. We cheered. We were happy. We thought we were saved. Free. Then … then … we were brought here.' She looked around the room. 'As soon as I looked at the barbed wire my mind was full of fear. Instead of freedom, I am in prison.'

Ally translated. She concentrated on Aminia and ignored the spikes of distress radiating in Stephen's brain. She would deal with him later.

'How do we know if she is a convert? She could be pretending.' Georgie looked up from the file.

'Aminia.' Ally concentrated her energy on calming Aminia. 'Do you know any verses or sections in the Bible? Anything to prove you really are a Christian?'

Aminia smiled. It was a flash of sunshine that lit up the dingy little interview chamber. 'I spent the time at the refuge in Negombo memorising verses in the Bible in English. I don't know what they all mean. But they make me feel loved and comforted. Should I say some?'

Ally looked at Georgie. 'She says she can recite Bible verses in English.'

Georgie shrugged. 'I wouldn't know the difference between Bible verses and the lyrics of a Lady Gaga song. Would you recognise what she says?'

Ally held back the disgust she felt towards Georgie. 'Yes, I can.'

'Okay then. Get her to recite something.'

Ally's sent vibes of encouragement to Aminia. 'Recite some Bible passages, Aminia.'

'The Lord is my shepherd, I lack nothing. He makes me lie down in green pastures, he leads me beside quiet waters, he refreshes my soul. He guides me along the right paths. Even though I walk through the darkest valley, I will fear no evil, for you are with me.'

'Psalm twenty-three in the Bible,' Ally advised Georgie.

Georgie scribbled it down in her notes.

Aminia continued. 'I am convinced that neither death nor life, neither angels nor demons, neither the present nor the future, nor any powers, neither height nor depth, nor anything else in all creation, will be able to separate us from the love of God that is in Christ Jesus our Lord.'

'Chapter eight of Paul's epistle to the Romans,' Ally reported to Georgie. 'Would you like Aminia to continue?'

'Yeah, get one more for the record.'

Aminia nodded. 'God is our refuge and strength, an ever-present help in trouble. Therefore, we will not fear, though the earth gives way and the mountains fall into the heart of the sea.'

'Psalm forty-six.'

'That'll do.' Georgie slammed the file shut. For the first time since they met her, the lines of her face relaxed. 'You can tell Aminia that we checked all the information she gave us. We have determined that she cannot return to Pakistan due to religious persecution and fear for her life. She will be granted a refugee visa for resettlement in Australia.' She waited till Ally translated.

Aminia bowed her head. Ally followed Aminia's silent prayer of thanks to God. Prayers for her family. For the people who had helped her. Even for the staff of the detention centre. Tears glistened on her eyelashes when she raised her eyes to Georgie. 'Thank you,' she said in English. She turned to Ally. 'Please tell madam that I will be a good Australian.'

'I know you will be, Aminia,' Ally responded. 'I know.' She translated for Georgie.

She connected with Stephen. She sensed his emergent determination. 'One in eight Christians worldwide are persecuted for their faith. Pakistan is high on the list of persecuted countries. Afghanistan and North Korea are at the top of the list. And no, Australia does not make the list. Not as yet.'

Stephen sat there, absorbing it all.

After Aminia left, Ally translated from Dari to English for an Afghan journalist from the minority Hazara ethnic group. He was under a death threat from the government for what they perceived as his subversive and unpatriotic poetry. He showed Ally some of his writing. She read it in Dari and translated it for Georgie. It didn't sound in any way dangerous or anything that warranted arrest or death in either language. Stephen listened as she spoke in Dari to the man, tutoring him on how to phrase his story of travel from Afghanistan and his encounter with people smugglers in Indonesia in a manner that would appeal to the sensitivities of the immigration department and Georgie.

Stephen listened and learned from Ally's discussion in Vietnamese with the refugee whose wife and two children had drowned when the boat they were travelling in capsized. With tears glistening on her lashes, she reported to Georgie that the one child who survived now refuses to eat and had cut herself. The child was isolated. On suicide watch. Diagnosed with a condition called resignation syndrome. The man asked Ally to tell Georgie to please take the child. He no longer cared about himself. He begged. Ally translated it in a way that the child be eligible for a protection visa.

'They all beg!' Georgie shut the file and shoved it back into her briefcase. She signalled the interview over and sent the man away. 'Okay, kiddos, we're done for the day.' She glanced at her wrist. 'Wow, it's one o'clock. You two want to have lunch with the staff? Not five-star cuisine, but it's edible. It's a long drive back to Kalgoorlie.'

'No thanks, Georgie.' Ally stood up. 'We have to return the car to the Rawlinna Station and catch a ride to Sydney on their private plane this afternoon.'

'Well, thank you for your help, Priscilla. I look forward to reading the report of your experiences.'

The two officers who had ushered them into the camp were waiting outside the building. They escorted Ally and Stephen past the refugees gathered in the compound to the gates.

The wind picked up as they passed through the outer gate. 'A dust storm! Run for the car!' Ally yelled.

The gates clanged shut behind them.

They scrambled into the car and slammed the doors shut. The wind howled and the dust swirled around them.

'We're not going to Rawlinna Station, are we?' Stephen shouted over the wail of wind and rattle of sand on the metal shell of the car.

'Hang on tight!' Ally turned the engine on and swung the car directly into the storm.

CHAPTER 21

Serendib, 2131

The rays of the afternoon sun slanted over the coconut palms and frangipani trees of Serendib. A gentle wind caressed the gold and white flowers and chased puffs of clouds across the sapphire blue sky.

Saint Thomas stood outside his nexus pod.

Ally slowed the car and braked in the paved drive. They both opened the doors and jumped out.

Saint Thomas stepped toward them. He pointed to the path leading away from his nexus pod and towards the buildings of Serendib. 'Aletheia, go. Get washed and changed and come back.'

'Appa, I'd like to stay.'

'No, Aletheia. I need to speak to Stephen.'

'Stephen needs to wash and change too.' She met Saint Thomas' gaze. 'Yes, I will come back.' With a wave to Stephen, she jumped on her skimmer. She flew down the paved path away from them.

Saint Thomas touched Stephen's shoulder. 'Come. We have to talk.'

Once inside the pod, Saint Thomas pointed to the table. 'Your favourite thambili drink and some pastries. Sit down. You can eat while we talk.'

A growl in his stomach reminded Stephen he was starving. He bit into the pastry and washed it down with coconut water. 'Sir … Saint Thomas …' He sank into the shell and looked into the eyes of the man sitting opposite him. Stephen was drawn into their deep charcoal grey depth. He felt a sense of calm. Strength. But above it all the stirring of a challenge. A challenge to a greater, purer purpose. For the first time since they met, Saint Thomas was allowing Stephen access to his brain.

Moments passed.

'Yes, Stephen Ashley-Cooper. You are ready. What happens after this is in the hands of God.'

'I don't understand …'

Saint Thomas silenced Stephen with a look. 'You have all you need. All it takes. You need to pull the threads together. And, Stephen, we don't have much time left.'

Anxiety gripped Stephen's heart. 'Is it my parents?'

'Your parents will be fine. It is only …' He shut his eyes. Stephen was blocked from Saint Thomas's mind. 'It is fourteen minutes and thirty-two seconds since you left the caravan.' The block lifted. Saint Thomas leaned forward and filled Stephen's glass. 'Let me tell you a story. I want you to allow what I tell you and what I transfer into your brain thought processes to weave into and consolidate with what you have experienced here in Serendib. Can you do that?'

The arc of connection between their consciousness was so real that Stephen felt he could reach out and touch it. 'Yes, Saint Thomas, I'm ready.'

'Ever since men and women were created, humanity has struggled with accepting those who are different,' Saint Thomas mused. He stopped and wobbled his head. 'Yes, good. Allow the threads of thought and emotion to interweave and coalesce. Take it slow, Stephen.'

Stephen gave his floating reflections a voice. 'It's always been us, and them. Countries, ethnicities, class differences, religion. And colour. The whites, the pure ones. The chosen race. The coloured and Blacks seen as inferior, undeveloped. Even cursed. It gave the whites the assumed right for what they saw as advancement. Colonisation. Slavery. The holocaust.'

Ideas and emotions chased each other through his neuronal circuits. Stephen felt as if his brain would burst out of his skull. He tore his eyes away from Saint Thomas' and dropped his head in his hands.

'Relax, son. Breathe.'

Stephen drew a shuddering breath. The Saint had called him son. The word consoled and soothed Stephen. His brain waves stopped jangling and stabilised.

Thoughts became ideas. Ideas became the nascent beginnings of plans.

'Saint Thomas, we're one humanity. Everyone. Countries. Colours. We're equal in God's eyes. We should be equal in the eyes of each other. There's no us and them on our planet.'

Saint Thomas kept the connection. But now, he was allowing Stephen to think independently. The impulses from Saint Thomas' emotions were bolstering Stephen's thoughts. And his courage.

'Sir … Saint Thomas.' The words tumbled out of him. He leapt out of the shell and paced up and down the room.

'My generation, Generation Alpha, are searching for a cause. Those who went before us tried to rally under climate change. Under sexual permissiveness. Gender equality. Nothing worked. We need a cause that's bigger than anyone. One that promises global enlightenment. Worldwide unity. Equity. We need a visionary leader who can give them a cause and a reason to follow him—or her.' He stood by Saint Thomas.

'Yes, Stephen,' Saint Thomas smiled. He hauled himself away from the shell. His touch on Stephen's shoulder sent a shiver of anticipation through him. 'Yes, you are ready.'

'Me? Wait! Saint Thomas. I'm here and …'

'You.' Saint Thomas's words reverberated in Stephen's brain. 'You are the Chosen One. We have done what we had to do. The rest …' Saint Thomas' eyes dimmed, and lines of worry creased his face. 'The rest is in God's hands.'

The front entrance to the pod slid open. Ally dashed in. 'Appa, have you told him?'

'Aletheia.' The command in his voice silenced Ally. She slid up to Stephen and slipped her fingers into his. Her fingers trembled in his palm. She was terrified. Stephen curled his fingers around hers. Giving rather than taking comfort. Ally accepted it from him. It felt good.

'Sit down children.' Saint Thomas pointed to a double shell.

'Stephen, I want you to listen to what I have to say. When I finish, you will have to make a decision. How you choose will affect you and the future of the world as you know it.'

CHAPTER 22

Serendib, 2131

'Stephen, the world as you know it is at a critical juncture. What happens next will make the difference between a world where all humans live as equals and the world as you see it here in Serendib.'

'I don't understand. You have a good place here in Serendib.' He glanced at Ally. 'You're at peace. Both as a community and as individuals. You have a global collaborative to maintain harmony between all people. Ally said your name of ... Sama ... Sama ...'

'Samaataanam,' Ally prompted silently.

Stephen nodded acceptance. 'Ally told me that Samaataanam stands for tranquillity, peace, and reconciliation. You've got it all here. Why would you want to change it?'

'Exactly what I keep saying,' he felt Ally's thought.

Stephen's thoughts and reflections were drawn into Saint Thomas' intellect. 'Except ... except ...'

'Yes, Stephen. Keep thinking. Tranquillity, peace and reconciliation. Do we have all three? Think. Think.' He waited in silence for a few seconds. 'Now express it.'

Emotions and observations slotted into place in Stephen's brain. 'You've got tranquillity and peace. But there's more. Reconciliation. Equality between you and the non-coloured people. The noncys. They're somehow less.' He stopped and connected with Saint Thomas. 'You want full reconciliation of all people. Whites and all people of colour. True equality of all humanity.'

The look of approval in Saint Thomas' face signalled to Stephen that he was on the right track. 'Ally's father told me that noncy brains don't develop beyond childhood. And that it's due to something that happened a long time ago. But what has this got to do with me?'

Saint Thomas' eyes softened, turning from platinum to the silver-grey of a night sky kissed by the first rays of the rising sun. Compassion and courage reached out from Saint Thomas and surrounded Stephen. He felt buoyed. Strengthened to face what he would hear.

Ally's fingers curled tight in his.

'Stephen.' Saint Thomas' voice gentled. 'Son, the something that happened is a virus infection. A virus developed in a laboratory. Meant for good, but changed and released into the community with disastrous results. And, Stephen, this event is happening in your world right now.'

The conversation between his parents flashed back into Stephen's mind. 'Oh no! My father? The virus strains he was working on? The research that his boss sold to a laboratory connected to some group called Myers …'

'Maius Bonum, translated "for the greater good",' Ally channelled.

'Yes, Maius Bonum,' Stephen repeated. 'They're located in Europe. My parents don't trust them.'

'Rightly so.' Saint Thomas wobbled his head. 'Maius Bonum was a conglomerate of Western European so-called superpowers. They were worried about the rising military capabilities and technological competence of developing nations—India, Africa, and China. They were exploring ways of controlling and limiting what they called the emergence of the coloured continents.'

Stephen shivered as the implications of what had happened shot across his conscience. 'My father's boss, Edward Ellis, sold the virus research to a laboratory in Switzerland.'

Saint Thomas shrugged. 'Edward Ellis sold the virus cultures and all research data to a laboratory in Geneva Switzerland.' He grimaced. 'He knew of their links to Maius Bonum.'

Stephen dredged up the memory of the conversation in the caravan. 'My father said that he'd developed a strain of an encephalitis virus in the Ellis lab.' He paused and collected his thoughts.

'Relax, take your time.' Ally's silent encouragement was accompanied by the pressure of her fingers on his.

'Dad said that since viral encephalitis affected people of different ethnicities differently, the first step was to find a specific … specific type … of encephalitis virus that would infect one group of people. And then make it less potent. I remember he called it the Herpes Simplex Virus Cos.' Stephen smiled at the memory. 'Cos for a cousin to the HSV virus. I think he had it sorted out.' He swallowed the lump that rose in his throat. 'It … the virus treatment and vaccine would work for whites. For … for non-coloureds.' He realized what he had taken for granted. Ellis Enterprises were developing a vaccine and treatment model for whites. Maybe they planned to do that for people of colour later. Maybe. Maybe not. He would never know.

Saint Thomas and Ally connected with him. Vibes of empathy and encouragement flowed from them.

He took a deep breath and clasped Ally's fingers. Another memory flitted through his brain. 'They talked about Dad's research assistant, Rachel Thomas, with the cute little two-year-old called Paul.' Stephen stopped. His mind did a quick calculation. Ally's giggle gave it away. He looked at Saint Paul Thomas. 'You … you … was it you?'

Saint Thomas' grey eyes twinkled. 'I have been told that I was a very cute and extremely rambunctious toddler.'

'Something happened, didn't it? After the virus was sold to the European lab?'

The lines on the old man's face deepened. The grey eyes darkened to a flint-like intensity. 'It has already happened, Stephen. The Geneva laboratory scientists, under instructions from Maius Bonum, decided to tamper with the genetic code. Tweaking the RNA and DNA genetic code of the HSV cos so that it would infect only non-whites.'

'Dear God!' Stephen gasped. 'That'd make it a biological weapon! They were never interested in vaccines and treatment, were they?'

'No.'

'But the noncys? You said that they are what they are because of what happened. How?'

'Fate. Sabotage. Retribution. God. Somehow the virus escaped the laboratory.'

Stephen gasped. 'Rachel told Dad that those infected were mainly whites. That they were calling it the 'White Plague'.'

Saint Thomas nodded 'Your father realised what happened. That is why he is so anxious.'

'And now it's infecting the whole world.'

Saint Thomas shook his head. 'Whites are infected globally. As you surmised, the Swiss team succeeded in tweaking the virulence, but not the ethnic specificity. The virus is super-infective for whites. Coloured people are carriers. They show no symptoms, but they spread the virus. In your time, back in 2030, there are cases of the 'White Plague' across all continents and countries of the world.'

The party at Dr Vijay's house. The relatives there from Switzerland, Germany, France. They were all Indians. Coloured men and women. Laughing. Singing. His parents dragged in with great reluctance to join the Bollywood dancing. Stephen pulled his fingers free from Ally and stared at her, and then Saint Thomas. The memory of his parents suddenly taking ill sent a cold shudder through Stephen. 'My parents,' he whispered. 'They have it. Saint Thomas, what does this virus do?'

'It starts like a bad flu. That is what your parents have. Within four to five hours, it penetrates the brain. Initially, it causes delirium. Then coma. Long term, in those who recover, it causes a significant decrease in cognitive higher-order thinking capacity and intelligence. It also acts on the emotional parts of the brain. The limbic system. It depresses emotions, learning and memory. All to a childlike stage. It changes the very genetic codes in the cells throughout the body, including the brain. Sadly, these are passed on to their children and their children's children.'

'I can't believe this is happening.' The immensity of what he was hearing ripped open his heart.

He felt Saint Thomas' hand on his head. A blessing. Stephen kept his head bowed. He accepted the calming effect of the old man's fingers in his hair.

'Son. Stephen. There is more.'

A shudder passed through Stephen's body. 'More?'

'You are also infected.'

Stephen leapt out of the shell. 'No! I came here looking for help, and you're telling me I've infected Serendib? That I've brought sickness and death to this beautiful place. I'm sorry. I'm so sorry.' He stopped and stared. Ally and Saint Thomas were smiling.

Ally chuckled. 'Stephen, look at me!' Ally stood up and faced him. 'We're coloured. We're immune to the virus. In fact, over the last one hundred years, we've developed an inbuilt immunity to all known viruses. And to unknown ones as well.' She chuckled and pointed to Saint Thomas. 'That's why we live so long. Over one hundred and twenty is normal.' She stopped and laughed out loud. 'And, Stephen, thank you for thinking that I will be beautiful even when I am one hundred years old.'

'Children,' Saint Thomas interrupted their conversation. 'Stephen, sit down.' He glanced at Ally. 'Yes, you may sit with him, Aletheia.'

They sat side by side. 'What happens now?' Stephen connected with Ally.

'Listen,' she responded.

'Stephen, you are infected. Every organ in your body has the HSV cos virus. You have no symptoms yet because you are young. The virus affects older people faster. They show symptoms earlier than younger ones. But ultimately, it affects everyone who is white-skinned. In your time, you will have developed the flu-like symptoms in about five to six hours.'

'Saint Thomas, you're in a world of artificial intelligence and super technology. You must be very advanced in medicine. Can't you use my blood or something to develop a cure for my parents? For this awful virus? Can it be done fast enough for Mum and Dad? To help people in my world? In 2030?'

For the first time since he met Ally and Saint Thomas, he felt an uncertain quiver in their brain waves.

'Stephen.' Saint Thomas spoke slowly. 'The answer to your questions lies with you.'

Stephen frowned. 'Me? How?'

Saint Thomas nodded. 'We have played our part in providing your brain with all the information you will need. You have accepted and integrated it well. That is proof to us that you are the Chosen One from the Before. And now … now you have to choose between two paths. What you choose will have consequences for you and the world as you know it. Now and into the future. We cannot influence you, only show you. This has to be your decision.'

Ally's fingers crept back into his.

Saint Thomas placed his hand on Stephen's shoulder.

Stephen breathed in. The sweet air of Serendib. The scent of frangipani that would stay with him forever. A deep wave of sadness swept over him. He knew that whatever decision he made would take him away from Serendib.

He also knew that Ally and Saint Thomas both recognised his uncertainty and fear. He opened his heart and mind to the strength and courage that radiated from their mind into his.

Yes, he was ready.

He pushed himself out of the shell. Ally rose with him.

Stephen met Saint Thomas' penetrating gaze. 'I'm ready.'

CHAPTER 23

Serendib, 2131

Ally's heart swelled with pride and love for Stephen. He stood tall. Every muscle primed for action. His blue eyes were fixed on Appa's grey ones. He was ready. And waiting.

She knew that they would soon be parted in one way or another. It would leave a gaping void in her life. She had come to know and understand him. She knew the choices he would be given. Appa was uncertain how he would choose. She knew. He would need her strength to make the decision. Her brain refused to accept how it may end.

'Our scientists, doctors and researchers are capable and resourced to identify and develop vaccines and treatments for any virus. All we need is access to the live virus in all its combinations and permutations in a person's body.'

Stephen's nod of comprehension was barely perceptible. 'I have the virus in my body. Use it.'

Appa sighed. 'For the first time in my life—yes, the very first time—I am uncertain.' He sank back into his shell. He was silent. The shell accommodated and soothed. 'I wish there was another way. We examined the noncys. But they have no trace of the virus. Only the after-effects in their brain.'

Seconds passed.

'You, Stephen.' Appa's voice shook just a tiny bit. Ally hid her concern at the barely visible tremor in the finger pointed at Stephen. 'You have accepted all our teaching. The understanding and integration you have done in the short time we have had together is truly incredible. And now, I must face the fact that it may be of no use.'

Ally felt Appa's pain. She knelt by him. 'Appa, maybe there's another way?'

'No.' They both looked up at Stephen. He stood as still as a statue. His brain waves were calm. Regular. He was at peace.

There was the shadow of a smile on Appa's careworn countenance. 'Aletheia,' he said to her in silence. 'You are right. He will make the right decision.'

'Sit.' He gestured to Stephen.

Stephen stepped forward and dropped to his haunches by Ally's side. 'Saint Thomas, forgive me if I'm being disrespectful in saying this. But I can see that whatever you have to tell me upsets you.' His eyes slipped to Ally. 'Ally's freaked out, too. Please explain it to me. Trust me. You've taught me so much. Give me the opportunity to use it.'

'That,' Appa sighed, 'is what I pray. That you will have the opportunity to use it.'

Stephen took Appa's left hand in both of his. 'This much I know. I'm infected. And your researchers can use my blood and organs to develop a vaccine and treatments for this 'White Plague'. What's this decision I have to make?'

'Stephen, harvesting the virus is not a simple procedure. We need many blood samples. We also need to get into your body and take tissue samples from all your organs. Brain. Liver. Spleen, kidney, lungs, muscles, even your heart and testes. Our guardians—you call them doctors, are not certain how a body from the Before time will respond to this massive extraction procedure.'

Stephen was silent. Ally felt his brain waves waver. They spiked and shuddered. She tried to calm him. He blocked her entry. She withdrew. He wanted to make this decision on his own.

'Saint Thomas.' Stephen's words rang clear as a bell through the silence in the pod. 'Do you think I won't survive the procedure? That I might die?'

'Yes, it is a possibility. Even a strong one.' Sorrow formed a dark aura around the old man.

'But whether I live or die, your doctors and scientists will successfully produce a vaccine and treatment?'

Appa responded with a barely perceptible nod.

'How will this treatment be sent back to 2030 if I die?'

Appa sighed. 'The same way it will be transferred if you live. Our people will travel to 2030 and visit your parents in their caravan. They will treat them and cure them. Then transfer all the information to their brain. Your parents will wake up well. With the knowledge of what they have to do and how they should do it.'

'And … and my body?'

Appa took a deep breath. His body shuddered as he exhaled. 'They will think you were bitten by a poisonous snake and struggled back to …to …'

'To die in my bed in the caravan.' Stephen finished what Appa couldn't bring himself to say.

'What would happen if I don't die in the harvesting of my tissues and organs?'

Appa's grey eyes flashed silver. 'You will use everything you have learned. You will live out your calling. Your purpose.'

'What purpose? I don't understand.'

'No, son. You don't understand. But you will. You will. It will be your destiny.'

'If that happens,' Stephen's gaze roved around the pod and rested on Ally and then Saint Thomas. 'Will I remember you? Serendib?'

Appa shook his head. 'No. But you will integrate it and use it all in your future.'

'I'll be alone. It'll be hard.'

'No, Stephen. You will have a suitable helper.'

Stephen brought his eyes back to meet Appa's. 'You said I had a choice? What is it?'

'Yes,' Appa sighed. 'You could choose to not undergo the harvesting.'

'Then the 'White Plague' will continue to spread.'

Appa nodded. 'We will come back with you to the caravan. We will treat you and your parents. You already have the disease, so we cannot stop that. What we can do is prevent the brain changes. For you three. Only for you and your parents. Not for anyone else in your world. We also cannot prevent it from affecting the rest of your cells.'

'Any children I have will be noncys,' Stephen mused.

'After we treat you three, it will be up to your parents to find a cure and a vaccine. They are brilliant. They may do it,' He paused for a moment. 'Maybe in time to save about ten percent of the white population. But those people will intermarry and in a couple of generations, you will see … you will see what we have here.'

He sat in silence as the seconds ticked by. 'By consenting to blood and organ harvesting, and potentially death, I'll save the lives and future of millions of people in my world. In 2030,' Stephen said.

A tear Appa had held back escaped and meandered down the furrows on the old man's cheek.

'And by choosing life, I can save my parents and myself. But not the millions of others.'

Appa remained silent. More tears trickled down his cheeks.

Stephen rose to his feet and looked down at them both.

'You've taught me courage. Love. Peace. And true integrity.' His eyes focussed on Ally. Her mind was troubled. He tried to send her messages of calm. 'I know what I have to do.' He turned to Saint Thomas and smiled. 'How soon can we start the organ harvesting?'

Ally and Appa rose to their feet.

Appa wiped his tears away. 'Ally was certain that you would choose to do it.' He turned and flicked his fingers to the back of the pod. 'Meet the guardians. They are ready and waiting.'

The wall slid open and three people walked in. Appa beckoned them forward. 'Let me introduce our global chief researchers and medical specialists.' He pointed to a diminutive, brown-skinned figure of a young woman in a white silk suit, similar to what Ally had on. 'This is guardian Priya Kumar. She is our representative from here in Samaataanam. The other two have travelled here from our centres in Africa and Europe.' He gestured to a tall, muscular, Black man dressed in a multicoloured shirt and trousers. 'This is guardian Elijah Kwashi from Nigeria representing Amani. And,' he gestured to the third person, a slim, distinguished, olive-skinned older man with distinct Jewish features, 'This is guardian Uzzi Binyamin from Shalom in Israel.'

Dr Uzzi Binyamin gestured to Stephen. 'Come, Stephen. We need to get started. Time is, as you would say, of the essence.'

'Wait!' Stephen swung back to face Appa. 'But if you find the cure and the vaccine and I take it back to my world—to 2030—and people are cured, what will happen to your world? Will you … will you cease to…' He stared wide-eyed at Appa.

Appa chuckled. The three guardians laughed out loud. Appa wobbled his head at the guardians. 'I told you he is worthy.' He walked over to Stephen and laid his hand on Stephen's cheek. 'There are no guarantees, son. We only know that whatever happens will be for the best. Both for us and for the world. Both for now and for the future.'

Stephen nodded and walked to the guardians. 'I'm ready. Do whatever you have to.'

Ally scurried across to stand by Stephen. 'I'm coming with him.'

Guardian Elijah Kwashi grinned at Ally. 'Aletheia.' His voice had a guttural bass rumble. 'You are a trainee guardian. The future leader of Serendib. It is right that you should be there. Come.'

Ally slipped her hand into Stephen's. Together they followed the guardians away from Saint Thomas' nexus pod and into the guardian's domain.

The exit slid shut.

Appa's whispered words followed them. 'God go with you both.'

CHAPTER 24

Serendib, 2131

He was sinking deeper and deeper into a quagmire. Every tiny breath was a knife thrust in his chest. Every erratic heartbeat a tightening knot of agony. Stephen tried to struggle. To drag himself free. To reach up to the ever-receding light high above him. He couldn't. He didn't have the energy to break loose of the force dragging him down. He drew on all the brain training Ally and Saint Thomas had given him. His neurons screamed in pain when he tried to concentrate. It would be easy to stop. To give up. To let go. To sink into oblivion.

'Appa …' Ally's voice was a million miles away. A mere rustle in the wind. He heard her soft sob. 'No.' Stephen worked hard to connect. 'Don't … don't … cry.' The effort was too much. He had to stop.

'Appa.' Excitement and exhilaration threaded through her voice. 'Brain waves. Stephen has brain waves. He connected. I felt it.'

'Aletheia.' The old man sounded bone-weary. Every word was weighed down with sadness. 'You heard what the guardians said. They did their best. There is hope. But very little. You have spent all night by his side. You poured your energy into him. There is nothing more you can do. Your brain circuits are fatigued. Maybe you are imagining the connection.'

Stephen wanted to shout, 'She's not imagining it!' But all he could manage was another momentary connection with Ally. 'Need … you.'

Ally leaned over him. 'I hear you, Stephen,' she whispered in his ear. 'Give yourself a few more minutes. I'll be here.' Her hair brushed softly on the skin of his shoulders and chest.

Stephen dragged his eyes open. His eyelids drooped shut again. He felt himself drawn back into the dark slime holding him. He almost lost his hold on reality. No. He had to hold on.

'Appa, he's awake!' Ally's voice dragged him back from the precipice of unconsciousness he was teetering on. 'Fight, Stephen. Fight. Don't leave us. Let the solacement—the bed you're on help you.'

Stephen focused every wisp of neural energy he had in his brain to draw back from the edge. Every part of his body ached. Every cell screamed in agony. Lancing pain shot through his chest and abdomen with every breath. But he was breathing. His heart raced and stuttered. But it was beating.

He wavered. It was easy, even enticing, to let go.

The bed— or solacement as Ally had called it, warmed under him. Gentle, massage-like movements soothed his back and legs.

A pulse of energy surged through him. A wave of power. Ally was channelling her strength to him. He let it wash over and into him, pulling him back from the dark place to her presence.

'Ally …' He reached out. His arms felt leaden and stiff.

Her fingers curled around his. 'Thank God. Thank God. You're back.' Stephen tried to return the pressure of her fingers. 'No. Stephen, relax. You're healing now. Flow with it.'

His tongue was swollen. It was stuck to his palate. He forced his lips apart and whispered, 'Thirsty. Water.'

'He's talking!' Ally squealed. The excitement in her voice made Stephen want to respond. But his lips and facial muscles refused to move. He connected with her instead. 'I thought you said I talk too much.'

'Welcome back, Stephen.' She touched her lips to Stephen's fingers.

'Stop dithering,' Saint Thomas moved to stand beside Ally. 'Here.' He handed her a container that resembled a silver water bottle with a straw-like spout. 'Give him the alimentation.'

She leaned over him and slipped the spout between his lips. 'Sips only to start with.'

The sweet, rich, syrupy liquid slipped down his oesophagus and pooled in his stomach. Tendrils of energy reached from it to his arms, legs and finally, his brain. Stephen opened his eyes and looked around him. Everything was white. Pure gleaming white. He was lying on the solacement, the Serendib version of a hospital bed. A light breeze flowed over his body. He forced his eyelids open and looked down at his body. His chest and upper abdomen were uncovered and crisscrossed with what looked like a flesh-coloured band-aid. To his relief, his nether regions had a shimmering white silk covering thrown over them.

He focused on Ally's face. He tried to say thank you. Tell her how much he appreciated her. Her devotion. He raised his right hand. Smiling, she placed hers over his so that their birthmarks aligned.

'Soulmates,' she whispered. He tried to reply. She spoke in his ear. 'No, Stephen, don't try to channel me. I won't, either. We need you to concentrate on getting well as soon as possible.' She slipped the spout back between his lips. 'Drink as much as you can. Direct it to all parts of your body. Feel the change in your muscles, nerves, liver, heart and brain. Conserve your energy.'

Stephen did as she instructed him to do. He relaxed and felt an energy flow through his muscles, abdomen, chest. His heart rate settled to a regular rhythm. The lancing pain in his head dulled. Then ceased. He took a tentative breath. His ribs expanded. He breathed deeper. The air flowed sweet and clean through his air passages. Stamina pulsed through his blood vessels.

He moved his fingers. Then his toes. It took effort. He tried to prop himself up on his elbows. 'Ally,' he connected. 'Help.'

She pushed him back down. 'No. Sleep.'

'My parents,' Stephen murmured. 'Did … did the … the guardians …?'

'Yes, Stephen. We have the formulae for both the treatment and the vaccines. It's going to be okay. Now, please, rest.'

Her fingers slid feather-like over his face and chest. It was a touch that comforted and healed. His eyes slid shut.

Stephen slept.

***

Stephen hovered between sleep and semiconsciousness.

The solacement rippled under his body. The ripples moved first up and then down his body. Muted lights of green, blue and purple swept over and into him. He lay still, submitting to their ministrations.

'Guardian Uzzi, what is your assessment?' Stephen recognised the guttural African voice of Guardian Elijah Kwashi.

The lights stopped and the solacement under him was still.

The voice that responded had a Yiddish lilt. 'His heart and lungs are back to normal. As are his abdominal and pelvic organs. Blood count, haemoglobin, and liver function are all holding well.'

'Brain cognition?'

Guardian Uzzi chuckled. 'I think his brain function is better than it was when he came to Serendib. Aletheia and the Saint did a great job! The circuits we tampered with resulted in improved neuronal synaptic transport velocities and overall improved whole brain function.'

'Hmmm. Good. Good. He will need every neuron and synapse when he gets back to the Before! How are the scars?'

The rolling Indian accent was an adult version of Ally's. 'He has healed well. The residual scars fit well with his foray into a slime-filled limestone Nullarbor cave.'

'Have you placed that memory in his brain?' Guardian Elijah Kwashi seemed to be the one in charge of the team.

'Yes,' Guardian Priya Kumar responded. 'It is what he will remember when he wakes up in his sleeping pod vehicle.'

'Which they call a caravan in 2030.' Guardian Elijah Kwashi laughed.

'He will awaken with the memory we have implanted in his memory bank. He will think he ran down the road to the Rawlinna Station. That he tripped and fell down a chasm. He will remember lying, shivering, on a slime-covered ridge. Losing consciousness. Waking to scramble out. He will say he ran further down the road and found only the derelict buildings. He then ran back to the … the caravan pod and collapsed on his shell … bed … bunk … whatever they called it.'

'And,' Guardian Elijah Kwashi continued, 'his parents will wake up and find him dishevelled. They will believe his story.'

'Our work with Stephen is complete. We will let Saint Thomas and Aletheia take over from here. Come, we have more to do.'

Stephen heard the soft whoosh that he had come to associate with the opening and shutting of the pod wall.

Stephen continued on the edges of sleep. Saint Thomas and Ally would take him back to his caravan in Rawlinna. To the year 2030 and his life. He realised he would need all the strength and energy he could muster for what lay ahead.

He also knew that the ache in his heart had nothing to do with the surgical or other procedures the Guardians had subjected him to.

CHAPTER 25

Serendib, 2131

'Stephen, it is time.' Saint Thomas's gentle fingers stroked Stephen's head. 'You need to get back to your world. To your time. Back to 2030.'

Stephen opened his eyes and looked around. Saint Thomas stood on one side of him, Ally on the other. Behind Ally stood her friend, Nathan. Stephen reached his hand to Ally. She curled her fingers into his.

Stephen pushed himself to the edge of the solacement and dragged himself upright. He staggered and clutched the solacement for support. He held on to Ally and remained standing.

He looked down at his body and gasped. He was back in the clothes he had on when he first came to Serendib.

'What happened to my clothes?' Stephen's words came out as a croak. He coughed and cleared his throat. 'They're filthy!' His jeans were covered in mud and a green mossy stain. There were bloodstains where the jeans were ripped at his knees. His shirt and leather jacket were ripped and dusty. Mud covered his leather boots. 'What the heck?'

Ally sat on the solacement and pulled him down beside her. 'Stephen, it's about your memory. The one the guardians implanted in your cognition. You fell …'

Stephen remembered what the Guardians had discussed while he was healing. 'Yeah, yeah, I fell down a limestone cave and hurt myself. Lost consciousness. Recovered. Then climbed out and ran back to the caravan.'

'Good, that's what you'll think happened. All that you'll remember.'

Stephen stood up. He felt strong. No. More than strong. A fire of determination and purpose burned through his body and centred on his brain. He looked at Saint Thomas. 'Sir, Saint Thomas, I need to get back. There's so much I want to do. That I *need* to do.'

Saint Thomas nodded. 'I will pray you accomplish it all, son.'

Saint Thomas looked at Ally and Nathan. 'Come, children, it is time for you to take Stephen back to his world. The window will close soon.'

Stephen's heart was weighed down by the sorrow of parting with the old man who had inspired and prepared him for the future. But he realised the time was right. His mind was bounding with ideas and possibilities. For himself. For the future. 'Saint Thomas!' He let go of Ally's fingers and reached his right hand out to Saint Thomas. 'Thank you doesn't even begin to cover everything you've given me.'

Saint Thomas drew him close in a hug. 'You are worthy of the responsibility, son.' The old man's body shuddered against Stephen's. 'You will not remember this place. You will have no memory of us. But we will be with you in your nerve cells. In the neurochemistry and synapses you use to make decisions about your future.' He placed a trembling hand on Stephen's head. 'Go in God's strength.' His voice wavered and cracked on the words. He turned and walked out of the pod.

The wall of the pod whooshed shut.

Nathan stepped around Ally. 'We assumed you would need help in getting back to your caravan. That's why I'm here. We also brought a conveyance pod to take you back. It's our equivalent of what you'd call a small Sedan.'

Stephen looked into Nathan's eyes. With his newly developed skills of connection, he recognised Nathan's deep affection for Ally. 'You're right,' Nathan flashed back to him. 'I want to be there for her when she says goodbye to you.'

'Thank you,' Stephen responded. 'Hey, guys,' he spoke aloud to them both. 'Thank you. But, as you can see, I've recovered. See?' He flexed his shoulders and jogged around the solacement. 'And I would *love* one more ride on the skimmer.'

Ally laughed. Stephen listened and tucked away the joyous tinkle of her voice. Surely, he would remember that sound. 'I told you, Nathan. Stephen's a tough one. Come on, you two.'

A translucent blue hemispherical object about the size of a Volkswagen Beetle stood at the exit. 'There should be three skimmers here in the conveyance pod.' Ally touched the side of the object and dragged them out.

'I'll lead,' Nathan hopped onto one. 'Ally can ride with you. Let's go.'

Stephen looked back. The structure they had just left was a sheer white pod overlayed with shimmering transparent waves. It reminded Stephen of a stylised and futuristic Sydney Opera House.

'Come on.' Ally gave him a shove towards the skimmer. 'Stop gawking at the healing centre! And, yes. Someone did have the bright idea to model it on the Sydney Opera House.'

They flew over the mud road with hardly a flurry of sand. Within a few moments, Stephen saw the outline of the family car and caravan in the parking bay on the main road.

'That's it!' Stephen called out. The skimmers seemed to catch their excitement and sped up.

They hopped off the skimmers by the caravan.

'Looks like the guardians are still here.' Nathan gestured to a black conveyance pod that stood by the door of the caravan. As he spoke, the door of the caravan opened, and the three guardians stepped out.

'Perfect timing.' Guardian Elijah Kwashi pointed back to the caravan. 'Your parents will get up in about thirty minutes, your time. They'll find you asleep. The rest …' he patted Stephen on his shoulder. 'The rest is up to you.'

The top of the conveyance pod slipped open and swung shut once the three guardians were in.

Nathan climbed into the caravan. 'We have to hurry. The time portal will close soon.' Ally and Stephen followed.

They walked past his sleeping parents. Ally stopped and leaned over them. 'I can see where you get your looks from!'

'Ally.' Nathan steered Stephen to his single bunk bed. 'It's time.'

Ally stepped around Stephen's sleeping parents and stood by him. 'This is it, Stephen.' Her touch on his cheek was light. 'You need to get into your bed and sleep. We can't leave until then.'

'How long have we been together?' Stephen pulled his mobile phone from the back pocket of his jeans. 'Five forty-five pm. That means that we ...'

'We've spent forty-five minutes of your time together. Come on.' Ally sighed and patted the sheet on his bunk. 'Bedtime.'

Stephen pulled his boots off and sat down on the bunk. He dragged off his jacket and dropped it on the floor. He swung his feet up and lay down. Nathan and Ally stood side by side looking down at him.

Stephen glanced at Nathan. He read understanding. A connection between two people who cared deeply for Ally.

He turned back to Ally. 'Will you remember me?' he connected.

'Always,' she channelled. 'Always.'

His eyelids were heavy. He tried to hold them open. They dragged themselves shut. His breathing slowed.

Stephen slept.

***

Ally watched Stephen sleep.

'He's back in 2030,' she whispered. 'His brain waves are regular. He's not connecting.' Reaching up, she drew the white araliya flower she had tucked behind her ear and placed it by Stephen's cheek.

'Ally! The blessing of the Araliya flower. You're leaving it with him. Do you think that's smart?'

She smiled and touched Stephen's cheek. 'There are times in life, Nathan, when wisdom is superseded by attachment. Anyway, he might throw it away when he wakes up.'

She felt Nathan's arms around her waist. 'Ally. We need to leave now. You've done what was needed. It's time to focus on your duties as our future leader. You'll move on. You're strong.'

She leaned back into him. 'Yes. I'll move forward.' She absorbed Nathan's strength and confidence. 'Thank you.'

'What are you thanking me for?'

'For saying …' She turned to face him. 'For saying you'll always be there for me.'

Together they stepped out of the caravan and clicked the door shut.

Saint Thomas and his noncy, Jake, stood by an open conveyance pod. 'Appa!' Ally gasped. 'When did you get here?'

Saint Thomas glanced at their clasped hands. 'I thought you may need support.' He chuckled. 'I should have known better.'

Nathan let go of Ally. He picked up two of the three skimmers. 'I'll take these back to Serendib. Ally, you should ride back with Saint Thomas.' He jumped on the third skimmer. He blew Ally a kiss and whizzed off down the path towards Serendib.

'Wise young man, that Nathan. Very suitable.' Saint Thomas' eyes twinkled.

'Appa …' Ally groaned at her great-great-grandfather. 'Don't you think it's a little early to start arranging a marriage for me?'

Appa chortled. 'Come, Aletheia.'

The noncy sat in the front shell of the conveyance pod. Ally and Saint Thomas in the double shell at the back. They travelled away from the main road they'd left Stephen on. Towards Serendib.

Ally didn't look back.

Serendib loomed in front of them. Domes of different sizes. Pods reflecting the setting rays of the tropical sunset. Coconut-laden palm trees. The fragrance of araliya blossoms welcomed her back. Her city. Her people. Her future.

'Appa, can I ask you something?'

He wobbled his head. 'You are worried, Aletheia. Voice it.'

'Appa, we've given Stephen's parents the cure and the vaccine, right?'

'Yes.'

'That means the encephalitis HSV cos epidemic will be stopped.'

'Yes.'

'And there will be no …' she tilted her chin to the noncy in the front seat.

'Yes.'

'What if, after the epidemic, the whites go back to being what Maius Bonum represents?'

Saint Thomas laughed. Loud, belly shaking laughter that shook the transport pod.

Ally had never seen him so amused at anything. 'Appa! It isn't funny!'

'Aletheia. We had our brightest and best people plan this. The guardians had our think tank working with them.'

'I don't understand,' Ally said.

'Of course, you don't, Aletheia. We kept you out of it so you could concentrate on Stephen's healing.'

'What have I missed?' she pouted at him.

'The vaccine and treatment will shield cognitive capacity completely in them.' He gestured to the noncy. 'Intelligence and thinking capacity will be as it was before the 'White Plague'. But the limbic lobe and emotional system will be very selectively protected. Some parts will change forever across generations.'

Ally frowned. 'How will that help?'

'The parts that affect peace-seeking, kindness, self-sacrifice, benevolence, unconditional philanthropy and love will increase in size and effectiveness. This will be at the expense of the selfish individualistic traits that we know are rampant in Stephen's world.'

'Appa!' A flash of excitement raced through her. 'That'll make Stephen's work so much easier.'

Saint Thomas slid back in the shell with a sigh. He permitted it to massage him. 'Young people in 2030 will have a larger empathy lobe. How they use it is up to them—only time will tell.'

'But, Appa …' Ally hesitated. 'This will happen only for the white people, the noncys. Can we be sure that the coloured people in the Before of 2030 will respond and work together with the whites?'

'Only time will tell, Aletheia. Only time will tell.'

CHAPTER 26

Western Australia, 2030

Stephen Ashley-Cooper lay on his back in the bunk bed of the caravan floating in that nebulous space between sleep and waking. He struggled to remember where he was. What time or day. Even who he was. He grabbed at fleeting memories and feelings. Struggled to bring coherence to his bewildered brain.

Stephen ran his fingers through his hair and rubbed his palm over his face. The grit on his palm scraped his cheek. He dragged open his eyes and stared at his hand. It was scratched and covered with red desert mud and traces of blood. He glanced down at his clothes. His shirt and jeans were covered in the same red desert mud. The jeans were torn at the knees. The leather jacket on the floor by the bunk was stained with mud and something wet and mossy. His boots lay beside the jacket, also covered with mud and the red-brown desert dust. On the bed by his hand lay his mobile phone.

Memories of what had happened seeped back into his conscience. His parents had been sick. Very sick. He had gone looking for help. He slid off the bunk bed, wincing as shards of pain lanced through his body. He stumbled to the double bed and stared down at his parents. They didn't look sick. In fact, they were sleeping peacefully. His dad was making little snores. His mum's breathing was soft and regular.

Stephen staggered to the shower recess in the caravan. He looked into the mirror and stared, stunned at his reflection. His face was scratched and streaked with blood, as were his arms. His hair was matted with sand and dirt. The memory of what had happened came crashing back into his conscience. He remembered his desperate dash down the mud road towards what he had hoped was a working cattle station. He felt again the gut-wrenching fear when he discovered only broken-down derelict buildings. He remembered running back to the main road. Then tripping over a rock. Sliding into a crevasse. The memory of the dark cave he had lain in sent a shudder through him. Cold. Wet. Slimy moss on the ledge he had landed on. Clawing for a handhold. Falling back. Screaming for help. Knowing there was no one to hear his call. He had no memory of finding his way up and out of the cave. All he could remember was stumbling back onto the road and getting into the caravan.

Stephen shut the door to the shower recess. Shedding the stained and torn clothes, he let the hot water sluice over his head and body. He watched the mud and dust drain out of the shower tray through the outlet. Wrapped in a towel, he tiptoed out and changed into a fresh set of clothes. He perched at the edge of his bunk. The horrific memory of what had happened receded. It was replaced by an urgency for action. A thousand disconnected thoughts flashed into his conscience. Stephen sat back and concentrated on pulling together the ideas and plans whirling through his mind.

The fragrance of frangipani tickled his nose. He sniffed and looked down at his pillow. A single, perfect white frangipani blossom with a bright yellow centre lay beside the indentation of where his head had laid. Stephen touched a petal with a finger. He remembered a tall red-bark gum tree near the derelict buildings. He couldn't remember a flowering frangipani shrub. But there must have been one. How else would he have found the flower? He picked it up and tucked it into the breast pocket of his shirt.

His mind cleared. Ideas and thoughts coalesced into concrete action. He had to wake his parents. Get them moving. They had to get back to Sydney and fight the plague raging through Australia and the world. There wasn't a moment to waste. Stephen stretched out his arms and legs. Rotated his head. There was no longer any pain. A wave of energy flooded through him. He knew what needed to be done.

'Dad,' Stephen slipped off the bunk and stepped across the caravan towards the double bed. His dad stirred and hoisted himself up on his elbows. 'Son, what time is it?' He looked around the caravan. A frown creased his forehead. He leapt out of bed and grabbed Stephen by his shoulders. 'What happened to you? You're all bruised and battered!' He stopped. 'Wait! I remember. We were sick. You went for help.' He dropped his hands off Stephen's shoulders. 'What happened?'

Stephen batted his concerns away. 'It's complicated. I'll tell you later. We have to get to Sydney, Dad.' He looked his dad up and down. 'You look better. How're you feeling?'

'I feel fine, son. Just fine.' Dad glanced at Mum. 'I should wake your mother. I agree. We have to get back to our lab. I've got to kill that monster we let loose.' He glanced at the clock over the television screen. 'Five forty-five. An hours' sleep and I feel great.' He glanced at the bed where Mum was stirring in her sleep. 'Mum looks okay.'

Stephen grabbed his dad's arm. 'Dad, call the lab. Now. Get us transport. A helicopter. A plane. Something. We have to act. Every minute counts.'

A loud yawn interrupted him. His mum sat up in the bed. She blinked and looked around. 'Jon? Stephen?' she mumbled. 'What happened? How long did I sleep?'

'About an hour.' Dad's words were rushed. Stephen sensed that his dad felt the same pressing need for action that he did. 'Anne, we need to get back to Sydney immediately. How are you?'

Stephen's mum slipped off the bed. 'I feel great. I can't believe a little nap can do so much good!' She stretched her arms up and shook out her hair. 'Yes, we need to get back. We need to do something about the virus Edward—Maius Bonum let loose.' She stared at Stephen. 'What happened to you?'

'I felt sick soon after you,' Dad responded. 'We couldn't get any satellite connection. Stephen went for help and got hurt.' He shushed her gasp. 'Scratches and bruises. He'll be fine.'

Stephen pulled two cans of chicken soup from the cupboard. 'Dad, you're okay. Mum's okay. Let's have something to eat and get going.' He lit the gas stove, opened the cans, and poured the contents into a pan.

Dad nodded. 'We need to get back to Sydney as soon as we can.' He picked up his mobile phone. 'Great, we have reception.'

Stephen's mum slid off the bed and joined them at the dining area. 'Call Rachel,' she said as she picked up a ladle and stirred the soup simmering on the stovetop. 'Ask her to get us tickets to Sydney from Perth. Do whatever you need to do.' She reached out her free hand and held Dad's. 'We'll work together to stop this virus spreading. I felt it in my gut the moment I opened my eyes. You did all that research to make the world a better place. We're not going to let a bunch of money-hungry racists turn it into a global disaster.'

Stephen blinked and stared at his parents. He remembered how his dad had been on the way to Rawlinna. His anger at what Edward had done. The fear, the anxiety, the helplessness. His mum's frustration and exasperation at his dad's plan to drive through Rawlinna. And now here they were, both Mum and Dad, determined to save the world.

It's as if that little head cold had changed their minds. Stephen pointed to the mobile phone his dad held. 'Go on, Dad, call Rachel. Let's get a move on this.'

Dad nodded. 'Yes, I need to get to the lab.' He fired up his phone and pressed Rachel's speed-dial. He switched it on speaker and placed it on the table. Then sat down. The dial tone purred once before Rachel's voice broke in. The words tumbled out. Fast and frantic. 'Jonathan! Thank God.' There was a sob in her voice. 'Where have you been? I've been calling you for over an hour! Are you sick? Please say no! We need you at the lab! Now!'

Stephen glanced over his dad's shoulder at the mobile phone screen. Ten missed calls.

'Yeah, sorry about that,' His dad responded. 'I'm on the road in Rawlinna, I'll explain when we meet. And yes, we need to get back to Sydney. We can get to Kalgoorlie in …'

'You're in Rawlinna?' Rachel cut him off.

'Yeah.'

'Hang on a minute.' He heard her tap on the computer. 'Got it! There's an old airstrip nearby. Find it and wait there. We've chartered a private jet. It's been on standby at Perth. Now that I know where you are, it'll come over and pick you up. And bring you straight to Sydney.'

They all three stared at the screen of the phone, dumbstruck.

'All hell's broken loose.' Rachel's voice cracked on an edge of panic. 'The virus—it's spreading all over Europe! And there've been cases in Perth and

Melbourne in the last half hour! People go from symptoms of a flu to delirium and coma in just hours! This is our virus, Jonathan! Encephalitis HSV cos! It's somehow mutated into a mammoth global epidemic!'

Stephen's dad sat frozen. In the darkening land outside, a dingo's howl wafted over the gusting of the wind.

'Jonathan,' Rachel's voice broke on a sob. 'You have to do something!'

His dad shook himself, as if he was waking up from sleep again. 'Yes. Okay. Sorry, I didn't realise how bad it was. Yes, we need to find a cure. Soon.' He stopped speaking, frowned and smacked his palm on his forehead. 'Wait. Why didn't I think of this earlier? It's so bloody obvious! Rachel, you remember the experiments we did on the virus when Edward was away on a cruise with his family?'

'Yes, we isolated small segments of the virus RNA from our culture and produced killer T-cells in the mice. Jonathan!' Rachel's voice vibrated with excitement. 'I remember you said that we could use that model to produce a multiclonal antibody cocktail. To enhance current antiviral medication to make it specific to encephalitis HSV cos.' She paused. 'Jonathan, did … did … Edward send those samples to Geneva?'

Dad laughed. 'He doesn't know they exist. They are at the back of the spare incubator of the cool room. The one where we tuck away our failed experiments.'

'Do you think … do you think we can use it to develop a treatment for the 'White Plague'?' Optimism threaded through Rachel's tone.

'I don't think, I know we can do it.' Dad laughed. 'Get us home Rachel.'

The sound of keys clacking came through the speaker.

'And then,' Dad continued, 'pack what you need for a couple of weeks and move into the accommodation unit at the offices in Sydney.'

The sound of typing ceased and was replaced by the quiet hiss of static.

'I'm serious. You, David and little Paul. Isolate. Don't go out anywhere. I'm sorry to scare you but …'

'I'm not scared,' Rachel cut him off. 'Not anymore. I'm … kind of excited. And grateful. That you'd look after me and my family like this.'

Stephen's dad smiled. 'I need you healthy. And focused. We need to work together on stopping this catastrophe.' He waited another moment, then said, 'One more thing. Text me the number for the Indian researcher we met last year at the conference. Arjun. He works in the Geneva lab. The one Edward sold our research to. I need to know what they did with the culture to make it so lethal.' Bitterness seeped into his voice with the last sentence.

'Dr Arjun Eswaran,' Rachel responded. 'I have his number. I'll send it to you in a moment.'

His dad sat silent for a moment, tapping his knee. 'That's all I can think of for now, Rachel. Is there anything you need from me?'

'Well, one thing's been bugging me, Jonathan. The news reports now confirm that coloured people aren't getting sick. Why is our virus only infecting white people?'

His dad gave a weary sigh. 'It's the strain we developed, Rachel. I'm guessing that the Geneva scientists must have tried to work on its infectivity and specificity. They seem to have increased the infectivity. Making it more deadly. But the virus escaped before they could change the ethnic specificity. Meaning it affects only whites. That's why I want you isolated. Your husband's Indian so he and Paul are safe.'

To their surprise, a chuckle came down the line.

'What?' Dad queried.

'Didn't you know? My grandmother was Indian.' Amusement threaded Rachel's voice.

The phone pinged with an incoming message. Dad swiped at the notifications. Seated by his side, Stephen saw that it was the contact card for Arjun Eswaran.

'Okay, I just got the contact info you sent me. Thank you.'

'Yup,' Rachel confirmed. 'And your jet has just been cleared to take off from Perth. They should be at Rawlinna airfield in about forty-five minutes.'

'Rachel,' Dad hunched forward in the seat. 'Who authorised this flight?'

'Dr Ellis himself. Jonathan,' Rachel's voice crackled over the phone again, 'you take care.'

'You too, Rachel,' his dad replied and ended the call. He pushed his chair back and stood up. 'What the hell is Edward up to now? I wouldn't put it beyond him to try to shift the blame for the whole sorry saga onto me! That way he can salvage some of the company's reputation and his own.'

'Dad.' Stephen stepped close to him and placed his hand on his dad's shoulder. 'Why not accept it at face value? Whatever his intentions may have been, I say we just use this as the opportunity it is. We've got a plane to catch and work to do in Sydney.' He took the ladle from his mum's hands and served the soup into bowls. He placed a steaming bowl in front of each of them. Then served one for himself. 'Come on Dad, Mum, get some nourishment into you. It's about a 30-minute drive from here to the Rawlinna airstrip. And that's without towing the caravan.'

Mum stopped between mouthfuls of soup to stare at Stephen. 'How do you know where the airstrip is?'

Stephen shrugged. 'Dunno. I must have picked it up when reading up for this trip.'

Dad picked up his phone and moved to the door of the caravan. 'I have another call to make. Can you two pack up some essentials and meet me in the Jeep?'

Stephen gave his dad a gentle shove. 'Go on Dad, call Dr Arjun. We'll be with you in a few minutes.'

CHAPTER 27

Western Australia, 2030

Shoving the phone into his pocket, Jonathan jumped out of the caravan and trotted round to the driver's side of the Jeep. He opened the door and climbed in.

The sun had dipped below the horizon. The stars sequinned the eastern sky as the sky turned purple in the west. The dim glow from the phone was the only light inside the car. And the twinkle of stars the only light outside.

Jonathan swiped his phone and brought up the number for Dr Arjun Eswaran. It was ten in the morning in Geneva. Arjun would be in the laboratory. Jonathan did not want any of the others in the Geneva laboratory hearing what he had to say. He hesitated, shrugged, and tapped the number, initiating the call.

The phone was picked up on the first ring. 'Who is this?' asked a female with the rolling drawl Jonathan recognised as that of an expatriate Indian.

'This is Jonathan Cooper. Is Dr Arjun Eswaran there?'

'Dr Jonathan Cooper? From Ellis Enterprises Laboratories in Sydney?' Her words exploded into the phone. 'You have a nerve to be calling my husband!'

Taken aback by the sheer vitriol in her voice, Jonathan took a second to gather his thoughts. 'Mrs Eswaran. I'm sorry, I don't understand …'

'Understand? You don't understand?' she yelled. 'You are the cause of it all. As if you don't know!'

He heard a male voice in the background, speaking in what he assumed was their native language. Jonathan could not understand what was discussed, but the raised voices and harsh tone implied a heated discussion.

Finally, Arjun came on to the phone. 'Jonathan,' he said, his voice overflowing with weariness. 'Why did you call me?'

'Arjun, I need to know what is happening in the laboratories in Geneva. You're the only one I can trust there.' He hesitated. 'I assume you're at home?'

'How can you not know what is happening, Jonathan? *You* made the virus. *You* sent it here!' There was silence for a couple of seconds. His voice was soft and sad. 'I thought more of you, Jonathan.'

'Arjun, please listen to me. Please.' Jonathan stopped. He marshalled his thoughts and chose his words with care. 'I did not authorise the transfer of my material. Edward Ellis did it without my permission. When I found out what he'd done, I was furious. I resigned. He refused to accept my resignation and put me on extended leave instead.' He stopped speaking for a moment. 'So, that's why I don't know what's been going on for the last few weeks, Arjun. That's the truth. Believe me. Please.'

The silence on the phone dragged on—and on. Jonathan clenched his hand on the phone. *Don't hang up on me, Arjun. Please don't hang up*, he silently prayed.

A deep sigh rumbled across the phone from the other side of the world. 'Edward Ellis sent your encephalitis virus culture,' Arjun said, 'together with the files of your research data to our laboratory five weeks ago. It was all very hush-hush. I remembered your presentation at the conference last year. On what you called encephalitis HSV cos. I was excited by your research into ethnic-specific vaccines and treatment. When I heard that we had bought the rights to work on the virus, I assumed that our laboratory was planning to work with you on this. But that wasn't how it turned out.'

Arjun fell silent. The seconds ticked by.

'What happened?' Jonathan prompted.

'I was put on leave. Paid leave. Without any explanation. So was the only other non-white person in the lab. A young African research assistant. He was thrilled. I was mortified! I might as well have been sacked! I was so interested in this project! Excited. I really wanted to contribute to developing this vaccine and treatment for encephalitis HSV.'

His voice trailed off and he was silent again. He said something in his native language. Jonathan heard his wife rattle off a lengthy response. He didn't need to understand the language. Her anger was obvious.

'My wife says she never liked or trusted the lab. She always felt they had some hidden agenda.' He sighed again. 'She was right.'

'What do you mean?' Jonathan asked.

Another long silence dragged on. This time, Jonathan let it continue. Until Arjun felt confident to speak.

'Have you ever heard …' Arjun dropped his voice. 'Of an organisation called Maius Bonum?'

Jonathan closed his eyes. This time it was his turn to be silent.

'Jonathan, are you there?' Arjun queried.

Jonathan's eyes snapped open and his brow furrowed in determination. 'Arjun. Yes, I have heard of them. I too think there's a link between your lab and that group. But, right now, we have to do something to stop this monstrosity.'

'What do you want from me?' Arjun's voice was hesitant. Laced with suspicion.

'Could your lab have reversed the ethnic specificity of the virus? Do they have the expertise?' Jonathan continued.

'Well, I am the one with the most training in virus mutation. There are others who have some knowledge in the area. I know what they would try to do. It would be slow and laborious.'

'And to increase the activity and infectivity of the virus?'

'That, they probably could do without me.' Again, Jonathan heard Arjun's wife bellow something in the background.

'I can understand why your wife is angry. You're the most qualified researcher there.'

'No, Jonathan. It's not just that. Anamika, my wife, works for the Indian firm that does the cleaning for our office. She's disgusted with how the lab staff treat the cleaners. Of the things they throw in the trash. Of course,' he paused and continued, 'no one in the lab realised we were married to each other.' He snorted a laugh. 'All of us Indians probably look the same to them.'

In the darkness of the Jeep cab, Jonathan frowned again. 'But, Arjun—your wife is as qualified as you are. You said you wouldn't have finished your

PhD without her help. What is she …' he stopped and swallowed.

'What is she doing as a cleaner?' Arjun barked a laugh. 'Jonathan. She is a woman of colour. No one would give her an academic position. Or any professional role within her field.' He laughed again, a dry and bitter sound. 'We had bills. A mortgage. Children's school fees. We migrants do what we have to.'

'Arjun,' he repeated. 'I am so sorry.'

Jonathan's mind whirled with memories of the Geneva research team at the conference last year. White middle-aged men from the Geneva lab. They had been happy to talk with him. Of course. A fellow white man. But now that he thought about it – he struggled to remember them with any of the multitudes of students and scientists of east Asian, South Asian, African and Latino background who were at the conference. Probably because they didn't talk to them. Or even look at them. Non-whites were of no consequence in the world of Maius Bonum. They tolerated Arjun because of his specific area of expertise.

'Arjun,' he repeated, 'I … I am so sorry.'

A quiet chuckle came down the line. 'Stop apologising, my friend! I believe you. It's not as if *you* did it!'

'Well … yes … but I feel like … never mind.' Jonathan stopped and collected his thoughts. 'Do you have any idea how the virus got out? Into the community?'

'No. I wasn't there.'

'Of course, of course.'

The line lay silent for a couple of seconds, both men lost in their thoughts.

'Is there anything else, Jonathan?' Arjun prompted.

All right, Jonathan thought. Time to close the deal. He started on his carefully rehearsed script.

'Arjun,' he said. 'You are one of the best virologists and immunologists in the world. I created this virus culture. And now it's decimating people. Your expertise in the area will speed up the process of finding a cure and a vaccine. I need you to help me stop it.' He swallowed to clear his dry throat. 'Please come down to Sydney. Work with me.'

Arjun said something to his wife. Her response was short and sharp.

'Jonathan—let's not mince words here. The lab was preparing a bioweapon.'

'I didn't ...'

'Not *you*,' Arjun cut in, 'The *lab*. *My* lab. No one's accusing you of eugenics, my friend.'

Jonathan's gut clenched. Arjun was right. Eugenics. That's what Maius Bonum was about.

And yet, the Indian had called Jonathan his friend.

'They wanted to create a bioweapon,' Arjun continued, 'to use against people of colour. A neo-colonial ethnic cleansing. But somehow it got loose. In a form that's doing the opposite.'

'It's become a bioweapon targeting white people,' Jonathan squeezed the words out of his tight throat.

'Precisely,' Arjun said, his voice heavy and flat. 'You could call it God or karma or fate or just blind bad luck. But that's what happened.' His voice was harsh. 'And you want me to help you stop it.'

'Yes.' Jonathan licked his lips and took a deep breath. 'Arjun. I appeal to you as a human being. Help us. We need you.'

The soft rumble of static filled the interior of the Jeep.

'Because I am coloured, I'm immune to the virus. I can travel freely.'

'Yes. But no one realises that yet.' Jonathan spoke quickly now. 'We need to get you here as soon as possible. Before international borders close.'

He was cut off by a burst of conversation between Arjun and his wife. She still sounded angry. He sounded like he was trying to placate her. Jonathan heard heavy footsteps and the slam of a door.

'Arjun?'

The Indian sighed. 'Jonathan, my wife doesn't want me to come.'

Jonathan stayed silent.

'She says you whites are all the same. All racists. And you can all go to hell for all she cares.'

With a silent groan, Jonathan dropped his face into his hands.

'Jonathan, I'm sorry. I don't think you are racist. I believe you mean well. But I want no part in this.'

'You won't join me?' Despair filled Jonathan's heart.

'No, I will not work with you. However, here is what I can do. I still have the keys to the laboratory. I will get in there and copy all the research documents. Everything they have done. You'll have them within a couple of hours. After that,' he continued, 'I'm sorry. But you're on your own.'

Despite his disappointment, Jonathan understood Arjun's feelings. 'Thank you, Arjun. Thank you so much.'

'Jonathan, if anyone can find a solution to this, you can. I am confident of that.' He cut the line.

Jonathan opened the door and stepped out into the cool of the desert night. A light wind caressed the low mallee scrub. He could hear his wife and son chatting in the caravan just behind him. He stretched his back, working out the aches and kinks caused by stress and sitting motionless in the car seat. Yes, he was white. As were Anne and Stephen. But, somehow, he knew it didn't matter. He was filled with a certainty that they would see this thing through.

Above him, the sky was carpeted with stars. They were so clear he could tell the different colours of the ones that must have been planets, maybe Venus, Mars and Jupiter. He squinted as he looked at two of them. They seemed to be blinking in a regular rhythm. Getting closer. Larger. It was the lights of an approaching aircraft.

He snapped a look at his watch. He had been on the phone for almost half an hour. That was their charter flight Rachel had hired coming in to land.

He bolted to the caravan, banged on the door and hollered, 'Stephen! Anne! Get in the car! Our flight's coming in, we have to go!'

The caravan door burst open and his son erupted out of it, dashed to the rear passenger door of the Jeep, and hurled himself in. Anne followed him. Jonathan fired the engine and put the car in gear. The aircraft's lights were now distinct on the horizon, blinking white and red. The distant, high-pitched whine of turbofan jet engines cut through the still Nullarbor night.

Jonathan glanced at the rear-view mirror as they sped away from Rawlinna. The silver starlight shimmered on domes of silver, white and blue. Wave-like shells shifted and glowed.

He blinked and looked again into the mirror.

It was gone.

It must have been a mirage.

CHAPTER 28

Western Australia, 2030

Engines idling, a sleek private jet crouched on the tarmac at the small Rawlinna airstrip. The plane's engines were mounted on its rear, with rear horizontal fins perched at the top of the tail. Wing tips curved up like dolphin fins. The plane was painted silver, with a purple streak running from nose to tail. Through the wraparound windows at the bullet-shaped nose, the silhouettes of the pilot and co-pilot were barely visible in the dim light of the cockpit.

'Wow! What a beaut!' Stephen couldn't contain his excitement. His heart raced in anticipation. Anticipation of travelling in this amazing machine, but even more at the prospect of getting back to Sydney quickly and working with his parents to stop the 'White Plague' ravaging the world.

Mum laughed. 'Rachel sure didn't cut corners!'

The Jeep rolled towards the plane. Dad pulled to a stop and the three scrambled out. As they did so, the door at the front of the plane cracked open from the top and folded down to become a set of stairs. A young, slim woman trotted down the steps and approached them. She was dressed in a duck-egg-blue uniform skirt and jacket and a white blouse. A matching blue sailor-style cap was perched at a jaunty angle on her velvet black hair, which was drawn into a low chignon. She had a white mask over her nose and mouth. Her high cheekbones indicated East Asian ancestry.

'Doctor Jonathan Cooper,' she greeted Jonathan, 'Doctor Anne Cooper,' she acknowledged Mum, 'and Master Stephen,' she nodded to Stephen.

'Please,' Stephen interrupted her. He stepped around his parents to stand by the young woman. 'Please, no honorifics! Just Stephen would do.'

He air-quoted the word honorific.

Her lips were hidden under the face mask, but her eyes crinkled in a smile. 'I'm Elisa Yen. On behalf of Captain John Chong and First Officer Tom Rutnam, welcome aboard.' She glanced at Mum and Dad. 'Do you have any luggage?' The mask muffled her words a little, but her slightly accented voice was understandable.

'No luggage. Only our Jeep.' Mum looked back at their vehicle. 'And the caravan in Rawlinna.'

'Someone will pick them up, ma'am,' Elisa replied, 'and drive them back to Sydney for you. Our instructions are to get you to Sydney. And to make it quick. Hopefully also,' she laughed, 'in comfort!'

Dad nodded. 'Let's get going, shall we?'

Elisa spun on her heels, and led them onto the steps and up into the aircraft.

Stephen followed his parents into the plane. He scanned the cabin. There were six single seats on either side of the cabin with a carpeted aisle between the two rows.

'Please sit wherever you like.' Elisa gestured to the seats.

She turned and pressed a button on the bulkhead at the front of the cabin as the three Ashley-Coopers sat down and buckled their seatbelts. With a whine of hydraulics, the airstair lifted back up until it sealed in place and became the outer fuselage of the airplane. Elisa pulled the lever to lock it, then picked up a phone handset, pressed it to her mask, and spoke into it. The whine of the jet engines at the back of the plane increased in volume, and the jet began a tight turn to align itself with the runway.

Elisa lowered a rear-facing seat from the front bulkhead, perched herself on it, and clipped a safety harness around herself. She picked up the phone handset again, pushed a button on it, pressed it against her face mask again, and started speaking through the cabin loudspeaker. 'Jonathan, Dr Anne, and Stephen. As you already know, my name is Elisa. I'll be looking after you during the flight.' She waved a hand at one of the empty seats. 'These seats fully recline to become sleeping pods. There are sheets and pillows and blankets in the rear storage. As soon as we're at cruising altitude, if you wish to get some sleep, I can make three very comfortable beds for you.'

The jet engines bellowed, making the loudspeaker essential. The plane began its take-off roll down the runway.

Elisa gestured towards the back of the cabin. 'Behind that bulkhead is a multipurpose dining, lounge, or workspace.'

Stephen swivelled his head to where Elisa pointed. 'That's awesome!' He raised his hand in a simulated high five to her. 'I'm sure Mum and Dad will find use for that.'

'We have satellite phones and unlocked laptops on board. I can set it up as an office space.' Elisa continued.

'Yes, please,' Dad yelled over the noise of the engines.

The plane bumped and jostled as the old tarmac taxed the undercarriage.

'There's a bathroom connected to the second cabin. With a shower cubicle.' Elisa gestured to the back of the plane. 'And a fully equipped galley. I can cook you up a hot dinner if you like.'

Stephen's stomach growled. He realised he had only had a few spoons of the soup they had made back at Rawlinna. 'Food!' he groaned. 'Yes, please!'

Elisa's eyes crinkled in another smile.

The floor tilted as they became airborne.

'You're flying aboard a Bombardier executive jet,' Elisa continued her announcement. 'We can go up to a cruising speed of ninety percent of the speed of sound. Our flight time to Sydney will be just under three hours. Give us a couple of minutes to get to a safe altitude, and then we can go to the cabin next door and get to work.'

***

'Within the four weeks when the first cases were detected, the numbers of cases of what is now being called the 'White Plague' are rising at alarming rates in Switzerland, France, Italy, and Germany,' the TV newscaster announced. The picture on the screen cut to a scene of large, tent-like structures in a park. 'In Geneva, where the first and most severe cases were detected, the military have set up field hospitals to deal with the overflow of patients from the emergency wards.' The picture changed again, to a graphic of an RNA spiral, rotating on its axis. 'Early testing of the virus' genetic structure indicates that it could be a mutation of a virus commonly known as herpes simplex virus, or HSV. A variant of the common shingles. But experts are at a loss to explain how it could mutate so quickly and in such an unexpected way. One virologist we spoke to in Geneva has raised the possibility of it being human-engineered. He would only speak to us on condition of anonymity.'

Stephen felt a strange sense of déjà vu. He felt like he knew of this unfolding catastrophe already. The feeling was followed by impatience to get to Sydney and do whatever was needed to stop it. He glanced at his parents. His dad's face was etched with lines of anxiety. Mum was biting on her lower lip. 'Dear God, Jon,' she rasped.

The screen showed only the silhouette of a man, his face deep in shadow. The voice which came through the speakers was distorted and out of sync with the man speaking. But the south-Indian accent was detectable. 'The early infections happened here in Geneva. I am fairly certain it started in one of the laboratories. This degree of mutation can only happen through human manipulation of virus RNA.'

'That's Arjun.' Jonathan gasped. 'He's going public.'

The screen cut to pictures of hospital wards full of people with ventilators over their faces. The medical staff attending them wore baggy overalls, gloves, and boots. They had masks over their mouths and noses, and in addition to that, a plastic spittle-shield over their faces. 'Encephalitis HSV starts with symptoms resembling a severe flu and moves into lethargy, confusion, and delirium,' the news reader intoned. 'Anyone with even the slightest of symptoms is asked to report to their doctor immediately.'

Dad swore and turned off the news feed. They had been watching the news broadcast on a screen Elisa had unfolded from the wall.

The rumble of jet engines returned to fill the central cabin. Dad and Mum stared at each other, apparently stunned into silence at the enormity of the problem they faced.

Stephen dragged his eyes off the screen of the tablet Elisa had just given him to speak to her. She nodded and got to her feet.

He slid out of his safety belt and turned to his parents. 'Mum, Dad.' He raised his voice. 'Elisa's going to fix us roast chicken and mayo sandwiches.

How about we start making an action plan for the development of a vaccine and treatment?' He raised his hands in a faux surrender gesture. 'Okay, okay. I'm being bossy, right?'

His mum smiled. 'That you are. But we need that right now.' She rubbed her forehead. 'I'm feeling shell-shocked at how fast it's all happening!'

Dad nodded. 'We haven't a moment to lose.' He turned his head around to where tantalising smells of roast chicken wafted from the galley. 'Elisa, can you set up a call on the sat phone?'

Elisa came out of the galley and walked to a cupboard recessed into a bulkhead.

'Who're you calling, Jon?' Mum asked.

'Rachel.'

Mum glanced at her watch. 'It's two am in Sydney!'

'Yeah. I should let her sleep. We'll just work on it ourselves. Elisa,' he called out. 'Don't worry about it. Can you set us up on a workstation instead?'

Elisa led the way to the mini-work space in the bulkhead. 'I can do better than give you a laptop,' she said. 'I can patch you through to your work's main computer if you have the access codes.'

Stephen joined his parents in front of a laptop.

'I hope Edward didn't cancel my access,' Dad muttered, as he entered his personal ID. The laptop connected to Ellis Enterprises' main computer. A few seconds passed. 'Great,' he punched the air with a closed fist. 'We can plan what we have to do. Hit the ground running when we get to Sydney.' He pulled up the diagrams representing the virus and he and Mum started brainstorming. Stephen watched, listened and learned. He picked up the tablet Elisa had given him and recorded their conversation. He stopped at intervals and sent the documents to his personal secure Dropbox.

Elisa came out of the galley and placed plates with warm, spicy chicken and mayo sandwiches on the table by their side. 'Take a break, folks. I'll get some food to the cockpit and join you.'

His parents nodded their thanks and grabbed a sandwich each without taking their eyes off the screen.

Elisa returned in a few minutes and settled into a seat opposite Stephen.

'Elisa, are you from China?' he asked her.

She shook her head. 'My grandparents were born in Vietnam. They came to Australia during the war.' She shrugged. 'Their story of time spent in a rusty, leaky boat is harrowing.'

A memory of another similar story stirred somewhere in the deep recesses of Stephen's brain. He tried to grasp it, but it slipped away.

'Our family name used to be Nguyen,' Elisa continued, 'but my grandparents shortened it to Yen because the Aussies refused to pronounce Nguyen.'

'That doesn't make any sense.' His voice roughened in annoyance. 'We expect immigrants to pronounce Wangaratta and Woolloomooloo, but we won't pronounce Nguyen?'

Elisa shrugged. Then laughed. 'It is what it is, Stephen. I don't mind. My grandparents and parents worked hard running a Vietnamese food store and cleaning business. And this country gave them plenty of opportunities to learn and develop and succeed. My family are very proud of me and my high-flying career!'

They both shared a laugh.

Stephen noticed his parents glance at each other.

His mum slanted a look at him. 'Who swapped our stuck-up snob of a son for this mature, empathetic young gentleman?' She teased.

Dad tapped his forehead. 'The head knock in Rawlinna has changed him.'

Elisa laughed.

Stephen pointed to the computer screen. 'Hey, you should get back to the task at hand, rather than psychoanalyse me.'

His parents turned back to the laptop. 'Yes,' his dad muttered. He clicked through the information on the screen. 'We have to deconstruct the genetic code of our virus and map all possible mutations. I can sync that with the work I've already done. I hope Arjun comes through on his promise to send us the documents from the lab. It will give us a head start on what the Geneva team have done to the virus.'

Elisa stood up and walked over to Stephen. 'You look exhausted. Let me convert this to a sleeping pod.'

Stephen nodded his thanks and slipped into the pod. He slept. And dreamed.

CHAPTER 29

Airspace above South Australia, 2030

A whirling wind shook the branches of the frangipani tree he stood under. A single velvet-white flower with an orange sun-kissed heart floated down and rested on the wavy black hair of the fine-boned and beautiful dark-skinned girl who stood by his side. She caught the flower and tucked it behind her ear.

Almond-shaped, deep brown-black eyes, shaded by long eyelashes, met and held Stephen's gaze. 'I feel like I know you. But … from where?' Stephen stammered.

She slid closer to him. The corners of her lips turned up in the mere hint of a smile. She reached up and placed her palm on his shoulder. 'I am a memory. An experience from the past. And from the future. Don't analyse what you feel. And don't grasp it, Stephen.'

Her touch calmed him. Something deep in his brain stirred. 'I know your name. You're Ally.'

She wobbled her head. 'We are proud of you, Stephen. And of your parents. Right now, your father is on the cusp of an important discovery.'

'Will it be in time? How can I help?'

'Stephen.' She slid her palm down to rest over his heart. 'You have everything you need. Look into your brain. Draw on all your learning. Goodbye, Stephen.'

'Wait.' Stephen placed his hand over hers.

She drew her hand away and stepped back. 'You need to wake up and get on with saving the world.'

She blew him a kiss.

Stephen stirred and blinked. The smell of freshly brewed coffee rather than frangipani swirled around him. Elisa stood at his side with a steaming carafe. 'You must have had very sweet dreams!' She filled a mug and placed it on the tray in front of him. 'You had a smile on your face while you were asleep.'

Stephen sat up and looked at his parents. His dad was staring at images of RNA strands and equations on the computer screen in front of him. Mum was fast asleep, her head pillowed on her arms folded on the table in front of her.

'More coffee, Dr Cooper?' Elisa filled Dad's mug.

Dad nodded. 'Thank you, Elisa.'

He turned to Stephen. 'I'm glad you're awake!' His eyes, though weary, brimmed with excitement. He gestured at the computer screen. 'I believe I have the basic framework for the vaccine and treatment worked out here.' He shook his head. 'Amazing! All I needed was to modify and finetune my earlier work.' He took a deep breath and let it out in a slow shuddering sigh. 'Arjun's information of the Geneva lab protocol just came through. We have time to plug that information in before we land in Sydney. We can sync all this into the cultures Rachel will have ready when we get to the lab.'

Dad turned to Elisa. 'Thanks so much for looking after us Elisa. You can take your mask off, you know.'

'Thanks,' she replied. 'But apparently it's safer to have it on.'

'You're perfectly safe,' Stephen piped in. 'You're Vietnamese?'

'Yep.'

'Parents and grandparents?'

She nodded. 'All four grandparents.'

'You're fine.' Dad gestured to Mum and Stephen 'The virus only affects white people.'

'Noncys,' Stephen added. 'The virus only affects non-coloured people. Creates noncys.'

Dad blinked and stared at Stephen. 'That's an interesting way of putting it. Did you think that up just now?'

Stephen shrugged. 'It kinda just came to me. Dunno how.'

'Well, he's right,' Jonathan said, looking back at Elisa. 'You're coloured. You're immune to the virus.' He paused. 'I know that. Because I created it.'

Elisa jerked backward, a startled look in her eyes.

'The news reports, they're true?' she whispered. 'About it being man-made?'

'It's true,' Dad said with a nod. 'I don't know how it got out into the public. Or how it became the monster it is … but I made it.'

Stephen pulled himself upright. 'Dad, stop blaming yourself.' He placed his hand on his dad's shoulder. 'He made it to save lives.' He glanced at Elisa. 'To develop vaccines and medications. But it's somehow got loose and is taking lives instead.'

'And that's why you're so determined to stop it,' Elisa whispered.

Dad nodded.

'He will do it.' Stephen added.

Dad smiled up at him. 'Yes. *We* will do it.'

Elisa stood still for a moment. Then she reached up, tugged the straps of her mask from the back of her head, and yanked it off.

The mask left a couple of curved lines on an otherwise flawless, fine-boned face.

The trill of the satellite phone startled them all. Mum jerked upright and looked around. She rubbed her eyes. 'Sorry,' she groaned.

Elisa snatched up the phone handset. 'Yes?' She listened for a moment, then held the handset out to Dad. 'Dr Rachel Thomas. From your office in Sydney.'

'Rachel. Good to hear from you.' Dad spoke into the handset. 'Just a sec.' He removed the handset from his ear. 'Elisa,' he called out. 'Can we put this on speaker?'

Elisa reached over and punched a button on the phone base.

'You're on speaker, Rachel,' Jonathan said. 'Go ahead. You're speaking to myself, Anne, Stephen, and our airline hostess, Elisa. What are you doing up at this hour?'

'Getting ready to come to the airport to pick you up,' Rachel's voice filled the cabin. The tension and anxiety in her tone was obvious. 'But that's not why I called. I need to tell you what's going on.' Rachel hesitated. 'Jonathan, I've got to share personal information about the Ellis family. And maybe proprietary information about Ellis Enterprises. Are you sure you want me to be on speaker?'

'Just say what you need to say, Rachel,' Dad cut her off. 'I trust everyone here. Secrets and lies got us into this mess. They won't get us out of it.'

Rachel stopped speaking. In his mind's eye, Stephen could see her shrug. 'Okay, if you say so. First of all, you need to know that Edward's not in the country. He's headed off to Geneva with his youngest daughter, Carly.'

'What does he think he's up to? And with Carly?' Dad's eyebrows arched with surprise.

'That's got to be a first.' Stephen interjected. 'She told me she hates working with her father.'

'Well,' Rachel continued. 'You know Carly has a minor role in the personnel department. She found out about your pseudo resignation and forced leave. That made her dig into the firm's records. And, well, she found out about her father selling the research and the virus cultures to the Geneva laboratories.'

Stephen punched the air. 'Go, Carly! Good for her!'

'Yeah. She was furious. She stormed into the lab and confronted her father. And her older sister, Jacqui. Right in front of all of us. She stood toe-to-toe with Edward and accused him of sending Geneva a time bomb. Jacqui laughed and called her an idealistic do-gooder. She started lecturing Carly about profitability. Carly stormed out declaring she was going to do something herself. She said she would go to the media and to hell with the company reputation. Edward went scurrying after her. Next thing I know, they're both on a flight to Geneva via London.'

'Are they bloody suicidal?' Dad snapped. 'That city is swimming with the 'White Plague'!'

'It's not the only one, Jonathan.' Rachel's voice trembled. 'There are cases in Sydney, Jonathan. It's here.'

It felt like all the air had been sucked out of the cabin. Everyone glanced at each other, tense.

'And the Ellis' have come down with it.'

'WHAT?' they all gasped in unison.

'Mrs Ellis, Roslyn, she called me just now. She said that both she and Jacqui had just woken up with all the symptoms. Wheezing, sneezing, coughing, shivering, sweating. Their middle daughter, Sarah, was about to drive them to hospital.'

Dad put his hands on his head and groaned. Mum covered her mouth with her hands. Tears glistened in her eyes.

'But that's not all,' Rachel continued. 'Edward left a letter with Roslyn. An envelope addressed to you. He told her that you would be returning to Sydney and she needed to give it to you.'

Dad frowned. 'What's in it?'

'I don't know. Her driver's bringing it round to our place. I'll bring it with me to the airport.'

'Okay,' Dad muttered.

'But here's the thing, Jonathan.' Rachel paused. 'Roslyn's sending it to me now because she's sick. But Edward gave it to her when he left for Geneva. Yesterday morning.'

Dad and Mum looked at each other. Stephen sensed their weariness.

'Rachel. Stephen here.' Stephen moved closer to the phone speaker. 'That's before Dad contacted you from Rawlinna. And before you organised this flight back to Sydney. In fact—' He did some quick calculations. 'That must have been while we were at the Kalgoorlie mine. When Dad,' Stephen glanced at his dad. 'When Dad refused to return.'

'Yes,' Rachel continued. 'He arranged for the plane to be on standby to fly you back to Sydney soon after he talked to you. All I did was make a call to get it in the air.'

'How did he know I would change my mind?' Dad growled. 'That I would come back to sort out the mess he created?'

'Because he knows you,' Mum cut in. Stephen and Dad glanced at her. Her hair was dishevelled, there was a crease on her face where she had lain on her arm, and there were bags under her eyelids. But she was smiling. 'You, Jonathan Ashley-Cooper, can't sit back and watch a global disaster unfold. You've got too much integrity for that. And Edward Ellis knows it.'

Dad looked first at his Mum, then at Stephen, and finally, the air hostess he had only known for a couple of hours. 'You all have trust and confidence in me.' He mumbled. 'I'm not sure whether to be impressed or intimidated.'

'Dad.' Stephen leaned forward. 'Edward Ellis trusts you to fix this. And he needs you to fix it. For the sake of his own family. And the world. Dad, I know you can fix it. You can do it. Don't ask how I know. But I'm certain you will. And,' he looked at his mum, 'Mum and I will be there by your side,' he grinned. 'As you save the world!'

Jonathan nodded. 'He steals my life's work. Sells it for his own profit. Brings down a plague on people and his own family. And now,' Jonathan shook his head. 'I have to fix it for him.'

Rachel's voice came over the sat phone again. They had almost forgotten she was there. 'Mrs Ellis' driver just got here and gave me the letter. It's more like a package,' she said. 'I'll leave now for the airport. I'll give the document to you when I meet you. In about an hour.'

'We should be wheels down in forty-five minutes,' Elisa interjected.

'I'll see you then,' Rachel said and hung up.

Dad stood up and stretched.

Mum stood up, stretched, and yawned. She eyed the door to the washroom. 'Do I have time for a shower?'

'Yes, as long as you're quick,' Elisa said. 'I'll get you some towels. Her smile, now unmasked, lit up the cabin. She held up a steaming pot. 'More coffee, anyone?'

'I'll have some, thanks, Elisa,' Stephen placed his hand on his dad's shoulder. 'Dad, you can do this. *We* can do this. And the world *will* be a better place for having been through the 'White Plague'.'

CHAPTER 30

Sydney, 2030

The airplane rolled to a stop in the private aviation bay of Sydney's Kingsford Smith Airport. The moment they stopped moving, Elisa jumped off her collapsible seat and started the process of unlocking and opening the main door. Stephen was out of his seat and by the door before his parents.

The airstair hummed and hissed as it extended, then locked in place with a clunk. Outside, the sky was still dark. But, unlike the Nullarbor, the stars were invisible, washed out by the city's constant background light. At this early hour, the private aviation bay was quiet and still. But at the commercial facilities at the other end of the tarmac, Stephen could see vehicles and ground staff scurrying around silent planes as they prepared for the early morning rush.

Elisa turned around and smiled at the three Ashley-Coopers, who had lined up to depart. 'Well, I guess this is goodbye.' Her eyes glowed above her face mask, which she had put on again to comply with airport safety regulations.

Stephen was first out of the plane. He grinned at Elisa and slipped on his mask. 'Yeah, I hope you make pilot sometime soon!'

Elisa laughed. 'I'll remember to invite you on my first flight, Stephen!'

Dad was a step behind Stephen. He took Elisa's hand in both of his. 'Thanks again, Elisa,' he said. Mum similarly held Elisa's hand in hers. 'I'm sure you'll continue to make your family proud of you.' Mum and Dad slipped on their masks.

Rachel Thomas stood at the foot of the stairs, waiting for them.

Clutched in her right hand was a large brown envelope. Behind her, parked on the tarmac, was the familiar black Ellis Enterprises limousine. Farid Younis, the Ellis' chauffeur, stood by it, holding open the door to the rear passenger compartment.

Dad jogged down the stairs towards Rachel. Stephen followed close behind.

The usually elegant Rachel looked like she had been through the wringer. Her blue jeans and white shirt were wrinkled as if she had slept in them or pulled them on in a hurry in the dark. Her brown hair, usually in a neat, low chignon, lay loose and windblown to her shoulders. Her face was devoid of makeup. A mask dangled from her right wrist.

'Look that bad, do I, Jonathan?' she asked with a tired chuckle.

'Sorry,' Dad muttered. 'I didn't mean to stare …'

She interrupted with a little shrug and a smile. 'When you looked at me—the way your eyebrows went up—I knew you were surprised and worried about me. Thanks. But relax, I'm fine.' She handed Dad the envelope. 'Roslyn doesn't know what's in it. And neither do I.' She looked over Dad's shoulder, raised her arm, and gave a wave. 'Thanks, Elisa!' she called out.

They all three glanced back to see the flight attendant, still at the top of the airstairs, return the wave.

'You two know each other?' Mum looked from Rachel to Elisa.

'School classmates.' Rachel replied. 'We were scholarship students. The only two non-Anglo girls in class, so we stuck together. Edward booked the plane after he talked to you. But Elisa helped me organise the flight in double quick time.' She smiled and gestured to the car. 'I'm sure Elisa looked after you like royalty. But there's a flask of coffee in the limo if you need it. And some refresher towelettes. And there are croissants in the insulated container. Oh, and the obligatory bottle of hand sanitiser.'

'Yes, Elisa was amazing!' Stephen turned at the vehicle's passenger door. 'Hey, Farid. Thanks for coming out so early to pick us up.'

The chauffeur blinked and smiled back at him. 'Thank you, Master Cooper. Just doing my job.'

'Hey, no Master. Just Stephen will do. It's an awesome job you do. You're a great driver.' He held out a fist to the dark-skinned man.

Farid grinned and gave Stephen a fist bump with his white-gloved hand.

Stephen grasped the handle of the back door of the limo. 'You start the car, Farid. I'll get my parents seated and settled.' He glanced back at his parents and gestured to the limo. 'Come on. Get in the car. The sooner we get to the lab the better. You've got to implement all those plans swirling around in your head.'

Mum scrambled in, followed by Dad. Stephen held the door till Rachel followed them. He jumped in and pulled the door shut.

His parents sat alongside each other facing forward. Stephen sat on the rear-facing seat in front of his mother, and Rachel faced his dad.

'Thank you, Rachel.' Dad's voice expressed his admiration. 'Edward will be proud of the way you're taking over running everything here.'

Rachel's eyes met and held Dad's. 'I didn't do it for him, Jonathan. I did it for you.' Her gaze moved to encompass Mum and Stephen. 'And your family. You gave me a job to do. You trusted me. I will not let you down.'

Stephen turned sideways to observe Rachel. He could see hints of her Indian heritage in the olive tinge of her skin. He remembered what Carly had told him of her father's racist views. He wondered if the mighty Edward Ellis knew of Rachel's subcontinental bloodline. And if that knowledge would have made a difference when he hired her to join his team.

Farid started the car and, with hardly a whisper of engine noise, drove them out of the airport premises and onto General Holmes Drive. They travelled at a sedate pace. Traffic into the city was heavy, even at this early hour.

'David and I personally supervised a deep clean of the labs.' Rachel continued. 'We made sure no one went near your cultures and cool rooms. Just the work areas. We also had a deep clean done of your house. Devi has done some shopping and cooking for you. Oh, and Jonathan, I talked to your mother. The residential village is already in lockdown. The government doesn't want a repeat of the COVID 2020 debacle with aged care. Your mum asked me to tell you that she's fine.'

'Rachel,' Mum cut in, 'is it bad here in Sydney?'

'There aren't too many cases reported yet. We'll know more at the morning news update. But …' She took a deep breath. 'There's panic all around at the news from Europe. I managed to source sixty sets of personal protective equipment and a dozen boxes of medical-grade P95 masks. They're now completely sold out. Not available anywhere. There's talk of people stockpiling canned and dried foods. Shops are selling out of them too. And of sanitisers and cleaning products' She waited in silence for a moment. 'There's footage circulating on social media of people fighting each other to get loaves of bread.'

They travelled in silence. Dad stared out of the window. Mum rested her head back and was soon asleep. Stephen rummaged around till he found the croissants. He held the box to his dad. Dad shook his head.

'Jonathan,' Rachel whispered. 'I've sorted out all the information on every experiment we've done on the HSV cos virus. Found and prepped the cultures you had tucked away. I've also primed the mice strain for beta testing of any drugs or vaccine you develop.' She smiled at Dad's stunned expression. 'You trained me, Jonathan! I'm a fast learner. We're ready to go when you get to the lab.'

The car purred along the Eastern Distributor, heading north past the mix of old double-storey terraces and new multi-floor unit blocks that made up the suburb of Waterloo. The buildings were shrouded in darkness, lit only by the reflection of streetlights and the occasional flicker from the lighted window of an early riser.

Stephen dozed.

He was back under the frangipani tree with Ally. 'Tell me.' He reached a hand towards her. 'What am I supposed to do now? How do I help?'

She placed her hand on his forehead. It felt like a blessing. 'It's all in here, Stephen.' She chuckled. 'You'll know what to do when—how do you say it—when the rubber hits the road.'

Stephen snapped awake to Rachel's voice. 'Jonathan, do you want to check the document Edward left for you?' She held it out to his dad. Then placed it on Dad's lap. It was a plain brown envelope, about a centimetre thick, with 'JONATHAN ASHLEY-COOPER FOR YOUR EYES ONLY' written on it in felt-tip pen. Under it was a scrawled signature.

Mum stirred and sat up. She yawned and pointed at the envelope. 'How long do you plan to stare at it, Jon?' She slid across the seat away from him and poured herself a cup of coffee.

'Open it, Dad,' Stephen joined in. 'Whatever it is, it's something Dr Ellis has entrusted to you, and you only. It might be important to your plans.' He reached across and hefted the envelope in his hand, dropping croissant crumbs on it and on Dad's lap. 'I'll do it if you won't!'

Dad dusted the crumbs off and ripped open the envelope. He pulled out the sheaf of papers, scanned the cover page, and flicked through the attached sheets of paper. 'It's a legal document,' he mumbled as he read. 'Written and signed by the company solicitor, Matthew Morrison.' His eyebrows climbed towards his hairline. 'Dear God! This document,' he jabbed the page he was reading with his index finger, 'gives me power of attorney to use the money in one of the Ellis Enterprises accounts at my discretion.' He glanced down at the page. 'To do so until Edward personally revokes it.'

Dad's eyes lost the sheen of weariness and shone with excitement. He waved the document at Rachel. 'Rachel, Edward has handed us millions of dollars! All the money in this company account,' he waved the sheaf of papers, 'is for us to use in our work! It's a fortune!'

'That can't be right.' Mum yawned and slid to sit alongside Dad. She stared at the papers in his hand. 'There's got to be limitations. 'What about the rest of the company executives? The board of directors? His oldest daughter, Jacqueline? Don't any of them need to authorise this?'

Dad shook his head. 'Strictly speaking, it's not about the company. It's about the money in this particular account.' He jabbed the page again. 'It's one which Edward has personal control over. He can delegate it to whoever he wants.' He flipped the page and continued reading. 'Wait a minute, there is one condition.'

'I see it.' Mum nodded. She placed her finger on a line of type in the document. 'Edward says here that he and his family must be the first to be given the vaccines you develop. And if they get infected, the first to receive the treatment. He says here,' she pointed to another line on the document, 'he wants you to go directly to human trials. To use him and the family.

And here,' she pointed again, 'he says he exonerates you of any responsibility if the trials on him and the family don't succeed.'

Rachel scrunched up her face in a worried frown. 'Is that ethical?' she muttered.

It was all coming together. His parent's knowledge of the vaccine and treatment for encephalitis HSV cos and now Edward Ellis' money. Blood money. He broke into the conversation. 'It's his penance.'

The three adults swung round to stare at Stephen. He was filled with the need to make them understand what he already knew. He injected all the confidence he felt into his words. 'Doctor Ellis feels the weight of what he did.' He looked at his parents and then Rachel. 'He made a deal with the devil and lost. And he's willing to lay his life on the line to redeem himself. And his family.' He gave a slow nod. 'That's why he's even bypassing Jacqui. Right now, he trusts you, Dad, more than he trusts his own daughter.' He fell silent, turned, and stared out the window. The shadowed shapes of the shops and cafés of Point Piper rolled past as they motored along.

They sat in silence. The limo motored on towards their home.

In his mind's eye, he saw a smiling, dark-skinned girl. She smiled at him. 'Well done, Coops.'

He heard Dad mumble to Mum. 'The last twenty-four hours have been the weirdest ever!' He tapped his fingers on the bundle of papers in his hand. 'Stephen has grown up overnight and Edward seems to have developed a conscience.'

'And you,' Stephen could hear the teasing tone of his mum's voice. 'Are buzzing on adrenaline to get to the lab.'

Minutes passed.

'I'll call the solicitor at a more civilised hour,' Dad announced. 'For now, let's get home, freshen up, and get ready for the hard yards in the lab.'

***

The Ellis Enterprises limousine swept up the drive and stopped at the entrance of the Ashley-Cooper residence. Farid shut off the engine. Stephen opened the door and hopped out before Farid could get out and come around to do it for them.

'Care to come in?' Dad asked Rachel as he clambered out of the vehicle. 'Breakfast? Tea? Coffee?' He glanced at the driver. 'You too, Farid.'

'Thanks, but no. I need to get back to the apartment and check on Paul.' She glanced at Farid, who responded with a nod. 'I will drive you, Madam.'

Mum slid out of the car. 'How is little Paul, Rachel? He must be about two years old?'

'Two going on a hundred and three, I think!' She turned to Stephen. 'He knows his father and I are upset. He can sense it. And he's somehow got it into his head that you're going to fix everything!'

'Me?' Stephen cocked his head and smiled.

'Ever since we visited here some weeks ago.' Rachel waved her hand to the stout mahogany double doors fronting the Ashley-Cooper mansion. 'He keeps talking about you. Last night he held my hand and said Stephen aiya—that means older brother, will make everything right.'

Rachel opened the front passenger door of the limo and slid in next to chauffeur Farid. The engine started with a quiet whine and the vehicle purred out of their semi-circular drive.

The double front doors burst open, and Devi came bustling down the front steps. 'Aiyoo, where are your bags and all? You took six bags, no?'

Mum smiled at their housekeeper. 'Don't worry, Devi, we're getting them delivered later.' She took the other woman's hand in a light touch, turned her around, and guided her back up the stairs back towards the front door. 'Thank you for doing all the cleaning and shopping. I don't know what I would have done without you here to help. I realise now …'

'No, madam, no. Only doing my job!'

'And Devi, you have to stop calling me madam.'

Their voices faded as they entered the building. Dad looked at Stephen, his eyebrows drawn together. 'You, Edward and now your mother all acting totally out of character. It's like someone sprinkled fairy dust over us all.'

Stephen nudged him. 'Maybe the virus thing has been a reality check for all of us? Come on, Dad. You've a document to read and experiments to plan.'

His dad nodded and watched the car as it disappeared down the road.

'That girl is amazing. I didn't realise how bright and capable she is!'

'She's part Indian.' Stephen turned to his dad and looked straight at him. 'Not what you expected from a woman of colour, Dad?'

Dad held Stephen's gaze for a moment. He dropped his gaze. 'Yes, son,' he breathed. 'I guess so.'

The two of them walked together up the steps towards the still-open front doors. At the top, Stephen turned around. So did his dad.

Their house was positioned on a slope leading down to the beach. From their front porch, they could look across the road to the Pacific Ocean. The first rays of dawn streamed over the horizon, staining both sky and sea with a golden hue. A fresh, pre-dawn breeze ruffled his hair and tickled his nostrils with sea spray. The chorus of birdsong greeted the new day. Stephen breathed deep, savouring the moment and praying that he was up to meet the challenges that he knew lay ahead.

He gazed into the sunrise. 'This pandemic is a reality check for all of us. It's a new beginning.' He turned to face his dad.

Dad nodded. He paused for a moment at the front entrance of his mansion. He hefted the brown envelope in his hand. Then turned on his heel and entered their house.

A wave of anticipation swept through Stephen. Yes. It was beginning. He followed his dad into the house.

CHAPTER 31

Sydney, 2030

The three of them had showered, changed and hastily eaten the breakfast Devi had prepared for them. They trooped into the study.

Dad sat at his desk and snapped open his laptop. His face was set in a mask of concentration. Mum dropped into an armchair, and Stephen perched on its arm.

Dad tapped his phone. 'I think we should call Roslyn to check up on her and Jacqui.'

Mum raised her hands to her cheeks. 'Dear God, I almost forgot that Roslyn and Jacqueline Ellis had contracted the virus.' She leaned closer to Dad as he scrolled through his contacts.

'Got it.' Dad waved his phone at Mum. 'If Roslyn's well enough to talk, we can ask her what she knows about this power of attorney.' Dad patted the brown-paper envelope.

'She won't know anything.' Stephen said.

'And how do you know that?' Both Dad and Mum turned to him.

'I know. Edward Ellis never shares anything about the business with Roslyn. Or Sarah. Or Carly. Jacqui's the only one he talks to about the firm.' Stephen stood up and faced his parents. 'His first love is his business. And he only married Roslyn so she could produce heirs who would carry on the family tradition. He was disappointed that he didn't have a son. He's moulding Jacqui to take over the business. An accounting degree and MBA. Now senior partner. He even calls Jacqui 'Jack'.' Stephen shrugged. 'I've met Jacqui. She's ruthless and will do anything to get ahead. Just like her father.'

Mum nodded as disparate shreds of information connected in her head. 'Whereas the second daughter, Sarah, is a homebody.'

'Like her mother,' Stephen agreed. 'And Carly's into theatre and music. And is passionate about helping the disadvantaged.'

Mum turned to Stephen. 'How did you get to know all this?'

'Carly,' he replied. 'She posts things on Instagram and Snapchat.' He shrugged. 'Sometimes.'

Mum gestured at the phone. 'Make the call, Jonathan. We need to get to the lab ASAP.'

Dad tapped the phone, starting the call. He put it on speaker so they could all hear.

The ring tone purred a couple of times before a muffled, faintly accented female voice said, 'Hello?'

Mum frowned. 'My name is Anne Cooper. Is this Roslyn Ellis' phone?'

'Yes, ma'am it is.' The accent was now more pronounced. 'She's not well, ma'am.'

'Where is she? And who are you?'

'This is the Royal Eastern Suburbs Hospital intensive care. I'm the nurse looking after Mrs Ellis and her daughter, Jacqueline.'

'Can Roslyn talk?'

'Only very little, ma'am. She is very weak.'

A cold shiver went up Stephen's spine.

'Can you please tell her Anne Cooper is on the phone?' Mum continued. 'I think she would like to speak to me.'

They heard a muffled conversation. A cough. A deep laboured breath.

'Anne ...' the hoarse voice was barely audible.

'Roslyn, yes, it's Anne Cooper. We're back here in Sydney.'

'Good ... good ...' Roslyn drew a deep shuddering breath. 'Edward left a document ... he said it was important ... said you would ... would know what to do.' her voice broke on a cough.

'Please, Roslyn. Don't get upset.' Mum cut in. 'We got the document.'

'Don't know what's in it. He never tells me ... us ... anything.'

They heard the nurse's voice. 'Ma'am, Mrs Ellis. Your pressure is going up. And your heart rate. You have to stop speaking.'

'Jacqui's sicker than me,' Roslyn's voice faltered. 'Sarah's all alone … at home.'

The nurses' voice came over the speaker. 'Ma'am, Mrs Ellis can't speak anymore.'

'I understand,' Mum responded. 'Please tell her not to worry about Sarah. We'll take care of everything. Also, please keep us informed of her and Jacqui's progress.'

'Would you like me to put you down as first contact? I'll use this number.'

'Yes, please.'

Dad cut the line. He stared wide-eyed at Mum. The tension that radiated between them was palpable. Stephen, however, felt calm and in control. 'Mum?' Her eyes jerked to Stephen. 'We said we'd take care of Sarah.' He jerked his chin at her mobile phone. Then picked it up and scrolled through till he found the Ellis' home phone.

The call was answered on the second ring. 'Hello?' The girl's voice was small and uncertain.

'Sarah Ellis?' Mum queried.

'Yes?'

'My name is Anne Cooper. My husband, Jonathan, works for your father. We've been round your place a few times for company socials.'

'Yes?'

'I know your father and Carly are out of the country. And your mother and older sister are sick.'

'Mummy and Jacqui are in hospital,' Sarah stammered into the phone. 'I think they've got the 'White Plague'. And Dad and Carly have gone off to Europe. Carly said something about it all being Dad's fault. And I'm not feeling well, either!'

Mum pressed a hand to her head. 'Okay, Sarah. Try and stay calm. Stay at home. Don't go to the hospital. Don't go out for anything—not shopping, not socialising—nothing.' She frowned. 'Is there anyone with you?'

'Our housekeeper, Rani, came this morning. She wants to stay with me. She's so nice. I don't know what to do,' Sarah's voice broke on a sob.

'Relax, Sarah. Put Rani on, please.'

After a moment of dead air, another female voice came on the phone.

''Ello?'

'Rani, this is Anne Cooper.' Mum spoke slowly. 'My husband Jonathan works for Mr Ellis.'

'Ah, Mrs Cooper, I remember you, madam. I have worked in the Ellis house for ten years. I helped organise Miss Jacqueline's twenty-first birthday party. I made the cake also.'

Mum pursed her lips and frowned. Stephen realised that she was trying to place the woman, Rani.

Stephen had a vague memory of a middle-aged, dark-skinned woman in a multicoloured saree who had served the food and cleaned up after the party. He could remember Roslyn Ellis ordering the woman to do this and that, and the woman scurrying around in response.

A flush invaded Mum's cheek. 'Rani, could you please stay with Sarah?'

'Yes, of course. I have looked after Miss Sarah for the last ten years, madam. I will not leave her now. My husband has a car. He will take her to hospital if needed.'

'Thank you, Rani. Can you see this number?

'Yes, madam.'

'Good. Call us if you need anything. Anything at all.'

'Thank you, madam.'

'No. Thank *you*. And goodbye for now.'

'Goodbye, madam.'

Mum ended the call. She looked at Dad and then Stephen. 'The Ellis's treated Rani like a servant. Not anyone important. But now they need her to look after their child.'

Stephen walked over and took his mother's hand. 'Just like we need Devi? And Rachel?'

She nodded.

CHAPTER 32

Sydney, 2030

The slam of the car door was followed by the sound of footsteps.

'Matt,' Dad spoke into his phone, 'Thank you for the confirmation that I can use the money in the account listed in the document. There are a couple more technicalities. Can I call you back later? My assistant, Rachel, has arrived. We need to get to the lab and start work.' He ended the call with his company's solicitor, slipped the all-important power-of-attorney document back into its envelope, and dropped it into the top drawer of his study table. He pushed his chair back and hurried down the hall towards the front door. Stephen and Anne followed.

The front door opened and Rachel walked in, her arms laden with mail. 'Edward has been out of circulation since you left. I thought you might want to check these.' She walked into the dining room and dumped the envelopes on the side table.

Stephen looked from Rachel to his parents. 'Can we leave for the lab now?

'I'm ready when you are.' Rachel pulled out her phone. 'Just a minute, there's a special announcement from the Premier just come through.'

Devi bustled out of the kitchen with three plastic food containers. 'You are going to work, no? I made food. Sandwiches and Master Stephen's favourite, pancake rolls.'

Stephen tried to take the boxes from her. 'They smell delicious Devi. But I told you. No more master or sir from you. And,' he glanced at his dad. 'I think Dad will want you to call him Jonathan.'

'Yes, definitely. Definitely.' Dad smiled at Devi.

Devi beamed at Stephen. 'You, I can call by name. I washed your backside as a little boy, no? But your father? No, no, no.' She wobbled her head. 'I can call him Jonathan *aiya*.'

Stephen grinned.

'I will put this food in the big car, Jonathan *aiya*.' Devi trotted out of the side door leading to the garage.

Rachel looked up from her phone. 'The Prime Minister has put Australia in stage four lockdown from midnight tonight. It's the COVID 2020 drill all over again. All businesses and schools are to shut. No getting out of home except for medical care and one hour of exercise each day.' She waved her phone at them, then placed it on the table in front of Dad. 'Don't worry. I anticipated this. I went to the police before meeting you at the airport. I have special passes for all of us. Our laboratory and the pharmaceutical manufacturing plants have been classified as essential services. We can stay open and function 24-7 if needed. I have passes for the company limo, and for your cars, Jonathan.'

'Rachel, thank you.' Dad acknowledged the information with a grateful sigh.

'Jonathan, have you studied the documents Edward left for you?' Rachel asked.

'I did. I also talked to our solicitor, Matt.' He acknowledged the question in her eyes with a nod. 'You can read it later. Suffice to say that money will not be a problem in our work.'

Rachel glanced at her phone. 'A message from Edward. He's on a flight back to Sydney. He wants me to send the limo to the airport.' She glanced at the clock on the wall. 'I think I can get there in time if Farid and I hustle.' She picked up her handbag. 'I'll update you when I get there,' she called out as she dashed for the front door.

Dad looked at Mum. 'Edward's on his way back. I guess we wait till we hear from him.'

Stephen stood leaning on the wall by the kitchen door. 'Dad. NO. You don't wait for Edward. You know what needs to be done. Just do it. It's your virus, remember? He's given you the green light and the cash.'

'Stop it, Stephen. This is all too much!' Mum snapped. Then burst into tears.

Dad pulled her into his arms. 'Hush Anne. Hush.' He stroked her back. 'It'll be alright.'

Stephen walked up to his parents. He placed a hand on his mother's shoulder. The other on his dad's. 'Mum, Dad. We have to be strong. We have to get to the lab and start work. We'll get through this together. I promise you that.'

'How can you be so sure?' His mum sniffed.

Stephen took his hands off his parents. He touched the frangipani blossom he had slipped into the pocket of his shirt. He looked at them both. 'I'm sure because Dad knows exactly what has to be done. And Rachel, you and I will support him to get it done.' He took a deep shuddering breath. 'I'm also sure that the future of the world as we know it depends on what we accomplish in the next couple of days.'

Dad's phone trilled. He glanced at the screen. His eyebrows shot up. 'It's Edward!' he exclaimed and thumbed 'accept' and 'speaker'.

Stephen moved closer to the phone. What he heard made his gut clench.

'Jonathan ...'

The voice at the other end of the phone was raspy and breathless. Edward stopped to cough. He then took a deep shuddering breath.

'Oh no, Edward,' Dad whispered.

'Yes, Jonathan,' Edward Ellis said. 'I've got it too.' He barked a short laugh, which brought about another cough. 'Which is no more ... than I deserve ... I suppose.' He grunted.

'Have you landed?'

'Just now. We're at Sydney airport arrivals.'

'Stay where you are, Rachel's on her way to pick you up.' Dad frowned. 'You couldn't have reached Geneva. What happened?'

'We got blocked in London. Switzerland had closed their borders.' He gasped. 'I tried to meet with some of my ...' He hesitated. Coughed. 'Some of the representatives ... of Maius Bonum in London. But they refused ... to meet with me. One of them didn't even pick up the phone.'

'Cowards!' a female voice muttered alongside Edward, followed by an explosive sneeze.

'Who's that?'

'Carly. She's got it too.'

Stephen groaned and dropped his face into his hands. Mum wrapped an arm around his shoulders.

'Typical!' Carly hissed into the phone. 'They just want to protect themselves! They don't care about anyone else! That's where all this started! With white supremacist racists who couldn't handle the idea that foreign natives might be equal to them! Heck, might even be better than them!' She sneezed again.

'Carly,' Edward pleaded, 'don't start that again ...'

'Why not, father dear?' the girl snuffled. 'You're no better. Your medical business has never been about helping people.' Her voice rose in pitch and volume. 'It's always been about you! Your money! Your ego!' She broke off in a fit of coughing.

'That's not fair, and you know it,' Edward rasped.

'Carly!' Stephen leaned close to his dad's phone and spoke straight into it, his voice strong, calm and measured. 'You're right. Racist prejudice got us into this mess. And I think we all know that your dad recognises it. And regrets his actions deeply. But,' he paused, then spoke with slow deliberation. 'Carly, listen to me. Reactionary. Anger. Isn't. Going to. Fix. Anything.'

Silence filled the room, except for the rumble of background noise that came through the phone. Stephen remained bent over the phone. He was aware of Dad and Mum exchanging bemused glances.

Stephen no longer cared what anyone thought. He knew what needed to be done. He also knew that he would have to drive it forward.

Somewhere deep in his mind he heard a tinkling laugh. He heard a soft voice say, 'Go for it, Coops.'

'Thank you, young man,' Edward Ellis panted. 'Thank you very much.' He coughed. Then drew a stuttering breath.

'Glad to help, sir,' Stephen said. 'Now, the most important thing is to get you both to the hospital.' He straightened and looked at the others in the room.

'Don't worry, Stephen. Jonathan.' Rachel's voice cut in over the phone. 'I just got here,' she panted. 'I'll take care of them.'

'Oh, thank God.' Everyone in the room breathed a sigh of relief. Stephen dropped into a chair.

'Come, come.' They heard Rachel coax Edward. 'The limos just outside.'

Edward rasped a laugh. 'We're being treated like lepers. Carly and I—we started developing symptoms a few hours ago. On the flight back here. When we started coughing and sneezing, everyone jumped up from their seats and moved away from us.'

Rachel cut in. 'We're just at the limo now. Farid's loading the luggage into the boot. We'll get Dr Ellis and Carly to Eastern Suburbs Hospital straight away.'

'Just a minute, Rachel. I need to let Edward know something.' Dad raised his voice. 'Edward, Anne and I are on our way to the lab. We'll deconstruct my version of the virus. And figure out what Geneva's done to it. I'm confident we can develop a cure.'

'Thank you, Jonathan, thank you.' Edward stopped to cough and heave a breath. 'You got the document I left for you?'

'The power of attorney? With your …' Jonathan hesitated 'the endowment?'

'Yes,' Edward panted. 'I want you to stick to the instructions,' he continued in a firm voice. 'In detail.'

'When we come up with an experimental treatment, you want us to inject you and your family? Without waiting for trials?'

'Yes. You and I both know that a day, an hour, can make a difference to the outcome. You have no time for trials! We can *be* your human trials.' His voice dissolved into a bout of coughing and wheezing.

A sound of scratches and clunks came over the phone. There was shouting and gasps and the muffled thump of a door slam. They heard Rachel say, 'Farid, let's go.'

'Rachel?' Dad yelled into the phone.

Rachel's voice came over the phone. 'Sorry about that. Dr Ellis was about to faint. Farid caught him and lifted him into the limo. I'm here in the back with him and Carly. Wow, he's running one hell of a temperature.' There were a few seconds of silence. Then Rachel gasped. 'So are you, Carly.' She spoke into the phone again. 'Jonathan—I'm going to get these two to hospital. I think we need to make time for a deep clean of the car before joining you in the lab. See you soon.'

Disconnected, the phone hummed on the table in front of the Ashley-Coopers.

Stephen looked at his parents. They stood with shoulders slumped. He pushed his chair back and stood up. He clapped his hands together. 'Right, Dad. Mum. We know what needs to be done. Let's get to the lab. Rachel will be there soon.'

Stephen turned and trotted towards the door which led to their garage.

'Wait a minute.' Dad hurried after him. 'Son, you're not a chemist. Or a biologist. You can stay at home and rest awhile. Farid can drive you to the lab later.'

'NO.' The Stephen swung around. 'Dad. Mum. NO. Trust me. I know what I'm doing. You need me.'

Dad hesitated. Mum stepped up to Stephen and put an arm around his shoulders. 'Yes,' she said with a smile. 'I think you've already demonstrated that. Several times.'

'Thanks, Mum.' Stephen returned the smile. He spun on his heel and yanked open the garage door. 'Let's go kill this monster!' he called over his shoulder as he clattered down the stairs towards the waiting vehicle.

CHAPTER 33

Sydney, 2030

Jonathan shut his eyes and rolled them around in their sockets. At the moment, that was the closest he could get to rubbing his eyes. It was, of course, impossible to do anything else while kitted out in full personal protective equipment. Including a full-face plastic shield.

Jonathan, Anne and Rachel had spent the afternoon reviewing all that Jonathan had done with the virus right up to the moment Edward had shipped it off to Geneva. They analysed every experiment that Jonathan had carried out, discussed all possibilities and avenues for vaccines and treatments, checked the cultures, and prepared the mice clones for testing when needed.

They assessed what they had done. And micro-analysed it all again. They studied in detail the information Arjun had sent on what the Geneva team had done to the virus' RNA structure.

Stephen acted as a scribe. As the team discussed what they'd worked out so far, and debated the way forward, he jotted down points on the whiteboards on the lab walls.

Stephen was staring at two of the genomic patterns projected from the laptop onto one of the whiteboards. 'Um – everyone,' he called out, 'the RNA sequence on these two proteins look different.' He pointed out the variation. 'Is that an actual change? Or are we making mistakes? Here,' He pointed to a section of the amino acid sequence.

'We've probably just copied it wrong,' Jonathan mumbled. He blinked his tired eyes again.

'No. No.' Rachel exclaimed. She swiped back and forth on a tablet that lay on the lab desk, comparing two pictures. 'He's right. The last phase of incubation ultraviolet treatment caused a change. We all missed it.'

A buzz of excited conversation broke out.

Rachel turned to Jonathan. 'Stephen will make one hell of a geneticist!'

Jonathan smiled to cover his confusion. 'Yes,' he responded.

Jonathan studied Stephen. He was seeing a whole new side of his son. A young man with both strength of character and knowledge of biology and virology far exceeding his age and education. He was proud. But also perplexed.

The intercom by the lab door pealed a two-tone chime. The voice of David, Rachel's husband, came over the speaker. 'It's nine o'clock everyone. I've got coffee and snacks. You guys wanna take a break? You've been working non-stop since dinner. And that was five hours ago.'

Sighs and murmurs of appreciation rose from the researchers.

'Let's take half an hour, folks.' Stephen glanced at the digital clock on the wall. 'Dad said we have to get all those,' he pointed to a list of items on one of the whiteboards, 'done before midnight.'

Anne nudged Jonathan. 'When did our seventeen-year-old son become the team leader?'

Jonathan responded with a tired smile. 'He's doing a pretty good job.'

'Okay, team' Stephen continued, 'we break for half an hour.'

They all entered the clean room between the lab and the corridor, where they peeled off their PPE and dumped the various items into a hazardous waste bin for sterilisation. They then went over to one of two washbasins and subjected their hands and face to a vigorous scrub. By the time they'd done all that, they'd used up nearly ten minutes of the allotted break time.

'Thanks for your help, Stephen,' Rachel said as they walked down the corridor towards the accommodation suite, which she'd moved into with David and Paul.

'Thank you, Rachel—whoops!'

The door of the accommodation suite burst open. Little Paul rocketed out of it and launched himself at Stephen. He was wearing green pyjamas decorated with pictures of white flowers with a golden centre. Stephen picked Paul up.

Weary laughter burst out around him.

'Looks like you've got an admirer!' Jonathan chuckled.

'Feel free to babysit him anytime!' Rachel smiled and patted Stephen's arm. 'David and I could use the break from his constant chatter!'

David wandered out of the suite. He scratched his head and looked at Paul, now snuggled in Stephen's arms. 'Well, that was odd. I thought he was asleep. Then all of a sudden, he sits up and says 'Appa! Go to Stephen aiya!' and runs out here.'

Stephen carried little Paul back into the suite, followed by the rest of the team. 'What did you say he called you?' he asked, as he lowered Paul to the carpet. The toddler curled his left hand into Stephen's right hand and popped his right thumb into his mouth.

'Appa,' David replied. 'It means father.'

'I know it means father!' Stephen frowned. 'And that's the point. I shouldn't know. I've never heard that word.'

Jonathan wandered up to his son, his hands around a steaming mug of coffee. 'Have you heard it at school? From one of your friends? A teacher?'

Stephen shook his head. 'I don't think so. Never mind. Dad. We've more important things to do.' Stephen spun to face Jonathan still holding little Paul's hand. 'We'll figure out a cure, Dad. I am certain of it. But I feel like this is only the start of something much bigger.' Stephen's eyebrows drew together in a frown. 'I've got ideas. They're gnawing at the back of my brain. But they seem so … so improbable. Even impossible.'

'Stephen, you're tired.' Jonathan blinked and rubbed his face with his free hand. 'Do you want to go home? Come back tomorrow?'

'No! We're all tired, Dad. I have to see this through.'

Jonathan nodded. He stifled a yawn. 'Coffee break's over, everyone.

'Yes,' Stephen opened the door leading out to the corridor. 'Let's get the lab ready for phase three.'

Back in the laboratory, Jonathan, Anne, and Rachel ran experiments and poured over the results. Stephen sat at the computer entering the data into an Excel spreadsheet, which he used to run various analyses. He reported back to Jonathan, Anne and Rachel at regular intervals. Frequently making suggestions that were gratefully received.

The clock clicked over to eleven o'clock. Jonathan stretched and stood up. 'I think it's time we break and review what we've done.'

Stephen picked up the laptop he was working on. 'I've prepared a PowerPoint presentation with a summary of what we've done so far. And,' he tapped the screen, 'what we have to do.'

They stripped off their PPE, washed, and trooped out of the lab.

The aroma of fresh coffee greeted them. Assorted cakes, sandwiches, and pastries were laid out on the long table in the middle of the room. On a side table, a pot of coffee bubbled on a hotplate alongside a row of mugs. David was slouched in a chair at the table, half asleep. He shook himself awake and stood up.

Jonathan smiled at David. 'Where are you getting all this food from?'

'Your very own house-help and chef extraordinaire,' David replied. 'Devi. Her husband Krish has been shuttling back and forth from your place to here. With boxes of,' he waved his hand over the midnight feast, 'all this.'

'But—that means she's been up all night.'

'Yup. And she says she's going to stay awake as long as you're awake. And keep you guys fed and watered. I think she's kind of enjoying it. Thinks of it as her contribution to the fight.' David guffawed. 'I think Krish is enjoying it as well. He works nights as a taxi driver anyway, so he said this isn't a major change. And by the time the boxes get here, well, let's just say there are some gaps in the pastries and cakes!'

Jonathan sat silent. He watched his family and his assistant unwind and enjoy the food. He met his son's eyes. The quiet assurance in Stephen's face calmed him.

After everyone had eaten, Stephen loaded his PowerPoint presentation and projected it onto the screen. Jonathan moved to stand by the computer and ran through what they'd done so far.

'Our first goal,' he said, 'was to find out what Geneva did to my culture.'

'Which we were able to deduce from the information Arjun sent us.' Rachel commented.

'With that information,' Jonathan continued, 'we've pretty much replicated their work. I believe we've got the genotype of their version of the virus. We can now work on how to counteract it.'

Rachel shook her head. 'They successfully changed the virulence. How did they screw up so bad on ethnic specificity, Jonathan?'

'Because …' Jonathan looked at the faces around the table. A slight smile played on his lips. 'Because the data and procedures on changing ethnic specificity are in here.' He tapped his forehead. 'It is what I was working on with Rachel in my spare time with those virus cultures I had hidden away in the spare incubator.'

'You didn't record it anywhere?' Anne gasped. 'I didn't know that!'

'Well, I did make notes and records of the early experiments.' Jonathan paused and pursed his lips. 'The records that Geneva received were the protocols that failed. Not the final, successful procedures. Those,' he tapped his forehead, 'are in here. I did it for security reasons.'

Stephen laughed. 'Well done, Dad!' Stephen stared in admiration at Jonathan. 'Geneva had to figure it out for themselves'

Rachel laughed softly. 'Idiots.'

Jonathan rattled through the rest of the preliminary work that he, Anne, Rachel and Stephen had done so far. 'This last slide is what we have to do now. A three-pronged strategy of prevention, treatment and restoration.' He left the slide on the screen. 'Prevention is obvious. We need a vaccine. Urgently. We know we've isolated the live attenuated variant of the special strain encephalitis HSV cos. The one that's causing the 'White Plague'. We're calling it cos1 since it's targeted at the current strain. It needs double checking.' He glanced at Rachel.

Rachel nodded. 'Great. We leave room for the future development of a cos2 vaccine for people of colour.'

Jonathan pointed to the second point on the screen. 'In terms of treatment, we're looking at a double-pointed pincer action. First, an enhanced version of a regular antiviral medication that will super stimulate killer T-cells specific to HSV cos virus. That is relatively simple. We are some way towards finalising it. Second, we've made good progress in developing a multiclonal antibody cocktail based on my earlier work. It'll provide an immediate boost to immunity. So far, we're working with mice. It would be great if we had someone who was infected with HSV cos and recovered. But so far, sadly, we have no reports of anyone recovering from the disease.'

Stephen jumped off his chair, sending it tumbling backward. 'Dad, use my blood—serum, whatever. And,' he pointed at Anne, '… and Mum's.' He swung back to face Jonathan. 'And yours, too!'

'Stephen,' Anne frowned. 'We were not inf …' she stopped mid-sentence. 'Wait a minute. On the road to Rawlinna! I was sick. We must have been exposed in Perth. You,' she pointed a trembling finger at Jonathan. 'You had it too, Jonathan. But how … how did we recover?' She finished on a note of awe.

Stephen looked at Jonathan. 'Dad, Mum, I think all of us were infected in Perth. We recovered. I don't know how.' He stopped and looked around the table, smiling. 'But I think we all know why.'

'Okay,' Jonathan took a deep breath and let it out slowly. 'We can discuss miracles later. Right now,' he gestured to Rachel. 'You need to get some blood from us three blue-blooded whites so we can save the world from the 'White Plague'.'

Anne laughed and rolled up her sleeve.

'Come on, Rachel.' Stephen straightened the chair he had knocked over. 'Your chance to play vampire with your boss.'

Rachel dashed off to the side room for the equipment to draw blood.

'Once we get the multiclonal antibody cocktail tested on our mice models, translation with infected human blood will be next. Finally,' Jonathan continued, 'as you're aware, the virus attacks the myelin coverings of axons.' His eyes pivoted to Stephen. 'That's the fat that acts as an insulation on the brain cell conduction wiring.'

Stephen rolled his eyes. 'Dad! I know that!'

A wave of hilarity swept around the table at Stephen's annoyance.

'I believe we have a drug that can reverse the effect of the virus on the nerves and remyelinate affected cells. We need to work out how to get it into the brain and to the affected cells. We think we can do this by anchoring it to a tiny fragment of encephalitis HSV cos virus protein.' He stared at his notes.

Anne put her hand up. 'I'll work on that, Jon. You know that I did my

PhD on a similar topic.'

Jonathan looked at Rachel 'That leaves Rachel and me to work on the vaccines. We need to isolate a suitable cell line. We've experimented with the standard cell lines available. My research indicates bone marrow would make a good culture.'

'Dad.' Stephen was lounging back in a chair as Rachel insulated a cannula to draw blood from his forearm. 'Use my bone marrow.' He gestured to his hip bone with his free hand.

Anne walked over and touched Stephen's shoulder. 'How do you even know that we draw bone marrow from the hip bone?' She ruffled Stephen's hair.

'Mum.' Stephen scanned the room. 'Just do it. Use my bone marrow. It'll work. Dad and you need to be fit to continue with the research.'

Rachel looked up from scrolling through the tablet in his hand. 'Stephen is right. Bone marrow, especially from someone who has been infected and recovered, will form the best cell line for the vaccine development.'

Jonathan stood up. 'I'll allow Stephen to do it. But only on the ground that he agrees to rest after he's donated blood and bone marrow.'

'Aww, Dad!' Stephen whined. 'And miss all the fun?'

'Only a seventeen-year-old,' Anne sighed, 'would think what we're doing is fun!' Jonathan and Rachel smiled.

***

Rachel withdrew the cannula from Stephen's arm and stuck a plaster on the site. 'Bend your arm,' she instructed. 'I'll take blood from you two,' she said to Jonathan and Anne as she carried Stephen's blood to the refrigerator. 'After that, I'll do the bone marrow. When we're done, Stephen can rest in the unit with his new best mate, Paul.'

'Well,' Jonathan looked around the room. 'That's all I can think of. Anyone got any questions before we get back to the lab?'

Silence descended on the room.

'In that case,' Stephen stretched and stood up. He yawned. 'I think I will need a sleep after Rachel rips out my marrow!' He yawned again.

Anne looked up at Stephen. 'You've earned some sweet dreams, son.'

CHAPTER 34

Sydney, 2030

The garden seat he was perched on moved under him in a gentle, massaging movement. Stephen relaxed into it. The rays of the setting sun over the Nullarbor lit up the silver-blue dome-shaped building in front of him. The side whooshed open and Ally stepped out. The opening shut behind her. She sauntered over and joined him on the seat. Picking up his right hand she ran a finger over the birthmark on his palm.

The tension of the past few hours flowed out of him. It was replaced by an immense sense of calm. An anticipation of good things to come. 'Ally.' He tightened his fingers around hers. 'My parents did it. They have the treatment. The remyelination medication is almost ready. They've started on the vaccine.'

She slipped her fingers away from his and clasped her hands together on her lap. 'Your parents have used the information the guardians gave them wisely.' She wobbled her head. 'The whites will be healed and remyelination happen.' She stared into his eyes. 'What then?'

'We'll be back where we were.' A chill spiralled up his spine. 'Or maybe we'll be in a worse place.' Her eyes burrowed into his. Circuits lit up and connected in his brain. 'Without remyelination we'll have a childlike noncy. Remyelination is like re-learning. Maybe we could direct it.' He paused. 'Could we, Ally?'

'Appa will be proud of you, Stephen. At this very moment, your parents are celebrating success. The rest is up to you.' She stood up. Then leaned over and placed her lips on his forehead. 'Go with God.' The side of the dome opened. With a smile and a wave of her hand, she walked away from him. The dome closed. He was alone.

Stephen sat up and looked around him. The first rays of a Sydney sunrise filtered into the room through the partially open blinds on the single window. David stuck his head in through the half open door. 'Good. You're awake. Rachel texted me to send you into the lab as soon as you wake. She sounded excited.'

Stephen leapt out of bed. He ran to the ensuite and splashed water on his face. Then dashed out of the bedroom.

'There's coffee brewing in the conference room.' David called out.

'Thanks.' Stephen stepped out of the accommodation suite into the corridor leading to the lab. The sound of laughter, raised voices and even clapping came floating through the closed door of the lab. He dashed down the corridor and flung open the door.

'Hey, what have I missed?'

His mum turned to him. 'Son, you haven't got your PPE on!'

'Forget it, Mum. We don't need it.'

Dad's voice was threaded through with excitement. He looked at Stephen, 'I think we got it! Thanks to your idea to use the antibodies in our blood serum.'

'Congratulations!' Rachel rushed over to give Stephen a hug. 'I don't know what's going on in your brain. But you have certainly been the drive and guide to what we have achieved!'

'What have we achieved?' Stephen asked the question even though he knew the answer in his heart.

'We're about to see it. The battle of the encephalitis HSV cos virus and the Ashley-Cooper antibody.' Rachel gestured towards the large screen on the wall over the computer she was working at. 'What you will see is the two million or so magnification of the multiclonal antibody cocktail meeting the encephalitis HSV cos 'White Plague' virus.' She paused and glanced at Stephen, 'We're using the virus titrated from blood drawn from Edward Ellis.' She switched on the video link to the screen.

They stared at the screen, mesmerised at the site of the dark brown spiked oval viruses drifting across the screen.

Dad shivered. 'Dammit.' He swore. 'This is my virus. I had such high hopes. For a cure. For good.' He took a shuddering breath. 'Now it's a killer monster.'

Mum reached for his hand. 'It'll be okay, Jon,' she whispered.

Rachel clicked on her computer. 'Jonathan, watch.' Shining golden fluorescent orbs floated onto the screen. 'This,' she announced, 'is when we introduced the multiclonal antibody complex.'

Their eyes fixed on the golden orbs. There was a collective inhalation. They held their breaths. Waiting. Even the air in the laboratory seemed to be heavy and still with anticipation. The golden orbs each attached themselves to a spike on the virus. The spikes quivered, shrank, and disappeared. The envelope of the virus split apart. One by one, the viruses disintegrated. The RNA strands released from their protective envelope swirled around.

'Now,' Rachel pressed another key, 'we introduced a sample of T-cells from blood treated with the enhanced antiviral medication.'

They watched as the floating RNA strands were engulfed—seemingly eaten—by the killer T-cells.

Rachel froze the screen. For several seconds, everyone continued to stare at the picture that epitomised what they had worked towards and achieved.

'It worked,' his dad finally whispered.

Stephen reached out and placed his hand on his dad's arm. 'I never doubted that you'd do it, Dad.'

Dad turned around and wrapped Stephen and his mum up in a three-way hug, his parents' plastic face guards clacking against each other. Tears streaked down Dad's cheek. 'We did it, guys, we did it.'

Stephen glanced at the clock on the wall. It was eight o'clock in the morning. Outside, the sun shone down on a city in the grip of the 'White Plague'. A plague for which his dad's team had just unlocked the cure.

Dad heaved a deep sigh, unwound himself from his family's embrace, and turned back to Rachel. 'Okay, we all know this is only step one. We need to stabilise the combination of the multiclonal antibody complex and the enhanced antiviral medication.'

'We should be able to finalise that by lunchtime,' Mum said, her fingers flying on the computer keypad.

'And,' Mum looked down at the data on her laptop. 'I'm confident we can fine-tune the remyelination medication by the end of the day.'

'Team,' Stephen's calm, collected words sliced through their enthusiasm. 'We have a human trial awaiting us. Five Ellis family members, all in a coma.'

There was silence for a few seconds.

'Rachel,' Dad turned to her, 'please tell the pharmaceutical production team to start gearing up for a limited run. We're going to need three production lines. One for the vaccine, one for the treatment, one for the remyelination medication. Once we have … have done the human trials …' he hesitated.

Stephen realised that his dad was exhausted and assailed by anxiety. He spoke slowly, injecting confidence and strength into every word. 'Dad. Mum.' He swept his eyes across the room. 'Rachel. This *will* work. It will. What are we waiting for? We have a global crisis to conquer!'

Dad's eyes regained their gleam of purpose. 'Rachel,' he continued, 'Instruct the manufacturing team that we're going to need them ready to produce all three lines in sufficient quantities for global distribution—as soon as we give them a green light.'

'On it,' Rachel said and turned to leave.

'Hang on!' Dad stopped her. 'After that, please contact Dr Nick Garett.'

'Our government's Chief Medical Officer?'

'Yes, him,' Jonathan agreed. 'Tell him … tell him …'

'Rachel, you can tell Dr Nick Garett that we are on the cusp of a treatment for the 'White Plague'. That we're ready for human trials. And that we'll have the vaccines soon.' Stephen cut in.

Dad's smile was tinged with weariness. 'Yes, Rachel. Do it.'

'With pleasure!' Rachel fairly skipped out of the lab.

Stephen looked at his dad. 'It's time to get started.'

His dad held his gaze. 'Yes, it's time to prepare for human trials. On Edward Ellis. And his family.' His voice was strong and confident.

CHAPTER 35

Sydney, 2030

'We got pulse oxy of twenty percent! Need to intubate!'

'This one's critical! She's losing consciousness and going into a coma!'

'Ms Greene? I need to put this cannula into your hand. We're going to give you intravenous medication to try and bring down your temperature, okay? Ms Greene? Can you hear me?'

'Ventilator! I need a ventilator! This one's stopped breathing!'

'Bring me a defibrillator! I've got a cardiac arrest here!'

Stephen pressed himself to the side of the corridor, trying not to hinder the frantic activity of the doctors, nurses, and orderlies who were trying to save lives. He was in the intensive care unit of the Royal Eastern Suburbs Hospital. No one paid him any attention. To them, he was another health worker. As far as he could tell, he was the only healthy white person there.

The patients, lying helpless on the gurneys, were all white.

The health workers racing around them, desperately trying to keep them alive, were all people of colour. All were in full PPE. They didn't need the PPE. But they didn't seem to have worked that out. Yet.

Stephen had convinced his parents and Rachel to go home for a rest while he came to the hospital. They should be fast asleep now. This was something he had to do. Alone. He knew it would work. But he had to see it. It was only then that he could start planning the next phase. Meanwhile, the fact that the registrar in charge of the Ellis family happened to be another school friend of Rachel's had helped in getting the necessary permits fast-tracked.

Stephen threaded his way through the chaos. He was dressed in full PPE.

He knew that he didn't need it. But the hospital had insisted on it. His gloved fingers clenched on the handle of the sealed, insulated metal case he carried. It contained the precious remedy, intended to save lives and minds. Synchóresi. The combination enhanced antiviral drug and the multiclonal antibody cocktail sourced from the virus' antibodies taken from Mum, Dad and himself.

His parents and Rachel had finalised and tested the two-stage treatment against the 'White Plague' that afternoon in the Ellis laboratory.

Ellis Pharmaceuticals, the medical manufacturing arm of the company, had configured their production processes in record time. They had prepared the first batch of both medications within three hours. They were now on high alert, awaiting Dad's go-ahead to launch into full production with Synchóresi as well as the brain recovery remyelination drug, Apolutrosin. The vaccines would be ready soon. Stephen was confident of that.

He glanced up at the numbers above the wards he passed. Twenty-four. This was the one. He pushed through the swing doors and entered.

It was now eight o'clock in the evening. Edward Ellis had instructed Dad to use him and his family for human trials. Dad had promised. Stephen intended to help keep that promise. The two-person ward had been repurposed for five. Their beds lay next to each other, three on the left, two on the right. Wires monitoring heart rate, breathing, blood pressure, and other vital signs ran from their body to banks of monitors above and behind them. Intravenous drips led from elevated bags into their veins. Each patient had an oxygen mask over their face. A plastic tube led from the mask to an oxygen tank lying horizontally under the elevated bed.

Stephen looked down at the grey, pallid faces of Edward and Roslyn Ellis and their three daughters. All were motionless and unconscious. They hardly seemed to be breathing. With the shut doors muting the cacophony outside, the only sounds inside the room were the beep of monitors and hiss of oxygen.

Behind Stephen, the ward doors burst open. Stephen spun around. A medical professional dressed in full PPE and clutching a stethoscope stood there.

'Are you Stephen Ashley-Cooper?' the male voice demanded.

'Yes,' He replied. 'You must be Dr Michael Chen. Dr Rachel Thomas called you. She said you're in charge of the Ellis family?'

'In charge? Is anyone in charge of anything?' The ironic laugh was muffled by the mask and protective shield. 'Yes. I'm Michael Chen. I'm looking after the encephalitis patients in this wing.' He looked at the metal case Stephen held. 'I had a call from Chief Medical Officer, Nick Garrett. He authorised the use of a special medication your father and his team have produced. Is that it?'

'It's the first trial version, yes. Edward Ellis gave my dad permission to use his family for human trials.'

Doctor Chen nodded. 'Doctor Garrett told me that you have the permission.' He pushed past Stephen and stood alongside Edward Ellis. 'Let's get it into them. Right now.' He reached out to take the box from Stephen.

'Do you need to see the document authorising …'

'Young man,' the registrar interrupted, 'this city—heck, from what I hear, this whole bloody country is a disaster zone. People are flooding into this hospital faster than any of us can keep up. We've run out of beds. Out of equipment. Drugs. Everything. Our staff are dropping like flies.'

Stephen shuddered. On his way in, he had stepped around people lying on mats in the corridor, their intravenous bags affixed to the wall with duct tape.

'Nick Garrett contacted me and told me you were cleared to test your drug on this family.' He waved his hand at the recumbent forms of the five Ellises. 'At the moment, only this family. But if the treatment is successful, we are authorised to administer it to all our patients.' He held out a gloved hand. 'No time to waste. Let's get started. Now.'

Stephen placed the box on a small side table, opened it, and lifted out an intravenous bag. 'This is the combination of the antiviral drug and the multiclonal antibody cocktail. We named it Synchóresi. I have 5 sets here,' he said. 'Here's the instructions.' He handed the printed sheet to Dr Chen. 'As you can see, it needs to be administered intravenously. Slowly, over two hours.' He gestured at the IV drips already inserted into the crook of each of the patients' elbows. 'Dad also instructed me to find out what you've treated them with so far.'

Doctor Chen's chuckle was muffled by the face shield and mask. 'Your dad named the medication 'forgiveness'? Are you asking for it or offering it to Edward Ellis?' Without waiting for a reply, he pointed to the intravenous cannula. 'Antiviral Peramivir and Prednisolone. Any danger of cross-reactivity?' He held out both his hands to receive the plastic bottle.

Stephen glanced at the written instructions his dad had given him. He shook his head. 'It'll be fine.' He stepped over to the motionless form of Edward Ellis and added the Synchóresi bag to the two others already hooked to the multipronged stand alongside the bed. He stepped back. Doctor Chen inserted the tube from the Synchóresi bag into the cannula in Edward's hand, then twisted the small plastic lever, which let the medication flow into Edward's bloodstream.

Stephen handed the bottles to Dr Chen as he did the same with the four other Ellis family members. 'Now, we wait.' Doctor Chen's pager beeped. 'Emergency. Need to go.' He hustled to the door and looked back at Stephen. 'Do you want to stay here?'

Stephen nodded. 'Yes, please.'

'I'll find a chair for you.' He waved his hand at the instruments around the patients. 'Any changes in the vital signs will be reported to the nursing station.'

Doctor Chen charged out of the room.

Stephen looked at Edward Ellis. The gaunt form on the bed was a sad travesty of the powerful business executive who had walked the corridors of the multimillion-dollar empire of Ellis Enterprises, a shadow of the flamboyant host of the parties on his private yacht for birthdays and anniversaries. He glanced at the form of his friend Carly. Lying under the covers. Far removed from the fun-loving party girl he had spent time with.

The door behind him banged open again. Doctor Chen elbowed his way in, a black plastic foldable seat under his arm. 'Chair!' He yanked it open, dumped it on the floor, and barged back out again.

Minutes ticked by. Stephen walked around the room and looked at each of the five still bodies. When he came to Edward, he stopped, blinked, and looked again. He wasn't imagining it. Edward's breathing was less laboured. Even as he watched, a tiny smile tipped the corner of Edward's lips. He had to be patient. Dad had said they couldn't predict how long the medication would take to act.

He knew it would work, but he had to be patient.

Stephen decided to ignore the pretence that he needed a full PPE for protection against the virus. He lifted the face shield over his head and placed it on the floor by the chair. He kept the blue plastic hair cap on his head but slipped off his face mask. He removed the thick protective gloves and dropped them and the mask on the floor.

Reaching into his protective gown, he pulled out his mobile phone and switched it on. He flopped down on the chair Dr Chen had given him. Swiping his phone unlocked, he scrolled through his apps. Facebook. Instagram. Twitter. Tumblr, Messenger, Steam, and Twitch. Even Tinder. He hadn't wanted that one. But his mates used it. He'd downloaded it for a laugh. Swiped through sometimes. Never followed up. 'Can't believe I was such a social media junkie!' he mumbled to himself.

His finger hovered over the icons. He hadn't checked his social media since that day on the Nullarbor. He glanced through TikTok and Instagram. Smiling to himself, he flicked 'like' on a few of the posts, comments and pictures.

He flicked to Messenger. A torrent of messages filled his screen.

'Wow!' Stephen exclaimed.

The older posts were light. Funny comments from classmates.

From Bert who spent his time on Tinder trying to find his soulmate: '*Hey Coops. Are the girls hot in Perth?*' with an emoji of a sparkling heart. And his maths study buddy, Nandan, with his customary flair for words: '*Missing you at the weekly catchup Coops. Equations quivering with the expectation of your return*,' with an emoji of an Abacus.

Stephen scrolled up. The more recent messages reflected increasing distress. From a rugby teammate: 'R U OK people dropping like flies.' And a few days later from the coach: 'All matches cancelled till further notice.'

He moved to the most recent message. It was from Caleb, the Israeli ambassador's son. He often partnered with Stephen on information technology projects: 'Stay where you are. Your rugby team hospitalised.'

Stephen messaged back. 'How are you and the family?'

The response was immediate. 'OK. Seems to not affect non-whites. My father wants to know where your dad is.'

Caleb's father, Dr Joshua Binyamin, a consultant physician, and Israeli ambassador to Australia was a friend of Stephen's dad. He hesitated with his finger on the keys. 'No,' he mumbled to himself. Best say nothing. Not yet. 'Back in Sydney,' he texted. 'Dad and Mum at work.'

He shut messenger and opened the television news channel on his phone.

'Please, stand by' the newscaster announced. 'We are crossing to a media conference with Doctor Nick Garett, the Chief Medical Officer.' The cameras panned to an empty podium set in front of the Parliamentary Building in Sydney. Dr Nick Garrett, dressed in a dapper blue suit and white shirt, a silk hanky peeking from his breast pocket, strode to the front to face the cameras. He whipped off his mask. 'I am happy to report,' he rotated his head to encompass the bank of cameras, 'that we now have a potential treatment for the encephalitis HSV cos virus epidemic. It is being tested on patients even as we speak. Even more encouraging is that we are on the cusp of a breakthrough on a vaccine.' He paused for effect as the cameras flashed.

'Damn!' Stephen jumped out of the chair. 'He isn't supposed to say anything till we have some results!' he raged to the comatose Ellis family. He slumped back in the chair and continued watching. Dr Garrett stood messiah-like with arms raised facing the clamour of the press. 'Please, be patient,' he continued. 'I am, for reasons I am sure you will understand, not in a position to tell you anything more at this time. Except to say that we are all extremely optimistic.'

He nodded to a reporter to accept a question. 'Yes,' he responded. 'The government will invest in the vaccine and treatment as soon as trials are completed and proven successful.' He listened to another. 'Yes, we will make it available to everyone. And yes, it will be provided free.'

And again, in response to a query: 'I am sorry, for reasons of confidentiality I am not in a position to tell you the name of the laboratory or the scientists involved.'

Stephen switched off his phone.

Everybody's hopes and expectations would be raised, now. All across Australia, and within seconds, all across the world. Spread at the speed of light by the power of the internet and social media. Everywhere, everyone—would be talking about a cure for this new brain disease. He closed his eyes and massaged his temples. They didn't know what this cure would result in. There was so much more to do.

He was tired. Bone weary. But he could not stop now. Ideas buzzed around in his brain and formed into an action plan. It was crazy. But with his tech friends on board, it just might work.

Lulled by the rhythmic whoosh of the ventilators and click of the monitors, Stephen nodded off.

Somewhere in the deep recesses of his conscience he heard her voice. Ally. It was gentle, comforting and confident. 'Keep strong. This is only the beginning, Stephen.'

CHAPTER 36

Sydney, 2030

'Hey, wake up!'

Stephen's eyes flew open. A dark-skinned angel in a white silk tunic and a long, flowing skirt floated above him, her hand on his shoulder, shaking him. She shook him again. 'Get your PPE gear on. Your …' she waved her hand at the figures on the beds. 'Your family are waking up.'

The angel above him materialised to become a nurse dressed in full PPE. The skin of her face around her eyes, which was all that Stephen could see was dark as ebony.

'The patient, Dr Ellis, is reacting. He's breathing on his own and responding to painful stimuli.' Her black eyes softened in concern. 'Is he your father?'

'No. A family friend.' Stephen responded. 'And, I've already had the virus. That's why I don't need the PPE.'

'Never heard of anyone recovering!' she murmured. Then, turned and looked down at Edward Ellis' recumbent form. 'He started improving within–' she picked up a tablet from a pocket at the foot of the bed and glanced at it '– forty-five minutes of starting the Synchóresi medication.' She shook her head. 'That's incredibly fast. Miraculous in fact! All other encephalitis HSV patients are still in a deep coma.' She glanced at Stephen. She picked up a small sharp object that looked like a large pin and touched Edward's palm. She raised her voice. 'Dr Ellis, can you feel this? Open your eyes if you can.'

Edward's eyelids quivered. Slid open a fraction. Quivered again. Dropped shut.

'That's very good, Dr Ellis. Very good. Now, flex your fingers if you feel this.' She moved to the bottom of the bed and touched Edward's sole with the pin. A soft groan emerged from under the oxygen mask. There was a minuscule movement of the fingers of Edward's right hand.

'Excellent.' The nurse gestured to the array of monitors and machines. 'His vitals are improving. I need to alert Dr Chen.' She turned towards the ward doors, then looked back. 'Don't worry if the dials jump around,' she said over her shoulder, 'we monitor everything from the nursing station.' She pushed through the doors and let them swing shut behind her.

Stephen looked again at Edward Ellis. He was lying still now, his chest moving with each breath. The other four of the family were still unconscious. But instead of being inert bundles of flesh and bone, dependent on machinery to keep them alive, they seemed to be resting in comfort. It was exactly how they had hoped the medication would work.

Stephen kept his eyes on Edward's face.

Edward's eyelids trembled. His eyes fluttered half-open.

'Edward! Dr Ellis, can you hear me? Can you understand what I'm saying?'

Edward's eyes were glazed and unfocused. Empty of emotion, they stared beyond Stephen towards the ceiling.

The ward doors crashed open. Dr Chen shouldered his way in again, followed by the dark-skinned nurse.

'He's awake?' Dr Chen demanded.

'Well, he's responding to stimuli,' the nurse replied.

'He opened his eyes,' Stephen said as the doctor and nurse flanked him and loomed over the patient.

'That's amazing!' Doctor Chen leaned forward and stared into Edward's half-open eyes. 'This is the most that any of our patients have recovered. All the others are in a deep coma.'

Edward blinked several times. Under the transparent oxygen mask, they could see his mouth open and shut.

Doctor Chen stood up straight again. 'Remove the oxygen. Let him breathe on his own.' He ordered. 'I think he wants to talk.'

The nurse slipped the oxygen mask off Edward. His lips twisted then opened. He made a gurgling noise.

'Doctor Ellis, you're in the hospital,' Dr Chen said. 'You, your wife Roslyn, and your three daughters were all infected with encephalitis HSV cos virus.' He leaned forward again and enunciated his words with precision so he could be understood through his mask and face shield. 'Dr Ellis, do you understand me?'

He turned to stare at Stephen. 'What the hell are you doing? Put the bloody face shield and mask on.' He demanded. 'And your gloves.'

Stephen shook his head. 'My family and I are immune. We've already been infected and recovered.' He pointed to the bottle of Synchóresi dripping into Edward's veins. 'The drugs were developed using our serum.' He put his right hand on his hip. 'And my bone marrow.'

Dr Chen and the nurse exchanged stunned glances.

'You guys don't need all that kit either. You're immune.' Stephen continued. 'All non-white people are immune.' He slipped off his protective gown, unbuttoned the sleeves of his shirt, and rolled them up to his elbows. 'It only affects white people.'

'Do you know that for a fact?' Chen demanded. 'I've heard it on the news. And it's certainly what we've seen here.'

The nurse gave a vigorous nod of agreement.

'All our white staff got sick straight away. The protective gear didn't seem to make much difference. Only us coloureds are still upright.'

The nurse nodded again.

'Yes, it's a fact. I know it–' he looked around at the Ellis family, 'because my father, Dr Jonathan Ashley-Cooper, created the virus.' He jerked his head at the billionaire medical entrepreneur lying on the hospital bed. 'With him.'

Stephen turned back to the registrar and nurse. They were staring at him, still wearing their full PPE. Doctor Chen's brows were knitted in a scowl. The nurse's eyes were wide in fear or surprise. 'Please trust me. You'll be fine.' He jerked his chin at the patient on the bed. 'He hasn't said anything yet, has he?'

Doctor Chen threw a glance at Edward Ellis, then looked back at Stephen, his eyes still glowering. 'No, he hasn't said anything.'

Stephen took a couple of steps to stand alongside the bed, between the doctor and the nurse. Edward's eyes were wide but unfocused, and his mouth hung open. Stephen touched his fingers to Edward's cheeks. 'Dr Ellis. Edward,' he said. 'It's me. Stephen Ashley-Cooper. My father, Dr Jonathan Ashley-Cooper, works with you.' Edward blinked. His eyes focused on Stephen, but his face remained slack, his mouth agape. 'Dr Ellis, we've met. Many times. Carly and I are friends.' He placed his fingers on Edward's arm. 'Do you recognise me? Nod if you can.'

Edward's eyes remained fixed on Stephen. His lips moved without sound. They formed a word which might have been 'Jon'. Or any other single syllable.

'You got infected with the virus, Dr Ellis. Encephalitis HSV cos. The one Dad was working on. Your whole family has it.' Stephen kept his hand on Edward's arm. 'I got infected too. Me, Mum and Dad. We were all sick for a couple of hours.' He paused a moment to smile and shake his head. 'I don't know how we recovered so quickly. It's like some crazy miracle. But we did. And we used our blood and bone marrow to make a cure.'

Edward blinked and his mouth worked again. This time he let out a soft, unintelligible moan.

'Dr Ellis, you left instructions that we test any drugs we develop on you. That's what we did. Just like you wanted us to.' As he said this, Stephen's eyes flicked to the two medics standing on either side of him. 'And it's worked. You're getting better.' Stephen glanced at Edward's wife in the bed alongside him. 'Which means your family will get better soon too.'

Edward's eyes flicked from side to side. His mouth turned up in a small vacuous smile.

Stephen also glanced to either side. The overhead lights reflected off the face shields of the two medical professionals alongside him.

Edward lifted his left arm and pointed a tremulous finger at Dr Chen. 'Space … space … spaceman!' he giggled.

A shiver went through Stephen. A memory slipped into his mind. A distant memory of adult men and women in grey suits, cavorting in fields of flowers, squealing and giggling like children. 'A noncy,' he muttered. 'He's become a noncy.' It was that sudden.

Edward giggled again. 'We in space?' His speech was slurred, his voice high-pitched and prepubescent. 'Eddie wants … to play … too! Eddie wants … to be … Martian!'

Stephen let go of Edward and straightened up. He looked at Dr Chen. 'His brain,' he mumbled. 'The encephalitis. The virus. Is this behaviour because of it?'

'I need to consult with a neurologist and conduct a full neurological assessment. I can't make a diagnosis right now. Maybe oxygen deprivation. He could be confused. Or hallucinating. It is probably a passing phase—' Dr Chen was silent for a couple of seconds. 'At least, I hope so.'

'Shall I page Dr Mitchell?' the nurse asked.

Dr Chen shook his head. 'No use paging him. He's been admitted with the infection. If what Stephen says is true, Professor Rasiah would probably be a safer bet.'

Stephen stared at Edward. Dr Chen might think it temporary, but Stephen knew it was not.

Stephen looked from doctor to nurse. He pointed to where Roslyn and the girls were stirring and whimpering. 'You see to them. I'll contact my father and get the next phase of treatment set up.'

'There's more?' Dr Chen and the nurse exclaimed together

'Yes.' Stephen smiled. 'We thought this might happen. We have a drug that will improve their brain function. The remyelination nerve cell recovery drug. Apolutrosin.' Turning on his heel, Stephen walked out of the ward and the hospital.

CHAPTER 37

Sydney, 2030

Farid was snoring at the wheel of the Ellis limo. Stephen used his key to open the back door and jumped in. He pulled out his phone and pressed quick dial for his dad.

'Hello.' Dad's voice was heavy with sleep. 'Stephen!' He had obviously just looked at the screen. 'What happened? Are you okay? I mean is Edward … are the Ellises okay? Did something go wrong with the treatment? Did it fail? Were there side effects? Are the Ellises … are they …'

'Dad. Dad.' Stephen laughed. 'Stop.'

He heard his mum's voice. 'What time is it?' she mumbled.

'It's past midnight, Anne,' Dad responded. 'Stephen's on the line. I'll put him on speaker.'

Stephen heard the rustle of bedsheets. He waited a few seconds.

'Dad. Mum.' Stephen collected his thoughts. Then gave them the good news. 'Synchóresi worked.' He heard their joint intake of breath. 'Edward is out of his coma and talking. The rest of the family were just coming back to consciousness when I left the hospital.'

'Where are you?' Mum queried. 'And what's that noise?'

'I'm in the back seat of the limo. And the noise,' he chuckled. 'The noise is Farid snoring!'

Farid woke up with a start. 'So sorry … Master … er … Stephen. Shall we go home?'

'Hang on a moment,' he looked up from the phone. 'Yes, Farid. Home it is.'

Stephen spoke into the phone. 'You still there?

'Yes.' His parents chorused together. 'Stephen, you said Edward is speaking. How does he feel about our experiments? The treatment and vaccines?'

Stephen took a deep shuddering breath. 'Dad, Edward is out of his coma. That's the good news. But,' he hesitated. 'The virus has affected his brain. It's what you anticipated. Edward. He's behaving like … a little boy.'

Stephen screwed his eyes shut, wondering what Dad must be feeling. Edward Ellis, billionaire businessman, medical expert, and his dad's ex-boss, behaving like a child. As a result of a virus his dad created. Created for good. But gone horribly bad.

'Dad.' Stephen whispered. 'I'm sorry.'

His dad didn't reply for a moment. Then he said, 'Thanks, son.'

Silence filled the airwaves for a moment again. Then the phone rumbled as his dad sighed. 'It's an effect of the demyelination.' He heard his mum say something. 'It means,' Dad continued, 'the virus changes the …'

'Changes the nerve pathways as well as destroying the myelin covering.' Stephen interrupted. 'I know.' Excitement bloomed within him. 'Dad, when did you plan to start the remyelination medication?' He couldn't keep the excitement out of his voice.

His dad made a thoughtful humming sound. 'We need to keep monitoring the five of them for side effects. And wait for them to recover enough. For their bodies and brains to cope with the remyelination process. So-o-o-o-o,' He drew the word out. 'I'm thinking at least a week. Two weeks to be safe.'

The concepts in his mind clicked into place. It was simple. He knew exactly what needed to be done. And if they worked fast, it could be ready in a week. And fast and competent were natural to the people he had in mind. He just had to convince Dad, Mum and Rachel.

'Dad. Keep me on speaker so Mum can hear.' Stephen injected calm and confidence into his voice. 'I've been online, reading up on nerve development in the brain. Demyelination, remyelination and neuroplasticity. Okay. Tell me if I'm right. Apolutrosin will cause remyelination. And it will cause a rewiring of brain circuits.'

'Correct,' Dad confirmed.

'And while the brain circuits are healing, they'll be influenced by external input. The environment. What the person watches. Hears. Reads. Learns. It'll all direct and shape those new brain connections.'

'Yes.'

'Dad, Apolutrosin isn't enough. Not on its own, anyway. We can't just heal their brain. We need to heal the environment the brain is growing connections in.'

Stephen heard his mum's indrawn breath. 'Stephen. That is a brilliant idea. But how would we do that?'

Dad sounded more hesitant. 'It is a long shot. But it is worth a try. But as Mum asked, how? It's a huge undertaking.'

'Dad.' Stephen stopped him. 'Listen. Please. We need to create a kind of—' He dived deep into his brain for the right concept. 'We need a therapeutic environment!' Yes, that was it. The words and ideas now tumbled out of him. 'A healthy, yet challenging environment. One that helps the brain wiring to heal. Heal in good and wholesome ways. That helps the nerve connections and thought processes to be reframed and envision a new world.'

He jabbed the air as he spoke. 'We need to create an audio-visual resource to accompany Apolutrosin. So that the patients aren't absorbing sex, gore and violence as they recover. We need them to be sensitised to global problems. And enable them to develop good and healthy responses in their brain pathways. Resources on climate change. Global poverty. Racism. Slavery of all types. Inequality. Problems and possible solutions. We collect information. Find ways to feed this to people as they recover on Apolutrosin. We give the input. Their brains make the connections.'

'Then the remyelination,' Dad cut in, 'will be accompanied by a selective rewiring of the brain circuits. Away from greed and irresponsibility. And aggression and selfishness. And towards empathy, sympathy and compassion instead.' He sounded revitalised. Excited even.

'Away from the kind of irresponsible greed …' Stephen pulled himself up short.

His dad finished the sentence for him anyway. 'That Edward displayed. Which got us here in the first place.'

Stephen chuckled. 'Yeah. Sorry. I didn't want to insult Dr Ellis.'

He was relieved to hear an answering chuckle come down the line. 'Don't worry, son. I like the way you're thinking. I like it a lot.'

'The idea of a therapeutic environment? Or the irony of testing it on Edward Ellis?'

'Both.'

Father and son shared another laugh.

The limo pulled up at the front door of their house. 'Thanks, Farid.' Stephen opened the back door and jumped out. 'You go have a nap. We'll need you in the morning.'

Farid clambered out of the driver's seat. He took Stephen's hand in both of his. 'I'm your driver, but in my country, I was a scientist. Actually, I worked in a neurobiology lab.'

Stephen stared at Farid. Shame flooded through him. "I'm so sorry. Farid, we didn't know.'

'No. No. I don't want you to feel bad. I'm telling you because I understand what you're talking about, Stephen. You and your parents are good people. I'm sure you will be successful.'

A sense of peace and confidence swept through Stephen. He thanked Farid and ran up the steps and into the house.

His parents met him inside the front door. 'Dad. Mum. We need to plan the next step.'

Stephen's phone pinged. He glanced down at the screen. 'It's Dr Chen. He's the registrar looking after the Ellis family. I gave him my number.' He switched on speaker.

'Dr Chen. Stephen here. Is there a change?'

'Yes, the rest of the family are out of the coma. Roslyn Ellis and all three daughters.' Dr Chen's voice, muffled by mask and face shield, was barely audible.

'And?' Stephen prompted.

The doctor's voice was even softer. Weary. 'All the same. Reacting like they're children.' He stopped and sighed. 'But at least they're alive. And awake. Unlike others with the disease.' He paused again. 'I have to get back to the ward, Stephen. I'm waiting for the neurologist.'

Dad took the phone from Stephen. 'Dr Chen, this is Stephen's father, Jonathan Ashley-Cooper. My team developed the drug Synchóresi.'

Dr Chen's voice rose in pitch. 'Dr Ashley-Cooper, please send us more of the drug. The medical staff here are desperate. Please. Please.'

Dad glanced at Mum and shifted his eyes to Stephen. 'Do it.' Stephen whispered.

There was the sound of raised voices. 'Got to go.' Dr Chen cut the line.

'Dad,' Stephen repeated. 'Do it.'

'Go into production with Synchóresi? Stephen, Synchóresi gets patients out of a coma. But it doesn't cure the brain effects of demyelination. Should we?'

'Yes.' Stephen nodded. 'Even though you'll create a population of noncys.'

'Stephen.' His mum cut in. 'You keep using that word. What is it?'

Stephen scratched his head. 'It means non-coloured people whose brains stay in a childlike happy state.' He shrugged. 'Still not sure where I got the term.'

Dad's phone pinged with an incoming call. He glanced down. 'It's the Chief Medical Officer!'

'Congratulations, Dr Cooper. I have just been informed that your drug works!' Dr Nick Garrett's voice was loud and shrill with excitement. 'I want you to go into production. Now.'

'Dr Garrett, it isn't a complete cure. Did Dr Chen tell you?'

'Dr Cooper, people all over the globe are dying of encephalitis HSV cos. Your drug keeps them alive. Brings them out of the coma.' He paused. The moments dragged on. 'Dr Cooper. Either you do it or I use my executive powers to order the production and distribution of Synchóresi.'

Dad looked at Stephen and his mum. He nodded. 'I'll ask our companies to go into production.'

'Keep me informed.' The phone went silent.

'Okay.' Dad turned to the study. 'You two get some sleep. I'll press the button for production of both Synchóresi and Apolutrosin.'

Stephen yawned. 'Tomorrow, we start collecting global resources for the therapeutic environment.' He stumbled up the stairs to his bedroom. He dropped his clothes in a heap in the corner of his room and slipped into bed nude. He was asleep in a moment.

The paved path he stood on was lined on both sides with plants and flowers. Beyond the foliage, domes shimmered orange and red in the gentle rays of the setting sun. A sense of comfort and confidence swept through Stephen. He knew this place. He was back in Serendib.

Ally slipped her fingers into his. 'You're doing great.'

'Great?' Stephen turned to her. 'We got them out of a coma. But we've created noncys.'

'You've got the remyelination drug and the neuronal reprogramming.'

'The neuronal reprogramming is only a dream!' Stephen protested.

She let go of his hand and tapped his forehead. 'No. You have it all. Relax. Consolidate your ideas.' She stopped. 'Appa just connected.'

'Appa.' Stephen whispered. 'Saint Thomas.'

'The same! He wants you to think back to what you were when you came to Serendib.'

Stephen groaned. 'I was a geeky, cyber-addicted teen.'

'Now, think of the man you have become.' She tapped his forehead again. 'You have all you need, Stephen.'

She pulled her hand away and stepped back. Her smile was sad. It was a goodbye.

'Ally. Will I see you again?'

Ally shook her head. 'Not in your dreams. But maybe someday. I'll come to you. If you need me.'

CHAPTER 38

Sydney, 2030

Devi had prepared an early morning meal of milk rice. Rachel had joined the Ashley-Coopers for breakfast. But there was more than just eating happening around the breakfast table. Phones, tablets and laptops lay open and active by the plates of each person.

Over morning coffee, Stephen had described how a therapeutic environment could be used to support the remyelination brain recovery process induced by their medication Apolutrosin.

'Your idea of creating a formative environment for recovering patients is brilliant.' Rachel mused.

'It is just what we need,' his dad added. 'To reinforce and guide the remyelination treatment.'

'And make it all worthwhile,' Mum concluded.

Having eaten an early breakfast in the kitchen with Devi, Stephen sat at the dining table with his laptop open, fingers flying as he tried to keep up with the discussions taking place between the three scientists.

He stopped and looked around the table at his parents and Rachel. These people deserved a prize for what they'd achieved. And yet, here they were, following him. His lead. He should feel overwhelmed. But surprisingly, he didn't. He felt in control. Confident that this was how it was meant to be.

Rachel looked up from her laptop. 'Stephen, how do we collect the resources we require for this project? It needs to be collected from all over the globe. How?'

Stephen smiled at his dad. He swung his gaze to his mum. 'You have international connections. This is the time to use them.'

'I don't know, son.' Mum sounded hesitant. 'Do you think they'd believe what we've done? In the time we took to accomplish it? Wouldn't they want to investigate how the virus got to the Geneva labs in the first place?'

Stephen nodded. 'Yes, to all of the above, Mum. The world will be surprised and grateful that you discovered a cure so quickly. At the beginning, gratitude will overwhelm any curiosity. Later, there'll be an investigation. But,' he stopped and looked at his dad. 'Dad has all the information documented on his computer. Everything they need to know is right there.'

Dad frowned. 'How do you know what's in my computer?'

Stephen tried to look contrite. And failed. 'Eh, you slept in this morning. I checked your data. And added everything we've done.' He stopped and grinned. 'We now have a detailed timeline of everything. From your very first experiments to treatment of the Ellis family. And—' He took a deep breath. 'I programmed your phone when we were still in the caravan to record all your conversations. Everything from your chat with Dr Arjun when still in the Nullarbor, through to your discussions with Rachel while on the plane to when you talked to Edward after he landed back in Sydney.'

Mum gasped. 'Wow! That was good thinking, son.'

Dad nodded. 'You did right. That information will prove very important.'

Stephen tapped his laptop. 'I've downloaded it all.'

The door to the dining room swung open, and Devi bustled in. 'Stephen baba, turn on the TV. They're talking about you'll.'

Stephen picked up the remote for the wall-mounted widescreen monitor and activated it. It blinked on. The Prime Minister was standing in front of a bank of microphones. 'Thank you everyone for coming here at such short notice.' He paused and scanned the crowd of reporters and officials. 'You've had the case numbers from the Chief Medical Officer already. I won't repeat them. I'm here to give you the good news. We've had a breakthrough in the treatment for encephalitis HSV cos. Initial human trials have been successfully completed. As I speak, pharmaceutical manufacturing plants in Sydney are gearing up to get the treatment available to as many people as possible, as fast as possible. Other companies globally will come on line as soon as they can also retool their production processes. We're all very excited, relieved, and proud, that our nation has taken the lead in combating this global disaster. I'll let the Chief Medical Officer describe how these medications work. I have a meeting with the State Premiers starting in five minutes. But I wanted the press to hear about this from me first. Okay, I'll take up to three questions.'

'Mister Prime Minister, sir. Can you tell us the name of the researchers? Or the laboratory involved in the development of the medication?'

'I'm sorry, the research team are still working on a stage two treatment to counter the long-term side effects of the virus. They've asked me to keep their names and the location of their laboratory confidential. At least until they have completed human trials on that stage two treatment.'

There was a clamour of voices.

'What about a vaccine?' one reporter yelled over the others.

'Even as we speak, the researchers are working on a vaccine.'

'Sir,' a third called out. 'Do we know where the initial viral infections came from?'

The four people seated at the table looked at each other.

Dad picked up the remote and switched the television off. 'Enough. The news will be on global news channels within minutes. Our contacts in the virology field all over the world will make a calculated guess that we're the lab mentioned in the Prime Minister's speech.'

Stephen looked at his dad's phone lying by his plate. 'Maybe it's time to get in touch with your colleagues before they …'

The shrill ring of Dad's phone interrupted him. He glanced down. 'Simon Kwashi. The lead scientist in the virology research institute in Africa.' He swiped the phone on and turned on the speaker.

'Hello, Jonathan. Simon Kwashi here.' It sounded like the scientist was in the next room. 'Should we be nominating you for the Nobel prize? It was your lab, wasn't it?'

Dad didn't pretend to not understand what he was talking about. 'Yes, Simon, it was our research group. And, Simon, do you have cases?'

'Of encephalitis HSV cos? None here in Nigeria. But South Africa's pretty bad.'

'The whites,' Dad stated.

The phone pinged with another call. 'Just a minute, Simon. There's another call. Please stay on the line.' He swiped to accept the other call. 'Joshua Binyamin,' he looked at Stephen, who knew immediately who it was. Caleb's father. The Israeli ambassador.

'Jonathan,' Dr Binyamin cut to the chase in his characteristic manner. 'We have to talk. Now.'

'Joshua, I'm on the line to a colleague in Nigeria, Dr Simon Kwashi. How about I make this a conference call and I can explain the situation to you both.'

'Well ... okay.' The hesitancy in his voice was obvious to them all.

Over the next twenty minutes, Dad explained in detail what had happened. Beginning from his initial experiments, he told them how Dr Edward Ellis had sold his work to the Geneva lab. He told them what he could of what may have happened there without betraying Dr Arjun Eswaran's part in it. He described the development and composition of Synchóresi and Apolutrosin. He stopped to answer their questions.

Stephen opened a new document on his tablet. He typed, 'Ask them for help in collecting resources for the development of a therapeutic environment' in large font. He swung the laptop towards his dad.

Dad's eyes brightened. 'Simon, Joshua, we need your assistance for the next phase of treatment.'

'How can we help?' Simon responded immediately.

Dad smiled. 'We plan to help healthy rewiring of the brain by combining environmental stimuli while using the medication Apolutrosin. The first step is to develop a global learning resource to channel neuroplasticity and brain wiring during medication. You could assist us by sourcing information. The state of the globe today and ways we could reverse it.'

Simon Kwashi cut in. 'Happy to help. My people will work on collecting information from Africa. Starvation. Floods. Destruction of the forests and the environment. We've already done hypotheticals of how these could be reversed.'

Dr Binyamin sounded less enthusiastic. 'I could get my contacts in the Israeli media on it. They can locate the programs we need. I can ask for docos on terrorism. Ethnic wars. Genocide. How all that racial hatred begins and is nurtured and passed on and inflamed. They can translate the newsbyte videos to all world languages within three days. And develop programs on how global cooperation could solve these. But I can't commit, Jonathan. I need to know more. I'll come by the lab in a couple of hours.'

Stephen stood up. He picked up his laptop and pointed to the study. Dad, Mum and Rachel could work on collecting resources. He had other things to do.

Rachel gave him a thumbs up and started taking notes on her tablet.

***

Stephen strode into the study, connected his laptop to the widescreen monitor, and opened his various messaging apps. Text. WhatsApp. Signal. Facebook Messenger. Google Hangouts. Slack. And old-fashioned email. Different people paid attention to different platforms. He had to fill the ether with his requests. Like an emergency beacon.

He set up a Zoom meeting and connected it to the widescreen. He started firing off messages to his classmates, using all the communication services each one used, requesting they log in to the meeting immediately. He copied and sent the messages on the various platforms.

Phyllis' chocolate-brown face popped up on the screen. She was a scholarship student from Kenya. 'Coops!' she wailed. 'Where've you been? We've been so worried about you. We've tried calling. Texting.'

'Yeah, uh, sorry about that,' Stephen said. 'Been kinda tied up with some … um … adventures.' Kevin and Kent, the identical twin brothers from China, appeared on screen next. 'Are you okay, mate?' They spoke in complete unison. It was as if their brains were synced to function together.

Caleb arrived a few seconds later. 'All right, all right, I'm here,' he said. 'You can stop with all the messaging spam.'

Indira, a second-generation Indian-background migrant, was quiet and composed as always. 'Good to hear from you, Stephen. I told them that you'd have let us know if there was a problem.' She was quiet for a moment and then continued. 'I saw the press conference. The drugs the Prime Minister announced. They're from your father's lab, right?'

Stephen nodded. 'Yes. My dad and his team developed the drugs. We were in Perth when it all blew up. We came back and isolated ourselves in my parents' lab. And developed the medication you've heard about. And now we need your help.'

'Knew it!' Caleb snapped his fingers.

'Knew what, Caleb?' Stephen asked.

'You have a project for us. And it's probably connected to whatever my father is getting excited about on the phone right now!'

'Oh yeah,' Stephen replied, leaning back in his seat so he could better include his five best friends. 'How would you like to change the world?'

CHAPTER 39

Sydney, 2030

Phyllis dashed into the conference room, mobile phone in hand. '*#newworld* is trending big time!'

'And –' Kevin pointed to his tablet '—the YouTube clip Phyllis threw together has a gazillion downloads and likes!'

'I'm getting hundreds of DMs on the Twitter *#newworld,*' Caleb added. 'Someone has set up a subreddit page for it too.'

After the Zoom video meeting with his study buddies, Stephen had gone to the Ellis Enterprises building and with the help of David Thomas, converted the conference room into a workspace. The next morning, his team had joined him, and they had worked through the day, implementing their plans. The setting sun now cast slanting beams of light through the windows.

'Hang on a minute.' Stephen glanced up from his computer screen. 'I have some awesome content coming in from Dr Binyamin's contacts in Tel Aviv. They've sourced stuff on climate change that will get people's neurones myelinating!'

Phyllis looked over Stephen's shoulder. 'Wow! Look at those glaciers. The waterfalls are ice melt, aren't they?'

Stephen clicked on another file. 'This is a simulation of what would happen in the next eighty to a hundred years. Maybe less.'

Indira joined them. 'Aww, look at that poor polar bear. He's stuck on that chunk of ice!'

The video sped up. The twins and Caleb joined the group at the computer. Videos of sea levels rising. Islands inundated. Sea water encroaching into fresh water. Flooded streets. Submerged houses. Ghost forests. Bare fields.

The group was silent.

Indira's voice was almost a sob. 'My people in the north of Sri Lanka. They won't have a country!'

Stephen cringed. He had assumed she was Indian.

'Surely,' Indira continued, 'people will understand? Want to do something to stop it?'

Stephen looked round at the group. 'They will. I'm certain of that.'

The twins grinned at Stephen. 'You've changed, Coops,' Kevin started. 'In a good way.'

'You've become a leader worth following!' Kent finished.

Stephen laughed. 'You mean I'm not the whinging, upper-class, stuck-up, white snob you knew me for?' The others were silent. Their expressions, however, gave away their agreement with Stephen's self-assessment.

Phyllis reached over and turned her laptop towards them. She clicked it open. 'This is heartbreaking.' She stopped.

'What?' Stephen stood up and turned to her.

'Rachel's contacts just sent this through. From India.'

They watched in silence at the hidden camera footage of forced labour in the sweat shops of South Asia, women and children abused for money, the images blurred, but the activity unmistakable.

'This—' Indira raised her voice and pointed a trembling finger at the screen '—must be stopped.'

Stephen placed an arm around her shoulder.

'It'll be stopped, Indira. It *will* be.'

Kevin and Kent sat down and scrolled through the data on their laptop. 'More coming in from North America and Africa,' Kevin announced. 'Interesting videos and discussions on drug lords and mafia.' Kent commented.

Stephen walked over to the whiteboard. 'Okay, team,' he called out in a loud voice.

Everyone stopped what they were doing and focused on him.

'We've got volunteers,' he said, 'and we've got resources. Plenty of both. Now we need a plan for how we're gonna use 'em.'

With a black felt pen, Stephen drew a line down the middle of the board. He wrote the words 'Humans' on one side, and on the other he wrote 'Media'.

He turned back to his team. 'That's what we got. How are we gonna put 'em together?'

Kevin put up his hand. 'Media first. What we have is all muddled up. I got more coming in here,' he glanced at his laptop, 'on racism. Intolerance. Religious persecution. We need a generic resource playlist everyone watches.'

'And,' Kent continued, 'specific playlists of problems. And solutions that are relevant to the needs of individual patients.'

'Great!' Stephen agreed with a nod. 'We can do that.' He wrote it down on the board. 'Who decides what's relevant to a specific individual in a particular country?'

'The other column,' Indira called out. 'Our contacts in Africa, Asia, US, UK, Europe, everywhere. We've got them all involved and interested.'

'But how …' Phyllis shook her head. 'How do we screen out the weirdos from the ones we can trust?'

'Yes, how?' Kevin scrolled through the page he was on. 'Here's one who calls himself "fruitcake", another who is unashamedly "the messiah". And … here's a girl who calls herself "Araliya". She looks a little like you, Indira.'

'Araliya. A subcontinental name for frangipani,' Stephen muttered.

'How'd you know that?' Indira laughed across the table.

Stephen frowned. 'Don't know. It just popped into my head.' He looked around at the group. 'Come on, folks. You're the best we've got. Get your thinking caps on! How do we screen our gazillion potential helpers?'

Silence descended on the group. They shuffled on their seats and glanced at each other.

The door to the conference room swung open and Dr Joshua Binyamin strolled in. 'I stopped by to see Jonathan. How are you all progressing?' His voice trickled off as he looked around at the six crestfallen young people. 'Glazed eyes and glum faces!' he exclaimed. 'What's the matter?'

Caleb sighed. 'Hi, Dad. These are my friends from the IT class at my school.'

A vague mumble of muted greetings rose from the table of young techies.

'Very pleased to meet you all,' Dr Binyamin said. 'Caleb has told us a lot about you. He's very proud to be a part of this project.' He gave a little chuckle. 'I must say, I've rather enjoyed working my networks and sourcing all those resources for you. I think the rest of our global contacts have enjoyed it too.' He smiled and looked around the room. 'How are you progressing with the program?'

'Well, that's the thing, Dr Binyamin,' Phyllis began. 'We want to develop video and infotainment playlists. To use with the remyelination drug.'

'Playlists which show information about the dangers we're all facing,' Indira continued. 'As one people. The human race. Across the whole world.'

'So, that as people's brains are recovering,' Phyllis went on, 'they'll know about the dangers we all face together. They'll see it from a perspective other than their own.'

'And want to be part of the solution, instead of part of the problem,' Indira echoed.

Dr Binyamin smiled and raised a finger. 'So that these needs, and possible solutions to them, will be wired into people's brains as they recover. Nice use of neuroplasticity!'

'We want to make online games!' Kevin and Kent blurted together.

'First-person adventures!'

'MMOs! Massive Multiplayers Online!'

'Where instead of shooting each other …'

'… and blowing things up …'

'… they work together …'

'… to figure out solutions …'

'… to climate change …'

'… poverty …'

'… persecution …'

'… and racial prejudice!'

Stephen suppressed a smile as he watched Dr Binyamin's eyes flick between the twins as they played tennis with their conversation.

'We expect to have the playlists ready within three to four days,' Phyllis said.

'And we have lots of young people ready to share them,' Indira added. 'And even more ready to help us develop the online games.'

'Gazillions of volunteers!' the twins chorused.

Dr Binyamin raised his hands, palms up, in a 'so, what's the problem' gesture.

'The problem, Dad.' Caleb's voice was heavy with irritation, 'is we don't know who these people are! Are they really who they say they are? Are they weirdos? Catfishing?' His voice rose in pitch and volume. 'Are they into some kind of extortion? Or even sextortion? How the heck do we find out?'

Doctor Binyamin sat down at an empty chair at the table. He leaned forward, steepled his hands under his chin, and gave the whiteboard a thoughtful gaze.

Stephen wrote the word "screening" in the column under "humans" 'We need to identify teens we can trust from across the globe. Once we pick them out, they'll supervise the use of our playlists and report back to us on the effects. We need integrity, loyalty, patience and a willingness to stick with us for the long haul.'

Dr Binyamin gave a slow nod. 'You need a fail-safe procedure for checking the background of all your contacts. And then,' He stroked his chin with his right hand. 'And then you need a shortlist. With location, personal characteristics and contact details. You can pick the key leaders in specific locations to coordinate the effort.'

'Yes, sir, that sounds exactly right,' Stephen responded. 'But …' He glanced around at his team of tech nerds. 'How on earth are *we* going to do that?'

Dr Binyamin's lips tweaked up. He fished a pen and small spiral-bound writing pad from his shirt pocket, tore a page from the pad, and scribbled something on it.

'Send the names of your contacts to this email address.' He stood up and reached across the table to hand the small piece of paper to Stephen. 'You'll have the details you need within forty-eight hours.'

'Dad,' Caleb protested, 'how can you do that? Most of our contacts are only hashtags and nicknames!'

Dr Joshua Binyamin turned to his son with a chuckle. 'That's all we need.'

Phyllis blinked. Her face was puzzled. 'Who's the "we"?' She used her fingers to insert air quotes.

Dr Binyamin's smile broadened. 'Very nice to meet you all.' He nodded to his left and right, his eyes twinkled as he looked at the assembled youth. 'But I need to get back to the lab. I believe they're on the cusp of completing the vaccines. I've asked to be present.'

And with that, he trotted out the door and was gone.

CHAPTER 40

Sydney, 2030, Six Weeks Later

'Thanks, Krish,' Stephen leapt out of the Chevy.

'I'll park the car and bring the food Devi made for your lunch!' Krish called after him.

Stephen dashed into the Ellis Enterprises building. His friends and he had met regularly in the conference room, monitoring the roll-out of the therapeutic environment recovery program or TERP as they now called it across the world.

He grabbed his phone and checked the time. Ten minutes past ten. He was ten minutes late for the tech team debrief meeting. He'd missed the last meeting too. Never mind. They would have texted if there was anything urgent. He glanced at his phone. No missed calls. No texts. Everything must be under control. At least he hoped so. He trotted up the two flights of steps without waiting for the lift. He stopped briefly at the sanitiser station and jogged down the corridor to the conference room.

The members of the tech team were strewn around the meeting room in varying stages of relaxation. All with laptops and tablets open.

'Did you bring lunch?' Kent and Kevin called out together when Stephen entered.

'Lunch is on its way!' Stephen scanned the room. 'How's everything?'

Phyllis giggled and wagged her finger at Stephen. 'He went AWOL for all of four days. Naughty boy!'

Kevin and Kent both pretended to gag. 'We are dying without our leader!' Kevin gasped. Then broke into guffaws of laughter.

Indira looked up from her laptop. 'Relax, Stephen. You'd think we can't function without you!'

Stephen dropped into a chair. 'Sorry, team. I should've known you'd be fine without me.'

'Jokes asides, where were you?' Caleb quizzed.

'I was with Edward Ellis and his wife, Roslyn. They're well into the remyelination medication. They've watched the playlists we made for them. When I visited the hospital four nights ago, I noticed that the improvement was progressing rapidly. So, I stayed with them.' He dragged out his tablet and put it on the desk. 'I recorded the changes for Dad, Mum and Rachel.' He tapped the tablet. 'Have a look.'

They gathered around Stephen.

'This,' Stephen explained, 'was taken by Dr Chen, just prior to the Apolutrosin treatment. That would be—' He glanced at the date on the video. 'A little over five weeks ago.'

Edward Ellis dressed in a protective gown and mask scampered across the room. 'Me Martian! Give Eddie a lolly!'

'Oh my God,' Phyllis gasped. 'He's behaving like a child!'

'So sad,' Indira's voice broke on a sob. 'I remember seeing him on TV. He was such a large personality.'

'Hold on. Watch this.' Stephen clicked on another video. 'This one is after two weeks of treatment.'

Edward Ellis and his wife, Roslyn, sat side by side. Their eyes were fixed on the wide television screen. Edward turned to Roslyn. 'Sad. Wish we could help.'

Roslyn nodded. 'Yes.'

'Can't think straight,' Edward mumbled.

'The doctor … what's his name?' Roslyn turned to Edward.

'Don't know …' Edward muttered.

Stephen stopped the video. 'This one's four weeks into treatment.' He clicked on another video and fast-forwarded it. 'Watch this,' he murmured. He turned the volume up.

Edward and Roslyn were seated at a table alongside a blonde-haired young woman. The young woman had a laptop open in front of her. 'That,' Stephen pointed to the young woman, 'is Jacqui. Their oldest daughter. She was like all the others, childlike. Four weeks into Apolutrosin treatment and she can read and interpret information on the computer. It seems like she improved faster than her parents. Watch.'

'Dad,' Jacqui looked up from the computer screen, 'did you know that Jonathan Ashley-Cooper worked with his wife, Anne, and research assistant, Rachel? They developed the medications we've been given.'

Edward nodded. 'I gave him the run of the labs. I also gave him,' his smile was a wry smirk, 'the money in Ellis Enterprises new projects account.'

'He used it well.' Roslyn spoke slowly enunciating each word. 'The neurologist, Dr Rasiah, says we would have stayed in a coma without the drugs his team developed. Or, if we came out of the coma, lived in a regressed childhood state of memory and emotion for the rest of our life.'

Edward nodded. 'Jonathan has been in regular contact with me. I told him I caused this. I also told him that I would do anything … anything to make it right.'

'What did he suggest?' Jacqui queried.

Edward laughed. 'He told me to talk to his son, Stephen.'

Stephen stopped the video.

They looked at each other.

'You waited?' Indira frowned.

'I talked to Dr Chen and Dr Rasiah. They suggested that I wait for further myelination of the cognitive decision-making pathways and further emotional stability.'

'So, that's what you've been doing the last couple of days.' Phyllis pointed to Stephen's laptop. 'Do you have more?'

'Enough to tell me that the treatment with Apolutrosin is helping the myelination and brain development. And that our playlists are pointing the Ellis family in the right direction.'

Kevin and Kent gestured to their laptops. 'We're getting similar reports from all over the globe,' Kevin began. 'With some interesting outcomes,' Kent commented.

'This one,' Phyllis pointed to an email open on her screen, 'is from New York. A billionaire businessman by the name of Nick Demos and his company have set up a foundation to assist the families of those who died in the pandemic. Other businessmen who were ill and recovered have joined the effort.'

'Here's an email from Western Australia.' Caleb's voice bubbled with excitement. 'A mining magnate who has promised a significant portion of his money for the development of renewable energy sources. And climate change studies.'

'How about this?' Indira's voice was soft and breathy with awe. 'A man called Phile in South America is working with the church there to rehabilitate abused children and women.'

'And,' Kent continued, 'from China, Korea and Europe, we're getting reports of plans for the dismantling of all forms of ethnic discrimination.'

Krish came in with plates of fried chicken, salad and warm bread rolls. 'Devi says, you're working hard.' He pointed to the plates of food. 'Eat.'

'Gladly!' Kevin leapt out of his chair. Kent beat him to it and grabbed the plates.

Stephen waited till they were all settled with their food.

'Now for the update from Edward Ellis,' he announced.

They all looked up at him. 'There's more?' Kent asked with his mouth full of fried chicken.

Stephen smiled, and said 'Dr Edward Ellis has recovered cognition. He tested one hundred percent yesterday afternoon. We spent the evening talking about how he can help us. He's totally committed to *#newworld*.' Stephen looked around the team.

'Tell us!' Kevin and Kent yelled.

'He's willing to fund whatever we have to do to harness and maintain contact with our international Gen Alpha teen team. I shared our dream with him. He's willing to support us.'

Caleb frowned. 'Please explain?' He tapped his forehead.

'You told him what you've been talking to us about,' Indira responded. 'A shared global vision among Gen Alpha's. Shared resources. Economic and social equality,' She paused and looked at the others.

'Can we do this?' Phyllis' face tightened in anxiety.

'I have a plan. And the Ellis coffers to fund it.' Stephen looked at each person individually. 'It's ambitious. But doable. I'd like you guys with me.'

'Count me in.' Caleb raised his hand.

'And us,' said Kevin and Kent.

'Me too.' Phyllis high-fived Caleb. 'Yeah!' He responded.

Indira nodded assent.

Stephen pushed his chair back and walked to the whiteboard.

'Come on. Tell us more!' Phyllis rapped her fingers on the table.

'The Edward Ellis Foundation will fund a state-of-the-art computer lab at Saint Christopher's College. He's confident that the Silicon Valley social media giants will come on board.'

'Okay.' Kevin stood up. 'We get a lab. That's nice. Then what?'

Stephen placed his palms on the table and leaned forward. 'We,' he drew a circle with his index finger to encompass the group, 'will have fast-tracked training in software development. Algorithms. Everything. Edward wants the project called "Cornerstone".'

'Yes!' Caleb fisted his right hand and brought his elbow down in a sign of victory. 'We can develop an app.'

'Wow!' Indira pushed her chair back and stood up. She clapped. 'A global program that links people. A global movement of mutual assistance and empathy. A harnessing of Gen Alpha energy.'

'We can call the app "One Humanity"' Phyllis added air quotes of emphasis to the last two words.

'Awesome!' Kevin and Kent shouted together

Stephen's phone buzzed. He glanced down at the screen. A WhatsApp video message popped up. He stared at the picture.

Black hair cascaded in curls down to her waist. Almond-shaped black eyes and generous red lips on her olive-skinned face signalled her subcontinental heritage. She stood in front of a frangipani tree in full bloom. The image of the girl and the flowering tree sent an instant frisson of awareness down Stephen's spine. A response he couldn't fathom.

Indira looked at Stephen's phone. 'Who's that?' She swiped up to accept the video call. 'Go on, Stephen.' She grinned and passed the phone to him.

Stephen switched on the speaker and placed the phone on the table between them.

'Hello. Is that Stephen Cooper?' Her voice sent another jolt through Stephen.

He heard Caleb whisper to Indira. 'What a beauty!'

The twinkle in the eyes of the girl on the screen indicated that she had heard the comment. Stephen gestured to the team to be quiet.

Shocked at his visceral response to the girl on the screen, Stephen struggled to sound detached. 'Yes, I'm Stephen Cooper.'

'I hope you don't mind my calling you. I'm Shalini Thomas. And, yes, I'm related to David Thomas. I'm his cousin. He and Rachel suggested that I contact you and offer to help with your project. I'm in Mumbai. You might still call it Bombay. And I'm happy for you to check my credentials with Dr Joshua Benyamin!'

'Shalini.' Stephen's brain struggled to reconcile the feeling of familiarity when he looked at her. 'I have you on speaker here with the team working on our tech project.' He rotated the phone and introduced each of them.

'Great to meet you all,' Shalini continued. 'To give you my background, I'm studying tech science at my high school. My father has been appointed ambassador to Australia. I've travelled with him all over the globe since I was a baby and have a working knowledge of a dozen or more languages. I read and write Tamil and a variety of subcontinental dialects, as well as Vietnamese and French. My parents and I will travel to Sydney where I believe all you guys are as soon as the travel ban to India is lifted.' She smiled. The smile sent a frisson of awareness through Stephen's brain. Shalini continued. 'I've been accepted at Saint Christopher's College, where I believe all you guys all are.'

'Hey, Shalini'. Kevin picked up the phone. 'A recommendation from Rachel Thomas is sufficient for us. We don't need Dr Binyamin to check you out! I'm Kevin.' His twin popped his head into the screen next to him.

'And I'm Kent.' Together, they chorused, 'Welcome to the team!'

Shalini's tinkling laughter spilled from the phone. Something in Stephen's mind stirred from the memory of a laugh like that.

Phyllis took the phone from Kevin. 'Do we call you Shalini?'

'I like to be called Shali. Shali with an 'i''

Caleb picked up the phone. 'Well, Shali with an 'i',' he said with a grin, 'our team leader Stephen seems a little dumb-struck, so on behalf of all of us, welcome.' He passed the phone to Stephen. 'Come on, Coops!' he whispered.

A wind shook the branches on the frangipani tree behind Shalini. A few white flowers with their deep, orange-gold heart wafted in the breeze and rested on her hair.

'Shali, I … we …' Stephen cleared his throat. 'We all … look forward to seeing you here soon.'

Kevin grabbed the phone from Stephen, 'til you get here we can WhatsApp. Or Zoom.'

'Works for me. I'll send you my details by text and email. I feel like I know you guys already. Bye for now.'

Indira interrupted. 'Wait, Shali.' She turned to those in the room. 'Come on. Right hands together.' Kevin, Kent, Caleb, Phyllis and Stephen joined their hands with Indira's. Indira held the phone to their clasped hands. 'Stretch out your arm Shali.' Shali did as Indira asked her to.

'To the Cornerstone Project.' Indira weighted every word. 'A new world. Starting with us.'

'Cornerstone for a new world!' the team chorused.

Epilogue

Sydney, 2042

The Coopers' vintage Chevy pulled up at the foot of the wide steps leading up to the Sydney Opera House. Stephen opened the door of the passenger seat and stepped out.

The cool breeze from Sydney Harbour carried a tang of salt. Seagulls wheeled and squealed in the air above him. On his left, across the bay from Circular Quay, a mighty passenger liner lay at anchor in the international cruise ship terminal. On his right, lay the historic ornate entrance to the Botanical Gardens.

He was surrounded by a kaleidoscope of colour and costume which made him, dressed in his navy-blue dinner suit, white and blue pin-stripe shirt, and purple bow tie and cummerbund, feel distinctly ordinary. He recognised the embroidered, silk two-piece khet partug and dyed leather sandals of the Afghan man getting out of the car behind them. The woman walking up the steps ahead of him wore a multicoloured heavily beaded dress with a striped blanket over her shoulders. The multiple beaded hoops of twisted grass and the copper and brass rings around her neck, arms and legs, together with the fancy embroidered headband, marked her out as a senior in her Zimbabwean tribe.

'Aiyoo, Stephen aiya!' Krish came bustling around the side of the vehicle, his face split in a wide grin. He was dressed in a brown suit with a brick-red tie, and had a brown peaked cap perched on his head. 'You must wait for me to open the door for you, no? Or else people will think I'm a very bad chauffeur!'

Stephen laughed. 'Well, I'll tell them stories of your driving prowess, and how you cut through traffic to get us here after we left home late!'

Krish chuckled as he scuttled around the front of the car to the other side of the vehicle. Stephen let Krish open the passenger door, which he performed with a merry flourish.

Stephen held out his hand. An olive-brown arm emerged from the vehicle in response. Long brown fingers entwined themselves around Stephen's.

Shalini Thomas Ashley-Cooper, Shali with an 'i' to her friends and to her husband Stephen, emerged from the vehicle with effortless grace. She was wearing a long-sleeved, full-length formal salwar kameez, made of green silk, and embroidered with a gold leaf pattern. Her left hand held the dupatta—the long shawl—around her shoulders. A rhinestone tiara sparkled on her head, and her lustrous back hair cascaded unrestrained across her shoulders and down her back.

'Shah!' Krish exclaimed. 'You are looking very nice today, chinnamma!'

'She looks very nice every day!' Stephen retorted and gave the driver a wink.

Krish gave a booming laugh.

Shali smiled. 'Boys!' she said, her eyes twinkling. She drew Stephen alongside her and slipped her arm into the crook of his elbow. 'Thank you, Krish. See you in a few hours. Come along, husband dear.' She started up the stairs with resolute steps. 'Let's go celebrate the future.'

They joined the rainbow mix of skin tones and clothing ascending the stairs, entered the large entrance foyer, and lined up at the registration desk marked 'A-K'.

Fourteen-year-old Paul Thomas, one of the high school student volunteers, dashed up to Stephen. 'Thank God you two are here! I'm your host. I'm supposed to welcome you both and get you settled. I was going crazy thinking I'd missed you. Caleb would have killed me! That's if my mother didn't strangle me first!'

'Calm down, mate!' Stephen patted Paul on his shoulder. 'We're here now.' He looked around at the name tags of the invitees. 'Hey, cool idea! Who thought of putting the hashtag title on the name tag?'

'One of the team. Indira, I think. Neat, eh?'

'Definitely.' Stephen could recognise most of the young men and women around him from their hashtag titles. They didn't recognise him. He was just another white man in a suit.

Behind the registration booths, people were milling around the foyer, snacking on canapes and making connections based on their hashtag titles. A young Jewish man wearing a skullcap embraced a dark-skinned Lebanese man dressed in a multi-layered trouser-like sherwal and silk shirt. The Jew's nametag said *#tikvah*, which meant hope. The Lebanese was more prosaic—his simply declared *#amal*. An Indian girl in a red-and-gold saree with the Tamil word for trust *#nambikkai* stood with her arm around a Pakistani girl with *#aminia*. A man in a clan kilt with *#peil* on his nametag chatted with a dark-skinned Indian man dressed in veshti and tunic, bearing the name *#puli* meaning tiger.

Paul slipped them both their nametags. 'Phyllis says,' he whispered in a conspiratorial tone, 'not to put them on till after you sit down. You might be mobbed if people recognise you. I can't be responsible for protecting you!' His eyes danced with mirth.

He led them through the mass of cheerful, chattering young men and women, to a side door leading into the opera hall. The door shut behind them with a soft whump, cutting out the noise of the voices outside.

Stephen's and Shali's parents were seated in the front row. Stephen's dad was in a lounge suit like his, except more conservative, with a plain white shirt and black tie and cummerbund. Stephen's mum was in a plain cut, ivory silk evening gown. Shali's dad was in a simple but well-cut business suit, and her mum wore a royal blue saree edged with silver. Next to them sat Rachel and David. Beyond them, were the young leaders of the Cornerstone project: Kevin, Kent, Phyllis, and Indira. At the end of the front row sat Edward and Roslyn Ellis and their three daughters.

'You finally got here!' Stephen's dad lurched to his feet. 'We were getting worried!'

'My fault.' Shali beamed a sweet smile. 'Took my time getting ready.'

Stephen and Shali greeted their parents with hugs and waved to the rest of their friends. Paul Thomas pointed them to their allocated seats.

'Where's Caleb?' Stephen whispered to Paul as he lowered himself into the seat.

'Backstage,' Paul murmured back. 'He's tonight's MC.'

An electronic bell signalled the beginning of the night's event. The Opera House's uniformed staff swung open the hall doors and permitted the multicoloured, multitude of laughing, chatting young people to stream in.

After a few minutes of controlled chaos as everyone found their seats, the lights dimmed. The noise of conversation dropped away, and a palpable sense of anticipation settled on the crowd.

The stage lights flashed on. The spotlight picked a solitary figure in full white. Shirt, bow-tie, suit and shoes.

'Caleb always enjoyed high drama,' Stephen muttered. 'It's surprising that he didn't plan a drum roll!'

'Shush, son.' His mother, seated next to him, patted his arm.

As if on cue, a drum roll sounded from the orchestra pit.

Stephen groaned, eliciting a nudge from his wife.

'Ladies and gentlemen!' Caleb stepped forward and stood at the edge of the stage. His amplified voice boomed throughout the hall. 'Thank you for your presence here today. You, the Gen Alpha of a decade ago, are gathered here representing every nation, tribe, people and language of the world. You are here because you,' he spread his arms in an expansive gesture which included the entire sweep of the crowd—'yes, every one of you, have played a part in the Cornerstone Project!'

He paused as waves of applause swept around the hall.

'In the year 2030 the world faced a catastrophe of global proportions. Today, we take time to thank the people who spearheaded the move that saved the world. Firstly, the scientific team who worked day and night, fuelled by coffee and curry, to discover the treatment and vaccine for encephalitis HSV cos. Doctor Jonathan Ashley-Cooper, his wife, Anne, and Dr Rachel Thomas. We would not be here if not for your hard work and wisdom.' He gestured for them to stand.

Another wave of applause went around the room, interspersed with cheers and whistles. The researchers stood up and accepted the accolades.

‘Thank you. Thank you.’ Caleb waited till they were seated.

‘We needed funding to get all of you, from all ends of the globe, linked and sharing knowledge, wisdom and resources. That came from our sponsors. These are too many to name individually. You will find them listed in the program you received. However, we must acknowledge the people who spearheaded the fundraising for the Cornerstone Project.’ Caleb gestured to the group in the front row. ‘Dr Edward Ellis, his wife Roslyn, and their daughters Jaqueline, Sarah, and Carly. Thank you.’

The hall erupted again with applause. The Ellis family stood up and accepted the praise.

‘Of course, I can’t pass over the Gen Alpha tech-heads who worked on the software that drew you all together. Thank you, Stephen, Kevin, Kent, Phyllis, Indira and Shalini.’

Stephen’s former classmates popped up from their seats for a few seconds to acknowledge the claps and whistles from the crowd.

Caleb gestured for silence. ‘We now come to the true business for today. As you’re aware, we’re here today to launch the International Peace Initiative, or IPI, as it will be called. You’ve all been involved in the discussions and consultations and have a pretty good idea of the structure. Each of you belong to one of the five global collaboratives and have elected your leader. I would now like to invite the leaders up on the stage.’

His words elicited a rumble of excited conversation from the crowd. He stood silent till there was silence.

‘Representing the Asia-Oceania collaborative, called Samaataanam, with its headquarters in Nuwara Eliya, the hill country capital of Sri Lanka – Indira Kandiah!’

The hall erupted yet again with animated applause. Indira stood up and walked up the side stairs onto the stage. She was attired in a violet saree decorated with sequins that sparkled in the light. When she reached Caleb, he took her hand and raised her fingers to his lips in a gesture that elicited hoots and laughter from the crowd.

Caleb released Indira’s hand and faced the crowd again. ‘The North and South Americas have decided to work together and be called Harmony. They will be located in Virginia and will be led by—' he paused for effect 'Anthony Byrne!' He waited till Anthony joined him in the midst of rolling applause.

'Representing Amani from Africa, our very own Phyllis Ngabo! She, not surprisingly, has not yet decided where she will have her offices!' Caleb greeted her with a hug.

'And representing Shalom from Europe, David Leiblum. He has told me he would like to, very appropriately, be located in the city of David—Jerusalem!'

Caleb waited till all five stood together behind him with their arms linked.

'And now friends, for the announcement you are all waiting for. I have great pleasure in introducing to you the unanimously elected president of the International Peace Initiative. A man whose brilliance and wisdom guided us and held us together during the dark times. A man who yesterday was awarded his PhD for his research on "The Movement from Global Pandemic to World Peace". Ladies and gentlemen, I present to you, Reverend Doctor Stephen Ashley-Cooper, and his wife, Doctor Shalini Thomas Ashley-Cooper! Better known by their hashtag names—Coops and Shali!'

The entire hall erupted in the acclamation of over one thousand men and women. Stephen stood up. So did everyone else. He and Shali were receiving a standing ovation. And they hadn't even got on stage yet.

He turned to the side and reached for Shali's hand to help her up. 'Are you feeling alright?' he asked.

Shali pursed her lips and nodded.

He tucked her arm into the crook of his elbow and led her up the steps and onto the stage. Caleb and the five other sector leaders were pounding their hands together and stamping their feet and adding to the cacophony. When Stephen and Shali entered the spotlight's pool of illumination, the crowd gave a sustained, ear-splitting roar.

Stephen stood there, clinging to his wife. His heart pounded in his chest and tears pricked the back of his eyeballs. He glanced around the crowd of people. Young people from every nation, tribe, people and language of the world. Representatives of all of humanity standing together, stamping and cheering themselves hoarse.

His parents were also standing and applauding. Tears sparkled on the faces of both his father and mother. Shali's parents were on their feet as well. As were his classmates and the Ellis family.

The applause continued for a minute. Two minutes.

Stephen raised his hand and mouthed. 'Thank you.'

That only made the crowd raise a cheer and redouble their applause.

Caleb, a broad grin on his face, stepped to the edge of the stage and said something to the orchestra conductor in the pit below the stage.

A flurry of drums followed by a majestic brass fanfare heralded the anthem of the International Peace Initiative. The applause finally died away to be replaced by raised voices. Voices in every language on earth, singing one song.

'We all, among the nations set, all racial hate revoke,' they melodied. 'And national pride subordinate, to serve the eternal good.'

Stephen moved closer to his wife. 'Shali,' he said into her ear, 'we are one humanity today. But will it last?'

Shali placed her right hand on her abdomen. 'We have to make it last Stephen,' she replied. 'For our children.'

THE BEGINNING

Acknowledgments

Special thanks to my son Kamal who put his love of adventure, thrills and spills to good use by helping me bring action and colour to this story. And to my husband Vasantha who is always available when I need an audience to bounce off crazy story ideas.

Judy Taylor, my dear friend and sister in Christ this manuscript would not have attained the standard it has without your expert editorial skills. Thank you.

To my readers, I hope you enjoy this first of three novels set in Serendib; the beautiful blessed land of the beati.